ENDLESS

Praise for *Embrace* and *Entice*

'The Twilight set will embrace the opener of a YA trilogy'
NEW YORK POST

'It's perfect…five star rating'
NICE GIRLS READ BOOKS BLOG

'You'll be hooked on this new series!'
GIRLFRIEND MAGAZINE

'Entice had me glued to every page'
STORYWINGS BLOG

'A page-turning novel full of passion, romance,
action and suspense'
IRRESISTIBLE READS BLOG

The
Violet Eden Chapters

Book One: *Embrace*

Book Two: *Entice*

Book Three: *Emblaze*

Book Four: *Endless*

Book Five: *Empower*

www.jessicashirvington.com

ENDLESS

jessica shirvington

ORCHARD

For Phil and Jenny –
thank you for all your love and support
(and all of the research material!)

ORCHARD BOOKS
338 Euston Road, London NW1 3BH
Orchard Books Australia
Level 17/207 Kent Street, Sydney, NSW 2000

First published in Australia and New Zealand in 2012 by Hachette Australia
First published in the UK in 2013 by Orchard Books

ISBN 978 1 40833 263 4

Text © Jessica Shirvington 2012

The right of Jessica Shirvington to be identified as the author of this work has been
asserted by her in accordance with the Copyright, Designs and Patents Act, 1988.

The author and publisher would like to thank the following for permission to use
copyright material: Estate of C. S. Lewis for a quotation from The Four Loves by C. S.
Lewis, copyright © C. S. Lewis Pte. Ltd. 1960.
Every endeavour has been made on the part of the publisher to contact copyright
holders not mentioned above and the publisher will be happy to include a full
acknowledgement in any future edition.

The author and publisher would also like to acknowledge the following works from
which the author has quoted: Douay-Rheims Bible; English Standard Version; The King
James Bible; The Nag Hammadi library; The Holy Quran.

A CIP catalogue record for this book is available from the British Library.

1 3 5 7 9 8 6 4 2

Printed in Great Britain
Orchard Books is a division of Hachette Children's Books,
an Hachette UK company.

www.hachette.co.uk

'Light and darkness, life and death, right and left,
are brothers of one another. They are inseparable.
Because of this neither are the good good, nor the evil evil,
nor is life life, nor death death.'

The Gospel of Philip

CHAPTER ONE

'Everybody, sooner or later, sits down to a banquet of
consequences.'
Robert Louis Stevenson

What do you do the moment your father discovers your dead mother is still alive, standing in his apartment looking not a day older than the day she died – over seventeen years ago?

It was a decision I never had the chance to make.

'You didn't need to punch him!' I screamed, lifting Dad's unconscious body onto the couch.

'He was going into shock,' Evelyn said, without the slightest hint of remorse. 'And you and I haven't had a chance to talk.'

This woman was unbelievable. 'I don't want to talk to you! Get it through your head!'

She put her hands on her hips, looking down at me like . . . like . . . like a *mother*. My mind scrambled, struggling to generate anything productive.

Maybe there's still time to call Beth. She could come and wipe Dad's memory.

But I knew it was too late for that. And hadn't I come home to tell Dad everything anyway?

But not like this! And not about her*!*

She was still staring at me.

I harrumphed. 'What? Did you hit your head tumbling down from your cloud or something?'

Evelyn blinked, stunned for a moment, before she turned away from me and placed a pillow under Dad's head. She wiped the hair back from his face.

Her hand lingered.

Mine fisted.

'Would you just leave before I call the cops!' I spat out, furious that she continued to make herself comfortable in my home and so easily ignore me – and my most venomous of death stares.

She felt for Dad's pulse and studied his face. 'He'll come around soon.'

Oh, my God. How can this be happening?

I had just faced off against Phoenix – lost – come home not knowing if my father would even acknowledge me after he'd seen my markings, witnessed him have an extreme panic attack before my returned-from-the-dead mother, Evelyn, oh-so-calmly shoved a fist in his face with supernatural strength.

Oh yeah. Family reunions-R-us.

'You could've broken his jaw!' I said, at a loss to do anything other than hurl abuse at her. My mother was a stranger to me. All I knew about her was that she'd traded me in the moment I was born, given my destiny to angels, and committed both Dad and I to a lifetime of unanswered questions. Now she was back and I had zero concept of how to deal with her.

'It's just a bruise,' she waved me off.

I stormed into the kitchen, wet a towel and scooped in a handful of crushed ice before stomping back to Dad's side to dab at where his cheek was already turning purple.

'Before either one of us says anything to James, we should talk,' Evelyn said, sitting on the coffee table opposite, her fire-blue eyes darting between Dad and me. I could just imagine what was going through her mind.

Bet you never thought you'd be faced with us again. And never wanted to.

'You *mean* you need time to think fast so you can bail on him, *again*.' Every word tasted sour. I needed to get a grip. I was damned if this woman was going to push me over the edge. 'Look . . .' I blew out a breath. 'You were right. Knocking him out was a good option. Don't bother with the balcony, it's a nightmare to jump down – just use the front door and hide your face from the security guys on your way. When Dad wakes up, I'll tell him there was an intruder and that he was attacked. He'll think he was seeing things and let it go.'

She looked at me, eyes wide. 'Do you really think I would just run out the door?'

I almost laughed at her offended tone. 'Do *you* really think you *won't*?'

She sighed and glanced at Dad again. 'You inherited his stubbornness.' She looked like she wanted to say more but shook her head, frustrated. The movement gave me a small amount of satisfaction. 'I'm not going anywhere.'

Come. On.

I stared at her, wondering if I had time to literally throw her out before he woke up.

Christ. I can just picture Dad waking up to see his daughter and dead wife ripping each other apart.

'Please, just go,' I said. Things would be better once there were several cities between her and us. 'You don't belong here.'

She crossed her arms. But I could tell she was tensed and ready, waiting to see if things were going to get physical.

My eyes narrowed and the temptation to force her hand rose to the surface. But we both knew I couldn't risk it.

'Does he know what you are?' she asked, her shoulders relaxing.

I slumped back onto my heels. 'No. But he knows something. He's read your letter and seen my markings. I was planning to tell him today.'

She nodded, taking it all in. 'Well, then, I arrived at the right time. We'll tell him together. Everything.'

'You're so thoughtful,' I sniped.

Dad started to stir.

'Fine,' I said. 'But when you start flinging lies in the air, don't expect me to go along with them. Unlike you, my version of "everything" will actually contain the truth.'

Before she could respond, Dad's eyes fluttered open.

'Violet?' he said, his voice crackly and uncertain.

'Dad, it's okay,' I responded, putting a hand on his shoulder. 'You're home and safe.' I gave Evelyn a warning look then turned my attention back to my father. 'No one will hurt you again.'

His eyes came into focus and, despite his confusion, he smiled at me. I smiled back. Then he saw Evelyn. He gasped and I had to grab hold of him to keep him steady as he scrambled to sit up.

'Dad, breathe. You're going to have another panic attack,' I said as soothingly as possible.

His eyes were so wide they were mostly white. 'Oh, God. I *didn't* imagine it. Who are you? You ... You look ...' he stammered.

Evelyn took a deep breath and locked her eyes on his. 'You took me on a carriage ride through Central Park on our first date. You only had enough money for half the trip so we were dumped in the middle of the park and had to walk back. You picked flowers for me along the way. When you said goodbye that night, you kissed me and said, "This is only the beginning." We met for breakfast the following day and every day after that, for the next six months. The first morning we didn't have breakfast together was our wedding day.'

Dad was frozen. I think I was frozen too. From one small speech I now knew more about their relationship than Dad had ever told me. And it only made me more livid.

How could she have done this to him?

Time seemed to stand still. Evelyn looking at Dad, imploring him to accept this impossibility, Dad staring back at her with disbelief. My eyes shot between the two of them ... My *parents*.

'Evelyn?' he breathed the word.

She nodded.

'Are you ...' he swallowed. 'Are you a ghost?'

'No,' Evelyn said calmly. 'I'm human. Mostly.' Her brow furrowed. 'I think.'

'Oh,' Dad said.

I rolled my eyes at her.

Great clarification.

'James, Violet and I have a lot to explain. We would like to be able to tell you everything if you're willing to listen, but we must warn you – once you know, you will become a part of this world . . .' She glanced down, a sadness creeping into her voice. 'And you can never go back.'

I ground my jaw. I hated that she was right. I also hated the way she united us. There was no '*we*'. She'd kept her secrets from Dad since the moment they had met. Everything had been a lie. Then, when I was born, she'd accepted an angel's bargain – probably for a penthouse suite in heaven – and committed me to a life as a Grigori. Sure, I'd had to choose whether to accept it, but I was learning fast: angels are determined beings and what they want, they usually get.

She would have known that, too.

Worse, not only had she handed over my fate the moment I was born, she'd given me to an angel of the Sole, making me the one and only human Grigori to have ever been empowered by the highest-ranking and most mysterious order.

Yeah, I'm high up in the freak department.

'Violet?' Dad said, interrupting my thoughts, his face still a picture of shock.

I sighed, drawing my eyes away from Evelyn. 'It's her, Dad. I . . . found her when I was in Greece. Are you sure you're up to hearing the whole story?'

He shifted position and began rolling up his sleeves, the way he did when he'd set his mind on something. He took my hand, gripping it tight, and cast a wary glance in Evelyn's direction.

'I know my daughter. I *knew* my wife. You look incredibly like her, but she died seventeen years ago and you . . . You look the way she did the day she died.' He glanced at her wayward hair. 'Almost.'

I smiled, proud of Dad for not just falling into her arms.

'I *will* hear the entire story, nothing spared.' He gestured to Evelyn. 'You know things other people wouldn't, but that doesn't prove anything as far as I'm concerned.' He let go of my hand, stretched his arm across the back of the sofa and raised his eyebrows. 'Start talking.'

It must have taken every ounce of courage not to break down right there, not to grab Evelyn and hold her tight – whether he believed it was really her or not. Dad loved her like he loved no other person in this world and I knew nothing had changed that over the past seventeen years.

Evelyn was staring at him, a thoughtful look on her face. 'You've changed,' she said finally.

'Apparently you haven't. Talk!' Dad demanded.

Go, Dad!

Evelyn saw the amusement in my eyes and rolled hers in response.

'I'm human, like you,' she began, 'born to two human parents, but when my mother was in late pregnancy she had a placenta rupture. The doctors were able to deliver me, but it was a different time then – they didn't have the resources they do now. My mother did not survive.'

My heart sank. I had always thought there was nothing worse than knowing my mother had only held me for a few short minutes. But there was, I could see it in her eyes when she told the story. Her mother had never held her at all.

Dad shifted in his seat. 'Evelyn never told me that,' he said cautiously.

She smiled sadly. 'I was scared to give away too much information. I was always careful – it was the way I was trained.'

Dad maintained a stoic expression. I think it was the only way he could go on.

'Continue,' he said.

Evelyn nodded. 'When a human life is brought into the world, the moments following his or her first breath are vital. Newborns are bathed in the aura of new life. If a child suffers the loss of like-blood, most commonly a parent, within the first twelve days of their life, he or she is also overwhelmed by the aura of new death. When the two opposing forces are so strong, a doorway can be created.'

'What kind of doorway?' Dad asked, now cautiously glancing in my direction. He was already connecting the dots.

'When new life combines with new death it creates a kind of tunnel.' She took a deep breath. I found myself doing the same. 'A tunnel that . . . an angel can use to transfer a piece of its essence to the body. At seventeen, the child is given the choice of whether or not to embrace the gifts and responsibilities that come with having that essence.' She looked at me.

I'd practically stopped breathing.

'An . . . angel?' Dad repeated slowly.

'Yes, James. Angels are very real. They aren't what you probably think they are – they aren't always kind and they aren't always cruel but they are definitely always active and a controlling force over our world. If a person who carries an angel essence chooses to embrace, he or she is given – among other things – increased strength, speed, weapons both internal and external, the ability to sense otherworldly beings, a healing capacity, a partner in arms and . . . while still susceptible to mortality by harm, a much-extended lifespan, ageing increasingly slower the older we get.' She looked down. 'We can live for many hundreds of years.'

I was impressed Dad was still in the room, and upright. He cleared his throat. 'How old are you?'

Evelyn didn't even blink. 'I was 187 years old when I died. Now I'm back, I guess you could say I've passed my bicentenary.'

Dad looked at me, wide-eyed. 'Violet, have you been *listening* to this? Surely, this isn't what has been going on with you for the past months? This can't be real.'

'I wish it wasn't, Dad.' I took his hand. It was hot and clammy. 'But she *is* who she says and what she says. And just as an angel gave his essence to Evelyn . . . I'm what they call a Grigori. Part human but also, part angel. I have abilities – but you've already seen my wrists.' I bit my lip nervously, remembering his severe reaction at seeing the swirling silver markings before I'd taken off to Santorini.

As he looked at them, they started to move with a magic none of us could comprehend, churning like a river of mercury around my wrists. Delicate feathered tips began to emerge in the patterns, matching the design on Evelyn's wristbands. Dad glanced between us and I noticed Evelyn staring, mesmerised too.

'She said you had to choose to do this. Did you *want* this, Violet?'

'Not at the beginning. I wanted to finish school, become an artist, be . . . normal. After everything that happened . . .' my voice caught at the memory of the attack.

Dad nodded, not making me say it aloud. Evelyn watched on silently. There was no way I was about to explain it to her – the way that teacher had attacked me at my old school. Dad and I had done everything we could to try and get life back on track after the court case and all the awful questions.

'What happened?'

I glared at her, and continued speaking to Dad.

'Grigori all have a partner. A person whose power complements ours the most. Grigori can help to start the healing process in their partners when they are injured. The only problem is, apart from me, Grigori can only heal their own partner. Lincoln's mine.'

'What do you mean, *apart* from you?' Evelyn butted in, impatiently.

'I'm not here to answer *your* questions!' I snapped. Again, I turned back to Dad. 'I have some extra . . . abilities. Nothing major,' I said with a shrug. Dad looked at me like I'd just turned green.

'Lincoln was hurt,' Evelyn said, putting it together.

I nodded, remembering what it had been like to know he would die without my help. The overwhelming fear of a world that didn't include him was all I needed to know I'd made the right choice.

'He was dying,' I said.

'You became . . .' he couldn't find the words. 'This!' he pointed to my wrists. '*This* was for Lincoln?'

His disappointment stung, but I stayed calm to give him time to process. 'He would've died. I don't regret my choice, Dad. And now I'm Grigori and that means I'm a warrior.'

'A warrior against what?' he barked, incredulous.

I took a deep breath. 'Angels who exile themselves from their rightful place and take on human form.'

'Fallen angels?' he clarified. 'You *fight* fallen angels?'

'Yes. They're strong and powerful and . . . evil. They can do things that others can't and they are intent on taking this world for their own.'

'Sweetheart, there are no fallen angels walking around in this world.' He shook his head, as if trying to bring himself back to reality.

'Yes there are. You even know one.' I braced myself and bit down on the inside of my cheek. 'Phoenix is an exiled angel.'

'Phoenix? That guy that you were hanging out with a while back?'

I nodded. Dad had never liked him.

'You brought Phoenix into your home?' Evelyn asked, her tone carrying both disbelief and accusation.

I flashed her a quick smile. I didn't owe her an explanation.

'But you just said they were all evil,' Dad continued.

I nodded again, this time with regret. 'Phoenix has human blood in him, too, and that means he can seem more human than other exiles. He fooled me.' I dropped my head, feeling the shame of my choices. 'Lots of people have paid the price, with their lives.'

'Violet, what are you talking about?' Dad asked.

I thought of the Grigori who had died fighting Phoenix's exiles on Santorini. 'People are dead, Dad. I just got back from trying to stop Phoenix from opening the gates to Hell. He could've killed thousands of people but Grigori came in force from all around the world. We fought, we saved Santorini, but . . . we failed anyway. He used me to bring something out of Hell that makes nightmares seem like fairy floss. He's determined to be all-powerful and ... he's the way he is because of me.'

I could see Dad struggling to process my words but there was little point in stopping now, so I ploughed on.

'Phoenix has gone for now but I don't think forever and even if it is, there are still more exiles. They'll keep coming and we'll keep fighting them. This is the truth that you deserve, Dad. The truth that she–' I jabbed a finger towards Evelyn, 'should've told you a long time ago – like, before she married you, or before she had a child with you. *Definitely* before she chose to die and leave us.' My plan to remain calm had come unstuck.

Dad seemed frozen with shock but somehow he managed to reach over and pull a tissue from the coffee table to pass to me. I dabbed at my eyes but otherwise ignored the fact I'd started to leak.

'Did you really do that?' Dad asked, now looking at Evelyn. His voice was even and low.

Evelyn closed her eyes briefly. When she opened them, they were resolute. 'A few weeks before Violet was born, I started to have dreams. As Grigori we all have strengths. I'm what they call a dream-walker – I can communicate with others in the dreamscape. That always made it easier for angels to contact me. One angel started to visit me before Violet's birth. He was *very* powerful. He told me that wars were coming. I was given a choice: exist in a world, knowing my family would ultimately suffer in a reality ruled by exiled angels or give up my life and yes,' she glanced at me, 'commit my daughter to a fate where she would become what I am.' She paused. 'From what I've seen she is a respected warrior.'

I rolled my eyes. 'Compliments don't mend bridges. And you forgot the part where in return you got to live happily ever after – until I plucked you out of heaven, that is!'

'Violet!' Dad said, abruptly.

I closed my mouth.

'Wait, what do you mean you "plucked her out of heaven"?'

I pressed my lips together. There was so much to explain, it was hard to know where to start. 'My angel maker told me she made a deal to give me up to them. It doesn't take a genius to figure out where she went after she died.' I forced myself to remain indifferent. 'Phoenix executed a sacrificial ceremony from an ancient scripture in Santorini and part of my blood ended up in the mix. He got his mother and somehow . . . I got mine.'

We all sat in silence for a moment, digesting.

'This is . . .' Dad shook his head, but then blurted out, 'What colour was my underwear on our wedding night?'

Evelyn's lips curled. 'You weren't wearing any.'

I think I'm going to be sick.

'When we drove out to our honeymoon cottage, what happened halfway there?' he shot back.

'You ran out of fuel and made me wait in the car for three hours while you walked to the gas station.' Her smile widened.

'What was the last thing you ever said to me?'

Her smile faded. 'I asked you to name our daughter Violet.'

'The *very* last thing,' Dad pushed.

Evelyn bit her lip, looking for the first time vulnerable. 'I love you . . . both.'

Dad dropped from the couch onto his knees in front of her.

'Was it all lies?' Dad pleaded, not moving any closer.

'No.'

'You died . . .' he said, a tear sliding down his face.

'Yes.'

'And now you're back.'

'Yes.'

He swallowed and stood up, still trying to appear indifferent. 'For how long?'

'I don't know.' And then Evelyn's eyes seemed to lose their focus and she slumped to the ground, unconscious.

chapter two

'I am not bound to please thee with my answers.'
William Shakespeare

things weren't going in my direction.

After Evelyn first came to, she'd continued to pass out intermittently as we tried to answer Dad's many questions.

After the fourth time she blacked out, Dad had taken her into his room and ordered her to rest.

That was three weeks ago.

She was still there.

I'd tried to explain everything to Dad, sat up with him, night after night, giving him various demonstrations of my power, but logic is a strong counter-agent to acceptance. Eventually I called in Griffin and Spence to help. Griffin had the ability to instil truth in a person as long as what he was saying was in fact true. After a few choice words, it became difficult for Dad to question him.

Spence hammered everything home with a showing of his glamour abilities, morphing into a number of different personas and settling on simply putting his hand on my shoulder and cloaking us both with invisibility. I couldn't help but notice during his display that Spence's power had grown significantly in the last few months.

Finally, Dad knew the truth.

His acceptance was closely followed by a demand to see Lincoln.

They sat across from each other at the dining table, Dad staring at Lincoln in a new – unfriendly – manner.

'I welcomed you into my home,' Dad said, threateningly. 'Let you spend time with my daughter, *despite* the age difference. I thought we had an understanding.'

'Dad,' I groaned from my perch on the kitchen bench, but it was useless.

I'd expected Lincoln to be on edge or at least cautious. I was wrong.

He stared right back at Dad, sporting his own steely glare. 'With all due respect, Mr Eden, I've been here many times and seen you very few. For the first two years I knew Violet, we were just friends who worked out together. I never encouraged anything . . . more than friendship.'

Sadly true.

'When I first met her, she was trying to put her life back together after the attack, though I only learned about that recently. Her world had been thrown upside down by that bastard.' His hands fisted on the table. 'It's no wonder she was desperate to find a way to get control of her life. I helped give her some of that.' He glanced at me as I paled, half expecting

Dad to leap up and throw a punch in his direction. 'And she did the rest.'

Dad flinched and glanced towards the hallway where Evelyn was eavesdropping. She didn't look happy.

'That is, in part, true,' Dad confessed. 'But I trusted you with Violet and I now hear you happily sent her, with an evil angel no less, to jump off a cliff in order to save *your* life!'

I had to give it to Dad, he did have a way of presenting things in an unfavourable light.

Lincoln's composure didn't falter. 'I was unconscious and had no idea that she'd gone to embrace. I never wanted her to make the choice for me.' His next words were heavy and slow. 'I have to live with that for the rest of my life.'

Dad shook his head. 'And so you should.'

I chose that moment to step forward. 'Would you rather I was a different person, Dad?'

He broke his eye-lock with Lincoln to look at me.

'Would you rather I had let him die? Chose *my* future over *his* life?'

Dad was silent.

I glanced in Evelyn's direction. 'That's not something *I* could've lived with.' I walked to stand behind Lincoln, the symbolism not lost on anyone. 'I've made choices. Some I regret, some will haunt me forever. But leaping off that cliff to become who I was supposed to be, to save him – that's one choice I will never regret.'

I couldn't see Lincoln's face, but his body was very still.

Dad eventually cleared his throat and stood up. He was far from ready to forgive and forget.

'I hear what you say, Violet. But I can't help but feel you've been forced into this world for the wrong reasons.' He glared at Lincoln.

Lincoln stood up. 'I understand your feelings, Mr Eden. I look forward to changing your mind about me one day. But until then, I can only give you my word that I value Violet as both a person and a Grigori. And . . .' he looked at me briefly, 'I'd do anything for her.' And with that, he made for the door.

I followed him out to the lift. I'd expected him to be angry, ranting that Dad had lost his mind. But he was silent. Too silent.

I pressed the lift button. Lincoln didn't look at me.

'He just wants someone to blame. It won't last,' I said quietly, wishing I could be there for Lincoln the way I wanted.

He tried to say something, but closed his mouth again, as if he couldn't speak, and shook his head.

'Linc?' I reached out, the tips of my fingers grazing his hand. The contact sparked the usual influx of soul-crushing hurt.

Lincoln gripped my hand and suddenly, without warning, pulled me into his chest and wrapped his arms around me so tightly it was as if he was trying to weld us together.

It was a rare display of raw emotion and an even rarer display of physical need. I held on to him just as tightly, neither one of us saying or doing any more. Just holding on. I breathed him in – sun and melting honey – my soul only craving for more.

We stood like that until the elevator doors slid open. Lincoln sighed and pulled away from me, his hand moving to my jaw as he did, his thumb smudging my cheek in that way I loved, his emerald-green eyes piercing into mine. Wordlessly, he stepped into the lift.

The moment the doors closed, my knees gave out and I dropped to the ground in literal agony. I gripped my chest and stomach as, from somewhere within, the magic that bound our souls was torn apart.

I didn't even hear the door open behind me, but suddenly Evelyn was there, crouching beside me. I felt a tentative hand on my back as I tried to hold back the tears of pain.

'Are you hurt?' she asked, her voice sharp and fast. I could feel her tension as she looked around for an enemy.

'No,' I managed to say.

'Then what?' she continued, looking me over. 'I don't under–' she broke off, looking at me, then the lift. 'Lincoln? This is–' she stopped again. Then, sternly, she grabbed me by the shoulders, hauling me to my feet.

'Tell me that you two are not involved!' She shook me. 'Tell me you are *not* in love with your partner!'

I tried to swallow back the pain, the punishment for touching him. I started to shiver.

'Answer me now! Are you sleeping with him?' Evelyn said, giving me one more shake, forcing my head up to hers. Her eyes were blazing and boring into me.

'No,' I said, tears streaming from my eyes, partly from physical pain, partly from my heart. I knew why she was asking – it was forbidden for Grigori partners to start relationships – it caused some kind of negative response in our angelic components and the results were dangerous; at best the Grigori's powers are weakened, at worst they are lost. But Lincoln and I were quite the opposite.

We were soulmates.

Our powers would become greater if we were together . . . But there would be other costly consequences that neither one of us wanted to bring about.

She kept her eyes on me as I tried to gain control. 'But there is something, isn't there? Between you two, something you're not telling me.'

Her demand gave me what I needed to pull myself together and step out of her hold.

'You know what, *Mother*, if you're so clever, figure it out yourself!' And with that I stormed passed her into the apartment.

Evelyn had made herself comfortable in our home, with Dad now sleeping in the living room and despite my efforts, she didn't seem to be going anywhere.

It didn't take a genius to see Dad was falling in love with her all over again. I tried to make him understand how awful she was – and he actually agreed with what I said, part of the time. Evelyn had lied to him for their entire relationship and he hadn't forgotten that. But even so, his eyes tracked her around the apartment constantly.

The day after Lincoln's visit, I spent the morning avoiding home and trying to run off some of the residual soul-ache his touch had left behind. I always felt a little better after a good workout.

When I got home I grabbed a bottle of water from the kitchen and noticed yet another cut-up newspaper in pieces on the bench. I held it up to Dad and shook it.

'Has she explained why she keeps massacring these yet?' I asked, joining him on the sofa. She had been destroying our newspapers daily and I kept finding international ones stuffed into the rubbish.

'I don't think it will go on for much longer,' Dad said with a smile that spelled trouble. 'I've shown her how to use the internet.'

Great, that explains why I can't find my laptop.

'We should just send her to a hotel or something. Griffin could arrange it.' I'd offered this solution a number of times to no avail, but I was determined.

Dad just shook his head and gave his usual response. 'She's too weak. Whatever happened to her in the transition back . . . here – she can't be on her own.'

I slumped against the pillows. 'She's probably faking the fainting spells. She doesn't belong here, Dad.'

He sighed and put an arm around my shoulder for one of our traditional awkward hug moments.

'Vi, I know what you're saying. She's made choices that we don't understand or agree with, but I think we need to give her the chance to get well. Once she is, then . . . we'll work out what to do.'

Yeah, right.

I pulled away from him. 'I've gotta have a shower,' I said, standing up.

'I was hoping to see you in your dress tonight. You know, have a photo together or something.'

I shrugged. 'I'm getting ready with Steph,' I said, omitting the part about us meeting up at Hades.

'She could've come here. There was a time when she was here more than at her own home.'

I took a final sip of water and re-capped it. 'It's a bit crowded here already.'

Dad stood and took my hands in his, looking down at the bracelets that were covering my markings. 'Any news?'

I shook my head. 'Griffin's in touch with the Academy daily. They've had some sightings but nothing concrete.'

In fact, it was as if Phoenix and Lilith had dropped off the face of the earth. But at the same time, I knew they hadn't. Something was brewing. I could feel it – and it wasn't a happy feeling.

'You're not "hunting" tonight, are you?' Dad asked-slash-insisted.

I smiled. 'Not tonight.' I'd been given the night off for our school dance.

He kissed me on the top of my head. He smelled like Dad – shaving cream and aftershave.

'She's awake you know, if you wanted to say goodbye before you head off.'

He moved towards the dining table, where he had set up a makeshift office.

I laughed. 'I'll keep that in mind.'

CHAPTER THREE

'Can you hear Destiny laugh as she tiptoes toward you?
Destiny is heartless.'

Anonymous

The days ahead were full of landmark events, starting with the end of year dance that night, the Fenton art course starting the next day – yes, weekend attendance was expected – and on Monday, my official graduation.

I can't say I was expecting great things from my graduation. There was no doubt my exam performance had been substandard. But I was at least proud I'd made it through to the end of high school. Plus, Steph's speech would be a guaranteed highlight. She was valedictorian – and not afraid of saying, well . . . whatever came to mind.

It was the Fenton course that I was really looking forward to. I hoped those six weeks would be my stepping stone into the arts community and, all dramas aside, a chance for me to be normal.

Steph had bought me an incredible leather portfolio so large it would fit full canvases and all of my supplies. I knew that walking down the street with it would fill me with pride.

As I entered Hades with my dress – in protective carrier – slung over my shoulder, I smiled at the thought of trading it in for my portfolio the next day.

I made my way to Dapper's apartment through the bar. I knocked on the heavy door and called out so they knew it was me. Dapper had been attacked by Phoenix's exiles a month ago, when we were trying to set up an exchange. Phoenix had double-crossed us. Dapper, Onyx, and most of all, Steph, had paid the price.

I felt the same twinge of guilt every time I went to his place now and saw the steel reinforced door and listened to the various locks being undone. Dapper had once prided himself on his position of neutrality, but Phoenix hadn't cared; his exiles came anyway. Dapper almost died that night and it had taken something from him that I wasn't sure he would ever get back.

'Remind me again why it is I don't seem to be able to get rid of you?' he mumbled in greeting before looking over his shoulder to Steph, adding, 'Or her.'

The truth? Both of us were currently avoiding our homes like the plague. The last I'd heard, Steph's mother had been 'entertaining' a particularly crude, wealthy and handsy businessman whom Steph could barely tolerate.

'Because you'd be lost without us and as much as it annoys you, you get satisfaction out of knowing our presence annoys Onyx even more.'

'I heard that,' Onyx's voice rang out from inside. 'And it is entirely true. It's some form of twisted punishment.' His tone held no bite.

Dapper grunted, but I saw the corners of his mouth lift to an almost-smile.

I patted him on the shoulder as I walked in to find Steph right at home; dress hanging on the edge of the stand-up lamp, shoes off, hair wet and dripping on the carpet where she sat cross-legged, snacking on biscuits and flipping through *Vogue*.

She glanced up at me. 'If you want food, eat now. Nothing permitted in the two-hour lead-up.' She patted her stomach. 'Otherwise it'll show.'

I rolled my eyes. 'Are you planning on not eating all night?'

She fixed a serious look on me. 'Violet,' was all she said.

I took that as a yes, dropped my bag and slung my dress over the sofa before sitting beside her on the floor and grabbing a biscuit. I didn't bother explaining I wouldn't be sticking to the no-food rule. No dress was worth that.

It wasn't like I had anyone to impress.

We were going as a group: Steph and Salvatore, Zoe and Spence – who'd somehow managed to qualify for graduation too – and Jase with me. I'd felt uncomfortable about going with Steph's brother, but Zoe assured me she would be doing everything to command his attention for the evening.

Jase, apparently, had developed a small interest in me. It was flattering, since I used to drool over him in the pre-Lincoln days. But even though I couldn't be with Lincoln there was no way I could consider anything else with anyone else and . . . My heart just couldn't take another male complication.

I looked over at Onyx, who was sitting at the minibar, with a large glass of something mind-numbing, I assumed, and an open laptop in front of him.

'What are you doing?' I asked.

'Trying to track down some old exile chat sites.'

My eyes widened. 'You're kidding, right?'

'Absolutely not,' he grinned.

'Why?' I asked suspiciously. The last thing we needed was Onyx getting back in touch with his old followers and leaking information to them.

'Don't panic, rainbow. I'm just seeing if the threads are still active. Thought one might mention a Phoenix or Lilith sighting. They're quite the celebrities these days. The "first exile", returned from the pits of Hell and her exile son that bested you.'

There was serious envy in his voice. 'Jealous, much?'

'*Very* much.' He smiled at me wickedly and it sent a shiver down my spine. Reminders that Onyx had spent the majority of his existence as a force of all things corrupt and insane was never something I could afford to forget. For now, though, it seemed his humanity was taking shape and somehow, he'd earned my trust. But that didn't mean I could be complacent. After all, he'd almost succeeded in killing both Lincoln and me in the past. That's a hard thing to forget.

'Have you found anything?' Steph asked, interrupting my thoughts.

'Some murmurs here and there around the world, a little activity in Europe and on the east coast of America. Whatever they're doing, they're getting around, which isn't good.'

'Why?' Steph asked.

He closed the laptop. 'Because it means they have a plan.'

He made a show of looking at his watch then back at me – up and down. 'You only have two hours left. Do you at least plan on looking half-decent for your date?'

I gave him a tight-lipped smile. 'It's not a date.'

He smiled back, broadly.

'It's not . . .' I warned.

Steph looked down, flipping through her magazine again.

'There's always one way to know for sure,' Onyx offered smugly.

'And what's that?'

'When he arrives to pick you up, if you're going as a group he'll shake hands with the guys and kiss each girl on the cheek. If he's there for you alone, he'll just nod at the others, before leaning in to kiss your cheek. Only you.'

I rolled my eyes and threw a cookie at him. 'You are such a weirdo!'

Dapper walked over to a cupboard, pulled out a hand vacuum and passed it to me with a growl. 'Every last crumb.'

'It was his fault,' I sulked even as I started to clean up.

When Steph and I finally emerged from the bathroom Zoe was there, dressed in a short midnight-blue dress that perfectly matched the coloured tips of her short brown hair.

Looking between her and Steph, who was wearing a beautiful vintage dress – golden silk, strapless with lace trimmings, the two could not be more opposite.

I'd opted for my uniform black. The dress was a simple halter-neck, set off by a delicate gold chain hanging low on the fabric. Hair up, I'd kept my make-up focused on the eyes, using a smoky effect – one I'd copied from Morgan – highlighted by golden edges.

'Can you believe we're going out for a night to have pure fun? No exiles, no angels, no Grigori strategy – just us, music, dancing and seriously spiked punch!' Steph looked like she was about to explode with delirium.

'And for some of us, the after party!' Zoe added suggestively, looking at her with raised eyebrows.

Steph's smile broadened. 'That might have something to do with it,' she said, slyly. But we both knew tonight was the night she was planning to take things all the way with Salvatore.

I smiled, despite the twinge in my heart.

Steph's phone beeped.

'The boys are here,' she said, before almost sprinting to the door and glancing over her shoulder to add, 'Okay, so I'm not quite up to the standard make-them-wait protocol tonight.'

Zoe and I laughed as we followed her out.

'You know I have every intention of stealing your date from you tonight,' Zoe said as we walked down the stairs.

'He's not my date,' I said quickly. 'Steal away.'

Dapper caught sight of us the moment we entered the bar area and something in his expression looked suspiciously like pride. Definitely. I beamed, even as I felt a stab of regret at not having included Dad in the preparations.

However, my attention was quickly diverted and I started scanning the room. I'd felt his presence before we came downstairs but now it was overwhelming. Sure enough, Lincoln was sitting at the bar with Nathan and Becca, his eyes on me. On autopilot, my feet started to carry me towards him.

'You look beautiful,' a voice said from behind me. I stopped and spun around to see Jase, looking quite beautiful himself in a well-fitting tux. Made to measure, I was sure – he was a Morris after all. His eyes, hooded by lush dark eyebrows that were in complete contrast to his platinum-blond hair, took in my dress and his smile made me blush.

'Thanks,' I said, feeling awkward.

'Hey, mate,' Spence said, slapping Jase on the shoulder. Jase stumbled forward. I glared at Spence, who shouldn't have been so careless with his Grigori strength.

Jase looked around at the rest of the group, giving them an all-inclusive hello nod before turning back to me, putting his hands on my shoulders and leaning in towards me with his whole body. Then he kissed me on the cheek.

Out of the corner of my eye I saw Onyx watching with a huge grin.

Son of a . . .

Onyx wasn't the only one who reacted. From behind me I felt the spike of Lincoln's fury. I couldn't stop myself from turning and looking over my shoulder into his green eyes that were ablaze. He was already on his feet and moving towards us. I sighed.

This will not be good.

He stopped beside me, but focused on Jase.

Jase held out his hand. 'Lincoln. Did you come by to see us off?'

Lincoln shook his hand in response and I could almost feel the effort it took him not to snap it in two.

'No. I just stopped in with Becca and Nate to have a drink.'

'Oh, right,' Jase said, showing his disbelief and following it up with a dangerous smirk. 'Well, I get that you have a big-brother thing with Violet, so I promise I'll take good care of her and not keep her out too late.'

Mother of God. Does he want to lose his life?

Lincoln shrugged, too calm. 'I wouldn't describe our relationship as the brother–sister type, Jase. I believe that would be frowned upon. Nate?'

Nathan looked up briefly, a twinkle in his eye. 'Definitely.'

Blushing? Me?

Jase was speechless, too, while Lincoln was looking increasingly satisfied with himself.

'Stop it,' I said, under my breath.

'Well,' Lincoln said, now considerably lighter in tone, 'have a nice night.'

'We will,' I answered before whatever comeback was lurking in Jase's mind came out and started World War Three.

Onyx chose that moment to walk past me, brushing my shoulder as he watched Lincoln stalk away and resume his position at the bar. 'I like him more and more.'

'Hey, Jase!' Spence called out.

'Yeah?' Jase responded, looking relieved for the interruption.

'I need someone who knows their way around this place.'

Jase looked back at me, eyebrows raised. 'This isn't going to be a good idea, is it?'

Spence had a familiar wicked gleam in his eyes.

'Not at all,' I said.

Nonetheless, Jase headed off to join Spence. And I spun on my heel to see Lincoln, perched on his stool and looking right at me.

I stormed over. 'That wasn't necessary,' I snapped.

'I know,' he replied, quietly, catching me off-guard. He sighed and looked guilty. 'I know,' he said again, his eyes on me in a way that somehow covered my whole body and caused an unstoppable tingle all the way down to my toes.

Damn, he knows exactly how to unhinge me.

'But what do you want me to do? Stand by and smile while he hits on you?'

He looked down at his hands on the bar. I glanced at Nathan and Becca, who were both pretending not to notice our conversation.

Now it was my turn to sigh. 'You know I'm not . . . You know it's not . . . like that.'

I reached out and closed my hand over his. Neither of us spoke for a moment. His hand flattened on the bar beneath mine, fingers splaying just enough for mine to slip into the gaps.

The tiny movements – the stroke of a thumb, the slow raising of knuckles – were somehow more sensual than anything I'd ever experienced.

Finally, heart racing, I cleared my throat. 'You could always come tonight. We're going as a group, you know.'

He breathed deeply, his attention still focused on our hands.

I powered on.

Ignore the hands. Ignore the hands.

'Maybe we could just have one night where we didn't have to worry about everything else? Maybe we could just have *fun*, dance.' I smiled cheekily. 'We could always give salsa a go.'

At this, he looked at me, a single eyebrow raised. 'Salsa?'

I shrugged, my blush returning. 'Yeah, well . . . or anything.'

'You can salsa?'

'Um, no – but I've always wanted to learn,' I said, starting to realise how silly I sounded.

His eyes lit up. 'Just when I thought you couldn't surprise me.'

I held my breath, thinking he might just decide to come along. But as I watched, he glanced around the room and his eyes dropped.

'You're not going as a group, Vi, and we both know it. Anyway, it's not a good idea despite how much I'd like it to be.' And with that, he shut down and the walls came up. Typical Linc.

And typical me, I bristled, retrieving my hand suddenly and stepping away.

Spence chose that moment to reappear, carrying a tray of shot glasses.

'Time to get this party started, Eden.' He glanced over his shoulder nervously. 'And preferably before Dapper comes back!'

Around me, everyone was smiling and tossing back their drinks. I glanced at Lincoln. He watched on, unimpressed.

I grabbed a glass and threw back the shot.

'Cars are here!' Steph called out.

Spence tilted the tray, holding a final glass in Lincoln's direction. Lincoln simply shook his head. Without delay, and just because it all hurt and I needed to take it out on him, I grabbed his shot off the tray and gulped it down, ignoring the burn in my throat as I smiled.

'Waste not want not,' I said with a shrug before turning tail and heading for the door.

chapter four

'Are not all angels ministering spirits sent to serve . . .?'

Hebrews 1:14

two hours and a couple of spiked cups of punch later, I escaped the dance floor to get some fresh air.

Everyone was buzzing, laughing at the dorky dance moves of Steph and Salvatore and at Lydia Skilton trying desperately to grope Spence – not that he minded. Jase and I danced along with Zoe and the others until finally I managed to slip away, hoping to give Zoe a chance for some one-on-one time with Jase.

I slipped out the sliding doors of our school-hall-turned-ballroom and onto the small balcony. The truth was, the night was kind of a let-down. Not what I'd imagined in all the lead-up school years and, in the grand scheme of things, less important, too.

Once I was alone, I let my facade slip. My smile fell away and the loneliness I usually kept at bay rose to the surface. As soon as I opened myself up, I sensed him. And realised just how close he was.

I straightened and walked back to the doors, looking into the ballroom. My heart skipped a beat when I saw him, standing just inside the entry, wearing a suit and open-necked shirt. There was something about the way he filled a suit – something that made me think it was the original reason for their creation. But suit-genetics only favoured the few. His hair was ruffled, light brown with golden streaks, his full lips were parted just enough, his golden-brown skin screamed to be touched and, best of all, his wickedly enticing green eyes looked right into mine.

He's here.

My heart skipped another beat and I wanted to run, or leap into his arms, something. But instead, I found myself walking slowly towards him as he glided closer to me, hands in pockets. It felt like the entire room fell away and it was just us, staring at each other, inches apart, my soul crying out for his. I narrowed my eyes and put my hands on my hips.

'Why are you here?'

He winced. 'You're slurring.'

'Choose to ignore it and answer the question.'

He considered for a moment then nodded, as if coming to a decision. 'Three reasons. One,' he glanced in Jase's direction, who was standing at the edge of the dance floor chatting with Zoe, his eyes on us, 'to keep his hands off you in that dress. Two, the last time I let you walk out of a room without telling you how beautiful you looked, I ended up fishing you out of a volcano and you left before I could tell you . . .' he swallowed, looking me up and down. 'You look stunning.' His eyes bored into mine, silence stretching until he blinked back to awareness. 'And three,' he smiled devilishly, 'if you're going to have fun and *salsa* with anyone, it'd better be with me.' His look slipped into something more basic, more predatory and decidedly like . . . a challenge.

Holy Hell. What has got into him?

My mouth was dry. I was cemented in a deer-caught-in-headlights moment when Jase strolled up, clearly unhappy at Lincoln's arrival.

'Everything okay, Vi?'

I looked at him, eyes wide, mouth agape.

What to say, what to say . . .

But Lincoln spoke first, putting his hand up to stop me. 'Jase, I'm sure I haven't been clear with you on this issue. I apologise for that. Entirely my fault.'

Oh shit.

'Linc,' I butted in, unsuccessfully.

'Allow me to rectify,' Lincoln continued, stepping a little closer to Jase. 'If you look at her again, that *way* you do – I'm going to be very upset. If you touch her in any way that you haven't first been invited to and, well,' he glanced at me, still frozen, before turning his full attention back to Jase, 'even then, I won't be responsible for my actions. Violet and I may not *be* together, but make no mistake; she is mine just as much as I am hers.'

Huh.

I don't know how long all three of us stood there in silence. It was Jase who spoke first, turning to me. 'Violet?'

But I was lost – somewhere between anger at Lincoln for deciding now was declaration time and love towards him for just saying he was mine.

As if best-friend intuition had magically kicked in, Steph appeared. 'Sorry to interrupt. I can see things are going swimmingly over here, but Griffin just arrived – and not for a dance. Party's over.'

Lincoln was already looking towards the door. He turned to me, 'I'll see you outside.'

I nodded and watched as he headed towards Griffin without so much as another glance in Jase's direction.

So much for salsa.

'This is to do with that stuff you can't tell me about that everyone else, including my sister, seems to know about, right?'

I sighed. 'I'm sorry, Jase. My life . . . My life has changed a lot this year. What Lincoln said was really rude, but . . .'

'Not untrue?'

I swallowed, hating myself. 'Right.'

'Then explain to me why you two aren't together.'

Sensational question.

'It's complicated.'

He shifted a little closer to me and put a hand on my shoulder. 'Vi, if you're frightened of him, I can help.'

My eyes widened. 'No, no, it's not that. Lincoln would never hurt me.' That was half the problem.

Jase shook his head. 'Whatever you're caught up in, we can get you out of it.'

I smiled, sad for him, sad for me. 'No, you can't, Jase. And that time has passed. This is who I am now and our lives – yours and mine – don't cross over. I'm sorry.'

With that, I kissed him on the cheek and walked away, hoping I'd done enough to keep him from coming after me again. I didn't want to put him in harm's way – it was bad enough I'd already involved Steph.

Lincoln was waiting in his car outside. I opened the door. 'Where are the others?'

'En route. Jump in.'

Once we started moving Lincoln mumbled, 'Really not the way I saw things panning out.'

I raised an eyebrow. I'd half expected he'd pretend the earlier conversation never took place. 'And where exactly did you see tonight finishing?'

'With you on your back . . .' He paused to see my eyes bug out at the painful pun before he chuckled and finished the sentence, 'after collapsing from too much salsa.' He didn't stop grinning.

'Ha, ha,' I said, but then burst out laughing. He laughed beside me and took my hand and I realised he was giving me my one night of fun.

'I think you've got that the wrong way round, Linc. I'd dance circles around you. Dancing is *my* thing.'

'You said you couldn't salsa,' he said.

'What – and you do?'

He looked entirely too smug and his laugh became lower and secretive. The sound was glorious, pulsing out warmth. My fingernails dug into the seat but the pain of my soul stirring was worth it.

'You realise you haven't ever seen me dance.'

True. Usually, he ran a mile from me when I asked him. Suddenly, I wanted to see him dance more than anything, see him relax for once.

I licked my lips nervously. 'Well, I guess you owe me one now – a dance, that is.'

He settled back into the seat, still smiling but focused on the road. 'I guess I do.'

'Do I get to collect at a time of my choosing?'

He swallowed, his expression now more guarded. 'Within reason.'

I looked out the window. If there was a god – I hated him. Apart from all the angelic reasons I'd been provided with, I mean, who could do this to someone – inflict this much torment? It was not right. Not natural.

Lincoln pulled into the kerb outside my apartment building. I saw everyone else at the front doors, waiting.

'Ah . . . Why are we here?' I asked.

'Griffin just told me to come here,' Lincoln said, turning off the engine and jumping out.

I followed and we joined Steph, Zoe, Spence and Salvatore at the doors.

Zoe raised her eyebrows at me.

'Sorry,' I said with a wince, knowing tonight – and Jase – had not gone her way.

She gnawed on the inside of her cheek for a moment but then shrugged, flicking a hand in the air. 'To be honest, it was all a little complicated anyway,' she said. 'Not my kinda gig.'

We smiled at each other, but I saw a hint of sadness cross her face. Or was it loneliness?

Steph took a long look at Lincoln. 'Are you wearing Onyx's Ralph Lauren suit?'

Lincoln looked bemused. 'How did you know?'

She shrugged. 'He's a good shopping partner and someone else,' she looked at me, 'is always busy training.'

'He offered and I didn't have time to go home and change.' He glanced at me again. 'There were things to be done.'

'Clearly,' Steph said dryly. 'I do hope you left my brother in one piece.'

'I didn't touch him,' Lincoln said.

'I meant emotionally,' Steph replied, following as we all entered the lift.

'Oh,' Lincoln said, and offered no more.

chapter five

'There is little struggle; the doom of the heroes is fixed on high, and they pass in sublime composure, to fulfil their destiny. Their sorrows are awful . . .'

Sir Thomas Noon Talfourd

Dad and Evelyn were sitting at the dining table. Both of their heads snapped up when they saw me walk in. Dad smiled ear to ear, one of his proud-to-be-Dad looks. 'Violet, you look . . . Wow.'

I smiled. 'Thanks, Dad.'

'Very beautiful,' Evelyn said, a strange expression on her face.

I rolled my eyes. 'I'm going to get changed.' And before she could say anything else, I took off for my room, where I proceeded to change into old jeans and a T-shirt and instantly felt more myself.

Walking out again, my eye caught on my portfolio and all my new supplies waiting to be used at the Fenton course. I bit my lower lip, shut off the light and headed back to the living room.

Griffin was standing at the head of the dining table, while Lincoln had moved to the back wall and was leaning against it. Everyone else had taken seats. I chose the empty space beside

Dad. It was strange having everyone together, and in my home. My two worlds had collided and I desperately hoped it was a good thing.

'Here you are, sweetheart,' Dad said sliding a coffee towards me.

I gripped the mug in both hands, took a sip and sighed with relief – coffee had that effect.

'I imagine everyone is wondering why we're here ...' Griffin started.

'Not particularly,' Evelyn responded, flicking her badly chopped bangs from her face. 'If you're here, you're here for me.'

Griffin nodded. 'I'm afraid so, Evelyn. The Academy, it seems, are well aware of your location. They've demanded that you travel to New York for a full evaluation. "Non-negotiable" were their words. And,' he looked at me and I knew my night had just gone from hopeful to hopeless, 'they've strongly urged that Violet makes the trip as well to attend formal Grigori assessment. If she doesn't, they'll consider it a hostile act against the Academy's procedures and will respond accordingly.'

'Meaning they'll send forces here,' Evelyn said.

Griffin's lack of response and weary downcast eyes were answer enough.

Evelyn sighed. 'Josephine?'

Griffin tilted his head to the side and half smiled in tacit acknowledgement. He turned to Dad. 'Josephine is second in command on the Assembly that controls the Academy.'

'I don't care. Neither of you will be going anywhere,' Dad said, looking between us and then to Griffin. 'Forces or not.'

Evelyn took Dad's hand in hers. 'It's okay, James. Josephine and I go way back. I know how she operates and I also know when not to push her.' She glanced at Griffin. 'I would never bring Academy forces into your city. You've already taken an undeserved risk harbouring me for the past three weeks and I'm very grateful.'

Evelyn's words seemed genuine but her tone remained clipped. I couldn't work her out.

'Of course. But with all due respect – it *was* deserved.' Griffin looked at me and nodded.

I swallowed the lump in my throat.

'Indeed,' Evelyn said.

Griffin settled into a chair. 'But you're right. In my position, I cannot go up against the Academy personally. I'm bound to the Assembly and it directly affects the safety of this city. I'd never normally put you or Violet at risk but there is another reason I believe you both need to go.'

Evelyn took a deep breath and closed her eyes. When she opened them I saw something new – her inner warrior. She stared at me and I had to work hard not to shrink back.

'Lilith has gone home.'

Griffin gave a weary nod.

'I guess the party really is over,' Spence said, slumping into his chair.

I couldn't have agreed more.

'What do you mean, gone "home"?' Lincoln asked, pushing away from the wall.

'As much as anywhere was a home for her.' Griffin rubbed his eyes, the weight of his words increasing. 'We suspected she would, but only just received confirmation. Lilith lived

— 42 —

long enough to travel to all corners of the world, but before Evelyn returned her she'd taken a shine to the state of New York. Manhattan is heavily populated by exiles. She will have strength and numbers there.'

Evelyn pushed back in her chair, paused, then stood up.

'I knew you'd keep this,' she said to Dad, fingering a large white ceramic vase that sat in its usual place on the table.

He cleared his throat. 'Of course.'

I, at least, knew this story. Evelyn, an artist herself, used to make ceramics. This was the last piece she'd crafted. Dad had always kept it on display.

She picked up the heavy vase, as though it were as light as a feather.

'I'm glad you did,' she said, before throwing it on the floor.

Dad jumped to his feet, hands out. 'No!'

'I'll make you another one. I promise.' She leaned down and pushed the fragments aside until her hand found what she was looking for. She stood, holding her Grigori dagger.

'Cool,' Zoe murmured.

Griffin was the one to gasp. 'I don't understand. Grigori blades are known to disappear if they exist without a Grigori owner.'

Evelyn turned the dagger's handle in her hand, getting reacquainted with it. 'Nothing about me is normal.'

My hand passed over the hilt of my own Grigori dagger, the dagger that Phoenix had thrown into the volcano at Santorini and that had somehow returned to me three days later. I'd woken up to find it on my bedside table. Not much was normal about me, either.

Evelyn passed Griffin the dagger. 'Would you mind holding on to this?' She took off her wristbands and handed them to Griffin as well.

'You're trusting me with a lot, considering I'm about to deliver you to the Assembly – where you *will* be held indefinitely.'

She put a hand on Griffin's shoulder and glanced at me. 'You've kept her safe. Guided her, when I could not. It is not a big thing to trust you with mere weapons.'

Griffin nodded at the same time as I rolled my eyes.

God, is he welling up? Buying into her crap?

'Gee, Griff – need a tissue?' Spence said, killing the moment.

'When are we leaving?' I asked, getting back to business.

Griffin pulled himself together. 'Tomorrow. The Academy has arranged a plane.'

'Okay,' I said as I grabbed my empty coffee cup and headed towards the kitchen, needing to move.

I made it to the corner where I was out of sight before I exhaled and, hands gripping the bench, dropped my head.

I'm going to miss the Fenton course.

I was being stupid – it was meaningless, just an art course, but it was *my* art course. I'd earned my place in it and had been looking forward to it for so long. It was the only thing I had that was separate from all of this and now I was going to have to give it up. I took a moment to pull myself together, then I walked back out, refusing to show any weakness in front of everyone. I felt Lincoln's eyes on me. I didn't look at him.

Evelyn was talking. 'There's something you'll need to know before we leave.'

'What's that?' Griffin responded.

'If I'm being held captive and can't get out when Lilith is found, she'll need to be stopped. The reason for my return isn't just to help fight her, it's to finally explain how I returned her.'

'You've never told anyone before?' Lincoln asked.

She shook her head. 'I can't explain why not. I just knew it was a secret I had to keep.'

Her words sent an inexplicable shiver up my spine.

Evelyn looked around, assessing us all. I wasn't sure she liked what she saw.

'Why don't you have more senior Grigori here?' she asked, looking at Griffin accusingly. But his Seraph-given authority did not waver for a moment.

'Because I can't get all my Grigori into the Academy. Spence, Salvatore and Zoe are all students and can return with us if they choose. I'll travel as an escort and Lincoln will come as Violet's partner. You won't find any more senior than the two of us.'

Evelyn fixed a challenging glare on Griffin before conceding with a small nod. Finally, power struggles over, she settled into her chair and began her story.

'Lilith was created first and she is more powerful for it. A Grigori dagger made by lesser angels will have no impact on her and even those weapons of higher ranking angels,' she looked at me, 'will not be able to kill her. Jonathan–' her voice caught. 'My partner and I spent more than half a century tracking down old myths and forgotten tales about a substance that could harm exiles in human form. The potion dated back to ancient Egypt and seemed to be extinct. We found imitations but learned the only chance of locating the real thing was by dating it back to the time when angels were still permitted on earth – the time before the flood – and trying to find an untapped source.'

'That must've been near impossible,' Lincoln said.

'It was. But it was also our only chance. We needed the combination of this potion – a type of poison – *and* the Grigori blade if we were going to have any chance of incapacitating Lilith. The potion itself had thirteen ingredients. Twelve were earthbound. However,' she closed her eyes briefly, 'the thirteenth was from the angel realm.'

'So how did you find it?' Griffin asked, enthralled.

'By looking in places where angels who were once on earth might have left it behind. We searched Egyptian tombs that predated the flood until eventually we found one small vial in a just-discovered tomb in 1922.'

Steph gasped. 'Tutankhamun.'

Evelyn nodded.

'Why Egypt?' Lincoln enquired.

'Some of the Pharaohs believed this potion eliminated evil spirits and would elevate them to angelhood after death. They called it the First Breath of the Afterlife.'

'If this potion's purpose is just to incapacitate her, wouldn't Violet's power do the same thing?' Griffin asked.

I rolled my eyes. Clearly Griffin and Evelyn had been talking. I'd never explained the extent of my abilities to her and had asked Dad not to discuss them with her either. But from the look on her face now, she wasn't surprised to hear that I was able to hold exiles immobile without the physical contact other Grigori needed.

'It could . . .' Evelyn said to Griffin. 'But I doubt very much she is strong enough yet.'

Nice.

I gritted my teeth, defensive. 'And I doubt very much that you have *any* idea just how strong I am!'

Evelyn ignored me and kept talking. 'And relying on Violet is a big risk to take. The more I think about it, the more I question if it will be enough. I'd prefer that this didn't all rest in her hands.'

I scoffed. 'Yes, God forbid. We both know the chances are much more in favour of me getting dead long before I can be of any real use.'

Evelyn looked right at me, her stare unfaltering. 'Yes.'

'What?' Dad snapped, looking at Evelyn as if seeing her for the first time. I couldn't help but be pleased he was finally start to see the real her.

Evelyn turned to face him. 'We may all die trying to stop her, James; I've seen countless humans and way too many Grigori fall at her hand. We must be responsible. We must plan for every outcome.'

'Tell us more about the poison,' Griffin interjected. 'How do we find it?'

She shook her head. 'That's the thing. It took us half a century to find the vial, and I used it. You'll never find any more.'

'What's it called?' Steph questioned. She'd been studiously writing down all the details Evelyn had shared.

'It has a few names. Qorot is one, but the most common is Qeres.'

'The perfume?' Steph replied. 'I've read about that – it was used in the mummification process.'

Evelyn looked impressed. 'Yes, though what they refer to as Qeres now is simply that – a perfume. The original concoction was something quite different. It was both an angelic weapon and, when treated with the potion, a way to elevate the sacred tabernacles to become more powerful than anything in the human world.'

I thought of the Ark of the Covenant that we'd opened in Moses' tomb in Jordan. It certainly had not seemed like anything from this world.

'Do you know of any books that might be able to help us?' Steph asked.

'No,' Evelyn responded. 'There were rumours of some ancient texts that had documented its history – but they were destroyed long ago. I know most of the ingredients – frankincense, myrrh and lotus to start – simple earthbound components. But we only ever knew of ten of the ingredients with certainty, leaving us to guess the last two. This problem and the unidentified thirteenth ingredient were the reasons we had to find the potion in its finished state.'

Steph stood up, staring into space.

'What are you thinking?' Griffin asked. He'd come to respect and appreciate Steph's geeky tendencies.

'We should talk to Dapper. If anyone would know where to find a reference to this stuff, I have a feeling it would be him,' Steph said.

'Dapper?' Dad asked.

I couldn't hold back my smile, looking at Dad and Evelyn. Lincoln seemed amused, too. Not only were they about to meet Dapper for the first time, but my parents were also about to be introduced to Onyx.

CHapteR SIX

*'Today there exist in temples book chests which we ourselves
have seen, and, when these temples were plundered, these, we
are told, were emptied by our own men . . .'*

Paulus Orosius

'**I**sn't this the restaurant we came to on your birthday?' Dad
asked as we all piled out of the cars and into Hades. Dapper
had painted the door again in what was becoming a monthly
occurrence. It was now a high-gloss lime green, deco-chic.

'One and the same,' I answered, suddenly worried about
how Dad would react if he discovered that Hades had become
a second home to me. 'Actually, Dad, I . . . I'm not sure you
should come up . . .'

'Not open for negotiation,' was all Dad said.

I glanced nervously at Griffin.

'He deserves to be included,' Griffin responded.

'Okay, but just stay away from Onyx,' I pleaded.

Evelyn shot me a sideways look. 'Was he the one on the
flight back from Santorini? The one you stripped?'

I nodded, uncomfortable discussing my ability to strip
exiles of their powers against their will. All Grigori could
remove exile powers, but usually the exile had to surrender to

it – which they never did. I looked at Griffin. 'Gee, Griff, did you leave *anything* out?'

He shrugged. 'It wasn't like you were getting set to give her the history.'

'Should we be prepared for conflict?' Evelyn carried on.

Steph snorted as we walked towards the bar area. 'Only if he doesn't like your wardrobe selection.' She looked at Evelyn's outfit of dated navy pleated pants and black oversized jumper. 'Which, no offence, is a possibility.'

'Steph,' Salvatore chastised. 'Apologies, Signora Eden.' He bowed his head and pushed Steph forwards.

Evelyn looked herself up and down. 'I haven't had a chance to catch up with the latest fashions yet, between the lack of consciousness and threats of imprisonment.'

'You look fine,' Dad said, a blush tinting his cheeks.

Unfortunately, he was right. Evelyn was tall with striking features highlighted by her intense fire-blue eyes and there was a gravitational force about her that seemed to attract people.

Onyx was working behind the bar, showing off his impressive physique in a tight black T-shirt and torn slim-fit jeans. Dapper was serving a group of girls to his right. Working in sync, the two of them had the entire bar covered. I was struck by the professional attitude Onyx seemed to have adopted as he expertly flipped a coaster onto the bar with one hand just before landing a glass on it with the other. It was quite a change. Almost as different as his casual attire, which had girls draped over the bar eyeing him up instead of crying and running away at some insult he'd launched in their direction – as had happened in the past. Onyx, however, didn't seem to care for or return their interest.

Dapper saw us nearing and scowled as he tossed a bar towel over his shoulder. It made me smile.

Onyx, in complete contrast, beamed. He quickly motioned for one of the floor staff to relieve him and before we reached the bar he was pouring himself a drink.

'Just when things were becoming predictable,' he said, winking at me. 'I should never have doubted you.'

Dapper moved over grudgingly, taking in all the women drooling over Onyx – I could've sworn his eyes blazed before he began jabbing a finger towards Spence.

'Don't think I don't know you got into my stock earlier tonight. I catch you pilfering again and not only will you never set foot in this place again but I'll haul you down to the cop station myself and press charges. You hearing me?'

Spence grimaced. 'Hear you.'

Dapper nodded with a grunt and then addressed the rest of us. 'Whatever this is, let's get it over and done with.' He motioned towards the unmarked door that led to his apartment. 'Try not to frighten away any of my patrons on your way.'

'He's not coming with us, is he?' Evelyn asked Griffin, gesturing to Onyx who was already holding open the door with a look of delight.

'Onyx has proven himself a useful source and ally,' Griffin responded.

Evelyn looked disgusted as she passed Onyx.

'Love a family affair,' Onyx chimed in as I passed through the door.

In Dapper's living room, there were more of us than there were seats so Zoe and I took the floor while Lincoln assumed his usual back-of-the-room standing position.

Griffin filled in Dapper and Onyx with the most important updates, ending with Evelyn's disclosure about defeating Lilith with the Qeres. After giving them some time to absorb all of the information he asked Onyx if he'd ever heard of the substance before.

Onyx brushed non-existent lint from his jeans. I waited for him to break into some drawn-out story, but he surprised me by leaning back in his chair and shaking his head.

'Not in my angelic memory. Even if I had known, some things leave us the moment we exile. But I've heard rumours over the years. I believe there is truth in what she claims.'

'Dude, you feeling okay?' Spence blurted out, taking the words from my mouth; Onyx *never* cooperated without getting something in return.

He grinned secretively. 'Keeping sight of the bigger picture is an important part of the game.'

Dapper cleared his throat and grunted at Onyx. 'Is it so impossible to admit you simply wanted to help?'

Onyx's grin faltered and he rolled his eyes.

'I've heard of the potion,' Dapper said, standing up and pacing the living room. 'I believe I have a book that can help you with the first twelve ingredients.' His brow furrowed. 'And I have a suspicion the thirteenth ingredient dates back to the Garden of Eden.'

'How?' I jumped in.

'There are stories about a poison there – either in the serpent's bite or within the apple, depending on which version you want to believe, but something in that garden changed humans from being as indestructible as angels to the mortals we are now.' He looked away and didn't seem comfortable with the conversation. 'I'll do some research.'

Evelyn shook her head. 'I'm sorry, but there's no book that has such details in it.'

Dapper gave her a condescending sniff. 'Yes, there is.'

Evelyn stood. 'No, there is not! We hunted this potion for over fifty years. The only chance of ever finding a written reference to it went up in flames a long time ago, along with the–'

'Library of Alexandria?' Dapper cut her off with raised eyebrows.

Her eyes widened. 'Yes. Who *are* you?'

Dapper moved over to the minibar, grabbed a towel, and started to polish it while casting suspicious glances towards Evelyn and Dad, before finally settling his gaze on me.

I nodded, interpreting his unspoken question. 'He's my dad, Dapper, you can trust him.'

He went back to polishing. 'And her?'

I gnawed on my lip and decided on the truth. 'Still deciding. But I can give you my word that I'll protect your secrets if she betrays you.'

I ignored the stunned look on Dad's face and the almost-proud one on Evelyn's.

'Good enough for me,' Dapper responded, putting down the towel. 'I'm human. A descendant of the first patriarchs.'

'The *first* patriarchs?' Griffin repeated, as if the connection made all the difference.

Dapper nodded.

Griffin looked taken aback. 'The first patriarch's line ended with the flood,' he murmured, as if mentally running through history.

'That's what we thought, too,' Evelyn said, equally shocked. 'And we looked, believe me.' Her expression morphed to one of suspicion.

Dapper gave a knowing smile. 'Not my fault you couldn't find us. We're very good at remaining unnoticed.'

Griffin looked at the rest of us, less historically blessed. 'The first patriarchs were the direct descendants of Adam – the bloodline that flowed all the way down to Noah. They had certain unique qualities, including lifespans that stretched to almost one thousand years – but they were all thought to have been wiped out by the flood.'

'But isn't Phoenix a descendant of Adam?' I asked.

Griffin nodded. 'He is, but Adam impregnated Lilith *before* Original Sin – from the immortal version of humanity. The first patriarchs descend from Adam in his mortal state, and from his mortal partner. It is they who are the forefathers of humanity as we know it.'

Dapper sighed, and I felt his fear at finally letting this secret out. 'After the flood, the bloodline continued in secret. Our family tree is extensive and our role has remained the same – collectors and scribes of knowledge, our lives are extended in order that we can provide as much service as possible. Our purpose is to remain in the background; we never take sides and only document events.'

'That's why you never wanted to get involved,' I said, feeling guilty yet again that we had dragged him into our messes.

He shrugged. 'Old habits. But I long ago left my position as patriarch to other, more willing, family members. I am, for all intents and purposes, just a long-lived barman with some regenerative powers that I can sometimes share.' He glanced at Steph and Onyx.

Onyx threw back a shot of something and slammed the glass back on the bar. He'd just realised it was Dapper who'd healed him after the exile attack. Steph's hand went to her face. She'd made the same connection.

'What is this book you speak of?' Evelyn continued, ignoring everyone's reaction to Dapper's revelation and getting back to business.

'Do you know how the Library of Alexandria was destroyed?' Dapper asked the room.

'No one does exactly,' Steph chimed in. 'Some say the fire was started by Julius Caesar.'

Onyx nodded. 'And, of course, Mark Antony pilfered thousands of scrolls to woo Cleopatra.'

Dapper nodded.

'Another theory was that the patriarch Theophilus had the books destroyed when he turned the Temple of Serapis into a Christian church,' Griffin added.

'Or that it was Caliph Omar, when he took the city of Alexandria and gave instructions for the library's holdings to be destroyed,' Dad said.

When everyone turned to stare at him, he gave a dry laugh. 'What? I studied history. Omar ruled the contents as "superfluous".'

'Happy times,' Spence threw in, earning a stern look from Griffin.

Dapper went back to the minibar and poured himself a long drink. 'And over what period were all of these events?'

'Six, seven hundred years?' Steph answered quickly.

Dapper gave her a smile. That was Steph – brainy with the best of them and not about to be outdone.

'The truth is that the patriarchs lost faith in the human world. Humans could no longer be trusted to keep this knowledge – and in particular, items of power – safe and sacred. At the time of each of these events the patriarchs used the distraction to remove the scrolls, starting with the most important and ending with the least. Over time, they converted them into books and translated them when possible – the previous translation always destroyed afterwards. There is only ever one version of any text in existence.'

'Why?' Lincoln asked.

'Patriarchs are untrusting people. Knowledge is power.'

Lincoln nodded. Enough said.

I eyed Onyx – who hadn't said anything since Dapper's disclosure.

'You knew, didn't you?' I asked him. I could see Dapper's words were not a surprise to him.

He smiled broadly. 'Of course, rainbow. I've been around a very long time.'

Dapper snorted. 'And I told him last week.'

Typical.

'Descendants of the bloodline spend a minimum of one hundred years in service, protecting the knowledge. I did my stint beneath the ground, living with three others of my line, guarding one of the prime knowledge wells in Egypt. It gave me plenty of reading time.'

'And that is where this book you speak of is now?' Evelyn asked, leaning forward.

'No. The well was discovered and destroyed. We saved what we could and decided it would be better to separate and divide up what remained. Over the years I've returned most of the books to those more devoted to the cause than I ever was, but . . .' the corner of his mouth lifted. 'Let's just say that everyone likes to be prepared for a rainy day.'

'Where is it then?' Evelyn snapped.

Dapper gave her an unfriendly look. I understood completely.

'You're all going to have to move back from that wall,' he said.

We all stood and shuffled back – Lincoln moving closer to me. Protectively.

Dapper closed his eyes and started to say something quietly – chanting.

'Gaelic,' Lincoln whispered in my ear, sending a shiver down my spine.

After a minute or two, the living-room wall started to move towards us, the mantelpiece splitting in the middle, opening up like two massive doors.

'Open sesame,' Zoe said, her voice filled with awe.

Spence was grinning ear to ear. 'I know, right! I'm waiting for the troll to come out and ask for a magic password.'

I smiled at him. Griffin didn't. He smacked Spence over the head instead.

Dapper, ignoring our banter looked around the room solemnly. 'My oath is now your oath. If any of you betray it, you would be betraying me, and my people would come with strength and in numbers that would surprise you. They would slay you.' He half smiled. 'It wouldn't be right if I didn't warn you.'

Dad gasped. The rest of us looked around, unsure, until Spence took a casual step towards the open wall.

'Same old,' he said.

Lincoln put a hand on the small of my back, pushing me forward. 'They'll have to be comfortable with a first-come first-served situation,' he – the normally so grave – said, as we moved into the secret room.

Spence slapped a hand on Lincoln's back as he pushed ahead. 'Truer words were never spoken, mate.'

Lincoln smiled at my expression and my heart melted. 'You said you wanted a night of fun. Just holding up my end of the deal.'

When I didn't immediately smile back, as if sensing all of my fears for our tomorrows and my sadness about the things I – *we* – had to leave behind, he grabbed my hand.

Honey and spice and all things dangerous are nice.

CHAPTER SEVEN

'Fate is not satisfied with inflicting one calamity.'
Publilius Syrus

Salvatore and Steph disappeared quickly for some 'alone time' after we left Dapper's, then Zoe and Spence invited me to join them for 'ice cream' which – judging by the not-so-subtle winks – I strongly suspected was code for shenanigans.

I opted to stay with Dad. He was basically trembling from the sheer volume of new knowledge. The kind of awareness never intended for humans.

Outside Hades, he'd watched Steph casually walk away arm in arm with Salvatore and shook his head. 'How does she take all of this so well?' he'd asked. 'Isn't she afraid?'

Among my many confessions to Dad I'd told him how Steph had been taken captive by Phoenix.

'Sometimes I think Steph was destined for this world more than any of us. She might not be Grigori but she's chosen to play her part. I've had to learn to accept that, Dad.'

Dad looked at his feet, his shoulders slumping forwards. 'Is that your way of telling me that's what I have to do – accept *your* place in this . . . world of exiled angels?'

I put a hand on his arm briefly, wishing I was better at being consoling. 'It would make things easier for you if you could.'

When Evelyn and Griffin joined us, I couldn't help but be irritated. I never had any time alone with Dad these days.

As if reading my mind, Lincoln opened the back passenger door to his car. 'Mr Eden, how about I give you and Violet a lift home? Griffin can take Evelyn in his car – I'm sure they have some things to discuss.'

Dad looked between Evelyn and me and nodded, slipping into the back seat.

I moved in beside Dad and if my eyes could have said thank you a million times to Lincoln, they did then.

As we drove, Dad's erratic breathing settled and he relaxed enough to talk.

'I just can't believe I never knew all these things. Evelyn has lived for over two hundred *years*.' He shook his head. 'How could I not have known?'

I put my hand on top of his. 'Dad, there was no way you could've. Judgement aside, there's no denying she's a master at her work.' I bit my lip and moved my hand away awkwardly. 'She's a manipulator. The only thing we can possibly know for certain is that she *chose* to lie to you for the entire time she was with you.'

'That doesn't mean it was all lies,' Dad said defensively.

'No, it doesn't,' I conceded. 'And I'm sure her feelings for you were real – it's just . . . She puts her Grigori status above everything and everyone else. Us included.'

'And you don't?'

I couldn't help glancing at Lincoln in the front seat. His face was expressionless as he stared ahead, but his hands had that tell-tale white-knuckled grip on the steering wheel that told me he was listening intently.

I gnawed at the inside of my cheek and decided on the truth. 'No. I don't. There are things that are more important to me.'

Dad slumped back into the seat, exhausted. 'Will she ever age?'

'Probably not in your lifetime.' It was a grim reality, but he deserved to know.

He sighed and I noticed the dark circles rimming his eyes. 'It's so strange. I look at her, hear her speak – her mannerisms are the same but she's different as well.'

He ran his trembling hands through his hair and again, I wished I was better at connecting with him.

'I hear her in the night, tossing and turning – whatever haunts her dreams . . . It's awful, Vi.'

I find that hard to believe.

Then again, maybe it was waking up to discover she was back with us that led to the screaming. It didn't inspire much sympathy.

'Dad, I know it's hard, but she's a liar. She traded our futures, our happiness, for her place in Heaven. I don't know why she's back or for how long, but I think you need to be prepared for the possibility that if she has the opportunity to help herself, she'll ditch us without another thought.'

Dad stayed silent. But I'd been there for the last seventeen years, I'd seen what losing her did to him. I just couldn't let him go through it again.

Or me.

No. The best thing I could do for Dad was prepare him for her departure.

'Dad, please, look at the facts. She's using you.'

I closed my eyes briefly, sensing his hurt, but I needed to look after him. He was my father.

'Have you even spoken to Caroline since Evelyn came back?' I asked, reminding him of the good things that had started to happen in his life recently with his PA. Finally, Dad had been acting like he was ready for a relationship.

He shook his head. 'I . . . I told her I couldn't keep seeing her. It just didn't feel right and I had no other explanation.'

Poor Caroline.

I hadn't been thrilled about her interfering in Dad's and my relationship, but she was a good person and I knew she genuinely cared for Dad.

'What did she say?'

His hands combed his hair again. 'She resigned. Said it was for the best.'

'Oh, Dad.'

It made me so cross. Dad was turning his world upside down for Evelyn and I knew it could only end badly.

'Just promise me you'll keep your guard up,' I urged.

And, as if accepting the cruel truth, he nodded. 'I . . . I can't go through this again. You're right, Vi.'

I breathed out a sigh of relief.

'I'll keep my distance, but what happens now? I can't just let you go off to face this Academy on your own.'

'She won't be alone, Mr Eden,' Lincoln said.

Dad sent a dubious look in his direction. 'If any harm comes to her–'

'I'll look after her,' Lincoln jumped in. 'I'd never let any harm come to her.'

I rolled my eyes. 'When you two are finished . . .' I pointed out the window. 'We're home.'

Lincoln didn't get out so before I closed the door I looked back at him as Dad crossed the road. 'Thanks for the outrageously fun night.'

He winked. 'I aim to please.'

'Then we're going to have to reassess your pleasure standards.' At the smile on his face and raised eyebrow, my cheeks pinked. 'Ah . . . I mean . . .'

'Goodnight, Vi.'

I bit my lip. ''Night, Linc.'

Dad and I rode the lift together and walked hand in hand to our apartment. For the first time since Evelyn had reappeared I felt as though we were back on the right track.

The front door was ajar. I could sense the others inside already – that faint buzz of Grigori. Clearly Griffin and Evelyn had arrived before us.

Dad paused outside the door and pulled me into a hug. 'I love you, Vi.'

'You too, Dad.'

But as we stepped apart and I moved to push the door open, we heard Griffin's voice from inside. There are times when you just freeze – times when you somehow know that whatever it is you're seeing or hearing is important.

'To be pulled back to earth in a ceremony like that – I've thought of it from every angle and I can only come up with one explanation.'

There was a long silence before Evelyn spoke. 'Don't do this, Griffin.'

'You made terms, didn't you? When Violet was born?'

I knew that tone. Griffin was on a mission.

I looked at Dad. He was listening intently.

Why is my heart pounding?

There was another delay before Evelyn responded. We both heard her heavy sigh.

'It was the only way I could protect them. Lilith is eternal. She will always find a way to return. I always knew that Violet may have to face her. I was the one who sent Lilith to Hell and she is vengeful. She'll come for Violet.'

'Is that why you wanted Violet to be Grigori? So she had a chance at defending herself?'

'No,' she responded sharply. 'Never. I would've taken her and James far away if there had been any option. I would've kept them safe on my own but . . . *They* needed her.'

I swallowed hard.

'You made a deal with the angels?' Griffin pushed on.

'Two things. That Violet be partnered with a Grigori who came from a Power and that if Lilith returns in Violet's lifetime, that I would return with her.'

My eyes went wide and I felt myself shaking my head at her revelations, refusing to let the words sink in. She couldn't be trusted.

'And the price?'

'This isn't the time,' Evelyn replied, the warning in her voice clear.

'I think it's well overdue, actually. Where exactly have you been for the past seventeen years, Evelyn?'

Dad was frozen in place, his palm flat on the door.

'Not now,' she insisted, but I knew Griffin wasn't about to let it go. I had a terrible sinking feeling.

'If the deal was for you to be resurrected when she was, then you had to have been connected to her life-force. It's the only way, and we both know it. Evelyn, stand in front of me and tell me you have not spent the last seventeen years trapped in the pits of Hell.'

There was the sound of movement and I guessed she must have started to pace the floor. It helped to cover Dad's whimper.

'There's no point lying to you. You already know the truth,' Evelyn said.

I practically stopped breathing. Griffin *would have* known if she was lying but I couldn't accept it. It couldn't be true. It couldn't.

She traded me in, gave me away. Not . . . this. No. No!

I looked at Dad. I'd never seen him so stunned, so *blank*. His eyes met mine and I shook my head.

'She's lying,' I whispered. 'She's lying!'

His expression changed, eyes welling, looking at me with something new – a darkness filled with fear and anger. No . . . with blame.

I shook my head again. 'You can't trust her!' I heard myself saying frantically. And that's when it happened.

Rage took over and he slapped me across the face.

I saw it coming. I knew what he was doing. And it didn't even occur to me to move out of his way. His palm struck high on my cheek – the sting greater than from any blow I'd ever received.

Dad gasped, his hand dropping into his other as if to restrain it, his expression filled with shock.

I stumbled back into the wall, one hand covering my cheek.

We must've been noisy because the apartment door swung open.

'James!' Evelyn said, looking between us. 'Oh, God, you heard.'

I stared at my feet – unable to look at either one of them – and felt tears welling.

Not now, not now. Don't cry.

'Violet?' At the sound of Griffin's voice I glanced up.

A slap barely tickles Grigori. Griffin had given me my own fair share of playful punches along the way to toughen me up. But what Dad had done, the emotion and intent that came with it . . . hit me in so many painful ways. Griffin must have seen it all in my eyes. And, worse, I saw the sympathy in his.

Suck it up, Vi.

I stood up straight, blinking back the tears, and cleared my throat. I wouldn't be weak.

'Griff, can you wait a minute before leaving? I'm coming with you.'

As I was zipping up my bag, Evelyn let herself into my bedroom.

'Don't,' I said putting a hand up to stop whatever she was about to say. 'Just . . . don't.' I slung my duffle bag over my shoulder and grabbed my other bag, not pausing to look at her again as I headed to the front door, where Griffin and Dad were talking.

Dad had recovered and found his voice. 'I'm going to New York, too,' he stated.

Griffin was trying to settle him down. 'I understand how you feel, but they won't allow it, James. The Academy do not admit non-Grigori.'

'I don't care. I'm going with her,' Dad said adamantly.

I knew the 'her' he was referring to was not me.

I joined them. 'It's fine, Griff. We'll find a way.' I glanced at Dad, my expression blank. 'You'll be able to go with her, I'll make sure of it.' Then I turned back to Griffin with a nod, signalling I was ready to leave.

'Violet, wait!' Dad said.

I paused, head down.

'I . . . I'm so sorry. I lost my mind. I don't know what's going on – I just snapped. The idea of her being in . . . All this time. Please forgive me.'

But I couldn't. Because I didn't know what was going on either but my response hadn't been to blame him. So I shook my head, ignored my welling eyes, and headed for the lift.

chapter eight

*'No man chooses evil because it is evil . . . he only mistakes it
for happiness, the good he seeks.'*
Mary Wollstonecraft Shelley

The car trip was silent – Griffin leaving me to my thoughts as I
stared out the window, wondering how things had come to this.

He cleared his throat, bringing me out of my thoughts as
we pulled up outside Lincoln's warehouse. 'Are you going to
be okay?'

I clutched my bags. 'Sure. Tell the Academy I won't go
unless Dad is allowed to escort her.'

'They might not agree.'

I shrugged. 'Then I won't go. Tell them those are my terms
for full cooperation.'

He nodded. 'Okay. I'll do that.'

I looked out the window and Griffin began to tap his hand
on the steering wheel. It was starting to rain and steam was
rising from the road.

'Violet, he didn't mean it.'

I wasn't so sure. Dad had been tested in so many ways
and his loyalty to Evelyn had shone through above all else. I
swallowed. 'Has she really been in Hell?'

'Yes,' he said, with the kind of certainty only Griffin, a seeker of truth, could deliver.

'Why did she do it?'

'She's a warrior. She knew what was at stake. I think she thought doing things this way would give you the best chance.' He gestured a hand towards Lincoln's front door, which was already open. Lincoln had obviously sensed my arrival. 'Is this the best place for you?'

Yes. No. Maybe.

Lost for an answer, I opened the car door.

Griffin grabbed my arm before I stepped out, his eyes full of promise. 'Thank you, Violet. I know you're only going to the Academy because I asked. I want you to know that you won't be alone. You're one of mine, and my Grigori stand together.'

I knew it was true. One thing about my friends: not a coward among them.

'Thanks, Griff,' I said, honoured but keen to change the subject. 'So, do you think Dapper will be able to find all the ingredients?'

By the time we'd left Dapper's place he'd found – among the hundreds he had hidden in his concealed library – the book he believed would point us in the right direction. He had, however, remained tight-lipped on his theory about the poisonous thirteenth ingredient, insisting he needed to consult with his brothers before sharing.

'If anyone can, it's Dapper.' Griffin sighed. He was exhausted. 'Let's meet with him in the morning and make a plan.'

I nodded. 'Breakfast at Hades?'

'Yes. And just us for this one,' he said, letting me know I wouldn't have to see Evelyn.

Lincoln stood by the door as I walked up the stairs, his eyes on my bags.

I threw my shoulders back. 'I'm moving in,' I said simply. 'For tonight, anyway.' But as I walked past him, with all my false bravado that he saw right through, he grabbed my wrist and pulled me into a hug – into which I sank helplessly. He knew me too well.

'Dad slapped me,' I said into his chest, tears now flowing.

Lincoln tensed, the way he did when he was trying to control his anger.

'And apparently Evelyn's been stuck in Hell for the past seventeen years,' I added.

He pulled me tighter and I was struck by the realisation that he'd already figured it out.

Was I the only one who hadn't?

And then came the sickening thought . . . Deep down, had I known, too?

'Can I stay?' I asked, my nerves now breaking through.

Lincoln's hand stroked my hair. 'I've already told you, you'll always have a home here.'

With that he relieved me of my bags, pointed me towards the espresso machine, and took my things straight to his room.

'Where's Spence?' I asked when he came back.

'Staying at Zoe and Salvatore's,' he answered. 'You hungry?'

I smiled sheepishly. 'Starving.'

It was almost two in the morning and it had been a long night, but Lincoln made pizza and we sat on the sofa watching an action flick, laughing at all the special effects between steaming mouthfuls of heavy-on-the-cheese pizza.

He didn't say anything about what had happened and we didn't talk about what was to come. We were still on our 'fun night' it seemed, and I was grateful for the reprieve. We pretended to be normal and some time after we'd polished off the rocky-road ice cream we fell asleep on the sofa – his arm draped around my body – guarding me from the world. It hurt – that soul-deep pain surfacing. And it was worth it.

'You're becoming increasingly difficult to track down, lover,' Phoenix said.

Startled, I looked around. 'How ... I don't understand ...' I stuttered.

We were standing in the cafe he'd once called 'ours', Dough to Bread. It was empty. No staff, no customers, nothing apart from one table and two chairs. I was seated on one, Phoenix on the other.

He rapped his fingertips on the tabletop to a non-existent beat. 'Things are not going the way I planned,' he said.

Still taking in my surroundings, I suddenly stood up. 'You've pulled me into your dreamscape!' I yelled.

The last time someone who wasn't my angel maker had done this to me, I'd woken up standing over a dead body with blood on my hands. I ran to the cafe door only to gasp when I opened it. Beyond the cafe there was nothing. Empty space. A vortex.

Phoenix stood behind me.

'We need to talk. This was the only way. It's already taken me weeks to break through your shields. You mustn't have been having a good day.'

The sincerity in his voice unnerved me. It infuriated me that he could use a dip in my emotions to get to me. I slammed the door and spun round to face him. He was so close. Instinctively, I struck out to hit him across the face.

He stumbled back. I moved forwards, using my small advantage. 'Send me back!' I demanded. All I could think of was the last time I'd been under exile power in a dream . . . I needed to regain control.

Phoenix smirked, wiping away a bead of blood that ran from his nose. 'Dreams hurt,' he said, shrugging, before his gaze returned to me. 'Not exactly news.'

I narrowed my eyes at him and, lightning fast, he crouched and kicked his leg out, taking my feet from under me. I landed on my back.

He was right. Dreams hurt.

He launched himself on top of me, pinning me down. 'I told you, lover, we need to talk. I've gone to considerable lengths to make this happen.'

It was then that I noticed the strain in his expression. In fact, he was all but trembling.

'You can't hold me,' I said.

He smiled. 'You're getting stronger, I'll give you that.' He leaned in closer. I was trapped beneath his strength, but even if I hadn't been, in that moment I was powerless to move under the intensity of his chocolate gaze.

'I could do it, you know. Even here, in our dreams, I could give you everything you desire and take away all that you don't,' he said, his voice barely a murmur, as he teased me with the prospect of his empath abilities. The same abilities that I fought so hard against remembering but never succeeded; Phoenix could deliver pure bliss when he chose.

I was acutely aware of his body on top of mine and hated that the idea of giving in to his power stirred something in me. I gritted my teeth against the temptation.

'Why don't you, then?' I challenged.

He leaned closer, his lips so close that when he spoke they grazed mine. 'I won't force you, lover. Despite what you think of me, despite my previous . . . slip-ups, I'm not that man.'

I turned my head to the side and started to concentrate on my will, the one thing I knew could pull me out of this dream.

'I thought you weren't a man at all. You told me you were all exile now.' I tried to get a handle on my emotions. If I couldn't control myself, I had no chance of getting out of this.

'Lilith's growing stronger every day,' he said.

I wasn't interested in hearing him gloat about how they were going to be all-powerful.

'Soon, none of your Grigori will be able to stop her,' he continued.

I felt a surge of power within me as I grappled to pull myself away from him. Suddenly we were both back on our feet, standing on opposite sides of the cafe. Any other time, that would have been cool, but not now.

Phoenix's eyes widened and his hand reached out. 'No, Violet, please! We need to talk.'

I shook my head, finally in control again. 'So you can tell me how we're all going to die? I don't think so.' I took a step back and the wall behind engulfed me.

Phoenix screamed. 'Wait! I need you!'

I woke with a start, sucking in deep gulps of air.

Oh God. Oh God.

I swept my hands through my damp hair. Lincoln was still asleep. I considered waking him but he looked so content that I just couldn't.

Why did he come to me? Was it just to torment me?

My hands shook and my thoughts raced.

Why do his final words keep replaying in my head? And that look in his eyes . . .

Eventually, sleep impossible, I got up and pulled back the drop-sheet on the wall that Lincoln had set aside for me to paint.

Somehow I knew I was standing on a precipice, that this was a now-or-never moment. The blank space that I'd bugged him to let me paint for so long and that sported nothing other than a solitary white lily stood before me. For the first time, I knew what I wanted the wall to represent.

By the time I'd finished painting it was 9 am. Today we would leave for New York and who knew what would follow. I repositioned the drop-sheet and cleaned up.

Lincoln woke shortly after. 'I can smell paint,' he said as he stretched. I tried to look away from the exposed band of skin between his T-shirt and sweat pants and felt the blush when he caught me peeking.

'Are you okay?' he asked cautiously.

'Coffee,' I said, passing him a cup. 'Griffin wants us to meet him at Hades in half an hour.'

He groaned, taking a grateful sip, then glanced at the now-covered wall. 'Do I get to see?'

'Once all this is over, okay?'

He opened his mouth to argue, but must have seen the plea in my eyes, and simply nodded.

Have I mentioned, I love you?

I put my empty mug down and sat beside him casually. 'So, Phoenix visited me during the night.'

CHAPTER NINE

'Absence from those we love is self from self – a deadly
banishment.'
William Shakespeare

Griffin hadn't changed from the night before. He was already sitting at what had become our usual table in Hades, Dapper beside him, a book between them as they spoke in hushed tones.

Onyx was behind the bar. Shock of all shocks; he was making coffees. When he saw Lincoln and me walk in, he didn't say anything, just passed me a cup over the bar-top. It was way too passive a gesture for Onyx.

'Griffin told you,' I said, taking the drink, embarrassed that everyone knew what Dad had done.

Onyx shrugged, flicking his dark hair back from his eyes.

My, my – he's speechless.

I gave him a deadpan look. 'You feeling sorry for me doesn't work for me.'

'Oh, thank Christ,' he exclaimed with relief. 'I thought I was going to have to pretend all day.'

'You're an ass, you know that, right?'

He bowed. 'I do, thank you.' He eyed my drink. 'Enjoy

that, there's more rum in it than coffee,' he said with a wink before sauntering off to sit beside Dapper.

I turned to Lincoln, a look of puzzlement on his face as he watched Onyx. 'Do you think there's something going on between Dapper and Onyx?' he asked me.

I looked at them again. They did seem very comfortable around each other. Dapper had never said out loud that he was gay and to look at him he didn't fit any stereotype – well, apart from his eye for interior design and diamanté-studded accessories. And, now that I thought about it, I'd never seen Onyx take up any of the offers made to him by the girls who hung around Hades.

'Definitely,' I said, realising I was happy for them.

Lincoln looked at them again and nodded. Enough said.

Griffin waved us over.

'Time to save the world,' I said to Lincoln, putting my 'rum' coffee back on the bar.

Lincoln made a show of looking at his watch. 'Already?'

'Ha, ha,' I said, as we walked over to join them. But I noticed his smile faded quickly. He was putting on a good show, but Lincoln had not been happy since hearing that Phoenix had found a way into my dream. The only reason he wasn't completely freaking out was because I'd managed to pull myself out of it.

'Anyone else coming?' I asked when we reached the table.

'Just us this morning,' Griffin said. 'I thought we could do with a little privacy. Once we enter the Academy we may not get another chance to talk privately.'

This was Griffin's way of saying we'd be watched like hawks once we arrived in New York.

Lincoln studied the book Dapper and Griffin had been looking at. It was old – the paper thick and worn at the edges, the spine peeling away.

'This is it?' he asked.

Dapper nodded. 'It took most of the night to translate.' Unlike many of the books, this one had not been translated into English. It had only made it to old Aramaic. 'Could've used that girl's help,' he added, meaning Steph. But 'that girl' had had other plans last night and not even her utter joy at discovering Dapper's treasure trove of knowledge would have persuaded her to postpone her time with Salvatore.

'Anyway, the book does reference a potion named Qeres. It's not easy to decipher but there is a list of twelve ingredients,' Griffin said.

'What are they?' Lincoln asked.

'Some we still need to get translations for, but nothing too drastic. Frankincense, myrrh, cedar oil, the blue lotus, mostly flowers and herbs native to Egypt, which would make sense, given the time this was documented.'

'Easy,' I said with a shrug. 'We can probably get most of it online, if not at a health food shop.'

Dapper took off his glasses and stared at me. 'Do you really think we could just pop down to the local store and collect the ingredients for a mortalising potion? *Please* tell me that comment was a misinterpreted joke.'

I sank back in my chair. Nothing like being put in your place. Dapper was normally rude, and gruff, but that was . . .

He sighed, looking at the ceiling for a moment. 'I'm sorry,' he said eventually. 'I'm sorry. I have no right to speak to you like that. *You* of all people.' He bowed his head in shame and I wondered why he'd said 'you' in that way.

'Oh, stop your fussing,' Onyx threw in. 'She likes it when we're mean to her, she said as much on her way in.'

I rolled my eyes, but at least he'd broken the strange tension.

'Here,' Onyx said, passing Dapper a mug and looking at me, trying to cover what looked suspiciously like concern. 'He's just pissed off because if you lot want to get your hands on these ingredients, then he's going to have to go home.'

'Home?' Lincoln asked, taking the word from my mouth.

Dapper grimaced. 'The ingredients must come from the earth and from their rightful place. Most will be found in Egypt, along the Nile to be exact.'

I shook my head. 'Dapper, we can't ask you to go traipsing around the world looking for flowers and herbs. We don't even know if there's any truth to this tale and you said yourself, we don't have the thirteenth ingredient anyway.'

Dapper stared at me for a long time and I couldn't help but feel he wanted to say something. But it was Griffin who spoke up.

'Until something better presents itself, this is the closest thing we have to a plan.'

Dapper sighed. 'I never thought I'd go back there, but this potion could end up making the difference. Travel in Egypt requires connections and a guide. I can provide both.'

I wondered how many years it had been since Dapper was last in Egypt.

'You're a good girl to give me the choice. But we both know it won't mean a happy world for anyone if we don't stop Lilith.'

I shook my head and looked at my lap. I still struggled to believe it, that my relationship with Phoenix had ultimately led to this. It was a cruel twist of fate and now everyone was paying the price. Finally, I lifted my head and looked to Dapper.

'Thank you,' I said, because what else could I say?

Dapper smiled weakly. 'Griffin, with your permission, I'd suggest I take the girl with me. She'll not be permitted with your lot and I could use her.' He coughed, trying to hide his genuine concern. 'God knows she won't agree to stay behind.'

Griffin drained his coffee. 'If Stephanie is willing, I have no objection. We're already going to have enough trouble trying to get James in with Evelyn.'

They both looked at me.

'On one condition,' I said, determined to at least make sure Steph had this. 'Graduation is tomorrow. You wait until after that to leave. She's the valedictorian, for Christ's sake. And since I won't be here, I expect you,' I looked at Onyx sternly, 'will *both* be there throwing confetti.'

Lincoln gripped my hand under the table. Yeah, it sucked I wasn't going to be there.

Dapper nodded. 'We can use the time to translate the rest of this text and make arrangements. We'll be at her graduation.'

'Speak for yourself. I'd rather take a loaded weapon to my head,' Onyx said.

'Actually, I believe I *can* speak for you, since I'm imagining you plan on coming along on our little trip as well.'

Onyx rolled his eyes and gulped down the rest of his drink.

Yep. Definitely more than friends if Dapper can make him turn up to a high school graduation.

'See what you've reduced me to?' Onyx glared at me. 'My only comfort is knowing you'll be stuck with your treat of a mother for the foreseeable future.'

I glared back at him.

'Oh,' he said, throwing a hand to his chest. 'Is that your evil stare? I'm quivering.'

I looked at Linc, incredulous. The traitor was hiding a smile.

'What's so funny?' I asked.

He shrugged. 'Now all you have to do is separate Steph from Salvatore long enough to convince her not to stow away on our plane.'

'Oh, crap.'

'Actually, that might not be the case,' Griffin said, capturing our attention again. Something told me there was another reason Griffin had decided we should have today's powwow in private.

CHAPTER TEN

'Wild, dark times are rumbling toward us . . .'

Heinrich Heine

'**I** don't need a babysitter!' Steph said. Again.

She collapsed onto Onyx's sofa bed. We'd commandeered the small flat for our conversation that was probably not so private given the volume level.

'I know you don't,' I said. Again.

Now I knew why Griffin had thought it would be better if I had this conversation with Steph in private. I was going to be sure to repay the favour at the first opportunity.

'It's bad enough that you've stuck me on the farming expedition with Dapper and Onyx, but now you're going to take my boyfriend out of the action he has every right to be a part of so he can hold my hand! He'll never forgive me, Vi.' Her attack mode was starting to crumble as her eyes became teary. 'You can't do this to us. We're only good if he doesn't have to worry about me all the time.'

I sighed. 'We want to keep you safe. Is that so wrong? Please, Steph, we're family. I'm not telling you what to do and neither is Griffin. But sometimes being in a family means putting your safety first, even if you think Salvatore might

ENDLESS

think of you differently. Because that's what families do – survive for each other.'

Steph quickly wiped away the tears that had slipped down her cheeks. 'And what about you? Are *you* going to survive? Don't think I don't know what you did on that volcano.'

Wow, I did not see that one coming.

'Spence?' I mumbled.

She nodded. 'Don't blame him. He was all messed up afterwards and you were too busy dealing with your new arrival.'

I felt terrible. I hadn't been there for Spence or Steph since coming back from Greece, Evelyn's return had been dictating everything.

'You're right,' I confessed. 'It was stupid. Phoenix has power over me and I don't know what's going to happen. The only thing I know for sure is that we have to stop them. But I can promise you this, I'll fight with every last breath in my body to make it back to you, to my family.'

Steph broke into full-on sobs, using her sleeve to wipe at her tears.

'I hate being the weak link,' she blubbed.

The funny thing was, I thought she was one of the strongest people I knew. 'Me too.'

She jumped up and snatched a tissue from the bathroom, returning as she blew her nose. 'This is all going to go to shit, isn't it?'

'Probably.'

'At least I can't die a virgin.'

Just like that, tears turned to shared giggles.

'Happy?' I asked, hoping she'd spare me the details.

'Very,' she replied. That she didn't give me a play-by-play was enough to tell me she really was in love. She settled back on the sofa beside me. 'What are you going to do about Phoenix?'

A knot in my stomach tightened. It was almost impossible to make my mind up about him. He'd done so much wrong, inflicted so much evil. He'd hurt people I loved, stolen from me, left me bleeding – hell, he left me hanging in a volcano – but, I'd seen something in his eyes on that volcano. And, as much as I'd been trying to forget it, I'd seen it again in those final moments of my dream. Something that reminded me of the way he was before all of this had happened.

But I couldn't excuse his actions. Ultimately, nothing had stopped him from bringing pure evil into this world.

'Phoenix has had his chance to change. He never will.' It was difficult to admit to Steph what I realised then I'd known for some time.

'You really think you can kill him?'

I shrugged, thinking again of the dream. 'He's stronger than I am, but my abilities are growing all the time.'

'I didn't mean in strength, Vi. I mean *can* you kill him? Can you put aside the way you still feel for him?'

I blinked. 'What do you . . . What are you talking about?' Unable to stay still, I jumped to my feet and started to pace.

'You know exactly what I'm talking about. The two of you were together, however briefly. I mean, Vi, he's the only guy you've ever–'

I cut her off. 'I really don't need to go down memory lane.'

She nodded. 'But it's true. You might not have loved him the way you do someone else, but you cared enough to consider the possibility of being in a relationship with him. I was there, Vi. It wasn't just him who felt something. And now what? The two of you are just going to fight to the death?'

I gnawed my lower lip. She was right, there *had* been something between us. But a whole lot had happened since then.

'Whatever was once there is long gone.'

'So you can, then? Kill him, I mean.'

I checked my watch and headed for the door. We were running out of time to get organised. I pulled on my jumper and looked back at Steph. 'Absolutely.'

'Well, thank freaking Christ for that! And about time, too,' Onyx said, standing outside the door I'd just opened.

My eyes narrowed. 'Were you listening?'

'Yes. Better than an episode of *Gossip Girl*. Sex, betrayal, scheming, murder, and, my personal favourite . . . denial. I applaud you!' He clapped.

I moved in closer to him. 'Remind me again why we let you live?'

'You claim it's your humanity. I question whether it's that you secretly hope my powers will come back to me so you will finally have a worthy adversary.'

I'm so not in the mood for this.

I took one more step so I was almost standing on his toes. 'You will never get any powers back, but if you did, just remember I'd be there to take them from you all over again.'

Onyx looked at me, a supreme confidence flickering in his eyes. '*When* I get them back, which I will, I look forward to seeing anyone try to take them from me again.'

'When you two are finished!' Dapper called out from the end of the hallway. 'Honestly, you're like children going at each other for shits and giggles. And you're the worst of all, girly,' he said, jabbing a finger at me. 'You know he's harmless now. Leave him to his snarky remarks, they're all he damn well has.'

At that, both Onyx and I glared at Dapper.

'I am anything but harmless. You people gravely underestimate my potential.'

'Then perhaps we should throw you back out on the street we found you on?' I sniped.

Onyx whipped a hand through his hair. 'I look forward to the next time you need to come to me for information.'

Steph snaked her arm through mine and tried to pull me to her side. 'We're leaving. And Dapper is right, the two of you need to remember we're all on the same side.'

'Funny, but when I look at him it's just so easy to forget.'

Onyx smiled slyly.

'What?' I snapped.

'Nothing. I'm just trying to decide who it is for?'

'Who *what* is for?' I asked, losing all patience.

'Vi, let's go,' Steph said, trying to pull me away. I didn't budge.

Onyx's smile broadened. 'All the pent-up sexual frustration, of course.'

My mouth fell open and before I knew what I was doing, I'd launched myself at Onyx, taking us both to the ground.

'Violet!' Steph screamed.

Dapper's feet thudded down the hall, but all I could see was red. Onyx had said the one thing he knew would get to me and I could still see him grinning beneath me.

I pulled back my hand to hit him, but before I could follow through, someone yanked me off him and locked their arms around me.

I wriggled to get loose from the supernatural grip.

'Eden, trust me, I know what it's like to want to beat Onyx. But we can hear you from downstairs and Lincoln just walked in. Do you really want him to get involved in this? The man has been known to have a fairly possessive streak,' Spence said, holding me as I struggled.

My whole body went into a kind of delayed shock and I sagged in Spence's arms, suddenly feeling Lincoln's presence.

How come I haven't felt it 'til now?

In fact, I hadn't been able to feel anything except for my rage towards Onyx.

Onyx crawled onto his feet. He brushed himself off and looked at me with surprisingly calm eyes, the honest eyes that I'd started to associate with him recently – those of an ally.

'You can take that as a small reminder of what it's like to have an enemy who can pluck on your emotions.' He tilted his head as if assessing me. 'I suggest you work on that, rainbow.'

I finally shrugged free of Spence's hold; he'd obviously given up trying to restrain me. 'That was all on *purpose*?'

The corners of Onyx's mouth lifted. 'Can't say I didn't enjoy myself.' With that, he spun on his heel and headed towards Dapper's apartment.

'You're damn lucky she didn't kill you,' Dapper mumbled as he followed him.

'He's seriously messed up,' Spence said behind me.

'Completely nuts,' Steph reinforced.

But it wasn't nuts at all.

Onyx had been helping me, and he was right. If Onyx could weasel his way into my emotions, then Phoenix still could, too.

The rest of the day panned out as expected. Much discussing and not much new. Griffin had to retell the story to date a number of times as groups of the city's Grigori stopped by Hades for their instructions in his absence. Griffin put Beth and Archer in charge in his place and told Nathan and Becca to be ready to join us in New York at a moment's notice. As warriors, they were not happy about being left behind, but I could tell Griffin was worried about leaving the city unprotected, plus he didn't want it to look like we were going into the Academy with troops. Sends the wrong message.

Once he'd seen to most of his Grigori he sat down with Zoe, Spence and Salvatore. He made Spence agree to be on his best behaviour back at the Academy – apparently it had taken Griffin's word for them to even allow him back in. It wasn't long ago that Spence had left the Academy without permission before his training was completed.

Then Griffin explained to Salvatore that he wanted him to accompany Dapper, Onyx and Steph on their quest for the ingredients for the Qeres potion, in case they encountered any problems.

Salvatore nodded and seemed enthused by his mission. I could see it had more to do with being entrusted with such a responsibility than anything to do with body-guarding Steph. From across the room I could see Steph biting her nails anxiously as she also assessed his reaction.

'It would be my honour. Although, I am concerned to be separating from my partner,' he said, looking at Zoe.

Griffin nodded, happy with Salvatore's reaction. 'Good man.' He turned to Zoe. 'The choice is yours to make.'

Zoe was no fool. Separating partners is never ideal, but if Salvatore was with Dapper that meant he could heal him if needed and if Zoe stayed with me, I could offer the same reassurance to her. That said, there was always a danger of being separated from one another, especially given my tendency to find trouble.

Zoe pondered her options. When she looked up, it was with resolve. 'We all need to be where we are needed most right now. If Salvatore escorts Dapper's crew, then I'm not needed there. As long as Sal's okay with it, I'll go to New York.'

Salvatore nodded. 'And we'll meet you there as soon as we have the potion.'

When Dad and Evelyn arrived later in the day, I didn't know where to look. It was obvious to see there had been a change. Dad was walking closer to Evelyn, more protectively than he had been before, and they both looked tired, as if they'd been up all night talking.

Lincoln, who was sitting beside me, settled his gaze directly on Dad and didn't move his eyes away. I nudged him a couple of times, but he ignored me.

I felt my phone buzz with a message while Dad made a feeble attempt to encourage everyone to stay until after my graduation, but even he knew it was useless.

Evelyn was happy with the progress Dapper had made in finding exactly what the components of Qeres were, but she maintained the potion would be useless without the mysterious thirteenth ingredient.

While they pondered options, I pulled my phone out of my jeans pocket and checked my messages.

> *I know what you're planning, lover.*
> *I'll be seeing you soon.*

I sighed and passed my phone to Lincoln, who tensed, before passing it on to Griffin.

'What is it?' Dad asked.

'It's a text from Phoenix. He knows we're coming,' I said calmly, still not making eye contact.

Griffin studied the screen and looked confused. 'It doesn't make any sense. He'd know the message wouldn't serve him. All it does is inform us that exiles are tracking our movements.' He settled his gaze on me until I began to squirm in my chair, then sighed. 'His motivations are often twisted when it comes to you.'

You can say that again.

'We leave in three hours,' Griffin said, ending the meetings for the day. He turned his attention back to Dapper to discuss logistics.

'He needs a new partner,' I said to Lincoln as I watched them walk away. 'He carries too much on his shoulders.'

Lincoln nodded. 'He'll get one, when he's ready. Until then, he has us.' But Lincoln wasn't watching Griffin. His eyes were fixed on Dad, who was coming towards us.

Lincoln cut him off before he had a chance to speak.

'It's bad enough that you've barely been there since she was born. Bad *enough* that she's had to endure things no one should have to endure. But to hit your own daughter is unacceptable. When we get back from New York, Violet will be staying with me until she decides otherwise.'

My mouth gaped.

Who is this guy and what has he done with the calm controlled Lincoln I know so well?

'Violet?' Dad said, looking both furious and hurt.

I bit my lower lip. Dad and I avoided confronting conversations as a firm rule. But I'd spent my whole life excusing his actions. And as crazy as what Lincoln had just said was, and as much as I knew he'd probably take it all back in about two minutes, I also knew I'd never be able to live with Evelyn even if I could forgive Dad.

'It's better this way, Dad. For all of us.'

Uh, sweet little lies.

Exactly how long would Lincoln and I be able to live together before it all became unbearable?

'Violet, I need to apologise, please.'

'No you don't. I get it, I do. But right now I just can't come second to her – so just give me some space, okay?'

He eventually nodded but his brow furrowed. 'You don't come second.'

I looked between him and Evelyn, who had been standing by, silently watching our exchange.

'Of course I do. I always have.'

Lincoln stayed by my side as I left Hades. I didn't speak to him until we hit the street. 'Now you've landed yourself in it.'

'It was only a matter of time, anyway.'

I paused on the footpath. 'How do you figure that?'

He brushed his finger along my forehead, picking up the stray wisps of hair and pushing them back. 'Haven't you noticed how that pain is significantly less when we're together for extended periods of time?' He shrugged, as if that somehow explained everything.

I wasn't so sure.

CHapter eLeven

'It is easier to forgive an enemy . . .'
William Blake

Lincoln left me at Hades, disappearing to chase down yet another source. He'd been on a mission since we returned from Santorini, tracking down informants and lower-rank exiles all over the city in an attempt to learn more about Phoenix's physical bond with me. And how to break it.

I'd argued, like always. He'd been adamant nonetheless, like always.

When I made it back to the warehouse, cross with myself for letting Lincoln insist on going off alone, Evelyn was sitting on the stairs outside the building.

I wasn't ready for this, but she clearly wasn't going to go away and we'd have to have it out sooner or later. And once we arrived at the Academy we couldn't trust that any of our conversations would be private. So I guess that left now or never.

I walked past her and unlocked the door, leaving it open. She followed, closing it behind her.

The coffee machine drew me like a magnet and I started to make two cups. Evelyn took her time joining me, looking around Lincoln's place with unsettling curiosity. I noticed her eyes linger on the blankets that were still draped over the sofa from last night and fix on the wall covered by the large drop-sheet.

I fleetingly wondered if Lincoln had peeked but quickly discarded the thought. He wouldn't.

When Evelyn finally joined me, I handed her a latte.

'Thanks,' she said, stirring in a spoonful of sugar. 'This is a great place. The light is amazing.'

That it was. Lincoln's warehouse had huge arched windows stretching the full height of a space that could easily accommodate another floor.

'You should see it first thing in the morning,' I said.

'You stay here a lot, then?'

I crossed my arms and leaned back against the kitchen bench, not about to go there. 'Do you know who he is?'

'Who?'

'My angel maker. I know yours was Semangelof. I know you made the deal with mine, he told me. *So*, do you know who he is?' Evelyn might have come to me but that didn't mean I couldn't ask my own questions.

'Yes.' She was irritatingly good at retaining the same neutral expression.

Now we're getting somewhere.

'Well, who is he?'

She took a sip of coffee. A stalling tactic. 'It's not for me to tell and better that you do not know. For now, anyway.' She sighed and put her hands down on the bench, leaning in. 'I didn't want to leave you and your dad. I felt every second of the time I was not with you and James. But I'd do it all again.

You can hate me all you want – I would if I were you – but I look at you and I see . . . I might have taken your family from you, but I gave you one, too. You're Grigori – *they* are your family, and you're a warrior.'

I looked away from her piercing eyes. I couldn't let her in. I just couldn't. I'd gone my whole life without a mother.

What does she want from me?

'Now I have a question for you,' she said, satisfied she'd silenced me.

'What?' I managed, still digesting everything.

'You and Lincoln – are you more than partners? Griffin refuses to discuss it. I need to know.'

I took a sip of coffee. She raised her eyebrows.

'Yes. No. It's complicated,' I answered.

She nodded. 'Griffin told me about Rudyard and Nyla. They were friends of mine.' Her tone dropped and I was struck by her genuine sadness. She seemed so cold most of the time but this wasn't – they'd obviously truly been her friends.

'They were my friends, too,' I said. When she didn't respond, I added, 'Phoenix did it. Phoenix was the reason Rudyard died.'

Evelyn's eyes became fierce. 'A demonstration?'

I nodded, guilt weighing heavily on my chest.

'You and Lincoln are soulmates.'

It wasn't a question but I nodded anyway.

'Oh, you bastards,' she mumbled.

I raised my eyebrows in question.

She shook her head. 'The angels did it on purpose. They knew you'd choose for love.'

This was news to me. 'How? I mean . . . *How?*'

She was still shaking her head. 'Because I told them your choice would come from your heart.' She pinned me with her gaze. 'And James? He hasn't been around much?'

I shrugged uncomfortably. 'He works a lot.'

'Nice try. How many family holidays have you been on?'

I thought back to our one weekend away that had ended in carnage. 'Not many.'

'And clearly neither of you cook,' she concluded, adding, when she saw my expression, 'your oven still has stickers on it. And . . .' her look softened and intensified at the same moment. 'I've heard enough to know someone hurt you a couple of years back.'

I looked down, bracing myself for the inevitable questions.

As if she'd read my mind, or perhaps my rigid body language, she sighed. 'I'm not going to ask. I'm sorry I wasn't here to kill the bastard for you.'

I blinked back tears.

We were both silent for a while. Neither one of us knew where to go from here, but I guessed it was my turn to say something.

'Your angel maker told me you made a deal. I thought it was to get into Heaven or something like that. It wasn't though, was it?'

She smiled weakly. 'Not exactly. My deal was to come back if Lilith did.'

'And for that you went to Hell?'

She sipped her coffee. 'It was the only way to be sure I would return at the same time as her. These things can be quite complicated. I don't want you to feel sorry for me. I knew the price and I made my choice without regret. That doesn't mean I don't wish I could've been there for you. For everything.'

I looked down and shook my head quickly. 'Did it hurt? I mean, in Hell?'

I could almost feel the room grow cold.

'Violet, promise me you won't ever ask me that question again and I'll promise you, I won't ever tell.'

Part of me wanted to insist she tell me. But the other part of me understood the warning in her voice. I was certain hearing the truth would break us both. So I just nodded.

I glanced at my watch, thinking of Lincoln.

I should've gone with him.

'She'll come for us, you know,' Evelyn said, matter-of-factly.

'Lilith? I don't think so. She just cares about destruction. Phoenix knows no good will come of continuing to fight with us. He'll make her leave us alone.' But even I didn't believe my words.

Evelyn fastened another fire-blue stare on me. 'What Phoenix wanted stopped being relevant the moment Lilith returned. She's the alpha of exiles and considers no one, not even him. And at the top of her kill-list will be me, and my daughter.'

I heard myself laughing as if I was listening from far away. I was finally losing it.

'Well, that won't be hard, then. If she doesn't care about Phoenix, then all she has to do is kill him and she'll kill me too.'

Before I had time to register she was on the move, Evelyn had a bruising grip on my shoulders. 'How can hurting Phoenix harm you?' she yelled, shaking me.

Instinct kicked in and I tried to push her away, but she held on and shook me again. 'How?' she screamed. 'How!'

'Because he healed me!' I yelled back, making sure my next push counted, slamming her against the pantry as I added, 'I was dying and he saved me!'

She lunged towards me again and I braced for attack but instead her arms wrapped around me. Her hold was so tight I could barely breathe and before I knew it, I was hugging her back, crying and hiccupping my way through the entire story, telling her how I'd trusted Phoenix, how I'd embraced to save Lincoln, how Phoenix had used his empath abilities over me, how I'd slept with him and how he'd then betrayed me.

I told her how much I loved Lincoln, how it hurt so intolerably to be near him. I told her how we'd thought we could be together in Jordan, how Phoenix had ripped apart our hopes by having Gressil kill Rudyard. How now, the only thing that kept us apart was the memory of Nyla and knowing that we could never allow that to happen to us. Finally, I told her about my first battle at Hades against Joel and Onyx, how Onyx's sword had speared me and that Lincoln had been out cold.

'I could feel my heart slowing, and then Phoenix was there. He healed me and saved my life. Afterwards, I told him to leave and never come back,' I confessed, knowing that it had been that moment that had unleashed his darkness.

'But he couldn't stay away,' Evelyn said, stroking my hair.

Somehow we'd ended up on the floor, me still folded tightly in her arms. 'You're not the only one addicted, my girl. He's drawn to you. That may end up being your greatest weapon of all.'

She pulled me up off the floor and sat me at the dining table before reaching for her bag and pulling out a folder of newspaper clippings.

I pulled myself together and checked my watch. Lincoln should be on his way home soon. At least he hadn't been there to witness my breakdown.

'So this is where all our newspapers have been going.' I tried for light-hearted but didn't carry it off. 'What are they?' I asked, tucking my hair behind my ear, increasingly conscious of having just had a total meltdown in front of this woman. My *mother*! And then another joyous realisation sprang to mind . . .

I just told her I'd had sex with a dark exile!

Feeling way too exposed, I started closing up.

Remember the rules: No running, no quitting, no fairy tales. I can't look weak in front of her.

When I pulled out of my mind spiral, Evelyn was staring at me. She had her hands on her hips and was standing over me.

'Don't,' she said.

I blinked, wiping my tears away with the back of my hand. 'Don't what?'

'Do you think you didn't inherit anything from me? You're doing exactly what I would've done if I'd fallen apart in front of someone I'd sworn to never let my guard down in front of.'

'Sorry?' She had hit the nail on the head.

'You're shutting down and if you keep going like this it's going to get us nowhere.' She sighed and set her jaw. 'It's time you decided what I am to you. I know I can't step into the role of Mum, I don't expect to. I know I cause a problem with your relationship with your father but I don't think it would help to just disappear on him, do you? So that leaves us needing to find some middle ground. I suggest we start by working together to kill this bitch.'

'Who *are* you?'

'I'm Grigori.' She smiled. 'And whether you like it or not, I'm your mother.'

Holy crap.

She eyed me as if she knew exactly what I was thinking. 'We're out of time and I need to know the rest, Violet. *And* I need to know exactly who knows it.'

'What are you talking about?' I asked nervously.

'I'm talking about your powers. I know about the senses, the extra strength, the healing, and I know about your ability to hold multiple exiles at a time. What I *need* to know is whatever it is you and Griffin have been hiding. And don't even try to pretend there's nothing.' She leaned back in her seat, drumming her fingers on the table, while I mentally ran through the pros and cons of telling her.

Griffin had drilled it into me that no one else could know about my 'Sight'. He and Lincoln had been researching it and while they claimed they hadn't found anything substantial and refused to speculate, I knew whatever they *had* found had them both freaked out. So I'd put Steph to work on it, too. At least she'd tell me if she found something. To date . . . nothing.

I adopted a casual tone. 'I can see things around me when I need to. We've started to call it a Sight.'

Evelyn's eyes went wide. 'A Sight? Who called it that?'

I shifted in my seat. 'Phoenix.'

'Jesus Christ! Is there anything our enemy *doesn't* know?'

I rolled my eyes at her outburst. 'It wasn't as if I knew what it was and we weren't exactly enemies at the time.'

'Do you leave your body?' she asked.

'In a way. It's like I can go anywhere if I just let myself. It's amazing, I see things differently.'

'You're seeing energy.'

Now my eyes went wide. 'How do you know?'

She pressed her lips together, looking up and shaking her head.

'Do you know of other Grigori who can do it?' I asked when she didn't say anything.

'It is not a Grigori trait, Violet. No human Grigori that has come before has ever had the power of Sight.' She sighed.

I swallowed. 'Then, who *does* have it?'

Evelyn studied the markings around my wrists for a long time, eventually reaching out and taking one of my hands when I let her. She ran her fingers over the patterns as they swirled around my wrists like a silver river, something deep within me powering them. When she looked up, there was fear in her eyes but also something else.

'Violet, *Sight* is not something that humans have ever had before because it's the power of the non-corporeal. *Sight* is the power of angels.'

Old fears rose to the surface. Since I'd first embraced, I'd questioned what I was becoming, what I had left behind. I shook my head, refusing to entertain this idea, whatever this *idea* was.

'Well, we're calling it the wrong thing then, because I have a very real body, as you can see,' I said, gesturing.

She smiled. 'Yes, you do. And you're going to have to make sure that you always remember that. Tell me, when you pull away from yourself and use your Sight, is it empowering? Do you feel like you are invincible?'

I looked down and didn't respond. The truth was, it was intoxicating. I knew I had barely begun to explore my ability, and while fear had kept me from testing any limits, the desire to see how far I could go was strong.

'You have to be careful of the lure. Use your Sight only when you have no other choice and limit the time you allow yourself to slip into it.'

'Slip into *what*?' I snapped.

Evelyn seemed anxious and that unnerved me. I could almost see her mind ticking over, carefully selecting the words she would use.

'You're human, Violet. Never forget that. But you also have angelic qualities from one of the most powerful angels to have ever existed. If I had to guess, I'd say that just as angels can exile to earth and become human, you may be the first human who has the ability to exalt yourself and become an angel.'

An angel.

I dropped my head into my hands and tried to stop my head from screaming at me.

'I don't want to talk about this.'

'Who else knows about the Sight?' Evelyn pushed on like she hadn't just dropped a gigantic – and potentially species-altering – bomb on me.

'Griffin, Lincoln, Steph, Phoenix . . .'

She huffed, unhappy with my response. 'Anyone else?'

I thought back. 'Spence. He saw me use it once.'

'Do you trust him?'

I nodded. 'With my life.'

She grabbed my shoulder. 'You had better be sure, because that might be exactly what it comes down to.'

I shook her off. 'Spence wouldn't betray me. Ever.' He'd proved his loyalty time and time again and he had mine in return. I raised my eyebrows. 'What would you have done about it anyway? What if I'd told you he couldn't be trusted?'

She looked away. 'It doesn't matter. You said you trust him. I believe you. But you need to make sure no one else ever finds out about this. Do you understand me? This proves you were created by one of the Sole and one of the most powerful of them, no less. There are people who won't be pleased to discover this. Are we clear?'

I nodded, unsure what else to do and checked my watch again as I picked up my phone to call Lincoln. But the moment I did, it beeped with a text message.

On my way home.
No joy.
L.

I let out a breath of relief that he was okay, even if I was disappointed that he hadn't found a miracle cure for severing my physical bond with Phoenix. I looked back at Evelyn, who had turned her attention to her book, which was now resting on the table.

I drained the last of my now-cold coffee. 'I can't talk about this stuff any more. How about you show me whatever that is?'

The book turned out to be filled with newspaper clippings and internet print-outs from all around the world, with every single one relating to a disappearance, kidnapping or suspected murder, sometimes of individuals, sometimes groups, many involving families.

'Why are you showing me these?' I asked eventually, not seeing what they proved, other than that the world was a twisted place.

'What is the one thing they all have in common?' she asked, tapping the scrapbook.

I rubbed a hand over my face. 'I don't know . . . Tragedy.'

'The only constant is that in every case there is a young child involved and that the child is missing or *presumed* dead. Whatever the circumstances, no bodies have been recovered.'

'What are you saying?' I asked, studying the articles and seeing the pattern for myself. I was starting to dread where this was going.

'Lilith has always been a bringer of death to children.'

I nodded, thinking back to the stories I'd read. When Lilith fled Adam she vowed to bring death and destruction to humanity and swore to take out her vengeance on children. It was why the amulet my mother had left for me as a child was so important. Lilith had struck a deal with the angels Sanoy, Sansenoy and Semangelof that she would not harm children who bore their names in an amulet, but all other children were fair game. Some described Lilith as the original cot death. I felt the blood drain from my face.

'If Phoenix gave her the Grigori Scripture, which she will have made him do, her first plan of attack would be to take out the children – it's what brings her the most satisfaction, her middle finger to the sky.'

Phoenix had promised he would never use the Scripture – he'd even indicated he'd be open to trading it with us for something he wanted more. The only problem was that that something happened to be me. But if Evelyn was right, Lilith wouldn't have had to do too much investigating to find out he had the Scripture in his possession, then . . .

'Oh my God! These are all children destined to become Grigori. She's taking them and killing whoever stands in her way!'

Evelyn nodded. 'These date back about two weeks. Knowing her, she'll want to stage something dramatic. At least that gives us a chance. My guess is she'll keep the children alive until she's ready to make her statement.'

'How did you figure this out?'

She shrugged. 'I know her.'

Super.

'Does Griffin know?' I asked.

Evelyn took our cups to the sink and began to rinse them. 'I showed him the clippings earlier.' She turned off the tap and looked at me with a grim expression. 'Violet, Lilith is not like any other exile you've faced. They're all insane but, Lilith . . . Lilith *is* insanity. She gives it to others, drives people to madness. I'm the reason she went to Hell and if she ever gets her hands on you she will punish me by breaking you. She won't just kill you, Violet, she'll destroy you and everything you care about. I'll go to New York, but it would be safer for you if you and Lincoln run. Get as far away from her as you can.' She watched carefully for my reaction.

I looked over the newspaper clippings again. Children, some as young as three years old, had been reported missing.

One article showed an entire petrol station had been blown up in Brazil, the body of a five-year-old still missing but presumed cremated in the flames. In all cases there were no known survivors and no witnesses.

Lilith was covering her tracks. And she was moving fast.

'We both know you didn't let me become Grigori and spend the last seventeen years in Hell so I could run and hide. I appreciate the offer but there is only one way to stop her and you put it perfectly – we have to kill her.'

Evelyn smiled and I couldn't help but be a little scared by the amount of violence promised in that one expression.

'Well, well. You are my daughter after all.'

And I realised – I'd just passed her test.

It totally pissed me off. Even if I did feel oddly pleased with myself.

chapter twelve

'Love is of all passions the strongest,
for it attacks simultaneously the head,
the heat and the senses.'

Lao Tzu

I stepped out of the limousine that had collected us from the airport. I wasn't sure of the exact number of Grigori that had been there waiting for us – there were a number lurking in the shadows, using their ghosting abilities to follow us. For the first time, I wasn't sure if they were there to protect us or secure us.

The New York air was dense, thick with an energy unlike anything I'd ever experienced. People flowed along the pavements in a constant stream.

So. Many. People.

Cars moved surprisingly fast, considering their sheer number, dominated by the fearless yellow cabs that featured in every New York movie known to man.

'Welcome to Manhattan,' Griffin said, standing beside me.

He had travelled with me, Lincoln, Zoe and Spence. The car in front had taken Dad and Evelyn and the four guards who had taken her into custody at the airport. And there were two more vehicles . . . that I knew of. Personally, I felt it was overkill. We'd already agreed to come to New York – it wasn't likely we'd travel all that way to do a runner at the airport. Then again, this *was* Josephine's turf.

'Amazing, right?' Zoe said proudly. She glowed as though just being in the city was somehow recharging her.

'Did you grow up in New York?' I asked.

She nodded. 'Born and bred. Wait till I take you to a Yankees game.'

I was about to respond, when I was struck by my angelic senses. The familiar apple flavour washed through my mouth, the sounds of cars fell second to that of branches crashing and wings flapping frantically. My vision faltered as images of pure light followed by pure darkness and morning and evening flashed before me.

'Exiles,' I managed to say, desperate to give everyone some kind of warning even as the smell of flowers overwhelmed me and I started to shake with the energy flowing through my body. Ice for bones, fire for blood.

Lincoln wrapped his arms around me, tilting my face up to his. 'Focus, Vi. Manage the senses,' he murmured, bypassing the senses and finding me. But there was so much, so many. I tried to tell him to run but I couldn't speak.

I could see he was talking again but I couldn't hear over the sound of wings flapping.

I began to panic.

Too many.

We couldn't possibly fight them all. Had Lilith brought an army to meet us? Were they already here?

Too many. Too many.

Lincoln kissed me.

His lips were soft, warm and felt overwhelmingly right against mine. I fell into it, oblivious to anything other than the safety in his touch. One by one, the senses flowed from me as he pulled them away and set them free. It must have hurt him. The senses hurt the hell out of me.

But he was unfaltering, taking from me what I could not manage. He was my partner, my soulmate. As my body started to weaken, he wrapped his arms around me, supporting me. He kept his focus until the last of the senses had floated from me to him and then, when it was just us, the kiss lingered as we stole a few extra seconds. We both knew it was wrong – but letting go seemed impossible.

Lincoln started to tremble – his fingers digging into my sides, holding on to me, to *us,* yet also somehow trying to move away. I didn't ever want to let him go, wanted to pull him closer. My soul demanded it of me. It made no difference that we were out in the open, in the middle of the pavement.

But he was already shutting down – the honey from his power encircling me as he rebuilt the walls between us – and I knew I had to do the same.

'Linc,' I whispered, trying to put myself back together.

He rested his forehead against mine. 'It's okay. We're okay.'

He took a few deep breaths. Acting as a conduit for the senses always took a hefty toll on him.

I wrapped my arms around him. 'I know.'

We stayed like that for only a few seconds before he pulled away, regaining the control we both fought so hard to maintain.

I wish I had his strength.

'Let's get inside,' he said, his voice hoarse.

It was only then that I looked around and saw both carloads, including Dad and Evelyn, were staring at us. Zoe was fanning herself.

'Exiles,' I blurted out. 'They're . . . they're everywhere. The senses were suffocating me!'

'We're in New York, Violet,' Griffin said, a smirk on his lips. 'There are over one and a half million people on the eighty-seven square kilometres of Manhattan alone. And this is the home to the largest population of exiles in the world. You *should* be bombarded by your senses.'

'How am I supposed to stay here then?' I asked, my panic levels rising.

Lincoln, who'd put a few feet between us, answered. 'You'll adjust. And inside the Academy it will be easier.'

'Why?'

He smiled grimly, still recovering from the power-drain, and pointed to the top of the skyscraper we were standing in front of. 'Because they have strong shields and occupy the top floor. You can be certain there are no exiles in any of their buildings.'

Did he just say buildings, plural?

The black-suited Grigori who had collected us from the airport held open the large glass doors of the building.

I took a deep breath and closed my eyes, concentrating on the senses, letting them come to me, but on my terms. I had to master this. If I was bombarded by another attack of the senses and it was during a fight, I needed to be able to control them.

I felt the senses come to me. There were so many exiles and all so close by. It took the concept of fear to another level altogether.

The senses built inside me and started to become unbearable but, breathing deeply and steadily, this time I managed to push them down and move them to the background. They were still distracting, but for now, it was going to have to do.

I looked at Linc, who was waiting, and nodded. He smiled, the type of smile he gave me when I'd done well in training.

As we walked through the doors I ignored the stern looks coming from Dad, who didn't realise Lincoln had just saved my ass, and moved ahead – now was not the time for explanations. I was fairly certain Evelyn understood exactly what had happened since she had a tight grip on Dad's arm and was steering him away from us.

I nodded to her in thanks.

She ignored me in that annoying way of hers.

As soon as the lift doors opened on the top floor I was washed with another bout of senses, but they were different – subtle and comforting – signalling the presence of my own people.

'How many Grigori are here?' I whispered to Griffin.

'Around a hundred students plus up to another hundred senior Grigori are based here at any given time.'

'Wow.' That explained the sensory influx.

Eight silent and heavily armed Grigori dressed entirely in black appeared to take Evelyn to their holding rooms. Griffin had prepared us for this, but Dad struggled to keep his cool as she was led away in restraints.

The waiting room – where the rest of us had been deposited – was massive, and ultra-modern. The walls of the building were glass, offering magnificent views over Manhattan. It was astoundingly beautiful, and a touch like being in a fishbowl.

'Come with me,' Lincoln said quietly, moving to the side of the room. I followed him to the windows.

'What?' I asked.

He pointed outside and then I saw it.

Nothing could have prepared me for the sight before me. And when his extended arm panned to the right, I gasped.

'How ... how? That's not ... Are they *flying*?' My eyes could not make sense of what I was seeing. People were walking around in mid-air, literally. Nothing below them, nothing above them, and yet they looked like it was the most natural thing in the world. I looked down to the street – there was a wind blowing, trees swaying – but when I looked back at the people wandering around in the sky no one seemed affected.

Lincoln grinned. 'The Academy owns a number of buildings. There are walkways between them.'

I couldn't take my eyes off the sky-folk. 'There are *people* wandering around in the *sky*, Linc. Explain this to me.'

He laughed one of his low, secretive laughs. One that echoed through my entire body. One that told me he adored me. One that somehow I knew, out of everyone in the world, was reserved for me. The laugh that broke my heart.

Breathe.

'I'm glad you find me amusing. Less laughing, more telling!'

He laughed again and I was about a second away from either throwing a punch or throwing myself at him, when a woman's voice caught our attention.

'I see we have all made it,' Josephine said, her tone of superiority cutting through all the other noise.

She stood tall and prim, dressed in a navy suit that was cinched at the waist, her dark hair held back in a bun. She was attractive, in a very severe way. Appraising us one by one, Josephine may just as well have called us riff-raff to our faces.

She nodded to Zoe and Spence. 'Welcome home. You will have the same rooms as before you left. I assume you remember where they are. Zoe, unless you have any objection,' she actually rolled her eyes, 'which I'm sure you won't, Violet will be sharing your room.'

'That's fine,' Zoe said, trying to suppress her smile.

'Spence, you will be expected to sit in a disciplinary meeting this afternoon before recommencing classes,' she said, with a look that dared him to challenge her.

Jesus. She really is scary.

Of course Spence rose right to the challenge. 'Actually, I've just graduated high school. I've brought a copy of my records with me. I'd be very happy to attend combat training and additional physical education, though, since I'm sure I've missed some while I've been gone.'

I had to give it to him, he didn't even break out in a smile. He delivered the whole speech of crap with the most sincere look on his face that Josephine was left with nowhere to go.

Wonder how long he's been practising that!

'We can discuss it later,' Josephine snapped. 'You can both take your bags to your rooms and get settled.' She waved her hand at them, dismissing him and Zoe.

She's awfully keen to get rid of Zoe and Spence.

I gave Lincoln a sideways glance but he shook his head, discreetly asking me to let it go. I did.

Josephine took her time to show her clear disdain for me before she turned to Griffin and Lincoln, showering them with false kisses. Her theatrics reminded me of Onyx's.

Same drama. Different channel.

'So you're the human ...' she said, finally turning her attention to Dad. She didn't bother to hide her dislike. It struck me as oddly similar to the kind of disgust exiles show us.

Dad nodded. 'James Eden,' he said holding out his hand. Josephine ignored it.

'James, excuse me if I don't pretend to be happy to have you in my Academy. Certain rights are afforded us within these walls and by insisting on coming here you have breached those rights of ours. Out on the street, I tolerate humans – I dedicate my life to your survival – but I have been Grigori for so long now that unless it is a matter of the greater good, I prefer to keep the company of my own kind.'

'And I'm only human,' Dad responded.

'Correct,' Josephine stated with no shame.

'He's my father, Josephine,' I said, stepping forward, but Dad put his hand up to stop me.

'It's fine. I'd prefer not to suffer pretences either. I believe it has been made clear to you, Josephine, that I am here to escort Evelyn, and I expect to be with her at all times.'

Josephine laughed. 'And what gave you the impression that I would allow that?'

Dad bristled. 'I will be taken to Evelyn now. If she is locked up, then I give you my permission to lock me up with her, under the condition that my daughter is given access to me ...'

He glanced at me. 'If she would like to see me at any time. And you will provide this for the exact same reason that you let me inside your precious Academy to begin with. You want Evelyn, you need Violet, and without me you cannot be sure you will get either.'

Josephine's eyes went wide and she cleared her throat.

Score one for the human.

Finally, she gestured to a guard standing silently by the entry doors. 'Take him down to the holding cells.'

'Dad?' I started when they moved in to cuff him.

He shook his head. 'Sweetheart, it's fine. You do what you have to do and come and see me . . . when you're ready.' Then his eyes settled on Lincoln. 'I'm trusting you to look out for her.'

Lincoln nodded. 'I will.' He said it as if he was giving an oath and it made me nervous.

When the guards had led Dad away Josephine turned back to us. 'And then there were three,' she said and, at seeing my stance – hands on hips and head down as if I was about to charge her – she chuckled lightly. 'Save the demonstrations for a proper audience. I'd hate for you to be exhausted before the main event.' She held her perfectly manicured hand out. 'The Assembly are waiting for you.'

'The *entire* Assembly?' Griffin asked.

Josephine smiled knowingly and replied slowly. 'Every last one of them.'

Griffin paled. Lincoln looked away.

Oh, that can't mean anything good.

chapter thirteen

'Beware of dark and secret things.'

Sir John Clerk

Josephine led us into a large oval room. Again, the outer wall was entirely glass but this time it was opaque so there was no view. The space was largely bare, apart from a semi-circle of chairs which sat on a slightly raised stage at the far end of the room that looked like they'd been carved out of incredibly large trees – each one a different shade of natural wood. All were taken but one.

Lincoln stayed close to me as we were led to the centre of the room. There were no seats for us. I was desperate to talk to Griffin and find out why he was so freaked out that the entire Assembly was present.

We'd talked incessantly before and during our travels, Griffin briefing me on each of the Assembly members. But he'd told me that there would only be four of them at the Academy itself, at most. It seemed this was one of the rare occasions where Griffin had been mistaken.

I made sure my supernatural guards were in place. Before getting on the plane both Griffin and Evelyn had made me swear that I would keep my shields up as much as possible when in the Assembly's presence and not tell them anything I didn't need to – especially about my ability of Sight and, secondly, about my angelic ranking. I wasn't to allow for any flashy displays of power. Overall, their suggestion was to do everything I could to look weaker than I really was – a concept that went against my nature. But I could try.

A man sat in the middle of the chairs on the podium. Four people sat to his right, another three to his left and there was a single vacant chair beside him. Obviously Josephine's.

Griffin had explained to me that her position on the Assembly was one of the reasons she chose to remain partner-less. According to Grigori law, if one partner is elevated to a seat on the Assembly, then so too is their partner. As a result, they had an equal vote. Apparently, Josephine deemed no one worthy of a seat beside her. Partners generally voted in the same way, which often left Josephine wielding the deciding vote – a privilege she had no intention of sharing with an undeserving partner.

Total power wench.

Josephine took her seat.

'Griffin, I believe you have met the members of the Assembly before?' she began, every word oozing satisfaction.

Griffin nodded respectfully. 'I have. Though I must admit, I have never known of the entire Assembly to come together for such an . . . informal occasion.'

That was Griffin's way of highlighting to us, just in case we'd missed it, that something was up. Big time. If, in all his years as a Grigori leader, Griffin thought this was major, I wasn't about to argue.

Josephine smiled, clearly enjoying herself.

Another bad sign.

'Well then, allow me to make the introductions, for Lincoln and Violet's benefit. In the centre is Drenson, the head of the Assembly and the ultimate face of Grigori around the world.'

According to Griffin, Josephine specifically chose not to be the head of the Assembly. She didn't want to be the face of all Grigori. She was a strategist and a fighter, and enjoyed getting bloody too much for such a detached role.

Drenson looked like he was in his late twenties, but I knew he was old, in his many-hundreds. His hair was long, past his shoulders, and auburn, almost red in the light that filtered through the opaque glass. He wore a modern double-breasted suit in steel grey. Not the type of suit Onyx would be caught dead in but one that screamed power and money nonetheless. His brown eyes looked down on Griffin first, then Lincoln, before finally settling on me. He inclined his head slightly. I nodded back.

'We have waited a long time to meet you,' he said, his voice so deep it echoed through the room. A very faint accent hinted at Spanish being his native tongue.

'I'm honoured to be meeting with you,' I said, reciting the words Griffin had told me to use.

'Beside Drenson is his partner, Adele,' Josephine said, gesturing to a slight woman who sat rigidly in her seat. Long black hair almost covered her mouse-like features.

She cast a sweeping gaze over all of us and said, 'Welcome,' before turning her attention straight back to Josephine.

'Sitting next to Adele are partners Seth and Decima. The oldest serving members of the Assembly,' Josephine said.

In turn they both cast their emotionless eyes over us and nodded in introduction. A shiver ran down my spine.

So old. So powerful.

We nodded back – but I noticed Lincoln's nod seemed more of a bow. Seth and Decima were both tall and incredibly slender, both dressed in light flowing garments. Decima in all white – in contrast to her long black hair. Seth in all black – in contrast to his long white hair.

Griffin had told me about them on the plane. Seth and Decima were the most religious members of the Assembly – which apparently made them two of the most vicious warriors. They came from a time when religion meant fighting to the death – though demonstrations were now very rare. Seth and Decima felt their presence necessary only at times of great war. Perhaps that alone was the reason it seemed so strange they were here today.

'On my right,' Josephine continued, 'sit partners Hakon and Valerie, who also run the training academy. You can expect to see more of them in the near future.'

I suppressed an urge to object to this. Griffin had warned me that it would be unlikely the Assembly would permit my stay unless I agreed to attend some Academy classes. I wasn't happy about it. Something about conforming to their structure rubbed me the wrong way. Josephine didn't try hard to hide her knowing smile.

Glad to see she can entertain herself.

Hakon was *huge*. I wouldn't have been surprised if one of his previous names had been Hercules. He had short blond hair that made me think he might be Scandinavian. His light brown eyes, almost topaz, met mine. He didn't look impressed with what he saw.

His sheer size was mind-boggling. I didn't realise muscles could *be* that big and it wasn't as if he was trying to hide them. He was wearing only a strip of brown leather over his top half. I could see his entire chest. It was . . .

Lincoln cleared his throat.

Crap. I'm staring.

Embarrassed, I blinked, nodded to Hakon and quickly turned my attention to Valerie, who looked tiny beside him despite the fact she was probably the most athletically built of the women on the Assembly, notably dressed down in black leggings and a white sweater. She looked like she'd just come off a training session, which made me kind of warm to her. Then she gave me a full up-and-down and – by the judgemental glance she shared with Hakon – made it obvious she wasn't impressed with what she saw either. I felt my cheeks flush.

'And finally,' Josephine spoke up again, after we'd exchanged nods and awkward hellos with Hakon the Hulk and Valerie, 'closest to you are Wilhelm and Rainer.'

It didn't take a genius to realise that these two were her least preferred Assembly members from the way she brushed over them so quickly, barely gesturing in their direction.

I guess that makes them my new besties!

'You can call me Wil,' Wilhelm said kindly, nodding at Lincoln and me. 'Welcome to the Academy.' His glance moved to Griffin. 'Good to see you, old friend. You've been sorely missed.'

Griffin nodded, a smile spreading. 'And you, Wil. You too, Rainer.'

The woman stood up – the first of the Assembly to make any kind of move – and walked to Griffin. She kissed him on each cheek and took his hands, emotion passing between them.

'I'm sorry for what Magda has done. Her actions have hurt us all, but you the most. She was lucky to have you as a partner and wrong to have betrayed your trust.'

I liked Rainer.

'Thank you,' Griffin said, his head bowed humbly.

I could tell his respect for her was genuine and his gratitude heartfelt. Rainer leaned in again and whispered something in his ear. Griffin nodded again and I was sure I spotted a tear in his eye before he blinked it back.

Rainer turned towards Lincoln and me. She was about my height. She was beautiful. Glossy black hair cut straight and sharp at shoulder length. She had an exotic look to her, more so than Adele's. In fact, her eyes were so striking she reminded me of . . .

'Nyla,' I whispered. The name fell from my lips before I could stop it.

She smiled. 'Nyla is my sister. My twin sister, though not identical, obviously.'

I stared at her – the similarities now clear. The way she conducted herself and the warmth in her eyes left no doubt she was Nyla's kin.

Nyla had never told me she had a twin. But then again, older Grigori rarely spoke of their families – it was a no-go subject. More often than not they'd either been lost or outlived.

'I . . . I . . . Nyla was . . . She was amazing,' I stuttered.

Rainer's smile broadened as I fumbled with my words. 'She was amazing. And I have every confidence she will be again.'

At that, a steely determination that was gone as quickly as it came flashed in her eyes, leaving me in no doubt – Rainer, like her sister, was a fierce warrior.

'You'll have to pay her a visit during your stay,' she said, returning to a lighter tone as she went back to her seat.

'Well, now that all the introductions have taken place,' Josephine said, looking decidedly bored following Rainer's interruption, 'there are a few matters we would like to discuss. The first of which is identifying exactly which rank Violet Eden has been created from. As exciting as the rumours have been, I believe it's time to put this issue to rest once and for all.'

Griffin stepped forward. 'Josephine, it has already been a long day for us. Surely Violet is entitled to some Academy training before any testing is carried out.'

Josephine's upper lip twitched. 'We've waited long enough, Griffin. Don't think we are not aware that you have been withholding information from us as well.'

Griffin dipped his head. 'Nothing that I believed was cause for imminent danger to my Grigori brethren or to the Academy.'

'And what about to the Assembly, old *friend*? Have you withheld any information that could be detrimental to the Assembly?'

Griffin took his time. He looked at each member, some returning his gaze, some, interestingly, averting it. Their reactions didn't give me confidence about what was to come.

'Nothing that wasn't in the best interests of the future of the Assembly.'

Rainer, Wilhelm and Hakon kept their attention on Adele, so I did too. When she inclined her head slightly, as if accepting what Griffin had said, I wondered if she was a truth teller, like Griffin. Whatever she was, her nod seemed enough for those who'd been paying attention to her.

'Have it your way, Griffin, but we will not allow Violet to leave without at least submitting to a small power gauge first. Drenson has offered his services for today.'

Griffin looked at me, his expression grim. 'Do you remember when you first met Rudyard?'

Did I ever! He had taken my hand and pushed his power into me, taking me over in a completely intrusive way. It wasn't something I ever wanted to experience again.

I nodded, looking back at the Assembly. It was easy to see who my adversaries were – they were the ones smirking. I swallowed down the bitter taste at the back of my throat and nodded to Griffin again.

He closed his eyes briefly and it set off every panic button in my body.

Seth stood up and moved to the centre of the room. He took off his loose-fitting shirt to reveal a slender body with tight muscles that reminded me of a racehorse. He turned his attention to Lincoln.

'Perhaps you would like to take your shoes off,' he said in a strong accent that I couldn't place other than knowing it was European. It made me nervous to consider that I possibly couldn't place it because it was simply *that old*.

This place is like the United Nations.

I looked between them as Lincoln took off his shoes and then his shirt. When I caught his eye he shook his head and said under his breath, 'Don't watch. Concentrate.'

What the hell does that mean?

I looked at Griffin, who was backing away, and noticed a white box marked out on the floor – a sparring field. I'd just spent hours being told that Seth was a master fighter – 'unbeatable' and 'unstoppable' were the words thrown around.

'Violet,' Josephine's voice sang out to me, 'would you please join us up here? I'm sure you'd agree the sooner we can have what we need, the sooner we will all be able to get on with our day.'

I walked towards her, keeping my focus on Lincoln and Seth as they started to circle one another like predators.

Shit.

'I don't understand. Are you making Lincoln fight?'

Drenson stood up and walked towards me. 'I'm afraid a little distraction always helps get this side of things done more swiftly,' he said. He held out his hand, just like Rudyard had done, and I knew that whatever Rudyard had done to me the first time we met would be nothing compared to what was about to happen.

At my hesitation, Josephine nodded to Seth and in less than a second he had launched himself metres into the air and come back down spinning with inhuman speed and strength, his foot colliding with Lincoln's face, sending him straight to the ground before he'd had a moment to react.

Lincoln leaped back onto his feet quickly, as my breath caught at the sight of the blood pouring down the side of his face.

And that had only been the first hit.

'Your hand, Violet,' Drenson said.

Oh, God. What have we walked into? These people are insane.

Lincoln took another hit and barely managed to stop himself from going down again. Before he righted himself,

Seth, at lightning speed, delivered another terrifying blow that I suspected dislocated Lincoln's shoulder, from the awkward angle of his arm afterwards. I heard a whimpering sound and realised it was me.

'The sooner you give me your hand willingly, the sooner we can stop this,' Drenson said.

So that was it. I had to give my hand willingly to Drenson or his power wouldn't work. I bet it had been Josephine's suggestion to beat the shit out of Lincoln until I cooperated.

Just her style.

Lincoln landed a fist in Seth's gut. The Assembly members seemed to stiffen as a unit. I smiled at Josephine's look of surprise. They'd underestimated Lincoln. Unfortunately though, Seth still had the advantage.

I put my hand in Drenson's.

It was slow to start and I concentrated, as Griffin and Evelyn had instructed me, on keeping up my barriers. But I couldn't keep my attention away from Lincoln and Seth, fighting like gladiators in the middle of the room. Lincoln was covered in sweat, Seth delivering lethal blow after blow. If Lincoln had been only human, just one of those hits would have killed him. But he kept getting up, kept fighting back, putting serious power behind his punches.

Then Drenson's true power hit, as if he'd only been peeking from behind a curtain before. He kicked open the front door and charged into me. My body would have fallen back with the impact, but his vice-like grip on my hand held me in place.

I fought to keep my guards up, tried to hide who I was, *what* I was, but all the while I could see what was happening to Lincoln. He was being beaten to death and his pain was taking me over even as Drenson pushed into me – all I could concentrate on was Lincoln.

And that's when I realised – *that* was the other reason they were doing this. Seth was pounding Lincoln not just to force me to let Drenson look into my power – but to force me to lose my concentration and let down my guard. When that happened – they would see everything.

Lincoln took another punch to the face, his head jerking back. I was sure he'd already had his nose broken and a number of ribs.

But instead of screaming for them to stop, instead of running in to fight with him, I fought every natural instinct and . . . I closed my eyes. I blocked out the sounds of his body being pounded. One by one, I put back the bricks that had slipped from my defences. I put back the barrier that kept me safe. That kept us all safe.

Drenson was powerful. He pushed, he shoved hard and didn't bother being polite. I could feel his energy edging around my bones like a serrated knife, scratching and slicing, looking for a way in, eager to reach the well of power that lay within me. But even as he pushed more, even as I felt the tears slip from my eyes with the pressure and felt the trickle of blood from my nose, I held strong.

I *was* strong.

Drenson gripped my hand tighter until I started to feel the sharp snaps. He was crushing it like someone would juice an orange. But his own hand was starting to tremble and that gave me all the encouragement I needed. He was weakening.

When Rudyard had first used his power on me, I hadn't been expecting it and I was new to the game. A lot had happened since then and I was stronger than I had ever been. I opened my eyes and stared right into Drenson's.

'If you haven't got what you were looking for by now, I suggest it might be worth considering you are *never* going to get it.' I knew my words would be taken as the threat I had intended them to be.

His nostrils flared and he tightened his grip on my hand. More small bones crunched. I didn't react.

'That's enough,' Wil said from behind Drenson. 'This isn't getting us anywhere.'

Drenson's eyes were locked on mine and I knew that I had not made a friend in him today. But we were both going to have to find a way to deal with that, because I wasn't going to let his power steamroll me. As long as I was breathing, I wouldn't let anyone control me like that.

He dropped his hand, the release sending a wash of relief through my body. It made me want to scream in pain as the blood returned to my hand. Instead, I held it behind my back and turned to where Lincoln and Seth had been fighting.

Lincoln was on the ground. He was breathing. I could feel his heart beating. But he'd been pulverised. I forced myself not to run to him.

Griffin went over instead and crouched beside him, checking his vitals as Seth made his way back to his chair. When Seth passed me he paused and glanced at me briefly, yet somehow seemed to look right through me, as if I was nothing more than a small distraction.

'Nothing personal. He won't be so easy to best next time, I imagine,' he said, then continued.

'Why Seth, I think that might be the nicest thing you've ever said,' Rainer chimed in.

I half expected Seth to rip her out of her chair, but he actually turned to her, gave a small bow and – shock horror – smiled. For like, half a second.

'If we are done here we'll be taking Lincoln to his room,' Griffin said, standing now with Lincoln in his arms, unconscious. Griffin's face was a mask of calm but I doubted anyone could miss the fury in his eyes. Lincoln was one of his.

My stomach sank looking at the damage that had been done to my partner.

Breathing shallow. Shoulder definitely dislocated. Cuts over both eyes. Broken nose.

'Surely Violet can heal him?' Josephine threw in, innocently. 'We've all heard so much about her extraordinary healing abilities. Perhaps a demonstration would help us understand a little more.'

Yet another motivation for having Lincoln thrashed.

I took a deep breath and tried to stay calm. 'Josephine, you have my parents locked up. You have had my partner beaten to within an inch of his life. I've just been subjected to an incredibly intrusive power struggle . . .' I moved my mangled hand out from behind my body. 'And my hand is all messed up. We came here at your request. I intend to stay and abide by the Assembly and Academy rules while I'm here.' I glanced at the other Assembly members. 'I would very much like to do anything I can to help stop whatever Phoenix and Lilith are planning. But right now, instead of standing around here playing games with you, I'd really prefer to take my partner away so that I can rest before what will no doubt be the rather exhausting job of healing him.'

All eyes darted between Josephine and me. I'd just challenged her in a way that was only going to make her look bad and hate me even more but I was damned if I was going to subject myself and Lincoln to any more of her bullshit.

Josephine put a hand to her chin. 'Will you submit to full Grigori testing in three weeks' time?'

My eyes widened. If I didn't know better I could've sworn her voice held a note of respect.

Surely not.

I looked over my shoulder to Griffin. We'd discussed this and knew that this was one thing I was going to have to do – all Grigori do.

Turning back to Josephine, I gazed over the entire Assembly, showing – despite Griffin's advice to the contrary – that I was not afraid.

'In three weeks,' I agreed.

Then, without waiting for permission, I marched out of the room, Griffin following with Lincoln in his arms.

Welcome to New York, indeed.

chapter fourteen

morgan and Max were waiting outside the doors.

'Hey.' Then, 'Oh my God,' Morgan said, hand over her mouth, when she saw the state of Lincoln. 'Is he . . .?'

'He's fine,' I snapped. 'Where can we take him?'

'Follow us,' Max said, already moving.

We stormed through the halls, Max and I clearing the way – people were smart enough to move fast.

'Seth?' Max asked.

'Yes.'

He whistled. 'Oh man, he never stood a chance. No one has landed a hit on Seth and lived to tell the tale.'

'Well, they have now,' I said, not slowing even as my rage towards the Assembly and Josephine in particular continued to build. 'Where?'

Max pointed to the right. 'Infirmary or his room?'

'His room,' Griffin and I both said.

'Right, here. We're going to have to cross the walkway.'

I led the way with Max but stopped in my tracks when we

came to the end of the corridor. We faced a gap in the wall, a huge opening in the building.

'Whoa!' I said, looking over the edge. We were more than a hundred storeys above ground level. One more step and I would be falling and I didn't imagine it would be the kind of fall that would land me in the angel realm.

'What's the hold-up?' Griffin called from behind.

'Violet's at the walkway!' Max called back.

'Hurry up, for Christ's sake!' Griffin yelled.

'What do I do? Where do we go?' I looked between Max and the open space before me.

Max rolled his eyes and pushed me aside, storming towards the edge. I reached out just in time to grab the back of his T-shirt before he fell.

'What the hell are you doing?' I screamed.

He steadied himself and turned to face me, his feet dangerously close to the opening.

'Violet, it's a walkway. Just because you can't see it . . .' he took a step backwards. I lurched forwards to grab him again, but before I got there, his foot landed on something in mid-air. Nothing visible – but something that supported his weight. 'Doesn't mean it is not there.'

I'm hallucinating. Drenson must've messed with my head.

Max took another step back and I was suddenly staring at a man standing perfectly still in the sky.

Morgan pushed past where I stood frozen, staring at the impossible. She marched right out onto the invisible walkway without so much as a second of hesitation, turned back to face me and then released her power. It flowed from her in a multicoloured mist, floating out. I watched, amazed, as it hit invisible walls, revealing the transparent tunnel they were now standing in.

'These tunnels connect all of our buildings,' Morgan said. And when she saw the question in my eyes, she added, 'Just think of it as a glamour. A really complex glamour.'

With that she started to walk towards the building ahead. I could see now a similar opening in its wall and a person stepping out into the open air, who started walking towards us as if it was no different from taking a flight of stairs. This is what Lincoln had been showing me earlier.

'Violet, we need to move,' Griffin said, now behind me. I didn't like the urgency in his voice.

I nodded, but didn't look at Lincoln. I couldn't, not yet.

Ignoring every natural defence in my being, I followed Max and Morgan and stepped into thin air. My foot found a solid landing.

'Whoa!' I said again, marvelling. But now I knew it worked, I was moving at full speed, my feet seemingly walking on air. Logic struggled to keep up – the sensation not unlike stepping onto a stationary escalator. I looked down. The streets below buzzed with activity.

'Can't they see?' I called out to Morgan.

She followed my gaze. 'Nope. The whole thing is glamoured. They can't see it, or anything within it. Once you know it's there, you can see it a little. It has a kind of golden glow, but unless you know it's here you'd never see it.'

I felt Lincoln's heartbeat, which I'd been tracking since the fight had started, speed up. 'Griffin, I think he's waking up.'

We both knew when he did he'd be in a world of pain.

'Let's go!' Griffin called out and we picked up the pace.

In the other building, Morgan and Max led us through a maze of halls, eventually coming to an area that was set up like dorms with several doorways close together, some open to show small and simple bedrooms.

They led us down another corridor, into a more updated area, stopping outside a door at the end. Max pulled out a set of keys, unlocked and held the door open for us.

Griffin carried Lincoln in, laying him on the bed.

His eyes were starting to flutter and I could tell the pain was registering as his body convulsed and he started to gurgle with sharp intakes of breath.

Griffin checked his vitals again then looked to Morgan and Max. 'Thank you, but you need to leave now.'

Morgan looked offended. 'But we can help.'

Griffin didn't even consider it. 'It's best if you go. You'll only be asked questions that are too difficult to answer if you stay.'

Max seemed to accept this first and nodded to us as he pulled Morgan towards the door. 'Let us know if you need anything. We'll be in the cafeteria in building A.'

How many buildings are there?

Griffin nodded.

I sat on the edge of the bed, looking at Lincoln. His eyes opened. Blood covered his face so I reached for some tissues and tried to blot some of it away so that he could see.

He winced, and swallowed heavily. 'Griff, you . . . go, too,' he mumbled.

Griffin shook his head. 'No, Lincoln. I'm not going anywhere.'

I knew what Lincoln was doing. He was trying to protect Griffin – and all of us. The more Griffin knew, the more he would be expected to report. He was a truth detector and deliverer, so if he was asked to give details and then couldn't deliver those details with absolute honesty, it would cause him big problems.

I ran into the small bathroom and wet a hand towel, bringing it back out, trying to wipe away more of the blood.

'His heartbeat is strong, he's going to be fine, Griff. Lincoln's right, you should go. The less you see the better for all of us and you know it. Go with Max and Morgan. We'll find you later.' I saw the conflict in his eyes. It just wasn't in him to walk away from one of his Grigori when they were hurt. Especially Lincoln. They were like brothers. But we both knew it was the right option.

'Jesus,' he said, admitting defeat. 'Call me if you need me.'

'I will.'

Lincoln moved in and out of consciousness. I spent a little time just sitting beside him, making sure I was fully in touch with my power. Apart from just after I first embraced I'd never had to heal Lincoln from injuries this severe – I really didn't want to make a mess of it.

As if he could tell what I was thinking, he slipped his hand into mine before passing out again.

'Oh, Linc,' I ran a hand down the side of his face. 'I'm so sorry they did this to you.'

It was my fault.

And he hadn't even tried to resist.

There was a time when I could only access my healing abilities by kissing Lincoln. But I was stronger now.

I closed my eyes, put my hands on his chest, and drew up on the well of power that simmered within me. It came to me easily, like an old friend, eager to help. Lincoln was my partner and despite anything else we were made for healing each other. It was the one thing I could do that felt completely good and natural.

My amethyst mist flowed from me, frosting the room and settling on Lincoln, searching out the source of his pain and gradually healing him. I was thorough, taking my time and starting at the base of his body before working my way up. I left his shoulder till last, wanting him to be as strong as possible. Because before I healed the pain – I was going to have to put his shoulder back in place manually.

Lincoln's eyes opened.

His nose was healed and the cuts on his face were now gone. I used the towel on his face again, wiping away the rest of the blood carefully. He tried to move a few times, an intensity that he rarely let out showing in his green eyes.

My breath caught but I kept going. He wasn't healed yet.

Before I could say anything, he lifted his good arm, wincing at the pain from his dislocated shoulder, and put his hand on mine. The one Drenson had crushed.

Over my dead body.

I shook my head at him. 'I need to fix your shoulder first.'

'You're going to need both your hands for that,' he said, breathless.

It wasn't exactly true. I was pretty sure I could do it with one hand. And I didn't want to be fixing anything about me until I knew he was okay. As if he knew exactly what I was thinking, he didn't wait. His power, the array of colours led by green, poured from him and into me.

'Violet,' he said, insistent. He could be irritatingly stubborn when he wanted to be.

Reluctantly, but knowing from his look that it wasn't worth fighting, I added my power to his. It wanted to go back to him, sensing he was still hurt, but I directed it towards my hand instead, each of the broken bones knitting together until they were completely healed.

Immediately, I broke the connection between us, not wanting to waste any extra energy.

'You should rest for a while,' Lincoln said, his eyes watching me with that same deep concentration. My heart picked up its pace.

To cover it, I narrowed my gaze. 'Would you stop ordering me around?'

'I can wait until you've rested. I'm feeling better. It's just my shoulder left. I don't want you doing too much.'

I ignored him and instead began to prepare his arm, but the angle was off. His shoulder had popped out of its socket in such a way that putting it back would require great pressure on him. It wasn't a huge ask with my strength but the angle had to be right.

'You're just avoiding me yanking your arm back into place.'

I knew it wasn't true, but he gave up on disagreeing with me.

'Just do it,' he said.

I batted my eyelids, trying to keep him talking and distracted. 'Oh Linc, you're so brave.'

He tried to roll his eyes but his attention was really focused on the impending joint adjustment. Grigori or not – it was going to hurt.

I took the pillows out from under his head so he was lying flat. He pretended it didn't bother him, but the muscles in his neck betrayed him, bulging. I moved up, straddling him to get in the best position, ready to push his shoulder back into place. Suddenly, Lincoln's attention shifted back to me. I gnawed on my lower lip, and an idea.

'Ready?' I asked.

Oh crap, what am I thinking?

He gritted his teeth. 'Do it.'

Screw it.

'Close your eyes,' I ordered.

Surprisingly, he did. Without giving it another moment's thought, I leaned down and pressed my lips to his.

Lincoln's body flinched at the contact, but it only took a couple of seconds for the shock to end and then he was kissing me back. All the emotion that had been building as I'd been healing him released. He made a sound low in his throat and I took that as my cue.

I thrust my hand down hard and fast. His shoulder popped right back into place. His body jerked with the pain and I released my power back into him, my strength healing him quickly.

Lincoln's lips stayed on mine even as he tensed in pain. In a matter of seconds his kiss had changed from one filled with surprise, to pain, to relief and then . . . to something else altogether more urgent.

Yes, my plan had a significant flaw, because just as desperately as he kissed me, I was kissing him back. Both of his arms, now fully operational, pulled me down to him and in a particularly stealthy move he somehow flipped us so that I was lying under him.

My hands found their way up his bare back. Lincoln made another sound and something within pushed me forward, demanding that I have all of him. When his hands started to push my top up, I felt myself repositioning and whipping it over my head.

Think, Vi. Think.

Can't.

Lincoln's lips were at my throat, his hands travelling up my sides. Everything about him was surrounding me. His warmth reminded me of summer days and seeped into me, igniting my desire. This was exactly where I wanted to be, exactly what I wanted to be doing. Mind, body, soul. I ran my fingers through his hair and he did the same to me.

But his body began to tremble.

No.

I knew what he was doing.

I could feel his power, the distinctive honey flavour beginning to flare while the sun sensation faded. He was putting up the walls between us again.

But my walls weren't up. Mine were all the way down and my soul was hungry, agonisingly so.

'No,' I heard myself say. 'No!' I was growling. I didn't care.

I pulled his face up to mine and I kissed him. He kissed me back and his power dwindled, but he continued to tremble, continued to try to put walls between us that did *not* belong there.

His lips moved down along my jaw, but they were slowing now. His hands stroked my hair, gently instead of frantically.

'Don't stop,' I almost yelled, overwhelmed by a sense of panic at losing him. 'I need you. I . . . No! You can't stop!'

I arched my body towards him, trying to break down the walls, but he didn't respond, he just kept kissing me up to my ear and started to talk soothingly.

'You've used up all your strength. Your defences are down. Listen to me, Vi. Come back to me. Remember all the reasons.'

I ran my hands up and down his back, feeling every groove that was meant for me.

We are supposed to be together, damn it!

Our souls were matched and not only that, they'd tasted one another and would settle for nothing else.

My mind and body were on fire with my need for him. Everything that made me who I was, was crying out to be with him.

He wrapped his arms around me and moved to the side of me, pulling me close. I couldn't let go and he didn't make me. I pressed kisses into his neck, his shoulder, I kissed his lips and he let me, all the while talking to me softly and building the wall between us. Eventually, my soul's demands overcame me. Tears poured from my eyes as I started to pound my fists against his chest, small screams falling from my lips.

He took it, let me hit him, let me scream. He just pulled me back to him, waiting patiently for me to remember. Letting me know he was there for me, letting me know it was okay.

Finally, my screaming and the hitting stopped, replaced by exhaustion and a feeling of loss. I fell weakly into his embrace, tears pouring down my cheeks as he kept holding me.

'I'm here. I feel it too. It's . . . crushing and it hurts. You're not alone. You're not alone.'

But I was alone. That was the whole problem. For as long as we were apart, I would always be alone. I buried my head into his chest. 'I can't do this. I'm not strong enough.'

He stroked my hair. 'You're the strongest person I know. You'd just gone up against the head of the Academy and pulled on a tonne of power to heal me, your defences were down. If anyone should be apologising, it's me. I should have stopped sooner.'

'I just wanted to distract you.'

He grinned. 'You did. I've never been so distracted in my life.'

The enormity of what I had just risked hit me.

Guilt didn't begin to cover it.

If Lincoln and I were together, if we let our souls join completely . . . If one of us died the other one's soul would shatter . . . I wasn't stupid. I knew just as well as everyone else, a war was on the horizon. And it didn't take a genius to work out that with Phoenix's physical hold over me it was more than likely that I wasn't going to be walking away from the inevitable battle.

I couldn't believe I'd been so selfish, so willing to just take Lincoln as mine when I was so close to my end. And there he was, still talking to me, soothing me.

Disgusted with myself, I started to pull away from him.

'Hey,' he said, tugging me back to him.

I shook my head, too embarrassed for words.

'Don't,' he said. 'Don't blame yourself. Hell, Vi, I declared my love for you in front of everyone on a volcano for Christ's sake! When Phoenix had you prisoner in Santorini I turned that island upside down looking for you and almost lost my mind in the process. We have to help each other. Staying away didn't work. We're going to get through this together.'

I half laughed. 'We're going to work out how to not be together, *together*?'

He chuckled back. 'Yep. And I made a promise to you, in case you've forgotten, and I plan on fulfilling it one day.'

I swallowed, remembering that night after we'd come back from Santorini, when I'd asked him to promise that one day we would find a way to be together.

He pulled me to him.

'Are you okay?' I asked, worried I might be hurting him.

'A hundred per cent,' he said. 'You've got that healing thing down pat.'

At least I could do one thing right. Even if it did come with sex-maniac side effects.

As if reading my mind, he added playfully, 'And anyway, it's not as if I'm complaining. I haven't seen so much action in quite a while.'

My breath caught. I didn't know what to say. I mean, I'd presumed since we'd discovered the soulmate thing that he hadn't been with anyone else. But that didn't mean I hadn't wondered about other girls before. I wasn't a fool. Lincoln may have only looked young, but he was really twenty-six. I knew he'd had other relationships. I'd just never dared to ask about them.

Sensing my hesitance he brushed a hand through my hair. 'Wrong thing to say?' he asked.

'No. I just . . . I don't really know who you've . . . I mean, I don't know if there has ever been anyone . . .'

'Oh,' he said, catching on. He was silent for a while, deciding what to say. 'I don't want to make things harder for us, for you,' he said. When I remained silent, he sighed. 'I'm not . . . I've had a couple of girlfriends.'

'I didn't think you hadn't,' I answered honestly.

He nodded, his chin resting on the top of my head. 'I guess I've only had one relationship that has lasted more than a couple of months and that was when I was nineteen. I went out with a girl for two years.'

Wow. Two years was the equivalent of living together, according to Steph's timeline.

'What happened?'

'We realised we were better friends than anything else. Even then, it felt like something else was pulling me.' He shifted against me. 'I . . . When we first met, I knew I cared about you more than I'd ever cared about anyone. I just wanted to make you strong and keep you safe. All of my focus went into that – not into picking up girls. I don't know exactly when I realised my feelings had become more but it was around the time that we started to hang out away from training, when we just got to be ourselves around each other. From there I was lost.'

I chewed on the inside of my cheek, trying to bottom-line what he was saying. 'So . . .'

His tone held a smile. '*So*,' he mimicked.

'So, you haven't been with anyone since . . .?'

'Since you came into my life.'

Any way you put it – that is damn impressive.

Guilt washed over me. I wished I could say the same thing.

I looked around his room properly for the first time since arriving. 'Do you realise your room is three times bigger than any of the other ones I saw on my way here?'

He shrugged. 'Maybe it's Josephine's way of apologising for unleashing Seth.'

'Max said no one has ever landed a hit on Seth before and lived,' I said.

'They have now.'

I smiled. 'That's what I said.'

'Did Drenson get anything from you?'

'Not much.'

'That's going to piss them off.'

'Yeah, well, the feeling's mutual.'

We lay in silence for a few minutes. I realised we were both lying there shirtless and I didn't even feel self-conscious. That alone spoke volumes. But if someone walked in it wouldn't be good.

'I should go,' I said. 'Griffin will be waiting to hear how you are.'

But he didn't let me go.

'Griffin will be fine for an hour. Rest,' he ordered, and, there in his arms, with his heart beating strong and healthy against my ear, I couldn't think of anything I would rather do.

CHAPTER fifteen

'The pure and simple truth is rarely pure and never simple.'

Oscar Wilde

I was in Hades. I couldn't hear the music, but I could feel it vibrating up from the dance floor and into my body.

I spun. Phoenix was behind me. He looked . . . older. No, grave. And somehow more beautiful for it. He wore black pants and a midnight-blue fitted shirt. He rolled up his right sleeve to match his left. Such a simple action and yet it commanded my full attention. As if each roll of his sleeve signified something greater and the weight of his cast-away gaze meant so much more. And yet, there was also the danger. The ever-present danger that lurked in the shadows and followed him.

'What do you want, Phoenix?' I asked, crossing my arms.

He tilted his head, glancing up at me, and began to speak. But I couldn't hear him.

I noticed then that there was something between us that looked like a wall of liquid. It went all the way around me. I didn't know if it was trapping me, or keeping him out. I also didn't know whose it was – mine, his or someone else's.

He realised what was happening and studied what was separating us. He sighed. There were circles under his eyes and I felt an unbidden

pang of concern for him, but that was enough to pull me back to my
senses. I shook my head, remembering my run-in with Onyx.

I needed to stay in control.

Phoenix's hand reached up to press against the veil of liquid and
his brow furrowed, lost for what to do next.

I squared my shoulders. 'Leave, Phoenix,' I said.

He nodded sadly. He could obviously hear me.

I started to back away from him and from the dream. The vision
began to unravel.

'Don't go!' he said clearly so I could read his lips.

I couldn't let him get into my mind. Couldn't let him manipulate
me the way he always did.

I willed the dream away.

When I woke up, Lincoln was already dressed. He'd obviously
been out and retrieved his things. He'd covered me with a
blanket – all the way to my neck – and was sitting on the edge
of the bed watching me. Phoenix's dream visit drifted through
my mind. I wasn't sure if the dividing wall had come from me
but I was sure I now had the ability to remove myself from any
shared dreamscapes in the future. That was a good thing.

So why is my gut twisting?

Lincoln cleared his throat. I blinked, and accepted the bottle
of water he passed to me.

'Bed-head?' I asked, finger combing my hair.

'Extreme,' he said, smirking.

'Any visitors?' I asked, a little more apprehensively.

Besides the one in my dreams.

'No. I popped out to see Griff. He knows you're resting and
has been keeping the mobs away.'

'How are you?' I continued, deciding not to burden Lincoln with my dream update. It would only worry him.

'I feel fantastic – actually, I feel a little guilty about that,' he said looking down.

I stretched and pointed to my top, now hanging from the end of the bed. As Lincoln reached over to pass it to me I said, 'Don't. I feel good, too. When we heal like that together we are so much more powerful. It always seems to recharge us both. It's like having a jumpstart.'

He nodded, but didn't want to linger on the subject. 'Do you feel up to moving about?'

'Sure. Why?'

He stood up, politely turning his back to me as I sat up. 'First, we get food and I show you to your room. Zoe has organised for all of your stuff to go there.'

'And second?' I asked, shrugging my top on and continuing to finger comb my hair.

'Josephine has requested to see you in her office.'

Lucky me.

'Do they have any more intel on Lilith or Phoenix?'

He hitched a shoulder. 'I'm hoping that's what we're about to find out.'

My room wasn't nearly as impressive as Lincoln's. *And* it had to fit both Zoe and me.

'No fair,' I mumbled to Zoe, as I unloaded some clothes on the bed, looking for a suitable change after my cramped shower in our tiny cubicle of a bathroom.

'Yeah, well, wait till you see the size of the single rooms. At least we can lie straight in our beds,' she responded, pulling posters out of her bottom drawer and proceeding to put them up on the bare greyish wall above her bed.

'Who did you used to share this room with?' I asked, deciding on a pair of black jeans and a light red sweater.

'A girl called Eleanor. She graduated a few months back. She and her partner are now in Germany, I think,' she said with a shrug. 'We were never close.'

'How come Lincoln got such a flashy room?'

Zoe kicked her bags under her bed and dusted off her hands. 'Don't know. He was given one of the best suites. Apart from Grigori leaders, no one gets those rooms. Someone obviously thinks he's very important.'

That was interesting.

Zoe kept her gaze on me and finally rolled her eyes. 'Are you going to tell me what happened? Everyone's talking about it.'

I sighed. I wasn't up to reliving my introduction to the Assembly just yet. 'Later?' I asked.

She paused and I thought she'd argue, but instead she just nodded, acceptingly. 'Fine. But I'll want details.'

After we'd finished settling into our room, Zoe walked me through the halls and over the skywalk, back into the glass building apparently known as 'Command'. It was where all the training and official Assembly rooms were located. Zoe explained there were five buildings in total. Building B, where our rooms were, and another building, C, were both dedicated to accommodation. Building A was fitted with gyms and recreational areas along with a massive food hall and another large cafeteria. Building D was for Academy classes and was where all new Grigori were restricted to when they first started their training.

I guess I should have been grateful Josephine didn't try to confine me to Building D.

Now that I had crossed over the skywalk a couple of times, I could see the light golden glow that Morgan had talked about around its edges.

'It's amazing,' I said as we walked across it.

Zoe nodded. 'Always a crowd pleaser.'

I bounced up and down on the invisible floor. It was completely solid. 'What is it?'

'Reinforced glass,' she said, pulling out a bag of M&M's. She seriously must have had some kind of never-ending supply. 'Valerie and Hakon just keep them under a very strong glamour.'

I was mesmerised by it. 'Don't birds fly into it? Or planes?' If no one could see them, then surely they were some kind of hazard.

She shook her head. 'We're in a strict no-fly zone and the glamour does something that repels birds.'

I still couldn't comprehend it. 'What about when it rains – don't people see the water splashing off them?'

'Nope. If you're looking up from the street the glamour just mirrors the image from above the walkway so even when it rains all they see is the rain falling from above the tunnel.'

'Wow.'

'Yep,' she said, shaking out some M&M's into her hand and popping a few in her mouth.

She stopped at the beginning of a long corridor and pointed to the double doors at the end. 'Josephine's office is behind those doors. I gotta go meet up with Spence. He had his meeting. Valerie has made him start back in training sessions from tonight. I promised to be his sparring partner.' She popped another few M&M's. 'I'm gonna kick his ass.' She waggled her eyebrows.

Poor Spence. Zoe fought like a cat – a particularly well-clawed cat. 'See ya,' I said, as she left me to take the rest of the hallway on my own.

Josephine's doors were slightly ajar and I could hear her voice from inside. I knew she must have been talking to Lincoln, who had been called in to see her just before me.

'You've always had great potential, Lincoln. I've had high hopes for you. I must say, after watching your display this morning against Seth, you have only confirmed my suspicions that you may one day be eligible for a seat on the Assembly. That would make you the first Grigori made by a Power to be elevated so high.'

'A position on the Assembly would be a huge honour,' Lincoln said.

'Indeed it would. But I have to be honest with you, if you continue on this path I can't see that happening. Your connection to this girl is clouding your judgement. You are putting her above your responsibilities to the Assembly.'

When there was only silence, I heard Josephine sigh.

'Lincoln, she is not one of us – I have an eye for these things. You're honour-bound to her, which is admirable, but you also need to look beyond her and see the bigger picture.' She gave another heavy sigh. 'I think you should consider putting forward an application for a partner replacement. Griffin and I are both capable of appealing to the Seraphim guides on your behalf.'

I was sick of hearing conversations from the other side of the door. Sick of being let down by people and only finding out what was really going on in the world by eavesdropping.

Lincoln's power caressed me lightly, sending a warm shiver through me. I smiled, realising he was reminding me he could feel me from a mile off, just like I could him.

'I'll take that under advisement, Josephine,' he said, his response so non-committal I almost laughed.

Her tone dropped down a notch. 'Why am I sure, then, that you will not?'

'Because she is my partner,' he said, as if that answered everything. 'Shall I bring her in now?' he added, not so discreetly telling Josephine I was standing right outside her partially *open* door.

Score one for us!

The door swung open and Lincoln stood behind it, gesturing me into the room with a wink. It seemed Josephine wasn't the only one who could play the word game.

Josephine had a long list of dos and don'ts she felt the need to run through with me. I paid attention to the headlines. Effective tomorrow, I would be expected to participate in Academy training. Like Spence, I would not have to attend normal classes, though special theory sessions would be arranged to bring me up to speed on Grigori history. Much to Josephine's surprise I was happy to hear that.

The part I wasn't so excited about was that I would be Academy-bound until after my formal testing in three weeks and had to choose an in-house senior Grigori as my mentor to prepare me. I had to nominate someone by the end of the next day.

I agreed to everything, then asked, 'Where are my parents?' I stopped short of adding, 'And when can I see them?' The truth was, I wasn't sure I was ready for that yet.

Josephine pursed her lips. 'They are in the holding cell on the level below here. They will remain in quarantine until Evelyn has been through a full debriefing. However, as per your father's stipulations I will arrange for you to have access to him in due course, though visits will be supervised.'

I gave her a level stare. 'You do realise holding her won't accomplish anything. She's Grigori, just like you. All she wants to do is stop Lilith, that's all she's ever wanted to do.'

'We have our reasons. They are not for you to question, Violet.'

Josephine sat back in her chair wearing a smug expression.

She was up to something. Why was she so keen to have Evelyn locked up? What would she gain from holding her here? Me? No, it was more than that. Every move Josephine made was calculated. I suddenly had a terrible thought: 'You want Lilith to come for her?'

Lincoln straightened in his chair beside me when Josephine didn't immediately deny it.

'You have her locked up and defenceless because you think Lilith is crazy enough to break into the Academy just to kill her!' I shouted, jumping to my feet.

Josephine still didn't respond.

'Is that true?' Lincoln asked.

Eventually, Josephine waved a dismissive hand in the air. 'Even if that were to happen, which I'm not saying is our intention, we have both of your parents well guarded and behind Academy shields. No exile, no *anybody*, could even get close to them.' She smiled tightly. 'Evelyn isn't going anywhere without my say-so.'

Before I could argue, Lincoln stood and placed a halting hand on my shoulder. 'Have you had any more leads come through on Lilith's whereabouts?' he asked.

She turned her attention to her perfectly manicured fingernails. 'Not yet, but we will. Griffin has passed on Evelyn's theories regarding the missing children. We're yet to form an opinion on that, but we're looking into it.'

I worked hard not to roll my eyes. She knew as well as us that all those missing kids were no coincidence. It was clear she had no intention of sharing any real information with us.

When Lincoln walked me back to my room, we passed Mia and Hiro in the corridors.

'Hey,' Hiro said, dressed in his ghosting uniform of all-black.

Lincoln and I nodded to him.

'Hi Mia,' Lincoln said. 'Good to see you.'

Mia nodded curtly. 'You too.' She barely glanced at me. 'Violet.'

'Hi,' I said, wondering why she was being so frosty. I hoped we'd all kind of become friends since Santorini, what with the shared battlefield and all.

'We're on duty,' she said.

'Sure,' Lincoln said. 'We'll catch up later on.'

She nodded and the two walked on.

'Was that weird?' I asked Lincoln when they were out of earshot.

'No. She's just focused on her work. She's always been like that.'

'I guess . . .'

Lincoln dropped me off at my room and promised to return later. We had plans to meet Griffin, Spence and Zoe for dinner. They were going to give me a full run-down of what to expect once my classes started tomorrow. From the smirk on Lincoln's face I could tell he was looking forward to seeing how I fared in prac classes. I resolved to make sure I did him proud. As my primary trainer he took my performance results personally.

In my room, I found a note that had been left on my bed.

> *Dear Violet,*
> *I'm glad you are here.*
> *My invitation still stands if you should like to visit*
> *Nyla at any time. I have alerted the guards on her door*
> *that you are an approved visitor.*
> *On another issue, I wanted to offer my service as a potential*
> *mentor in your preparations towards your final testing.*
> *I would consider it an honour.*
> *Rainer.*

I smiled, slipping the note into my pocket. I'd just found myself a mentor.

After spending some time exploring Building B, I returned to my room to find Zoe sitting on her bed looking way too pleased with herself.

'I take it you beat Spence?' I asked, wondering how bad a mood he would be in at dinner.

'That would be one description,' she said. 'It was the most fun I've had in days.'

I laughed. 'You're evil!'

'Yeah, but I see my evilness as a service to the greater good. My superiority will only make Spence a better fighter in the end.'

We both laughed.

When we had calmed down and were reclining on our respective beds, Zoe rolled onto her side and pushed herself up onto her elbow.

'So?'

'So, what?' I responded, pulling out my ponytail and running a brush through my hair.

She raised her eyebrows expectantly. 'Are you going to tell me about it?'

I wondered if my meeting with the Assembly was supposed to be kept confidential but no one had told me it was. And Zoe had been incredibly patient.

So, I told her everything – how I had met the Assembly, about Lincoln's fight with Seth and Drenson's power test, which made her sit up, eyes wide, on the edge of her bed.

'Then, we took Lincoln back to his room and I . . . you know . . .'

She raised her eyebrows. 'Violet, *why* are you blushing?'

In the absence of Steph for the foreseeable future, Zoe was my closest girlfriend. And I needed to be able to talk to *someone* about this stuff.

I groaned. 'I kissed him.'

Zoe blinked. 'Oh, you're going to have to give me a *lot* more details!'

'It helps my healing – it makes it easier for our powers to merge and makes us both really strong.' I grimaced, realising I wasn't being entirely honest. 'Okay, I don't have to do it that way any more, but his shoulder was dislocated and I thought the distraction might . . . you know, help . . .'

Zoe nodded, keeping a serious expression. 'Practical and convenient.'

I rolled my eyes.

'And?' Zoe pushed.

'And . . . It worked. I popped his shoulder and healed him but . . . We were still kissing and I . . . I guess I was weakened from using so much power already and I kinda . . .'

'Kinda?' Zoe prompted.

'Jumped him,' I admitted.

Once Zoe had stopped laughing, she gave me her thoughts. 'First of all, Lincoln is gorgeous and he clearly loves you just as much as you love him. The fact you guys are being torn apart is the definition of tragic. So, don't beat yourself up about it – if I was on top of him half naked I'd totally be dishing the moves!' When she saw my narrowed gaze she quickly added, 'Hypothetically, of course.'

After I settled my head back on my pillow, Zoe carried on. 'The question I have is this: You said that when you and

Lincoln heal each other together it makes you both strong, rejuvenates you or whatever, right?'

I nodded.

'Then . . . wouldn't it make more sense that the two of you were at your strongest when you were finding it so hard to pull yourselves off each other rather than exhausted and at your weakest like you said?'

I opened my mouth to argue. Closed it.

Silence.

My mind went blank.

What the hell am I supposed to do with that?

chapter sixteen

'Fairly examined, truly understood, No man is wholly bad
nor wholly good . . .'
Theognis of Megara

The next morning I stood in the middle of one of the sparring rooms facing my opponent, who also happened to be one of the Academy Grigori I most liked.

'Morgan, I don't want to hurt you,' I said, after I pulled her up. Again.

Morgan shrugged. 'I'm okay.'

And she was. Morgan was a great fighter, but I was better. On natural strength and speed alone I outclassed her. On top of that, Lincoln had trained me so I was also tactically more aggressive. The Academy taught from the one book of moves and it hadn't taken me long to decipher their predictable pattern. Lincoln, on the other hand, drew from a number of different disciplines – kickboxing, judo, army-combat training – and had the final clear directive of winning at all costs, allowing for unsportsmanlike conduct when required.

It was an approach I shared wholeheartedly, one that many of the Grigori I was training with would no doubt share once they'd been fully exposed to the wrath of exiled angels.

I'd been allocated to an intermediate-level group since, according to the Academy, I was technically 'untrained'. Griffin had recommended I go straight into Advanced Combat – the level Zoe and Spence now trained in – but Josephine had vetoed the suggestion. It quickly became clear that although my group were naturally fast and strong, they had little idea what to do with their Grigori strength.

Valerie was running the class and had thrown me into it first thing. That was three hours and five opponents ago. I could tell she'd planned on teaching me a lesson and putting me in my place.

Guess that isn't going to happen.

I didn't think it was okay to beat down people who had had significantly less training than me, but it *did* seem to be helping in my assimilation with the other students. The Academy was a place where strength was respected.

'Cause strength means not getting yourself killed. Or anyone else.

'Again!' Valerie ordered.

Morgan pushed herself to her feet. In her training uniform of short fitted tights and black singlet top, the fresh bruises were clear to see. I'd already managed to send my first three opponents to the infirmary, before I'd stepped off the gas. I was glad Lincoln wasn't around. If he'd seen me holding back he would've gone mental.

I frowned, thinking of him, knowing that he'd be busy with Griffin. We had agreed at dinner last night that while I was showing up to my Academy training and putting on a good face, Griffin and Lincoln would be out sourcing more info on Lilith and Phoenix.

It annoyed me that I wouldn't be doing my bit, but they'd insisted that having me to concentrate on might keep Josephine from watching them too closely. In addition, Academy members in training weren't permitted to leave the buildings without prior consent and before my testing was complete it was unlikely any of the teachers would grant me permission to leave. I added my house arrest to the extensive list of reasons I hated this place.

Morgan came at me. She was learning and avoided my right leg. She got in a few good hits, and I dodged rather than taking her out straight away. When I saw my chance I lifted her into a tackle, taking her down with as little force as possible. But at the last second, to make sure I wasn't going to have to do it again, I landed on top of her.

'It would be nice if you fought with a shred of honour. Ninety per cent of your moves are illegal,' Valerie chastised me.

Suppressing a sigh, I stood up, offering Morgan my hand and helping her up. I glanced at Valerie and noticed Rainer standing near the entrance to the room. I wondered how long she'd been watching.

With a shrug, I explained. 'In my experience, exiles aren't so much concerned with honour as they are with ripping off my head. If it's them or me, or if I'm trying to defend a human I'll make any move I can to put them down and contemplate what kind of person that makes me afterwards.'

'That's one view. The other is that if you walk too close to the edge the lines between the monsters and yourself can start to blur. You risk waking up one day to discover you've become just the same as them.'

I stared in disbelief at Valerie as she waved a hand at the class.

'We've seen enough today. Dismissed.'

As Morgan walked out with me I started to apologise.

'Don't,' she said, putting her hand on my arm. 'I learned more today, fighting you, than I have since Nyla was taking this class.'

I nodded, accepting the compliment with a sense of pride.

'Did Valerie just call me a monster?' I asked.

Morgan cringed. 'She's not as bad as she comes across. I think she was just surprised you were so strong.'

'Isn't that what you said about Josephine?'

She cringed again. 'What can I say? I like to see the best in people.'

I guess I couldn't complain about that, since I was more than happy with her seeing the best in me. I needed all the friends I could get.

'Violet, do you have a minute?' Rainer asked as we passed.

I stopped as Morgan continued on with an apologetic wave. She thought I was about to be told off.

Probably right.

I threw my training bag over my shoulder and followed Rainer into a side room. The space was dimly lit with several golden artefacts dotted along the dark wooden shelves. In fact, the room was at odds with the bright and modern fit-out of the rest of the Academy buildings. Rainer sat down behind a large mahogany desk.

She motioned for me to take a seat.

'I live here full-time at the moment. I needed at least one place where I felt myself,' she said, as if reading my mind.

I put my bag on my lap and leaned on it. I'd been training for hours. My body was in a world of hurt.

'Did you get my note?' she asked.

'Yes, thank you. I . . . Um . . .' I didn't know how to talk about Nyla with her, with anyone, really.

She shook her head again, as if knowing exactly what I was thinking. 'Take your time. She's not going anywhere in a hurry, but I believe there is still hope. If I didn't,' she flashed me another glimpse at her warrior eyes, 'I'd finish things myself.'

I admired her optimism but . . . I was there when Nyla's soul shattered. She wasn't coming back.

Rainer kept going. 'I wanted to ask you if you have considered my offer to be your mentor?'

I had discussed it with Griffin last night and we had agreed it was very generous of Rainer and something I should jump at, but after the class I'd just been through . . .

'I don't seem to fight to the Academy standards. And I don't intend to change, either.'

She lifted one eyebrow.

Nifty.

'Did you see Seth adhering to Academy protocol when he took down your partner yesterday?'

'No.'

'I believe Nyla and Rudyard included you in some training when they were staying with you, too?'

I nodded, remembering how fierce a fighter Nyla had been.

'Precisely. Valerie is all about rules and regulations. She has to be in order to run the Academy effectively, but make no mistake, when you stand in front of a roomful of Grigori seniors and the Assembly for your final testing, only one thing is going to matter.'

'What?'

'Winning.'

I shifted in my seat. 'And you can help me do that?'

'Yes.'

I had to respect her confidence, given that we both knew there would be a number of Grigori, including Drenson and Josephine, who would like nothing more than to boot me out of the Academy for good.

'Okay, then. When do we start?'

'Tomorrow. We train before your classes and directly after every day. Be prepared – I plan on working you hard.'

I'd been so glad to have an ally as my mentor I don't think I'd been listening when Rainer had explained the working-me-hard part.

Two weeks after signing on with her I felt like the walking dead. From the first day of our training she'd been collecting me at 5 a.m. and not dropping me back at my room until 8 p.m. after our evening session.

My heavy schedule meant that I'd only seen Spence and Zoe in classes and due to the fact that more than a few sets of eyes were trained on everything I did, if Lincoln hadn't taken to sneaking me dinner in my room, I wouldn't have seen him at all. Or eaten.

Luckily, we both knew spending too much time apart was not a good idea. Somehow we seemed to have found some kind of medium for our souls. It wasn't perfect and although the physical pain – not to mention heartache – of being away from each other *and* around each other was constant – it was always intensified by extended periods of separation.

Hence my nightly room service.

'I'll talk to her,' he said, as we sat on my floor eating cold pasta. Well, Lincoln was eating it – I was basically inhaling it. I had missed lunch, again.

I'd thought Lincoln had been a hard taskmaster, but Rainer took training to another level. When I wasn't running laps in the enormous rooftop gym with its glass bubble ceiling – I was going through drills, lifting extreme weights, handling weapons or getting hit in the face. Repeatedly. By Rainer. She hit every other part of my body as well, but she focused on my face – reassuring me we'd always be able to gauge my progress by the amount of times I allowed her to smash it in.

I tried to explain I wasn't *allowing* anything.

She disagreed.

I shook my head at Lincoln. 'No you will not.' The last thing I wanted was him coming to my rescue. 'Only one more week to go and I'm learning a lot.'

Like what the ground looks like from close up.

He nodded, but remained focused on the food I could tell he wasn't enjoying. I might be fine with microwave dinners but Lincoln was a fresh-produce kind of guy.

'Is Zoe ever in here?' he asked, looking at her mess of a bed and opting for a subject change.

I took another huge mouthful of spaghetti. 'She's usually hanging out with Spence and the other students.' From her late-night stumbling around in our room, it was clear they got up to no good – aka . . . a lot of fun. But I was always too exhausted to tag along and find out what they really did.

'I tried to call Steph today, but I can never get through. Has Griff heard from them?'

Lincoln nodded. 'Today, briefly. Nothing new. Still on-track,' he said discreetly, not wanting to go into any more detail while within Academy walls. 'Griffin saw your parents today,' he added, trying to sound casual.

We'd had this conversation before. 'I'll go and see them soon. I haven't exactly had a lot of free time.'

'That's not the reason and you know it.'

True. It had more to do with still not knowing what to say to Dad and my inability to process the fact that I'd spent so long hating Evelyn – thinking she'd traded me off for her own advantage – that I couldn't even look at her now. I'd treated her so badly and I didn't know how to fix it. And . . . I had a feeling the two of them were growing . . . close, and I just didn't know how to deal with that.

'Is she still having fainting spells?' I asked.

'No. They gave her something to jumpstart her internal organs and it seems to have worked. They think it was something to do with her body readjusting to its earthly form.'

Made sense. Griffin had said something like that, too.

We sat in silence for a while. I finished off my pasta, cleaning the plate with a piece of bread. Lincoln had given up on his dinner.

'What do you think it was like for her?' I asked quietly.

'I can't imagine. According to her official debrief, she has no memory of being in Hell. Only that she was there.'

But I knew better. She'd told me never to ask her and not because she didn't remember – it was because she did. I suspected Lincoln knew that too.

'She's your mum, Vi. She gave up her first seventeen years with you, but she's here now. I . . .' He put his plate down on the tray beside him and stretched out his legs. 'I was so mad with my mum after she died. I was mad at her for getting sick – thought she'd been too weak and made it easy for Nahilius to brainwash her.'

'That's not true.'

He half smiled. 'I know, but it was what I felt for a time. I guess it was my way of dealing with things until I was able to see the truth, that I just missed her.'

I leaned my head back against the bed. 'I'll think about it.'

He nodded and passed me a bowl of melted chocolate ice cream.

Yum.

I ate while he filled me in. More missing children. Phoenix had been spotted in a few places, a couple of times in the New York area. There hadn't been any sightings of Lilith, but exiles in the area seemed to be moving in mixed packs. It was clear that Lilith had them out doing her dirty work for her – and it made sense since the lure of the Grigori Scripture would be the only explanation for exiles of both light and dark continuing to work together.

'I hate being stuck in here. I feel like I should be out hunting.'

'Right now, I think this is the best place for you. If you were out in the open they might've come for you. At least this way you're training and getting stronger. There are Grigori searching worldwide and all the senior Grigori in New York are hunting her. We'll find them.'

The problem was – I didn't feel stronger. I was exhausted. I slumped back even further. Lincoln smiled and started to get up, collecting the food trays as he did.

'I'll leave you to get some rest.' He paused at the door. 'You know, I'm really . . . You're doing great. The testing will be a breeze. I know it isn't easy and being locked up is hard but I've been really . . . proud to be your partner.'

I swallowed hard at the praise. Lincoln was talking to me as my trainer and it was a big thing for him to hand over a compliment like that.

'Thanks,' I said, wishing he wasn't leaving but knowing I couldn't ask him to stay.

He nodded. 'I'll see you tomorrow.'

After he left, I tried calling Steph again. We hadn't been having much luck reaching each other. She was either off hunting ingredients for the Qeres or I was busy training. Tonight was no different, my phone going straight to her voicemail. I left a message telling her I would try and email, but we both knew that however we made contact, neither phone nor email was secure so she wouldn't be able to tell me much.

From what Griffin had gleaned from Dapper, they'd already found nine of the ingredients they needed and Dapper had enlisted a few old friends of his family to help keep them hidden. We didn't know exactly what that meant but he assured us they were all safe and together. The last three ingredients were proving more difficult to find – the original sources of one, seemingly extinct. If we had to, we would use an inferior mutation of the herb but Dapper still felt it was worth persevering and since we hadn't got any further at our end, Griffin agreed. No one seemed to want to deal with the outstanding problem of the angelic thirteenth ingredient.

The odd text I had received from Steph mostly complained about her lack of 'alone time' with Sal, until, two days ago, a simple smiley-face message, which I presumed meant she'd finally found a way to rectify her problem.

I had a shower, washing off the blood from the evening's session with Rainer. When I walked out of the tiny bathroom, wrapped in my towel, every muscle aching to the extreme, and considering giving myself a quick healing once-over, I found Zoe and Spence both sitting on her bed.

'Hey,' I said. Then I saw the clothes – not mine – laid out on my bed.

'What's going on?'

My confusion didn't last long when I saw the smiles plastered on their faces.

I shook my head. 'No.'

They kept smiling, sitting there in the kind of clothes that screamed: planning no good.

'No!' I reinforced. 'I can barely stand up and Rainer will be back here banging on my door in,' I looked at my watch, 'six hours.'

'Oh, come on, Eden. You used to be fun. We've barely seen you and some of your classmates are starting to talk . . .' Spence said, trailing off.

'Talk about what?'

'That you think you're too good for us. I mean, look at it from their point of view, you haven't even been showing up to meals.'

I knew there was probably truth in what he was saying. I hadn't been showing up for things because of my training but that didn't mean people wouldn't take it in another way. I didn't want to be an outcast.

'A few of them will be out tonight and it'll give them something else to talk about over breakfast if you show.' Spence's eyes were alight. I knew he was baiting me, setting me up to give in.

I bit my lip.

'Come on.' Zoe chimed in. 'I've even put out a hot outfit for you so you don't have to think, and don't pretend you can't swing a little of your own power on yourself for some healing. We all know you can.'

I gave her a snarky look. 'In case you've forgotten, I'm not allowed to leave the buildings.'

Spence rolled his eyes. 'Technically, neither are we, but in case *you've* forgotten, we have particular talents when it comes to getting out of high-rises.'

At that, I couldn't hold back the smile.

Fifteen minutes later, I was in Zoe's favourite pair of black leather pants, high-heeled boots and a gold beaded halter-neck, which was crying out to be danced in.

Zoe yanked my hair up into a high ponytail while I smudged on some eyeliner and a layer of mascara.

Spence stuck his head back in the door. 'Coast is clear. Mission Bridge is a go.'

Mission Bridge?

Zoe grabbed my hand and yanked me down the corridor.

It was getting late so not many people were walking the halls. We stayed close, travelling through three buildings and over two skywalks, Spence hiding us under glamour whenever we were at risk of being seen. Finally, on the lowest of the Academy levels in Building D, Spence and Zoe came to a service lift.

'Zoe, you're look-out,' Spence said.

She nodded and kept a watch on the hallway while Spence started to pry open the doors.

'Are we going to die trying to get out of here?' I asked.

'Don't think so,' he said, as he pulled them apart. 'Zoe, let's go,' he whisper-yelled.

She ran straight for the lift and . . . jumped.

'Holy hell!' I yelped as I looked over the edge to see she had grabbed onto a ladder on the far side of the shaft.

Spence chuckled. 'After you, sunshine.'

My shock quickly morphed into a smile. This was going to be fun.

Following Zoe I leaped into the lift shaft, landing easily on the ladder and following her down. Spence was close behind.

When we reached the second floor, Zoe stopped climbing down and started heaving open the doors there. When we had clambered out, she led us straight through a fire door onto a balcony.

'Why are we going this way? Why not just use the front doors?'

'Motion detectors,' Spence replied. 'They'll still pick us up, even when I'm using a glamour.'

'How often do you guys do this?'

Spence shrugged. 'The service elevator is like . . . Like a rite of passage. We've both spent almost a year here confined to the buildings – use your imagination.'

'Right.'

With that we walked to the edge of the balcony and, despite the two-storey height, jumped off, landing easily before hailing a yellow taxi.

'Look up,' Zoe said.

I gave her a dubious glance but followed her line of sight.

'Oh, my God,' I whispered.

For the first time, I saw the skywalks connecting – *curving between* – the Academy buildings. Now that I was conscious of them, they shone in luminous gold.

'Is that . . .' I couldn't finish the absurd question.

Surely not.

'Yep,' Zoe said. 'Josephine built a halo over the city.'

I followed my friends into the waiting taxi, still amazed that Josephine had actually *haloed* New York.

'Brooklyn Bridge,' Spence said to the driver.

I wound down the window and sucked in the air that spelled temporary freedom. It was actually kind of dense, but when I looked at Zoe and Spence, both buzzing with adrenalin, I couldn't fight a smile spreading across my face. 'Mission Bridge?' I asked.

They nodded in unison.

'It's time to show you *our* New York.'

Chapter Seventeen

'Love is a familiar; Love is a devil. There is no evil angel
but Love.'

William Shakespeare

'**M**ission Bridge' turned out to be *under* Brooklyn Bridge.

After the taxi had left us, we stood in front of the massive supporting pillar that held up the Brooklyn side of the bridge. It was a warehouse district but the art community had clearly taken hold – many of the buildings showed signs of recent face-lifts and restaurants spilled onto the streets.

Zoe said the area we had just driven through was called Dumbo. Seeing all the art galleries reminded me of who I was, of the things I loved – the *human* me.

I stared up at the stone pillar noting with surprise that there seemed to be fewer exiles in the area. My shoulders relaxed and I breathed a sigh of relief at not having to work so damn hard to keep the senses at bay.

'Okay. So . . . I hate to tell you guys, but I think most of the nightlife was back a few blocks,' I announced. I looked out over the Hudson and towards Manhattan's city lights, sparkling on the other side. 'Though the view from here is pretty spectacular.'

Spence snorted. 'We're not here for the view, Eden,' he said, walking into a dark tunnel that went right through the middle of the pillar. It was the kind of shadowy underpass that the pre-Grigori me would've avoided like the plague – one that even the Grigori me wasn't thrilled about. But when Zoe skipped after Spence with a wink in my direction, what else could I do but follow?

Halfway through the tunnel, which was acting as a shelter for a number of homeless people, I started to feel a familiar buzz.

'Are there Grigori here?' I asked, when Spence stopped and knocked on a door that was almost hidden in the midnight black of the tunnel.

'You could say that,' he said.

The door opened, and a woman looked all three of us up and down before giving a small nod. 'Masks or not?' She didn't introduce herself but she was obviously Grigori.

'Masks,' Spence said.

With that, the woman stepped aside and we walked in. As we passed her, our hair changed colour and she handed each of us a small crystal mask. Spence's was black, Zoe's was pink – much to her satisfaction – and mine was gold, to match my top I guessed.

I looked at my new hair – it was still high in a ponytail but when I pulled the ends around they were at least a foot longer and now a dark burgundy. Zoe's hair was completely pink, another thing that had her beaming, and when we looked at Spence we both burst out laughing.

'No way,' he said to the woman. 'Anything but orange!'

Zoe and I were in hysterics, gasping for breath and holding our stomachs. The woman at the door laughed too, but must've taken pity on him because she waved her hand and his hair changed to marine blue. He put on his mask. It fit so well, like a second skin. If I didn't know it was Spence, I would never have guessed.

Zoe and I positioned our own masks.

'You know the rules?' the woman asked.

'No forcing identities, no powers, no photos, masks off only by choice, no fighting, no drawing weapons,' Spence replied.

She nodded and gestured to a set of stairs. 'Have a nice night.'

We walked up, the buzz of Grigori now surrounding me.

'What *is* this place?' I asked when we reached the top of the stairs. We were now inside the bridge's pillar, and the space – which was far larger than the impression given by the outside – was filled with people. No, *Grigori*. On the outer edges, tall metal scaffolding spiralled up for what must have been a hundred metres, parting at one point into three separate columns. Overhanging balconies and small rooms embedded into the high walls overflowed with Grigori, all drinking, laughing, dancing, partying. Most with masks, some without.

'This is *Ascension*. New York's Grigori-only club,' Spence said.

'Why the masks?'

''Cause this is a place where we're supposed to be able to let loose. A lot of Grigori are positioned in the military or within the government and don't want their identities to be common knowledge. Some are the Rogue. Others just like to come here and not have to be who they are in their normal work. This is strictly off-duty. Let's get a drink. Morgan and Max said they'd meet us at the bar.'

'We don't have ID,' I said, following in starry-eyed amazement. This place would make Dapper salivate.

'Doesn't matter,' Zoe threw an arm over my shoulder. 'They don't check ID. Half the Grigori here look like they're underage and are definitely not. It takes too much time and an all-Grigori club has its own laws,' Zoe had to yell over the music.

'Nice,' I said, my smile growing as the bass beats of the music reverberated through the floor and all around me. The vibe was incredible and I found myself laughing as Spence passed me the first of what would become many drinks. Looking around, I realised for the first time since arriving in New York that no one was watching me. No one knew who I was and no one cared to find out.

Okay, just because a person is Grigori. Just because that means they are warriors that fight to protect humanity's right to free will and existence – does *not* mean they are responsibly recreational.

My eyes bugged out at some of the things I saw. Once let off the leash, Grigori partied hard. I could understand why. Some of them would have been hundreds of years old, constantly caught up in the battle against exiles. I guess they figured that if they couldn't completely let go when among their own people, then when could they?

Once I'd managed to sneak off the dance floor – which took a major effort as Morgan, once she'd realised it was me behind the gold mask, refused to let me leave her sight – I set off to explore. The music was a line-up of retro dance at its best, with a few tracks tossed in that I'd never heard before but would now be forever hunting down online.

As I made my way up the spiral stairs, and along the balconies, I surveyed the cave-like rooms in the walls. Each was lit with either burning candles or chandeliers and each seemed to serve its own purpose. Some were for winding down with pillow-loaded sofas, some were for group get-togethers with tavern-style tables, others – I discovered after some investigation – were behind invisible sound-barrier curtains, and on the other side . . . a completely different theme and style of music. Ascension catered for all generations. The rockabilly room was like a time warp – and totally amazing.

Taking all of this in, I was halfway up the tower, just beyond the casino rooms, when I started to feel him. If I hadn't indulged in so many of the mint-delicious, alcohol-fuelled drinks Zoe and Spence had kept handing me, I would have felt him sooner.

What's he doing here?

I tapped a masked Grigori on the shoulder. She turned away from her conversation to look at me. She was wearing a tasselled red dress and had come out of the high-rollers room – one thing older Grigori were not short of was money.

'Sorry, but do you know what's up in the top rooms?' I asked.

She winked. 'Private parties, if you know what I mean, hon.'

I swallowed the lump in my throat. 'Got it.' I nodded, my smile fading. 'Thanks.' I moved back a few steps, or maybe stumbled, leaning over the railing and looking down at the dance floor.

Think.

If I knew Lincoln was here, it was only a matter of time before he felt me too.

Breathe. Think.

Maybe he was just hanging out with people from the Academy. Maybe they'd been hunting.

But why the private rooms?

The woman had made it clear the rooms were used for the kind of thing that would only break my heart to see. Not to mention my soul.

I had no claim on him.

Damn. I feel sick.

Lincoln had said himself; things with us hadn't exactly helped him in the action department. What had I really expected? That he'd just wait forever? At best, if I charged up there, I was going to look like some kind of crazy stalker.

The room started to spin. I needed to make a decision. Up or down?

Down, down, down!

I started walking faster, even as I felt the spike in Lincoln's power. He knew I was near and now he was moving, too.

Move, move!

I made it back to the dance floor and pushed through the people to find Spence and Zoe towards the back. Morgan and Max were nowhere in sight. I pulled Spence close.

'Can you put us under a glamour?' I asked, looking around frantically. 'Lincoln's here and we're about to be busted.'

He was getting close. I could feel his agitation.

Spence shook his head, looking around too. 'No. It's against the rules. And this is *not* a place where it is good to break the rules.'

'I think I see him,' Zoe said. 'Or at least, someone his size who's almost at the bottom of the stairs and looking in our direction. He can't see you yet through the mask and hair. But he could be here with anyone and if he spots you, we're toast.'

We all knew that was only a matter of time.

I pushed Zoe towards the stairs. 'Go, go, go!'

As we ran, I looked back over my shoulder and saw him on the opposite side of the dance floor. Although he was wearing a silver mask and his hair was dark and hanging to his shoulders, I'd know him anywhere and he was looking right at me, shaking his head. I couldn't tell if he was angry or just disappointed with me. After all his praise earlier on . . . I'd gone and blown it. I closed my eyes briefly with regret.

'Eden!' Spence called out.

I leaped down the stairs and we ran past the doorwoman, throwing back our masks to her on the way.

Spence and Zoe were laughing, on a high from both the near-escape and the drinks, but all I could see was Lincoln's eyes. We ran up the street at full speed, taking as many turns as possible, losing ourselves until, by luck, we stumbled onto a main road.

Spence slowed to a walk. 'Well, there's good news and bad news. The good: we've lost anyone who might have followed us. The bad: we just ran off all the alcohol.'

I rolled my eyes. 'So sorry,' I said, but my mind was still a livewire trying to work out what I was going to do. Should I race back to the Academy, jump into bed and feign ignorance? Should I confront Lincoln and ask what he was doing? Should I apologise? Get mad? Cry now or later?

Spence pointed to an all-night cafe. 'Don't beat yourself up. You can buy me cake to make–'

'Stop!' I said, grabbing his arm, trying to sift through the senses I was feeling.

Zoe and Spence froze.

All of my attention focused in on the café. 'Exile,' I said.

Spence and Zoe had to concentrate for a little while to pick it up, too, but they both nodded.

I was getting good at using the senses. They were so overwhelming here I'd had to work at them. Suddenly I had a new appreciation for Rainer's relentless tuition.

'I recognise this ... Roses and ... spearmint ...' My forehead crinkled. I'd definitely sensed the combination before, but I couldn't place it.

We moved back into the shadowed pavement opposite the cafe.

'Any ideas?' Spence asked. He already had his dagger out. And he was grinning. He'd formulated his plan quickly and it involved immediate confrontation.

'Let's wait here. He has to come out eventually and then we'll see what we're dealing with. If he's one of Phoenix's crew we may be able to follow him if we keep our guards up and stay back.'

Zoe looked between the cafe and us. 'You know we're gonna get nailed for this?'

'Yep,' I said. But we were already busted and at least this way we could actually be of use.

'I'm in,' Spence said.

Zoe nodded. 'Me, too. Just making sure we're all on the same page, *people*,' she said, imitating Griffin.

Half an hour later the excitement had worn off and we were freezing cold, and still waiting for our exile to show himself.

My phone vibrated in my pocket. I pulled it out and looked at the screen.

'Lincoln again?' Spence asked, blowing into his hands.

I nodded. All three of us had been ignoring his several calls.

Spence dropped his head in his hands. 'We're in so much shit. Hate to say it, Eden, but maybe you should answer.'

I looked at the phone, my finger hovering over the accept button. Spence had a point but something told me to wait. Before I could make up my mind, the cafe door opened and out walked our exile.

'Holy hell,' Zoe whispered.

Yep. Holy hell.

I put my phone back in my pocket and prepared to follow.

We'd just hit the jackpot.

Chapter eighteen

'In His angels he found wickedness.'

Job 4:18

We didn't need to tail Olivier – Phoenix's second-in-charge – for long before we saw him stalk into another building, this one a residential block. Something twisted in my gut.

We deliberated over whether to follow him in, but decided to stay outside for now.

Minutes later, Olivier came back out, a child wearing blue-and-white pyjamas in his arms, head resting on his shoulder as if he was sleeping. But we all saw the blood trickling down the side of the boy's face.

'Look,' Zoe said, pointing up to the third floor of the building where smoke was billowing from a window.

I panicked. People were still inside the building! I prayed that the boy's mother or father – destined Grigori only had one or the other – was still alive.

'I'll go,' Zoe said, not hesitating. 'You two follow Olivier.'

There was no time to delay. This shadowing mission had just turned into a rescue and none of us was about to turn our back on what needed to be done. This was what we were made for.

Zoe flew across the street and into the building while Spence and I followed Olivier.

Olivier hailed a taxi and took off in the direction of Manhattan. We almost lost him while we waited for our own taxi, Spence all but hauling a woman, who was still paying, out of the first one we could find.

'Follow that cab!' Spence said to the driver, throwing all the money in his pocket at the taxi driver.

We leaned back as we headed over the bridge and into lower Manhattan. Spence looked positively exhilarated.

'You've always wanted to say that, huh?'

'Every man's dream!' he said, not taking his eyes off the taxi ahead.

While he kept watch I used the opportunity to text Lincoln the name of the street where we'd left Zoe and told him to send fire engines and a clean-up crew, just in case.

He texted back.

On the way. Where r u?

I chewed on my lip.

In taxi. Following Olivier. Don't be mad.

Now wasn't the time to lie.

Lincoln's reply was instant.

NO! 2 dangerous! Wait for me and Griff.
DON'T follow on foot!

I showed the message to Spence without saying anything. This was his choice too.

'If we wait, we'll lose him.' He kept his eyes on our target. 'Eden, you need to decide. Are you going to be the Grigori everyone else tells you to be or the Grigori you know you are? He's going to City Hall!' He yelled the last part to the driver. 'Look, I get my partner in a couple of months. I'm going to have to bring her into this messed-up world and hope she can survive. I'm scared shitless that I might let her down, or that she might get hurt, but this is what we do.'

Spence never talked about his partner-to-be. He wouldn't even tell anyone her name. In case she decided not to embrace, he wanted to leave her with anonymity. He was good people.

My phone buzzed.

Violet?

It really was that simple to Spence. He was part of the Academy but he would not be defined by it. He had one objective and that was to be in the fight – to be Grigori.

I texted Lincoln.

He has a kid. Gotta go.

I shoved my phone back in my pocket. I felt it buzz again but ignored it.

'Here, stop here!' Spence instructed the driver. He pointed to Olivier who was now on foot and walking into a park. 'City Hall Park. Are we following or not?'

I opened the door. 'What do you think?'

He gave me a megawatt smile. 'Never doubted you, Eden.'

'Keep your guard up or he'll sense us,' I reminded Spence. He nodded and we let ourselves fall back as far as we could, just to be sure.

As Olivier walked through the park, past a water fountain, we hid in the bushes and I let my power flow from me to reveal what he was showing the rest of the world. He was hidden in a glamour. No normal humans could see the kid – not that there were many people around at this time.

'He's dressed himself in some kind of uniform.'

Spence nodded. 'As one of the City Hall guards. He can go wherever he wants. Look, he's heading down those stairs.'

'Where do they go?' I asked.

'Not sure. There's supposed to be some old subway station round here. It got shut down a while back – security risk or something.'

I could see why. Wherever Olivier was headed, it was right beneath City Hall.

Spence started looking around our immediate surroundings.

'There,' he said, pointing to a square metal manhole about fifteen metres away. 'That would get us down in the area. Better than trying to follow him past the guards and into the unknown.'

'Agreed.'

We moved out into the open, Spence putting a hand on my shoulder so he could glamour us both and keep us hidden. The large metal cover was locked in place with two padlocks.

I slipped my fingers beneath the edge of the cover until I had a good grip and glanced at Spence, making sure he was ready. We would have to move quickly.

He nodded, taking hold of the other side.

We yanked.

The padlocks snapped apart with our supernatural strength and the metal cover flew open. We slid down into the hole quickly, making as little noise as possible, easing the cover back into place above us.

Thankfully there was a ladder, but unfortunately there was no light, so we had to fumble our way blind until we hit a dimly lit junction. I pushed out my senses, looking for Olivier, and found myself pointing towards a brick wall.

'I don't know how we get there – but it's like he's inside the wall,' I said, increasingly confused.

'Power?' Spence suggested.

I walked up to the wall and put my hand on it. It felt real and solid. I moved back a couple of steps. 'Only one way to find out.'

Pushing out the power within me, my amethyst mist spread out, eagerly finding its way to the wall. The mist represented my will – an extension of my angelic side that I was still learning to master. Before our eyes, the wall dissolved, revealing a new passageway.

The power that had created this hidden tunnel was the work of exiles. And they'd been down here for a long time.

'Son of a bitch,' Spence whispered, obviously sensing the same thing. 'They've got the run of the whole city down here.'

We walked through the passage, checking behind a number of doorways that led to more tunnels. 'Oh man, right under the Academy's nose.'

'They don't know about these?'

Spence shook his head in awe.

'Maybe this isn't something we should be the ones to tell them about,' I added.

Spence lifted an eyebrow sarcastically. *'You think?'*

We both knew Josephine would not believe us. It also raised the question: Who was running this labyrinth? Lilith had only just returned to New York so it stood to reason another exile or group of exiles was responsible.

We followed the power trail along the tunnel, moving quickly and quietly until we came to an archway that opened into another wider tunnel, the ground lined with railway tracks and further up a raised platform. It must've been the abandoned subway station Spence had mentioned. Olivier's towering silhouette was unmistakable.

'We have to separate Olivier from the kid first . . .' Spence started to say.

I nodded. Olivier could snap that boy's neck faster than lightning. We were almost at the station and it was going to be hard to get closer to him without him sensing us.

Remaining on the tracks, we crouched below the edge of the deserted platform and watched Olivier pace back and forth. Dim lights revealed the station as quite beautiful – green-and-cream square tiling lined the curved tunnel walls, while the ceiling was decorated with leadlight glass patterns. A secret treasure beneath the city.

'What's he waiting for?' Spence asked just as a breeze lifted a stray strand of hair around my face and my breath caught. I gripped his arm without realising.

'Shit, Eden. Want to ease off a little?' he whispered, trying to pull his arm away. But when I didn't he put a hand on my shoulder. 'What?'

Jasmine and musk. That's what.

I felt the blood drain from my face. 'Phoenix is coming,' I hissed.

Olivier is waiting for Phoenix.

'Well ... That changes things. What now?' Spence asked. It was obvious the two of us were not going to be able to take on the two of them *and* save the little boy – especially when Phoenix could take me out with a simple thought.

The wind picked up. We shuffled back into our hiding place, watching as Phoenix arrived.

He was in a fitted black suit and polished black shoes. His hair had grown longer and it still rippled in that way it did – something powerful emanating from every strand, roots so dark they were purple and some sparkling silver to give that opal effect. The result was as dazzling as ever. In spite of all logic, my heart started to thump in my ears.

Phoenix slid his hands into his pockets. His confidence was coming off him in waves. I'd never seen him like this. So detached and yet ... composed, with a rigid determination that frightened me even more than his usual arrogance and manipulative game-playing.

He looked Olivier up and down without even casting an eye in the direction of the still-unconscious boy.

He's so cold.

Even after everything that had happened, I never would've believed Phoenix would be so devoid of emotion for a beaten child.

I was furious at his behaviour but it made me sad more than anything else. A tear formed in the corner of my eye.

Phoenix's jaw seemed to tense and he tilted his head to the side as if he'd heard something.

I held my breath, realising my mistake. Time stood still.

Idiot!

Desperately, I tried to lock down my thoughts. But it was too late. I'd just sent him my own personal emo-signature. Phoenix knew I was there.

I braced for the attack . . . But it didn't come. He simply turned his attention back to Olivier.

'Any problems?' Phoenix asked in a controlled tone.

Olivier grinned wickedly. 'None. Left the kid's place on fire. No one will track him.'

Phoenix nodded.

Why isn't he telling Olivier I'm here?

Phoenix paced the platform, his steps crisp against the concrete. 'I thought I told you not to beat the prisoners,' he said calmly, still not even glancing towards the boy. Or me.

Olivier shrugged. 'What do you care? We're just going to execute them once she's had her fun, anyway. She said she doesn't care what we do to them as long as they're still breathing. He's still breathing.'

In a flash, Phoenix grabbed Olivier by the neck, single-handedly hoisting him up against a wall.

'You answer to me!' he growled.

'I answer to the one who is going to cut down every human at the knees so they will forever know their place. That means, I answer to *her*,' Olivier choked. Phoenix loosened his hold. 'For now, anyway,' Olivier continued. 'This is all simply a means to an end. You forget, I am of the light.'

He might have once been an angel of light, but there was nothing but a deluded insanity about Olivier now.

Exiles still held onto their origins even after they had abandoned their rightful place. The war between light and dark was eternal, despite the current truce. If not for the Scripture's promise of Grigori destruction, there would be no way the two sides would tolerate each other.

Phoenix's grip tightened again around Olivier's neck. Distracted by this task, his defences slipped away and some of his emotion leaked into me.

I slapped a hand over my mouth, falling back into Spence with the intensity of Phoenix's ... hatred. It seeped into me like poison – so strong my eyes watered and my lungs constricted.

It was hatred for Olivier. For himself. For what they were doing. And impossible control. It was taking everything he had not to kill Olivier right there.

I trembled, experiencing just a taste of what Phoenix carried with him. Spence steadied me.

Oh, Phoenix. What have you done?

Sill holding Olivier, he looked down the platform, as if he could see me. I inhaled sharply and watched his eyes close. An outpour of sorrow flooded through me, as if somehow he was answering my unspoken question. And in that moment, I wanted to cry for him.

Oh, God help us.

Olivier laughed. 'You really thought Lilith was going to be grateful to you, didn't you? You were a fool not to realise she'd be so disgusted to find you had the Grigori list all this time and hadn't even used it!'

'Be very careful – I can rip out your heart with barely a thought,' responded Phoenix.

'Yes, but everyone would know it was you and after having Gressil killed, killing me . . .' He shook his head, smiling maniacally. 'She'll kill you. I'm too useful to her and you know it.'

Phoenix tightened his hold again but then, as if realising there was nothing more he could do released Olivier, pushing him to the ground.

'Once this is done, I am going to pull every organ from your body before I start on your eyes and heart, just so you can watch.'

Something flashed in Olivier's eyes and for the first time he backed away from Phoenix and stayed on the ground.

'I have work to do,' Olivier growled.

Phoenix turned to the child, his face emotionless, but I felt the trickle of concern he'd been working so hard to hide as he lifted the limp body from the ground. 'I'll take this one back to the estate. Lilith wants you to collect another one tonight. She's moved up the schedule.' He handed Olivier a piece of paper, glancing in my direction before continuing. 'The building is on East 79th, between Lexington and Park. I suggest you don't delay.'

'What?' Olivier scoffed. 'You're not waiting for me?'

Phoenix smirked. 'I'm sure you can manage to get back to the highlands on your own.' With that he walked towards our end of the platform, his back to Olivier and, before he took off with the wind, he nodded right at me.

Is Phoenix giving us information? Can we trust it?

Olivier went off in the other direction and Spence and I didn't wait around either. As soon as the coast was clear we ran back the way we'd come, racing along the tunnel and up the ladder leading back out into the park at City Hall. As soon as we were above ground I called Lincoln.

'Where are you?' was his answer.

I kept pace with Spence.

'City Hall.'

'I'm on the way,' he said, I could hear him running too.

'No! Wait! Where are you?'

'Southeast corner of Central Park.'

Shit. I didn't know this city well enough.

I shoved the phone towards Spence. 'Talk to Lincoln. He's at the southeast corner of Central Park.'

Spence grabbed the phone. 'You're closest,' he told Lincoln and then told him the address of where Olivier was headed before tossing the phone back to me.

'He said he'll go there with Griffin and that we should go back to the Academy and wait for them,' Spence explained.

But Olivier is going after another child.

We couldn't take any chances. I'd already stood by and watched one little boy be taken.

'Not going to happen. We'll meet them there just in case,' I said, throwing my arm out to hail a taxi. I shoved the phone in my pocket. 'What the hell, right? It's not like we can get in any more trouble tonight.'

'So true,' Spence said, clapping a hand on my back as I jumped in the car. 'It's an outlook I often take in life.'

When the taxi pulled up we saw Lincoln and Griffin standing outside a building. They were talking to a young woman, who held a little girl, wrapped in a blanket, asleep in her arms. The woman was crying.

We headed towards them, Lincoln spotting me straight away. I could almost see him relax as I felt myself do the same. In that instant I knew that whatever my concerns had been earlier tonight, they were meaningless. He might be mad at me for not doing what he said, but it was more important that we were both okay.

Spence and I stopped a discreet distance away, not wanting to interrupt, but close enough to hear what they were saying.

The girl must have been the one Olivier was after. Griffin and Lincoln had already fought him off – I could see their fresh bruises – but neither of them seemed satisfied.

They were telling the mother that she and her daughter were at risk in their apartment and would be taken somewhere secure tonight. Tomorrow they would be moved to a safe-house. Griffin was pushing a lot of truth into his words to get past her disbelief and uncertainty about not contacting the police.

Another car arrived and Rainer stepped out, holding the door open for the woman and her daughter. She glanced at me briefly and then away again as she followed them into the back seat wordlessly. I couldn't read whether she was pissed with me or not but my next training session was only a few hours away. I'd find out soon enough.

Griffin and Lincoln joined us. Griffin gave me a disapproving up-and-down. 'Fun night?'

I put my hands on my hips to cover my flush of guilt and focused on the problem at hand. 'We discovered a maze of glamoured tunnels connected to the subway under the city. And we found Phoenix in them, too.'

'Are you okay?' Lincoln asked, his face blank, despite the tension in his stance.

I nodded.

Griffin looked from me to Spence.

'What she said, boss,' Spence said.

I didn't need to look at him to know he was smiling.

'You get him?' Spence asked.

Griffin rubbed a tired hand over his face in typical Griff fashion. 'No. He actually ran. First time for everything, I suppose.'

'He'd already been shaken up by Phoenix,' I said. No wonder Griffin was keen to get the young family to a safe place. Olivier would be back.

'Did you get the kid?' Lincoln asked.

I shook my head. 'It was too risky. Phoenix took him, but he's still alive. I think Evelyn was right – they're collecting the children for some sort of mass execution.'

We stood for a few beats, all of us speechless. Things went to another level entirely when you were talking about innocent kids being slaughtered.

Griffin spoke up first. 'You three really landed yourselves in it tonight. Josephine's probably allocated a cell for the two of you down with your parents by now.'

'Griff, you might want to hold off on the lecture until we've told you everything,' Spence said, oh so casual, milking the fact that we'd come away from our night with some of the best intel in months.

It really did help, having a pro rule-breaker on one's side.

Griffin nodded, looking around. He was a leader but he wasn't averse to rule-breaking either. 'We can't talk here. A team's on the way to watch the building in case Olivier or any other exiles come back.' He passed what looked like a black credit card to Lincoln. 'Take them back to Ascension. I'll meet you there once I've handed over.'

Lincoln was already hailing a taxi.

'Why Ascension?' I asked Lincoln when we were in the car.

'You'll see.' His body was tense as he focused on the window.

'We had to follow him, Linc,' I said, assuming he was about to launch a verbal attack at me.

'I know,' he said, and then, as if he couldn't fight it any longer, he grabbed my hand and pulled it into his lap. He exhaled, his tension seeming to ease.

When I looked up, confused by his response, he shook his head and gave me a knowing smile. 'I wasn't keen on you tracking Olivier. I thought it could be a trap, Phoenix or Lilith luring you in. But when you told me he had a kid . . .' he shrugged. 'You did the right thing.'

I scrolled through my phone and selected the unopened text message I'd ignored after I'd told him Olivier had a kid.

Be careful.

There was no stopping the flutter in my heart or my hand that was squeezing his back, and not letting go.

Later that night, or rather *morning*, I discovered that Ascension was one of the only Grigori places over which the Assembly *didn't* have control and exactly why Lincoln had hidden behind a mask in one of the club's exclusive private rooms.

They were sound-proof. And free from prying eyes.

Ever since we'd arrived in New York, while I'd been stuck within Academy walls, Griffin and Lincoln had been using the privacy offered by the club to discuss all of their theories and plans. It turned out they'd been rather busy.

CHAPTER NINETEEN

'Evil draws men together.'

Aristotle

Determining whether or not Rainer was upset with me proved more difficult than I'd imagined. Judging it by the fact she still turned up at my room at 5 a.m., devoid of sympathy and clearly expecting me to be on my feet and running then, yeah, she was pissed.

But she had turned up.

I decided that punishment by way of hard-core training was preferable to cold-shoulder treatment. Seeing Phoenix, although troubling, had served as a solid reminder of what lay on my horizon. I needed to be ready. Plus, as strange as it was, I knew the Grigori testing was important and a desire to be accepted by the Assembly had kind of crept up on me.

Then again, when Rainer carved another wound into my upper arm, it was hard to remember all of that.

'Jesus!' I exclaimed, twisting to see the damage.

'You're sloppy,' she said, whipping her katana through the air in front of me then pointing it towards my arm. 'You keep dropping your right arm.'

For a nano-second!

'Might be because it has no blood left in it,' I mumbled.

Rainer shook her head. 'You can't afford to make a mistake, ever. Not if you plan on living. Start again, from the top. Drills first and then we fight.'

I swallowed. My mouth was parched and my body hurt in ways it was not supposed to, but I nodded, pushed the pain back and carried on through the monotonous and repetitive exercises. I wasn't sure if Rainer's training techniques left me feeling more like the Karate Kid or Sarah Connor.

The next time we fought I kept my arms up and ready. Our katanas clashed as we went at each other like feral animals. Fast fights were always preferable, and the only way to ensure that was with a fierce offensive. I wanted to be my best, to be my strongest. I had all the motivation in the world.

A rare opening presented itself; Rainer had made a slight error in the angling of her body. It wouldn't give me a kill shot but if I was lucky it should be enough to take her down.

I made my move, got a foot to her leg and followed with my blade, just nicking her thigh.

Rainer righted herself quickly, her eyes now alight with a fighter's intent.

I planted my feet and braced for the attack, but instead . . . she smiled.

'What?' I asked, wiping my sweaty brow.

'That's more like it,' she said, giving me a nod of respect.

It was the first time she'd done that and it had a surprisingly deep effect on me.

'You fight well with swords. You're best with a dagger, but then swords. You should remember that and always be armed. You can fight with bare hands when needed but you're a technician and most lethal with tools.'

I nodded, agreeing. 'I'll remember.'

Stepping forward, Rainer put a hand on my shoulder. 'We both know you hold back, Violet. The question *is*, how much?'

She didn't wait for my answer and I was grateful, since I didn't have one.

Rainer started to pack up for the day and when I started to help she put up a hand. 'Go. You've got time before your classes start and I hear you have somewhere else to be.' She gave me a knowing look.

She was right.

Not that I need the reminder.

Last night at Ascension I'd agreed it was time I visited Evelyn. I'd been putting it off, worried about what to say to her, and to Dad. But we needed her information and Griffin seemed convinced, despite his many visits, that Evelyn would tell me more than she'd revealed to him. I was surprised Griffin had obviously confided in Rainer. She might have been mentoring me, but she was still a member of the Assembly.

'Okay,' I said.

'Violet . . .' Rainer continued as I collected my things. Her voice was different now. No longer my teacher. 'I know that you and Lincoln are . . . Like Nyla and Rudyard were.'

I looked at my feet.

'I miss them both so much, but even now . . . I envy what they had.'

I blinked. 'What do you mean?'

She shrugged. 'All of it. They were much more powerful than they ever let others see – always worried it could endanger them if the strongest among us realised their potential. As bonded soulmates their union meant they could draw on one another's powers when they needed to. They transformed from two good fighters to one incredible warrior.' Her voice grew quiet. 'If they'd wanted to, they would've been sitting in Wil's and my seats at the Assembly, but they refused.'

It didn't surprise me that Nyla and Rudyard had declined places on the Assembly. It wasn't their kind of thing.

'Incredible, but not incredible enough,' I said. 'Rudyard is gone and Nyla is . . . lost, and everyone who loved them is left with the awful reality.'

'That's true,' Rainer agreed.

I hitched my training bag on my shoulder and made for the door.

'One other thing is true as well, though,' she continued.

'What?'

'Rudyard and Nyla were nowhere near as powerful individually as you and Lincoln. Not even close.'

I paused and turned back to her. 'The risk is too great, Rainer. Power isn't everything.'

She fixed a gaze on me that sent a shiver down my spine. 'Until it is.'

I didn't respond.

She couldn't possibly understand what it was like knowing that you could bring about the end to the person you loved. Only Nyla and Rudyard could understand that and they weren't here. Rainer had the luxury of being able to look at it from the outside. She'd been around for hundreds of years, seen Grigori come and go, all simply casualties of war. She probably wouldn't hesitate to use the added power that came with being bonded soulmates, but then, she wasn't taking into account all of the other realities that were a part of it. She couldn't begin to imagine.

Despite Rainer's encouragement, I still had my doubts – and anxieties – about visiting Evelyn and Dad. But as I loitered in the halls I thought about all the reasons why this was important – why confiding in Evelyn and having her opinion could make all the difference. In the end, it was the image of the child I'd seen Phoenix take off with that forced my decision. We were running out of time.

It was a task just to get through all of the security on the lower level until I was permitted into the holding cells.

I'm not sure what I'd expected, maybe jail cells, but Evelyn and Dad had been given something more like a small apartment. They had been allowed to share the same space – two single beds, which had been shoved close together. They had a small kitchenette with a good supply of fruit and vegetables – probably prison enough for Dad, who preferred his vegetables to come in a Chinese takeaway box and covered in oyster sauce.

The only thing that screamed lock-down was that the entire area was contained within some type of barely visible force field that reminded me of the liquid-like wall that divided Phoenix and me in my dream. I could see everything except for a small cubicle I assumed concealed their bathroom. At least they'd been given some privacy.

I walked down the narrow white corridor, alongside their cell. Dad and Evelyn were sitting at a small oval table, playing cards. They both looked up and saw me at the same time and I was struck by the weirdness of it all. The Academy, Grigori, Hell, Lilith, Lincoln, Phoenix, the Scriptures – and there were my parents, playing blackjack in an impenetrable box. It took me a moment to realise I was laughing hysterically.

Maybe they thought it would be good therapy, or were just pleased to see me, but within seconds, the parents I'd been so nervous about seeing for the last two and a half weeks burst out laughing too.

Just what every kid wants, right? Happy family moments.

As we all sobered, one of the guards patted me down, taking my dagger from me. He looked at my wrist markings with a puzzled expression. Normally, they would ask Grigori to remove their wristbands.

I turned my wrists up and smiled. 'Sorry. Permanent.'

He grunted and then surprised me by opening a door in the force field.

'Is it solid?' I asked.

He shrugged. 'In a way. But it's charged by Grigori power, which makes it more, and less.'

'Like the walkways?'

He gestured me into the room. 'Similar,' he said, shutting down the line of questioning. He wasn't going to tell me any more.

'Ten minutes,' the guard said, with a look that said he'd be timing me. Griffin had called in a bunch of favours to arrange the full-access visitation.

I stepped in and watched, as the door seemed to reseal behind me. Once the guard left the area, I took a seat at the table with my parents. I observed them both. Dad looked tired but otherwise fine. Evelyn looked terrible. Her eyes were dark and she had bruises up and down her arms. I suspected her elbows on the table were there to help hold her up more than the cards.

Griffin had warned me that the Academy had been putting her through the wringer, testing her both mentally and physically. I felt a surge of rage and it surprised me to realise I'd stopped thinking of this woman as my enemy.

But what does that make us now?

'Violet, I've missed you ... *We've* missed you so much. I can't begin to tell you how sorry I am for what happened. I am so ashamed. I can't ask for your forgiveness but I ...'

'Dad,' I said before he could ramble any more. 'It's okay.' I shook my head, at myself more than anything. I'd been a fool. Sitting there in front of Dad put everything into perspective. 'Trust me, I've done and said a lot of things I wish I could take back recently. You had a huge amount lumped on you all at once and you made a mistake.' I glanced at Evelyn. 'I think I've made my fair share of those and it might be time we all started letting some of them go. And ... I've missed you, too.'

Dad nodded quickly and looked away.

I rolled my eyes. 'Don't cry, Dad.'

He turned back to me, eyes wet, and smiled. 'I'm just ... I'm so scared and so proud. I don't know how to be the father in this world.'

I took his hand. 'It's okay. I'm struggling to know what my boundaries are as a daughter who's also Grigori.'

He gave me one of his proud-to-be-Dad smiles. Whatever I'd done over the past few weeks to convince myself I didn't need him disintegrated and I smiled back, a huge weight lifting from my heart.

One down.

I turned my attention to Evelyn. 'We don't have long and we may not be alone.'

Evelyn nodded, something like pride glinting in her eyes.

Oh no, I can't cope if she starts tearing up as well.

Blessedly, she reined it in and nodded in agreement.

'Give me your hands,' I said.

She raised an eyebrow, curious.

I stared back at her. 'Just do it, and hurry up. This isn't going to be pleasant.'

Evelyn placed her hands in mine.

My power moved slowly compared to how it did with Lincoln. It would work my will but it felt less natural to merge with anyone other than my partner. I pushed it out, ignoring Dad's gasp when my markings started to swirl. At least his human eyes didn't have to witness my power, which had begun misting the room with billions of tiny amethyst crystals and flowing into Evelyn.

All I saw or felt was the slight tightening of Evelyn's grip on my hands. She was tough. I'd give her that.

Spence had screamed to high heaven when I healed him. Admittedly, his injuries were far worse than hers but still . . . it had to be seriously uncomfortable.

When my power seemed to be satisfied, it settled back into me and I released Evelyn's hands.

She took a moment, shaking them out as if trying to regain control of her body.

'Thanks,' she rasped. 'You were right. That wasn't pleasant.' She coughed. 'But I feel . . . Thank you.'

I shrugged. 'You're going to need your strength.'

Dad's mouth was hanging open. 'You, you . . . I mean, Violet, you healed her.'

He'd been told, but seeing was believing. As if reminding himself what he was really dealing with he whispered one more word. '*Angel*.'

I decided to let him have his moment and focused on Evelyn.

She nodded, clearly thinking the same thing. 'Tell me.'

With relief, I filled her in on the latest events, not much of which was different from what Griffin had already told her. Nonetheless, Evelyn listened intently to every word, particularly my quick recap about seeing Phoenix in the tunnels beneath the city. Dad, to his credit, managed to shut his gaping mouth and remain silent the whole time.

'Lilith has taken up from where she left off,' Evelyn said when I had finished. 'Phoenix told you they were staying in the highlands?'

I nodded again.

'She'll be in one of the bigger estates along the Hudson and not too far outside of Manhattan – within an hour's drive, I'd say.'

'How do you know?'

'Because I know her better than anyone, and Lilith has a weakness for the water. She likes to be close to it, in case she needs to make a quick escape. Jonathan and I followed her all around the world, but eventually she came to America and took a shine to that area.' She raised her eyebrows. 'Old money and lots of it. She took pleasure in annihilating families and destroying their lineage by first dirtying their reputations. She would pick the best of the estates along the Hudson, putting entire towns under strong illusions to ensure that family disappearances were never investigated. She drove many of them to their own gruesome suicides. It was horrible. But Lilith took so much pleasure in their destruction that instead of fleeing she stole their fortunes and their houses, keeping them as trophies. Even now there would be many that are well hidden that she would still believe to be her rightful spoils.'

'Griffin says the Academy is preparing to launch an attack when they find a location. This information will help them narrow it down,' I said.

'She'll be ready for them and expecting it.' Evelyn sighed. 'The toll will be high, but I don't know that it can be avoided.'

I caught her gaze drop to my markings. 'What is it?' I asked. Her eyes often went to my wrists when I thought she was about to say something.

She reached out and touched them. 'Just a theory. Not one to speak aloud.'

Because we were being watched.

'Violet, if anything happens I need you to promise me one thing,' she said, staring at me like she wanted to say a thousand things. 'Do what Griffin says.'

'Why?'

She smiled softly and changed the subject. 'You're angel maker is one of the most powerful angels to have ever been created,' she said, carefully avoiding naming his rank. 'Angels are creatures of pride, even the best of them. He knew when he created you that this day might come. He would not have left you without a fail-safe. Remember that.'

I tried to find the meaning in her words. 'Is this about Lincoln and me?'

'Possibly. I don't know. The very fact he selected your soulmate to be your partner . . . There is always a reason. But it is *their* reason and don't ever forget it. Free will is yours until you choose to relinquish it. That you are soulmates may be their choice, but whether you make the bond is *yours*.'

'Doesn't exactly help,' I said, more confused than ever.

'I'd be happy to offer my opinion on the matter,' Dad deadpanned.

I'm sure you would.

I settled for a snort.

'I wish I had the answers but it's complicated,' Evelyn continued. 'Your being soulmates could be the very thing that saves you both or . . .'

'The thing that destroys us,' I finished.

'Yes. Which is why no one else,' she glanced at Dad, 'can tell you which way to go.'

The guard reappeared and tapped his watch. I nodded and stood up, returning Dad's embrace.

I turned back to Evelyn, who was now standing, looking considerably better.

'Would you do things differently? If you could go back and change things?' I just had to ask.

She looked at Dad, love in her eyes. 'I would've put more faith in the people around me whose lives were to be affected by my choices.' She turned back to me. 'But I don't regret some of the things you probably wish I did and if I had to do them again, I would likely make the same decisions even though that means having a daughter who hates me.'

'I don't hate you. And I'm sorry it took me this long to understand. But . . . you scare me.' I looked at Dad. 'For him *and* for me.' Whether I was ready to deal with it or not, she was my mum and she was here. 'Do you . . . Do you even *know* what will happen to you once Lilith is returned? Was that part of your agreement?'

She walked me to the doorway, Dad following silently. 'No, we never got that far. What drew me here with her may well take me back again when she is returned. We'll all have to accept that if it happens. James knows that. As for the rest . . . well, if we survive to see the other side of this – there will be a lot of things that need to be worked out.'

Yeah. Like the fact that Dad already looks too old for her and is the only one getting any older!

The guard cleared his throat. It was time to go.

'Bye, Dad,' I said, and turned to Evelyn. 'Griffin is still trying to get you out of here.'

She nodded back, a little sadly. 'Something tells me I won't be in here much longer anyway.' Before I could ask what she meant, she grabbed hold of my arm and pulled me close, whispering in my ear. 'No matter the price, when you have the chance to destroy her, you take it! No second thoughts.'

I swallowed, and nodded even as her words sickened me.

Because when Lilith is returned – it might mean the end of Evelyn, too.

Like mother like daughter. She was possibly tied to Lilith just as much as I was tied to Phoenix.

'Good luck in your testing,' was Evelyn's parting comment before the door closed and I was escorted back to the top level of the Command building.

chapter twenty

'What you are comes to you.'

Ralph Waldo Emerson

The Assembly had scouts looking up and down the Hudson for the estate where Lilith was hiding out thanks to Evelyn's intel. Nevertheless, the next few days went by with little progress, our frustration levels reaching breaking point as we dreaded what might be happening to the captured boy Spence and I had seen and every other missing child who was possibly being held captive by Lilith.

Nothing but dead ends so far.

Although the Assembly still refused to confirm that Lilith had taken the children, Griffin and Lincoln had been collecting all the data on disappearances, presumed deaths, unexplained kidnappings and more. So far, there were over sixty children on the list whom they believed Lilith had been responsible for taking from around the world.

It was tragedy enough for the children and their families, but for the Grigori population, it spelled disaster. These children were future Grigori recruits and our numbers were simply too few to endure such devastation if Lilith was successful.

The Assembly hadn't taken kindly to being delivered this information by Griffin. Drenson and Josephine had gone as far as to call into question Griffin's loyalties. But every time I asked Lincoln and Griffin for more details they became cagey. It wasn't that they didn't want to tell me, but I was still restricted to the Academy buildings and therefore under constant surveillance.

And they're protecting me, as always.

But for today, at least, I had other things to concentrate on. It was my official testing day and if I passed I'd be able to join in the hunt for Lilith and Phoenix, so that was what I planned to do.

I was in the training area with Rainer, the only person permitted to escort me to the Assembly. Apparently today was momentous, it being the first Grigori testing in over three centuries where all members of the Assembly would be present.

I do love being special.

'Why does the whole Assembly come together so rarely?' I asked Rainer, after finishing my warm-up.

'Seth and Decima deem very little to be worthy of their presence. They vote on some issues, but have not sat in their Assembly chairs in over one hundred and fifty years. Plus, Wil and I are usually based in London. We only moved here after . . .'

I nodded. She didn't need to finish for me to know she meant – *after Nyla.*

We started walking towards the main hall.

'There will be a lot of people watching. Try to ignore them. It's Drenson's choice who you will fight so I can't tell you what to expect, but I'm sure even if they throw a senior Grigori at you, you'll be fine.' I couldn't hide the smile at her praise. 'The mental obstacles will be more difficult, but you can do it. At the end, the Assembly will vote for your position as an official member of the Academy and of the Grigori population.'

'How do you see that working?'

Rainer's eyes exposed her apprehension. 'Unfortunately, Drenson and Josephine are unlikely to be swayed in your favour, so that means you need to get Seth and Decima on side as well as Valerie and Hakon if you want to be sure of a win.'

'What about Adele?'

Rainer didn't even consider before answering. 'She's never voted against Drenson. She never will.'

I could understand that, although it didn't help me much. Valerie had made it clear I wasn't her nearest and dearest and I'd been in history lessons with Hakon for the past three weeks and we hadn't exactly bonded. Probably my fault since I was guilty of paying more attention to his sheer size than listening to the history he'd been attempting to bring me up to speed on. As for Seth and Decima – they were almost primordial; I had no idea what I could do to win them over. I was too scared to even look in their direction.

Rainer and I carried on in silence until we reached the double doors to the Assembly. 'You ready?'

I nodded.

Rainer pushed the doors open to the massive room and I entered my official Grigori testing.

Lincoln stood just inside the doors and I paused only to hand him my dagger. I wasn't permitted to have it in the testing but I trusted no one else with it. His eyes met mine briefly, reflecting nothing but confidence.

Rainer took her seat with the other Assembly members, and I assumed my position in the centre of the room. Grigori lined the walls and more people watched on from the large balcony above. I spotted Griffin standing with Zoe and Spence, their attempts at hiding their concern not exactly successful.

'Violet Eden,' Drenson addressed me.

'Yes,' I answered, trying to appear at ease.

'Do you come here today willingly to submit to Grigori testing?'

'Yes.'

Drenson was so formal, but I could see the challenge in his eyes.

'Are you willing to recognise the Assembly as your superior council and abide by the decisions that are made here today?'

It was a loaded question and we all knew it. But I couldn't back down now. The only thing I could do was pass the tests if I wanted to maintain not only my position in the Grigori community, but Lincoln's position as well. As my partner, whatever happened to me, affected him directly.

'Yes,' I replied, noting Josephine's smirk.

She sat to Drenson's left, wearing a steel-grey pantsuit, her hair tied up in a French roll that looked too soft for her features.

'Let's begin, then,' Drenson said.

A senior instructor stepped forward and began calling out movements for me to perform. After all of Rainer's training the actions came as easily as though I was doing them in my sleep, but I ensured I completed each one carefully.

Satisfied, Drenson stood up again and gestured to a woman stationed by a door to his left. When it opened, three senior Grigori entered the room and stood on the edge of the sparring floor. Each one dressed in black loose-fitting fighting clothes. The first carried two traditional Dragonfly katanas, the second, two Grigori daggers, while the third simply held his palms up, empty handed.

'Select your weapon,' Drenson instructed me.

Frankly, I was surprised.

Am I really being given a choice of weapon and *opponent?*

Out of the corner of my eye I saw Rainer leaning across her chair talking to Valerie and Hakon, her hands chopping through the air. Whatever she knew, it wasn't good.

Okay. Be smart.

I looked at the weapons. There was no doubt the dagger was my best option, but then again, it was also weapon of choice for most Grigori. Bare hands were okay, but like Rainer had said, I was strongest with tools.

I stared at the katanas. I was good with them. I could be better, but then again, I always felt that I could do more. Something about holding a katana felt natural.

It was a risk, but I took it, moving into position opposite the Grigori holding the two Dragonfly swords.

'You have selected your weapon?' Drenson asked.

'Yes.'

'Then take it in hand and assume your place on the floor.'

I did as instructed, taking one of the katanas, twisting the handle as I resumed my post. I couldn't help but notice that Rainer was looking decidedly unhappy.

I waited for the senior Grigori holding the other katana to move in opposite me, but he stayed where he was. My eyes started skirting the area, looking for movement, for any indication of who would be my challenger.

The tension in the room was palpable, everyone wondering the same thing. I darted a look at Josephine, her grin was widening.

Finally, I saw why.

Decima had stood up, letting her overcoat slip to the floor to reveal her all-white fighting wear.

I'm dead.

The room roared with a deafening silence. Decima stalked like a tiger, moving first to take the other Dragonfly katana and then into position opposite me. Suddenly, my clever weapon selection seemed stupid.

Shit.

She didn't look at me. Her head remained bowed to the ground.

'First to draw blood three times wins,' Drenson said, satisfaction sounding in his voice. It was enough to make me stand a little taller. 'Are you both ready?'

I nodded. Now or later, I didn't think it would make much difference. Josephine and Drenson had sabotaged my testing.

I felt Lincoln's power caress me, his way of telling me he was there with me. I let it flow over me for a moment, basking in the strength of our partnership before I pulled back into myself, locking down everything else and focusing on the task at hand.

The task of getting my ass kicked.

Decima answered Drenson by parting her feet, letting her blade hang loosely to her side and finally looking at me. Her eyes were pale gold like those of a cat and showed the enormity of her wisdom, experience and cunning – it was not an encouraging sign. But I dug deep and returned her stare even as she looked right through me.

Something told me Decima's interpretation of drawing blood would be different from most.

'Begin,' Drenson ordered.

I responded quickly, stepping back to increase the distance between us. It was a defensive tactic but also – I'd never seen Decima fight. I needed to see her move before I could know how to engage her – putting space between us was the easiest way.

Decima's only movement was a slight tilting of her head as if she were listening to something far away.

That's reassuring.

We stood facing each other, Decima's expression decidedly bored, mine decidedly freaked out. But she didn't move.

She's waiting me out to make me go to her. Fat chance.

I knew enough not to be played this way. If she wanted to wait, I'd wait.

A few minutes passed, both of us simply watching the other, until Decima's head tilted once more. Then, finally, she moved. If I thought she stalked like a tiger, she struck like a snake. Her feet never seemed to leave the ground and yet her speed was phenomenal. I'd been ready and waiting for her to attack, but nothing could prepare a person for that. Just before reaching me, she leaped into the air, clearing my head and landing behind me. Before I had time to spin, I felt the sting of her katana drawing a line along half the length of my spine.

Decima had just taken first blood, leaving a gash down my back.

I heard the collective gasp of the Grigori spectators, their excitement at watching Decima in action boiling over.

'One, Decima,' Drenson said.

He didn't need to say any more, there was no break. We both knew the rules – the fight continued until one of us won.

I moved back a couple of steps to get myself together and did everything I could to block out the rest of the world.

I can do this.

I had the advantage that they didn't understand. I was of the Sole. I was the highest-ranking Grigori present, whether I wanted to be or not. Technically, whatever she could do, I should be able to do better.

And maybe in several hundred years that will be true, a taunting voice whispered within.

Right then, if I didn't find a way to tap into whatever made me powerful, I was going to find myself in a world of pain.

I ignored the warmth spreading out along my back and concentrated on Decima again. She was waiting once more, the snake preparing to strike.

Drawing from my well of power within, I called it forward and out to my fingertips.

I am fast. I am strong. And I will not be bested, or defeated.

The thoughts came to me as if they were not even my own. My warrior instinct was taking over. I felt it like a force anxious to be released and I knew it was important to keep control.

Decima moved suddenly to the side and then back at me. This time, I moved too. And instead of dodging her, I headed right into her path, dropped to my knees and rolled, coming back up as she passed me, just in time to extend my katana and cut into her thigh.

This time when the audience gasped, it was for me.

'One, Decima. One, Violet,' Drenson umpired.

I jumped up onto my feet, knowing enough to not get excited. Decima was already in position, ignoring the wound in her leg. But it had been a deep cut and it had to hurt.

Decima repaid the favour quickly, her katana only nicking my forehead with one of her fast swipes. But blood was blood.

That gave her two. Drenson confirmed the score.

The next round went to me, thanks to landing a lucky kick in her side and being ready to take full advantage of my temporary gain, my blade making a swift incision on her exposed side.

Again, the crowd gasped. This time some cheering began. Several people chanted for Decima. A few crazy ones hollered my name. I heard one distinctive voice above the rest. 'Come on, Eden! Stop messing around – bring it home!'

Hi, Spence.

Decima and I took our positions again. This time, I didn't wait. I moved, using my katana like a sword and engaging her in a traditional fight. She was fast and sparks flew as the blades hit. We both had close calls, reaching for each other and just missing. She landed a solid punch in my face and I barely had enough time to throw out a defensive kick before the pain flared. I felt it then I ignored it.

No time.

Don't quit, Vi. Don't back down!

I saw Decima lunge towards me. It was perfect, nothing for me to work with. I knew as I saw her coming that she'd beat me. But I couldn't let her have this one – this was the decider.

I could do only one thing. I switched my katana to my other hand and as she spun in mid-air, perfectly aligned with my upper chest, my left arm came up and my blade skimmed her extended forearm, drawing blood.

The room fell silent. We had struck, almost simultaneously.

Decima paused to look at the insignificant wound on her forearm. I didn't bother looking at my chest. I could feel the blood soaking into the fabric of my top. It didn't matter right now.

It had been a low blow, taking the blade to her arm like that. Defensively, it achieved nothing. If we'd been in real battle she would probably have taken me out with her strike, but this wasn't a real battle and drawing blood was drawing blood.

Three all.

I kept a grip on my katana, not ready to relinquish it until I knew I was safe.

What now?

Decima took it upon herself to answer that question, giving the audience another reason to gasp as she bowed her head and held her arms out, her katana resting flat across them in an offering to me.

Unsure, I glanced at Rainer who nodded at me, so I stepped forward to take the sword from Decima's hands. She lifted her gaze to meet mine and tilted her head. This time her eyes truly saw me.

'Warrior,' she said.

I nodded.

Drenson stood, abruptly. 'Decima, there should be a tie-breaker.'

She shook her head, not even glancing at him. 'No need. Her blade touched my skin before mine touched hers. She won.'

I replayed the fight in my head. It had all happened so fast, but she was right – by a margin, I'd touched her first. She was honourable to admit it.

'With a superficial wound,' Drenson scoffed. 'Hardly impressive.'

Decima gave me one last inquisitive look before returning to her seat. Seth passed an assessing gaze over her, as if checking her for any serious injury.

'You made the rules, Drenson. The girl played by them and won.' If I wasn't mistaken, Decima seemed slightly entertained.

I felt Lincoln's power again at my back, supporting me. Proud.

And then . . .

The silent crowd erupted into cheers. Spence and Zoe wolf-whistling from the balcony.

It was overwhelming, but I kept my composure after a quick look around.

Maybe I'll make it through this after all.

Josephine's smirk was well and truly gone.

The mental elements of the testing went on for hours. Different Grigori presenting their powers to me – glamours, perceptions, barriers – all for me to break down and overcome. Some were easier than others and a couple, that Griffin had warned me about earlier, I chose not to even try. Josephine had deliberately included them to test whether I was of a superior rank or not. But I didn't have to be able to do everything and my continued protection was more important than acing every challenge.

As the testing dragged on, I felt myself growing weary. I hoped it was nearing an end but then I saw Josephine lean over and whisper in Drenson's ear. He nodded, whispered a reply and stood up.

'Your final challenge will be a test of solidarity with your fellow Grigori. Are you ready?' he asked.

Rainer and I hadn't discussed what this test would be, but it wasn't the first attempt to unnerve me.

I nodded. 'I'm ready.'

'Griffin Moore, if you could join us?'

Once again, the crowd fell silent as the assembled Grigori watched Griffin move into the arena. From the look on his face, this was a surprise to him, too. He took up position beside me and faced Drenson.

'We are going to ask Violet three questions. They will be answered in full and Griffin will read the sincerity in her response and in turn, deliver its truth to the Assembly.'

This was not good. Griffin could see truth if it was there and could only deliver it in full if it was in fact truth. There was no way around this and depending on what questions they asked we were now in trouble.

'Do you both understand?'

'I do,' Griffin said.

'Yes,' I said.

'Violet Eden, are you aware of the ranking of your angel maker?'

I looked between Drenson and Josephine. Both carried that arrogant air of superiority. The rest of the Assembly members watched on curiously.

Griffin kept his expression passive, emotionless, playing his part.

'Yes,' I answered.

There were a few murmurs but most people remained silent.

Griffin turned to the Assembly. 'This is her truth.'

The Assembly members waited for Adele to nod first before proceeding to do the same. I wondered how her power differed from Griffin's. Perhaps it didn't and they were making Griffin do this for another reason.

'Violet Eden, were you involved in a relationship with the exile, Phoenix, son of Lilith, that led to an event where he healed you of injuries, thereby forming a connection between the two of you, which he can manipulate to control your survival?'

I didn't know where this was going. I swallowed nervously. 'Yes.'

Griffin's mouth thinned into a straight line. 'This is her truth.'

The Assembly nodded.

Final question.

'Violet Eden, is it true that you gave the Grigori Scripture over to Phoenix, son of Lilith, after he threatened to hurt your human friend, Stephanie Morris, thereby endangering the lives of all Grigori in order to ensure her safety?'

Shit.

I couldn't apologise for that. I now had an idea where this was going, but I couldn't show remorse for those decisions.

'Yes,' I said, standing tall.

Griffin turned to the Assembly. 'This is her truth. Though I must add, this is also my truth as this choice was made together and without regret.'

'Mine, too,' Lincoln said, stepping out of the crowd.

Griffin turned to Lincoln and then looked back at the Assembly. 'This is our truth.'

The considering eyes of the nine Assembly members watched the exchange and finally nodded in acceptance of Griffin's word.

Drenson cleared his throat. 'The testing is complete. We will cast our votes.'

Rainer stood first. 'Pass,' she said, not holding back her smile.

Wil stood beside her. 'Pass,' he said.

They were the only two votes I was confident about. I held my breath.

Valerie stood. I suspected where her vote would be going. She wouldn't have liked my cheap trick against Decima. 'Fail,' she said.

Hakon stood. 'Fail,' he said, supporting his partner.

Seth stood. 'Pass.'

Decima stood. 'Pass.'

I kept my expression neutral even if I did feel it was already a victory in itself to have their votes. Somehow their approval counted for more than a simple ruling.

Adele was on her feet next. She looked at me for a moment and then to Drenson. She pursed her lips. 'Fail.'

Drenson glanced at Josephine, who clearly had every intention of saving her vote for last. It was clear, then, who was really in control, because Drenson stood.

'Fail,' he said, his voice ringing out into the arena.

You could have heard a pin drop as Josephine slowly rose from her seat and moved forward so she was in clear view of the entire room.

'Violet, you have fought well, there is no doubt. Decima is undefeated and while she remains that way, you have shown your various skills and willingness to use them. Not a soul in this room could deny that, in time, your fighting skills may one day only be matched by those of your own partner.'

Did she just compliment me?

'But being Grigori is about more than being able to fight. Grigori must be able to put the greater good first and above all else. It is clear to see that you are willing to put the people *you* care about first, above yourself, above all others. But what, then, for everyone else, Violet? I fear the day that your choices will come at a great expense to the rest of the world.' Josephine worked the crowd, casting her gaze around the room and nodding at several important members of the Academy. Her words were building anticipation to her vote. The worst thing was, even though I hated her, even though I knew she was doing this for her own agenda . . . she was right.

'On top of that we cannot ignore an anonymous accusation that has been made against you, one that you have done nothing to dissuade us from here today.'

What the . . .?

'As members of the Assembly we must consider the implications of an allegation that you are in fact still involved with the exile Phoenix and indeed aided him in his attempts to resurrect Lilith and utilise the Grigori Scripture.'

My mouth fell open. 'Who said that?' I exclaimed. 'That's not true! I would never have done that. And in case you've forgotten, he dropped me into a volcano not so long ago. That hardly says "same team"!'

My words fell on deaf ears, Josephine lifting a patronising hand to silence me. I wanted to scream.

'I'm afraid I have been left with no alternative,' she addressed the room. 'Violet Eden is simply *not* one of us. I must vote therefore, fail.'

Whispers rushed through the crowd. Murmurs of agreement, sounds of horror, as arguments sparked and I simply stood in silence as one by one the Assembly filed out of the room, Rainer and Wil both looking at me apologetically as they followed.

That was it.

Testing complete.

I'd failed.

I turned on my heel and walked at a steady pace out of the room, not looking at a single person. The rules still applied.

I don't run away.

That didn't mean I didn't power through the Command building, over the skywalks and to my room, all the while forcing back the threatening tears. Once there, I grabbed my backpack and started shoving my things into it. If I had failed then at least I didn't have to stay here. And just because I wasn't part of their stupid Academy, that didn't mean I wasn't Grigori. I could hunt just fine without them.

My door swung open. I didn't stop packing. I'd felt him coming.

'They were wrong and everyone knows it. Josephine set you up to fail. Griffin will fix this.'

I kept packing. I couldn't even speak.

Suddenly he was there, his arms wrapping around me from behind, supporting my weight as I crumpled from sheer exhaustion.

'You were amazing. No one can stop talking about how you took on Decima.'

I leaned back into him, ignoring the sting from the gash in my back and instead drawing in all that he was.

'I'm sorry, Linc,' I said, mortified that I'd just ruined his future as well.

He hushed me, his arms tightening around me, using the moment to heal the worst of my wounds.

'You have nothing to–'

But his words were cut off as an explosion rocked the building. Lincoln threw me to the ground and himself on top of me. Everything shook with the force of the blast. As soon as the vibrations settled we heard several smaller explosions further away. By then, we were already on our feet and running in their direction, back towards Command.

CHapteR twenty-oNe

Charging through the halls, Grigori were running everywhere. Lincoln and I picked up the pace, people moving out of our way as we passed them, our legs and arms pumping with all we had. We made it onto the skywalk just as we heard another explosion, which shattered more of the glass walls containing Command.

Lincoln and I saw our problem at the same time: the explosion had hit part of the skywalk we were racing across. Lincoln didn't stop running but looked over his shoulder to shout, 'Faster!' to me, and then to the Grigori following us further back, 'Go back! Go back!' His voice held the kind of authority one did not argue with. We kept running, faster and faster, the walkway threatening to give way beneath us.

Without slowing, Lincoln thrust his hand back and I grabbed it just as he leaped forwards, pulling me with him as the glass gave a final sensational crack and fell. I landed in his arms, and he held me to his chest until he was sure I was safe. We looked down and watched the skyway fall, but before the largest piece of glass hit the ground it stopped and hovered, suspended in mid-air.

Confused, I looked back over to the building we had fled. Hiro and some of the other telekinetic Grigori were using their powers to hold it there, preventing a catastrophic collision with the pedestrians that swarmed the pavements beneath.

'Okay?' Lincoln asked, eyes searching me as he pushed the hair back from my face.

'Yes,' I breathed.

Two Grigori ran towards us from Command, as if they were headed for the walkway. 'Get a clean-up crew on the ground,' Lincoln ordered shoving them back in the other direction. They didn't need telling twice.

'Linc!' I yelled, as we started to run again. 'They're everywhere!' It was all I needed to say. My senses were buzzing, but his would be too. We both knew where we needed to go. 'They're going for Evelyn!'

This was what Josephine had been waiting for, but I was willing to bet she'd never counted on an assault of this magnitude.

We ran through the open reception area – Grigori and exiles were already fighting, many badly wounded from the explosion. My stomach lurched, thinking of our friends. It had been perfectly orchestrated – so many of them were in the arena and the explosions went off right beneath them. We would have been there too if I hadn't taken off.

We barged through, Lincoln pulling out our daggers and thrusting mine into my hand. We made for the stairs, leaping down the flights in full jumps to the floor below, where the main explosion had erupted. When we reached the lower floor, my stomach knotted and a cry fell from my lips. More than fifteen guards lay motionless in a pool of blood. They looked like broken toy soldiers. So surreal.

Oh, God, no! Please, no!

I heard movement coming towards us from the cells and I grabbed Lincoln's arm. He stopped.

Phoenix strolled down the corridor, apparently not in the least surprised to see us waiting.

'Finally,' he said, drawing out the word, ignoring me and giving Lincoln a smug look.

That was all it took. Lincoln and Phoenix went for each other hard and fast, fists and legs flying as they went up against one another for the first time. But they were so evenly matched that for every punch Lincoln delivered, Phoenix retaliated. What Lincoln lacked in speed he made up for in strength and vice versa.

I used their distraction to look over the Grigori on the ground, checking to see if any of them were still alive in case I could heal them, stopping only when I heard footsteps behind me. I spun in my crouched position in time to see Griffin explode into the room, take one look at the scene in front of him and settle on Lincoln and Phoenix.

He pulled out his dagger and moved in to help Lincoln, leaving me to check the last of the guards.

'No!' Lincoln yelled, stopping Griffin in his tracks.

I stood up, sickened and terrified – none of the guards needed healing. They were gone. I joined Griffin, eager to step into the fight myself.

How could Phoenix have done this? I need to find my parents!

Lincoln had already held Griffin back, demonstrating his unwillingness to finish Phoenix – and we all knew it was because of me. But Phoenix would never let Lincoln capture him alive. I tightened my grip on my dagger, but before I made my move, it struck me that Phoenix wasn't fighting with his usual zest, he was just going through the motions.

'He's stalling!' I yelled.

Phoenix's eyes cut to me for just a second and he grinned.

Another smaller explosion sounded from the end of the corridor – where the holding cell was. A few seconds later, a figure emerged from the smoke.

Lincoln and Phoenix pulled back at the same time. They were both badly beaten, but no real harm had been done.

I watched as everything I'd feared played out in front of me. A woman, undoubtedly Lilith, walked towards us, two exiles following behind, Evelyn held between them.

Both Evelyn and the exiles were in bad shape. At least she hadn't made it easy for them.

Phoenix looked at Lilith. 'Where are the others?' he asked calmly.

Lilith hissed, her golden hair burning vividly through the smoke, her power coming off her in waves.

I found myself smiling.

Evelyn kicked their asses! That's where they are.

Evelyn looked satisfied, too.

Lilith turned her gaze to us, settling upon me.

'Oh, how I have looked forward to this moment.' She cast a scrutinising glance over me then raised her precisely shaped eyebrows at Phoenix. 'I can't say I'm impressed, son.'

I started to build my power. We'd see how impressed she was when I froze her and rammed my dagger through her chest.

Lilith sighed. 'We'll be off now – schedule to maintain. Violet, your father is still alive. Consider it a gift – you will merely have to kill the exile I left to guard him and allow us to pass without any . . . childish behaviour.'

Instantly, I dropped the power I'd been on the verge of releasing. I couldn't risk it.

'Rest assured,' she continued, unleashing a smile with her Christmas-red lips. She was dazzling and her beauty hit me like a lightning bolt, literally taking my breath away. I heard Griffin inhale beside me. 'We will see each other shortly.'

I reined myself in – and also my power, which was pushing at me, wanting to be used. But I wasn't about to jeopardise Dad's life.

'Phoenix will find you in two days and give you an opportunity to . . . retrieve your mother.' She laughed, the sound carrying like music through the room. 'Or, at least, die trying.'

Lilith motioned to the exiles with her, before walking right past us and into the waiting lift. I could barely stand it, watching them shove Evelyn roughly against its wall. My hands fisted but I did nothing, fear for Dad stopping me.

My blood began to boil.

Phoenix was last out.

He paused at my shoulder. 'That's good, lover. You're going to need that,' he said quietly, reading my emotions. 'That and more.'

I looked at him, nothing but determination on my face. 'I will be getting my mother back,' I said, through gritted teeth.

He smiled, stepping into my personal space. 'I'm counting on it. Two days, and I'll find you, but just remember . . .' He moved closer, his voice dropping to barely a whisper, 'If you so much as leave a window open, I can find you before then.' He pulled back, something passing over his eyes as they locked briefly with mine before he turned the look to one of triumph, entered the lift, and left with his mother. And mine.

As soon as the doors closed I was running down the hall towards the cell. There was not one but two exiles ready and waiting. It didn't matter. I made quick work of the first, barely slowing down as my blade went straight into his stomach and then across his neck. I wasn't stopping to give exiles choices today.

You take my Dad; that is *your choice.*

Lincoln dealt with the other exile in much the same fashion and soon I was dropping to the ground beside Dad, my fingers grappling to find a pulse. When I felt the steady beat I cried out in relief.

Another series of explosions started to rock the building. Griffin ran in behind us. 'Troops are coming!' he yelled, grabbing hold of Lincoln and telling him something. I remained focused on Dad, trying to wake him, but there was no use – he was out cold.

I started to get up, planning to lift Dad and take him to safety, but Lincoln grabbed me by the arm and started to pull me back towards the corridor.

'What are you–' I started. He cut me off, yanking me after him.

'We have to go. Now!' He kept moving but I shrugged a hand free, looking back at Dad. There was no way in hell I was leaving him.

Griffin dropped beside Dad and looked at me. 'I've got him, Violet. You have my word. Do what Lincoln says! Run! *Now!*'

I don't know if it was the terror in his eyes or the force of his voice – whatever it was made me give in, letting Lincoln take my arm once more as we ran towards the exit and left Griffin and Dad behind. I tried to head for the door to the stairs, but Lincoln pulled me towards the lift, yanking the doors open.

But the lift wasn't there – Lilith and Phoenix had just taken it to the ground floor. It would take too long to come back up. It was then that I heard the sounds of people coming down the stairs, yelling out orders.

Looking at Lincoln I saw the same fear in his eyes that I'd seen in Griffin's. Whatever was going on wasn't good.

Lincoln pulled off his belt. 'Get on my back!' he ordered.

I looked down the lift shaft at the multi-storey drop and baulked. A fire smouldered at the bottom.

'They blew it up!' I said. 'We can't go that way!' But Lincoln wasn't moving. I looked at him, wide-eyed. 'Are you insane? We can't jump!'

'We don't have a choice, Vi. Just stay on my back and protect yourself. You hear me? Protect yourself so you can heal me at the bottom. If we're both hurt we're no good.'

This can't be happening.

I shook my head back and forth. 'No, no, no! This is crazy!'

He grabbed me by the shoulders, the sounds of Grigori approaching getting closer. 'We don't have time. You have to trust me!'

His eyes held mine and in that split second so much passed between us, so much love and yes, trust.

Stupid, stupid trust.

I gripped his shoulders and leaped onto his back. 'We're going to have words about this later,' I said.

'Looking forward to them,' he said, and jumped.

Lincoln was so strong, he carried my weight as if I wasn't there, manoeuvring himself to hook his belt around one of the steel cables to guide us down the centre of the shaft. But we both knew there was only so long his belt would hold. Moving at breakneck speed, the belt gave way and split in two when we were little more than halfway down. Lincoln quickly replaced it with his bare hands.

The smell of flesh burning was instant. But, stubborn as ever, he held on for as long as he could, even as I screamed, watching the trail of blood left behind on the cable.

Finally, he let go, using the momentum to push himself forward so that he fell with his chest facing down for the last ten floors, protecting me from the impact of the fall.

He's going to take the hit!

Everything in me wanted to stop him, wanted to use my own momentum to roll his body so that I was on the bottom. But I didn't. He was right; we were no use to each other if we were dead or unconscious. The only way out of this was if I was in good enough shape to heal him when we stopped.

What the hell is going on? Why are we running from the Grigori?

We hurtled towards the ground and I braced, not wanting to hurt Lincoln when we landed and determined to remain breathing.

The landing sent a violent shock through my body and I instantly felt consciousness slipping away. But Lincoln was beneath me and he wasn't moving, so somehow I held on, summoning my power as I crawled off him and, avoiding the flames that were licking the walls around us, flipped him onto his back. I didn't let the blood, the broken bones or the shoulder that had dislocated again sink in or slow me down. Because on top of all of that I could still hear people, *Grigori*, yelling from the top of the lift shaft for us to hold still.

My power flared and I let it flow hard and fast. Never before had I willed it to work so quickly. Responding to my urgency, the space around us filled with my amethyst mist. So much so that it hid us beneath a purple cloud as it worked to find Lincoln's injuries while I shoved his shoulder back into place. His burnt hands were stripped to the bone and the smell made me gag, but I kept going. When Lincoln's eyes finally opened, he screamed in agony, grasping my arms as I stared at him, concentrating all of my power to fix him. Nothing, not even the sound of people nearby, took my focus away.

When Lincoln's hands, face and shoulder were healed I went over his legs. One had snapped in two, bone piercing through his torn pants.

'Jesus!' I cried, failing for a moment to supress my horror, before forcing my healing into him as he screamed again.

Once his breathing was steady and his leg was mended, he grabbed my hand. 'Let's move!' He jumped up, the man who had been on his deathbed just seconds ago, and yanked open the lift doors with his inhuman strength.

Once we made it outside, we fell into pace alongside each other, running through the New York streets, putting five, then ten, then fifteen blocks between us and the Academy buildings. We didn't slow to a walk until we hit a pedestrian-heavy street.

'What's going on?' I asked finally. I needed to know what the hell had happened. But then I noticed that Lincoln was limping. 'Damn. We need to get you somewhere. You're still hurt.'

'We'll be there soon,' he said, not stopping.

'Linc!' I shouted, exasperated. 'Why are we on the run?'

'Because Griffin told me to get you out of there. I don't know everything yet but he said they'd take you prisoner if we stayed.'

'Why?' I pushed, confused.

He started to pick up the pace again. 'I think Griffin believes Josephine will try and pin this whole thing on you. She's already started to claim you're sympathetic to exiles.'

Oh my God.

They'd lock me up and throw away the key. I never would have made it out without Lincoln and would have had no chance of going after Evelyn.

'Griff is going to meet us at midnight. Until then, we need to stay hidden and make sure no one follows him to us.'

'How do we do that?'

'By being prepared.' He started to lead us down a side street.

'Where are we going?'

He almost smiled, but the limp and the fear killed it. 'We're going to church.'

chapter twenty-two

'He will order his angels to protect you wherever you go.'

Psalms 91:11

'The Church of the Guardian Angel?' I asked, sarcasm dripping from my voice as we stood across the road from the unassuming red-brick church, scoping it out. 'You're kidding, right?'

Lincoln grinned briefly and gestured to our surroundings. 'Would you prefer to stay out here?'

Only then did I actually register the people staring at us in our torn and blood-soaked clothes. We looked like we'd just walked away from a car wreck – or a massacre.

Lincoln was doing better now that we weren't charging through peak-hour crowds, but he was clearly hurting more than he'd admit. He stubbornly refused to let me look at him, insisting we get inside first.

I accused him of having a hero complex.

He ignored me.

My head was spinning. Everything seemed to have been turned upside down so quickly. A few hours ago I had been fighting to earn my place in the Academy, and now I was running from them.

Lincoln inspected the church from all angles, taking his time to walk the perimeter a number of times. Once satisfied it wasn't some kind of set-up he went to the front doors and pulled them open. We entered silently, taking in every detail, Lincoln pausing to bless himself with holy water. I wasn't sure if he had done it out of faith or as a stalling strategy to continue scanning the interior. Both, maybe.

I couldn't bring myself to follow suit settling instead for looking around like a tourist – a fitting description for me when it came to religion.

The church was simple yet handsome. Small statues and stone engravings decorated the interior perimeter, stained-glass windows were set high in the walls beneath dark wooden beams. Polished cherry-wood pews lined the knave, while hanging lanterns gave the whole space a welcoming feel. Before we'd even been there for a minute, a small door opened to the side of the altar and a priest stepped out.

He looked us up and down. Lincoln paused, assuming a non-confrontational stance. I, on the other hand, took my dagger in my hand and stepped forwards, positioning myself between the priest and my injured partner.

'Violet,' Lincoln said calmly. 'Relax.'

But my protective instincts had kicked in. Stubbornly, I held my position. I could already sense this priest was not human. Not *only* human, anyway.

I concentrated on what I was feeling. He was dressed in a black cassock, though his collar was open and the stiff white insert was missing. His hair was beginning to grey but his features remained young, and he had kind and knowing brown eyes. His physique, though hidden beneath robes, was obviously fit. I guessed he was no more than thirty, making him on the younger side for both the greying hair and to be a priest. I measured our new risk carefully, the priest remaining still while I did, but his eyes darted between us, intrigued.

'Violet,' Lincoln said again. 'Father Peters is a friend.'

My eyes narrowed. 'That's not all he is,' I said, keeping my eyes on the priest.

At my comment he smiled and bowed his head. 'Very perceptive,' he said, his gentle voice carrying through the room. I felt it move into me, reassuring me and instilling a sense of calm. 'I was once Grigori, now retired.'

I blinked, realising that my senses weren't playing tricks on me. The priest smiled, as if he could read me.

'Stop using your power on us,' I said, putting my dagger away and placing my hands on my hips.

His eyes widened.

Yeah, that's right. I can feel you leaking your calm crap into me and I've had about enough of my emotions being messed with to last a lifetime.

He didn't need telling twice. The trickle of his power moved away from us and he gestured to the front pew.

'My apologies.'

I nodded. 'Accepted.'

Lincoln sighed – probably relieved I hadn't taken down a priest. He moved to the front pew trying to hide his weakness as he collapsed onto the bench.

I rolled my eyes at him. 'Are you going to let me heal you now?'

'In a minute,' he said, dismissing me and then waving a hand between the priest and me. 'Violet, meet Father Peters.

He's an old friend of Griffin's and, this church is one of the only places in Manhattan that we can hide from Josephine's sources.'

'And only for a short time,' Father Peters added. 'Griffin called ahead. He didn't say much, but enough to know I could expect trouble.' He put his hand out to shake mine and then to Lincoln.

Lincoln slumped a little further even as he took his hand. 'I'm sure you don't remember me–' he began but Peters cut him off.

'Lincoln Wood. I remember you. Griffin speaks highly of few and age is not thy enemy. Now, what are we expecting? And just how pissed off are they likely to be?'

Lincoln smiled. He liked Father Peters' candour. So did I.

'No company we hope, we didn't spy any followers and we were careful. We just need a place to stay until Griffin arrives. We don't want to bring trouble your way.'

Father Peters raised a knowing eyebrow. 'But you had nowhere else to go, which says enough.'

Lincoln nodded. I sat beside him, desperate to reach out and help him, but knowing that he didn't want my help. Not yet.

The priest looked around the quiet church. 'Well, it's times like these when the house of God puts it best, and most stubborn, foot forward. We'll hope no trouble comes to us, but best we prepare for it anyway.'

Priest or not – he's a fighter for sure.
Good.

Father Peters wasted no time. He gave Lincoln and me a quick tour of the areas in the church we could use for defence and attack, showing us all the entry points and possible weaknesses in the building's structure. Finally, he took us down to his private chambers. Lincoln and I both took a moment to absorb the sight before us.

'That's a lot of weapons to have in a house of God,' I said.

He shrugged. 'It won't be the first time Christians have needed them. Nor the last.'

He had a point.

'And on top of that,' he continued, 'we're in New York city and I'm trying to run an honest church – if I have to blow something up occasionally to get rid of some of the darkness . . . I'm not above it.'

I *really* liked him.

Lincoln snorted beside me and when I looked at him I realised it had been directed at me.

'What?'

'You didn't trust him when he was just a priest, but now you know he's willing to blow things up, you look like you've just confirmed him as a friend for life.'

I nodded, smiling. 'I have.'

Father Peters laughed even as he shook his head. 'Griffin always finds the good ones.'

When we returned to ground level, the priest flicked a switch and metal shields started rolling down over all of the upper-level windows, going far beyond standard church security.

'Is that . . .' I began.

'Titanium?' he finished my sentence with a raised brow. 'You're a smart cookie.'

'Why?' I asked, nervously. Titanium was metal that exiles used as a defensive tool. It helped them stay hidden from Grigori. Phoenix had an entire Antanov plane lined with the stuff.

Peters shrugged, waiting for the last covers to click into place before taking his hand off the lever. 'Titanium doesn't just protect exiles. It works both ways.'

'You mean it affects exiles' ability to sense us too?'

He nodded. 'Not as effectively, but still, every little bit counts in these situations. Grigori generally stay away from it because they think the advantages are greater for exiles. I disagree.'

I hadn't considered it before but, especially in our current circumstances, I had to agree with Peters' logic. If nothing else, the physical strength of the titanium shields would help hold any attackers at bay for a time.

I turned my attention to Lincoln. Almost all the colour had drained from his face.

'We still have a while before Griffin arrives. Sit,' I ordered.

Lincoln hesitated for a moment, but finally dropped into a chair so that I could heal him. I knelt in front of him and rolled up his ripped, blood-soaked jeans.

'Don't fuss,' he said, quietly.

'Don't back-seat drive,' I retorted. I was so relieved to finally have my chance to fix him, I didn't even care that Father Peters was watching. I pulled back the remaining scraps of fabric to get a good look at Lincoln's leg. 'Mother of–'

'A-hem,' Father Peters cleared his throat loudly.

'Sorry,' I apologised then glanced at Lincoln. 'You should've let me look at this earlier,' I said, cross with him. His leg was twice the size it was supposed to be and bubbled with red welts and black bruises.

He closed his eyes, trying to hide the pain. 'It wasn't important.'

I continued to fume even as I let my power surge into him. He tried to stop me a few times, saying I'd done enough, but I wasn't having it.

After healing his leg, I checked the rest of his body, finding more problems in his ribs that he hadn't mentioned and that his shoulder was still very weak.

Lincoln couldn't contain a sigh of relief when the pain that must have been torturing him finally eased.

Eventually, I sat back on my heels. Both of us were silent as we pulled ourselves together.

'Well, well,' said Father Peters. 'And they say miracles don't happen these days.'

I gave him a sceptical look as I settled down beside Lincoln for the wait.

'No offence, but you should know my jury is well and truly out on the God issue,' I said to Peters.

My comment only seemed to amuse him. He sat on a low step at the base of the marble altar. 'You might not have made your mind up about Him, but He sure seems to have made a decision or two about you.'

'I'm not buying what you're selling, priest,' I responded, refusing to go down that road.

He laughed. 'Consider it on the house.'

Ha.

CHAPTER TWENTY-THREE

'Be bold, and mighty forces will come to your aid.'

Basil King

Griffin arrived at the church exactly on midnight. We watched from the small, elevated look-out not covered by titanium. He was careful, like we'd been, taking the long route, going down side streets and circling back in case anyone was following. We couldn't spot anyone from our vantage point.

Finally, he headed around to the back entrance, where Father Peters was waiting to let him in.

I could barely breathe with anticipation and when Griffin walked in I leaped from my chair.

'Your father is fine,' he said immediately.

I staggered forwards with relief. I'd been trying so hard not to think the worst, but running like that, leaving him behind, had gone against every natural inclination.

'Thank you,' I said, throwing my arms around him.

'I told you I would look after him,' Griffin responded, hugging me back. 'He came around not long after you left. He's in the infirmary – a few cracked ribs, bruises, nothing major – but after everything that has happened I'm not too hopeful the Academy will be willing to release him any time soon.'

I nodded. That wasn't exactly good news, but far better than it might have been. I was just going to have to go and get him out of there, the first chance I got.

After Griffin embraced Father Peters and thanked him for taking us in, we settled down to hear Griffin's account of what had happened at the Academy.

'Josephine has been raising suspicions for a while now about your motivations, Violet, calling into question Lincoln's and my loyalties at the same time. No small allegations to make. But highlighting your relationship and bond with Phoenix has enabled her to inspire some support within the Assembly and more broadly throughout the Academy.

'We knew Josephine was hoping Lilith would try and come after Evelyn, that it was why she'd kept Evelyn so close and well guarded even though she'd come in willingly. You saw what happened to the guards and another dozen Grigori have been badly wounded, too.'

Griffin paused then answered the question I'd just opened my mouth to ask. 'None of our people were hurt. A few students are rather worse for wear, but it was Hakon who bore the brunt of the explosion.' Griffin ran a hand through his hair and looked at us with dismay. 'Josephine hadn't counted on Lilith's willingness to literally blow everything up.'

I glanced at Father Peters and we exchanged a small smile.

'Now that Evelyn has been taken – and as a hostage, no less – my fears have become reality.' Griffin sighed. 'Josephine has been looking for an excuse to control you, Violet. Partly, I think she actually believes what she said to you in the testing – she fears you wouldn't put the greater good above someone you cared for. But more than anything, she knows you're a threat to her position. Ironically, her motivations are good – if delusional. She believes in Grigori and the role we play, and she believes she is the only one who will put that loyalty above everything else.'

'So where does that leave us?' Lincoln asked.

'Josephine has accused Violet of orchestrating the exile break-in for the purposes of her mother's escape. She claims Violet has been working with Phoenix all this time – initially because of love, now out of her loyalty to their bond. In return, Phoenix enabled the resurrection of Evelyn.'

'But that's bullshit!' I said.

Griffin barely paused. 'Of course it is. We all know that, but Josephine's presented it to the Academy and claimed that the fact that everyone who came into contact with Lilith is now dead or gravely injured apart from us is evidence enough. Plus, of course, there is the additional implied guilt because you and Lincoln ran.'

Oh my God.

'Griffin, are you in trouble?' I asked.

He smiled, sadly. 'Not yet. It will come, but for now I'm too big a fish to fry and Josephine and I have always had an understanding of sorts. She'll resist bringing me down if she can. Strangely enough, she considers me a friend.'

I wondered if Griffin considered *her* a friend.

'So why did we have to run, then?' I asked, trying to put it all together. 'Wouldn't it have been better to stay and explain?'

Griffin accepted the cup of coffee Peters passed him with a nod. I all but yanked mine out of his hand. It was drip-brewed, but I sucked down the scalding liquid anyway and wondered if it would be rude to ask for an immediate refill.

'Trust me, the alternative was not preferable. Lilith and Phoenix have kidnapped over sixty children that we know of, not to mention Evelyn – the time for dealing with the politics of the Academy is over. Our only hope of stopping this runaway train is trapping Lilith. And our only hope of doing that is going to be by using the right bait.' Griffin took a gulp of his coffee.

'Violet,' Lincoln concluded.

Joy.

'How do you know that Josephine has been doing all of this?' I asked Griffin.

'Evelyn and I discussed the possibilities before coming to New York. We both know Josephine well enough to have made some assumptions and expected her to use Evelyn in an attempt to lure Lilith. The rest came in from Rainer. She and Wil have been feeding me information whenever they could. They're tired of Josephine's games.'

Evelyn had known exactly how things would play out – that Lilith would take her – and yet, she'd stayed there patiently and waited. I wouldn't be surprised if the only reason she'd put up a fight at all was to protect Dad. I hoped I'd get my chance to say thank you and . . . tell her some of the things I should have told her already.

'Why do I get the feeling you have a plan, Griff?' Lincoln asked, leaning forwards now.

Griffin nodded. 'Because you know me.' He turned to me. 'You trusted me to come to New York. You told me if the roles were reversed you knew I'd be there for you. Well,' he held his hands out, 'this is me, here for you. You two need to leave the city. Get rid of your mobile phones and anything else electronic. I have everything you need here.' He heaved a bag onto the table. 'Zoe and Spence helped me pull as much together as I could. Passports are still good, but no credit cards. There's plenty of cash in the side compartment. I've got clothes but not much else, you'll have to buy what you need along the way.'

I shook my head. 'I have to stay, Griff. I have to get Evelyn back.'

He nodded. 'I agree. And being outside the Academy walls will make it easier for Phoenix to find you in two days, but never lose sight of the fact that this is all a trap. Lilith is setting you up to fall.' He dug a piece of paper out of his pocket and passed it to Lincoln. 'Evelyn gave this to me before we came to New York in case something like this happened. She and Jonathan had a safe-house on the Hudson. This information will take you in the right direction and she was confident everything you needed would still be there. She said to make sure you checked the basement.' Griffin glanced at the note, handing it over to Lincoln. 'It's a little cryptic, but she was worried it might be found. When you arrive, contact me with the missing details so I can send Steph and the others to you when they get here.'

We nodded.

'Wait. What about you?' Lincoln asked.

Griffin put a hand on his shoulder. 'I'm staying here. I'll keep an eye on Josephine and try to get any intel on Lilith and Phoenix to you when I can. If you need me, go through Dapper and Salvatore. They'll act as our go-betweens for now. I spoke to them before coming here – they're on their way to collect the final ingredient now. None of us knows if this potion will

JESSICA SHIRVINGTON

work, but we have to hope. Most importantly, I'll be gathering the cavalry for when you call. Something tells me this fight is going to find you two before anyone else.'

With that, Griffin rose and embraced us all, a promise passing between us.

He turned to Father Peters. 'Do you have a way to get them out of here safely?'

The priest nodded. 'Safe from Grigori, anyway.'

'Show us,' Griffin said.

After Lincoln and I exchanged our bloodied clothes for fresh jeans and T-shirts from our new supplies, we followed Peters down to the basement, where he pulled aside a loose covering over one of the walls to reveal what looked like a bank-vault door.

I had a terrible suspicion where it would lead. 'The tunnels?' I asked.

Peters took hold of the large spinning circle to unlock the door. 'Like titanium, exiles aren't the only ones who like to have a good escape route. I owned this property long before it became a church. The original tunnels have been down here over four hundred years and have been added to over time. Some of us managed to add our own hidden entrances without the exiles noticing. When all else has failed, these tunnels have saved me. Just move fast and kill anything you see.'

'That's do-able,' Lincoln said.

I smiled, keen even, for a little confrontation that I could actually handle.

Father Peters pulled the heavy door back that probably would have taken six human men to shift. 'You'll hear the trains when you get near the subway. Head down the east

— 246 —

tunnel – it will take you all the way to Grand Central. You can jump a train up the Hudson from there.'

'How will we know when we're at Grand Central?' I asked.

He winked. 'Because there will be a door with a sign above it saying "Grand Central Station".'

'Oh.'

He pushed us into the tunnel. 'This door doesn't open from the inside so don't rely on getting back in through here.'

'Phones?' Griffin ordered.

Lincoln and I handed them over. We didn't have anything else electronic on us. Griffin gave us a replacement mobile. 'Untraceable. But short calls only, just in case. Don't do anything foolish,' he cautioned, also offering us a couple of flashlights from the wall.

We both nodded.

'God be with you,' Peters said, right before he slammed the massive door shut.

Flooded by the darkness we quickly turned on our flashlights. We stared down the old tunnel and I pointed in the direction I thought was right. 'East?' I checked.

Lincoln nodded, his hand reaching down for mine. 'East.'

We ran.

The tunnels changed shape and size as we crossed from one to the next in the complex network, having to regularly stop and use our abilities to reveal the hidden way. Grigori may be able to use these paths but there was no mistaking the dominating exile signature that pulsed around us.

Every now and then the path opened into a broader tunnel or crossed over a subway track, we even found ourselves running through what seemed to be an abandoned aqueduct at one point.

We noticed a few marked doors along the way – one labelled Central Park, and another, the Empire State Building – before we finally reached one with an engraved plaque reading Grand Central Station.

We slipped through the door, which opened into a garbage room. The rotten stench was more than offensive but I was relieved to be out of the tunnels. We made our way through the bins to the other side, where there was another door.

'This is disgusting,' I said, while Lincoln carefully opened the door just wide enough to scope out our new surroundings.

He glanced at me. 'Yes, but imagine how disappointed you would've been if it had come out in a janitor's closet.'

He was right. That kind of cliché would have just annoyed me.

I smiled, even as my nerves were fighting the jitters. Things had become very bad, very fast, and now we were on the run. Again. Lincoln peered through the crack in the door, looking for an opportunity for us to slip out. Watching him, I felt sick to the gut.

Lincoln valued his role in the Academy, as a Grigori, and now he had turned his back on everything he knew to help me escape. Josephine would already have Grigori out there looking for us. And God only knew what Lilith was up to.

What will happen to him after all of this? Will he lose his place in the ranks of Grigori?

I couldn't let that happen.

'Linc . . .' I said, tugging his arm and drawing his attention. 'I think you should go back.' I bit my lip.

He blinked. 'Excuse me?'

'You heard me. I think you should go back. I'll be fine on my own and then you won't be in as much trouble.'

Still watching through the gap in the door, he must've spied an opportunity to move because he grabbed my hand, opened the door and pulled me through behind him. Suddenly, we were in the very public Grand Central Station. Lincoln didn't slow, dragging me along until we turned a corner. There, we stopped, Lincoln checking back around the corner in case anyone had followed us. Satisfied, he turned a severe look on me.

'Let's get this straight right now. I'm not going anywhere.' But even as he stared at me, I noticed his breath hitch as he became aware of just how close our bodies were.

His expression softened. 'You don't need to protect me, Vi. I'm by your side and nothing you say will get rid of me.' His voice became rough. 'This whole thing would be easier if we could get along, okay?'

'Getting along isn't exactly our problem, in case you've forgotten,' I mumbled.

But he kept his eyes fixed on mine until I sighed. 'Okay, okay. Got it. We're in this together.'

His hand went to my face, warm and all-encompassing. 'We're going to make it through this.' His forehead dropped to meet mine and we stayed like that for a few precious seconds before we were moving on again. Lincoln knew the station and led with purpose. Within minutes we had tickets and were boarding the first available train, taking our seats at the back of the last carriage after doing a walk-through of the entire train, monitoring every other person who stepped on after us. We were relentless in our focus. Now was no time for dereliction of duty.

chapter twenty-four

*'This is how it will be . . . The angels will come and separate
the wicked from the righteous.'*

Matthew 13:49

Lincoln only bought tickets to get us half way. Due to the pre-dawn hour and Lincoln's paranoia that we'd be followed, he decided to 'borrow' a car for the remainder of the trip.

In spite of our frantic situation I found myself fascinated by the prospect of seeing Lincoln hotwire a car. And, he put on an impressively stealthy show, selecting a well-blending four-wheel drive parked close to the train station, and managing to start it in less than thirty seconds before tearing up the freeway like a madman while I searched for a map in the glove box.

I grabbed hold of my door handle as we took a sharp corner.

Lincoln finally slowed down when we merged with the other traffic, suddenly making us one of the many.

'Who *are* you?' I asked, as I stared at the normally by-the-book Lincoln.

He kept his eyes on the road. 'Mum taught me to always be prepared for desperate times.'

'Did your mum also teach you how to boost a car?'

He smiled, keeping his eyes on the road ahead. 'Not exactly, but I'm sure she wouldn't argue under the circumstances.'

I had to agree. I started unfolding the map I'd found, twisting it around until I figured out where we were. 'Okay, what's the name of this town?'

'Cold Spring,' Lincoln replied. 'We should be about twenty minutes out.'

I searched the map. 'Got it,' I said.

Well, it sounded nice enough. 'Stay on the US-9,' I instructed.

It didn't take long and when we arrived in Cold Spring, it was still pre-dawn. The small town was misty and silent. The main street – the *only* street really – was deserted and we knew it would still be a couple of hours before any shops opened. We considered trying to find Evelyn's safe-house but the instructions had told us only to get to Cold Spring and then to the general store.

We parked the car in a small side street and tried to rest, but despite our lack of sleep neither one of us could relax. In the end we settled for a walk along the river, the sky slowly brightening as the sun rose.

'It's beautiful here,' I said, taking in the picturesque scene. Cold Spring was perched along the river, walkways, small boats and huge old weatherboard homes lining its banks. I stared across the river into nothing but greenery. The view was so natural – untainted by human development.

'There are towns like this up and down the Hudson,' Lincoln said, an ease in his voice that reflected our environment.

'I used to try and get away from the Academy and explore whenever I could. I never made it to this place, but I think it's popular for its antiques.'

We walked back through an underpass beneath the train line and into the centre of the town.

'I can believe that,' I said, taking in just how many quaint little shops edged the street.

'Look,' Lincoln said, pointing across the road to where a window glowed and, above, soft plumes of smoke escaped a vent. 'Can you smell that?'

I sucked in a deep breath and almost moaned. 'Fresh bread.'

He grinned. 'Yep.'

We made our way over to the bakery and pressed our faces against the windows until we caught the attention of the tiny man pulling first-of-the-day bread from the ovens. After he had recovered from the fright he opened the door.

'Travelling through?' he bellowed in a deep voice that seemed far too powerful for his size.

We nodded. 'Any chance we could buy a few loaves of bread?' Lincoln asked.

A few minutes later we walked out with a bag of five-grain rolls, a loaf of sourdough and a slice of still-warm pumpkin bread hanging from each of our mouths.

Delicious!

While we were there we had asked the baker if he knew what time the general store opened. He told us we had another hour's wait ahead, and looked amused as he warned us that the owner, Merri, wouldn't take kindly to us leeching onto her windows.

But we were done waiting and headed to the shop anyway, knocking on the weathered green door, rattling its glass pane inserts.

A light came on in the upstairs window and we heard some moving around. Footsteps sounded and finally came to the front door. Lincoln put a hand on me as if to move me behind him. I cut him a look. He dropped his hand.

I should think so.

'You realise you can be very difficult,' he whispered.

'I do,' I replied, batting my eyelashes and making him laugh.

A slim woman answered the door. Her grey wiry hair was heaped in a messy bun, an old yellowed robe was wrapped around her and a very pointed scowl was focused on us.

'We ain't open for another hour,' she said, pointing at the trading hours sign.

'We're sorry to bother you . . .' I started. But somewhere in those words she straightened, her eyes narrowing.

'You look awfully like someone I used to know.' She studied me a moment longer, her expression suspicious.

'My name is Violet. Are you Merri?'

The woman coughed as she nodded, a hacking, unpleasant sound.

'I believe you knew my mother, Evelyn.'

She surveyed us for a moment longer, staring at Lincoln then back at me. She shook her head and opened the door for us. 'You'd better come in.'

We followed her up the stairs and into a small kitchenette, where she dropped her robe on the chair, revealing that she was fully dressed in brown pants and a white shirt. She smirked when she saw my surprise and sat down before a cup of tea.

'If folks round here knew I was up and about at this hour I'd have people expecting me to open the store earlier. Sit. I've got tea and I can smell you've already got the bread.'

We sat, accepting her offer of tea and handed her our loaf of bread. Merri put butter and jam on the table, passing us each a knife. We didn't hold back.

'So, you're Evelyn's daughter?'

I nodded.

She smiled at that, as if pleased by the idea.

'You headed to her place up here, then?'

I nodded again. 'She told us to get here and that you'd be able to tell us the rest of the way.'

'Why didn't she tell you the way herself?'

I shrugged. 'Things have been complicated. She had to be careful what she said. She knew if we could get this far, you'd help us with the rest,' I said, hoping that was the case.

'Humph, things were always complicated with that woman. You have a car?'

'Yes,' Lincoln replied. 'An off-roader.'

Merri nodded. 'Good.'

'You wouldn't by chance have a map to her house, would you?' Lincoln asked.

'Ha!' she exclaimed, almost losing her mouthful of bread, using her fingers to catch the crumbs. 'That woman never gave no directions to anyone. But I expect I came as close as anyone to knowing. If she sent you to me, I must've. Over sixty years ago now. I was just a girl and curiosity often caused me troubles. I followed her and that fellow. Two of them were like brother and sister, fought like it, too. They were trekking through the woods when I spied them. Thought I was right clever, too, following like that. The town folk were always whispering about them, wondering where it was they stayed. I wasn't into the gossip, but I sure wanted answers to my own suspicions. I followed them all the way down a long dirt road. It led to the river and then just stopped. No purpose to it at all. Anyway, I lost 'em there.'

'So, you *don't* know where it is?' Lincoln asked, his ever-polite tone beginning to waver.

She tutted at him. 'I ain't no fool, lad. That road went somewhere and just before they disappeared from sight, Evelyn looked right at where I was hidden behind a tree. The years went by and I never went back to look for them and never told anyone about that day, till now.'

'Why?' I asked.

Merri stuffed a large piece of pumpkin bread into her mouth and spoke while she chewed. 'Sometimes you just know to leave well enough alone. Those two weren't no honeymooners and I knew the likes of me had no right in knowing their business.' She shrugged, swallowed. 'Every now and then I'd see them back in the area.' She raised her eyebrow. 'I got older but the two of them never seemed much different at all. They stayed out of sight of the other town people, but for some reason she always let me see her when they came through town for supplies. Once I took over my pa's store, she took to visiting me every so often, late at night or early in the mornings.'

There was a look of longing in her eyes. Was that why she was up and dressed at this early hour? Was she still waiting for Evelyn to return?

'You became friends,' I offered.

'As much as that woman could be friends with anyone, I expect. Stubborn as hell, she was, and always looked like she was carrying the weight of the world on her shoulders.' She harrumphed again. 'She looked like you two do now.'

Lincoln and I both twitched in our seats. Merri smiled, but it quickly faded as she went back to her story.

'The last time I saw her she was on her own, and in a bad way. She was never without that fella so I knew something terrible had happened.'

It must have been after Jonathan died.

Merri got up and reached into one of her kitchen drawers, pulling out a large old-fashioned key. She put it on the table, her hand hovering over it protectively.

'I patched her up as best I could and she gave me this, told me to keep it safe for her. Said I'd been the closest to ever finding them that day when I was a kid. She knew I'd never told anyone or tried to find 'em again. She said time was the best test of trust. That was over thirty years ago, and the last I seen her.'

'Would you be able to point us in the right direction?' Lincoln asked.

She took a sip of tea and ripped off another piece of bread. 'You two look like you're headed for trouble.'

Lincoln kept his voice calm and neutral. 'We're just going up there for a night or two then we'll be on our way. We don't want to bring any trouble to the town,' he said.

Merri considered this and nodded, before casting a curious gaze on me. 'You got your mother's eyes.'

'No, I . . . I . . . She has blue eyes,' I stammered, caught off-guard by the statement.

'Not the same colour, maybe, but still . . . Same eyes. You're a fighter, like her.'

I swallowed, realising with surprise I was glad she thought I could be like Evelyn.

'And you're all but a billboard screaming the same thing,' she said to Lincoln, who smiled in response.

'I'm sure you've seen your fair share of strange happenings, if you knew Evelyn for so long. We're just trying to keep our people safe.'

'And am *I* your people?' Merri asked.

Wise woman.

'Yes, you are,' Lincoln answered, not missing a beat.

Merri stood. 'Collect what you need from the store. I'll get you a map to point you in the right direction. Best we get you two back on the road before the town wakes up.'

We didn't delay, heading back downstairs.

We moved through the store, grabbing anything we felt might come in handy. Lincoln went for the practical stuff – batteries, radio, gas cookers, blankets, candles, matches. He even grabbed two sleeping bags and then several large bottles of water. I prioritised food, mainly things that could be eaten raw or straight from a can. When I spied a kettle, I couldn't resist grabbing it along with a packet of coffee. Lincoln saw and rolled his eyes, but he was grinning.

No way I'm going indefinitely without caffeine!

Lincoln piled his selections onto the counter and I loaded mine alongside them.

'You were in the boy scouts, weren't you?' I teased.

He laughed, that laugh he had just for me, and I melted from the inside, my soul tugging at me, desperate to reach out to him. I resisted, busying myself with the supplies.

Merri brought us our map and gave us the key. She put all of our goods into bags, while Lincoln fetched the car. She even threw in a few extras like bug spray and a jar of homemade jam.

'Thank you for helping us,' I said.

She sniffed and I braced myself for another of her hacking coughs. 'I know there is something bigger than us going on out there. Evelyn was part of it. You are, too. Offering a little help when I can . . . It's the least I can do. But I recommend staying hidden, unless you want to be dealing with small-town gossip.'

That was definitely something we didn't want. We thanked Merri and set off to find Evelyn's safe-house.

The map was easy to follow and ten minutes later we were on the dirt road Merri had described. And, just like she'd explained, the road finished abruptly at the edge of the river, as if it had no real purpose. Lincoln pulled over and we stared into the forest surrounding us.

What now?

It was early morning. Birds were going nuts chirping in the trees, their songs sounding practised and regimented. The sun was now up, the sky pink with the promise of a clear day ahead. Frustrated, I got out of the car, slammed the door and started pacing aimlessly.

Unlike me, Lincoln radiated composure, even though he'd had just as little shut-eye over the past twenty-four hours. He stood at the hood of the car, breathing deeply. He looked around slowly, purposefully, eventually pointing towards a clearing at the river's edge.

'There,' he said.

'What?' I snapped, all patience gone.

Lincoln looked at me as I seethed and nodded back in the direction he'd just pointed, a smirk playing on the corners of his lips as he registered my hands-on-hips pose.

'You didn't really think it would be that easy to find, did you? I looked up Evelyn and Jonathan's documented histories at the Academy. Jonathan was one of the most powerful glamour-wielders of all time. It's amazing,' he marvelled, looking back at the cleared area. 'It's as if he left a piece of himself here. Even now, so many years after his death, his glamour still holds.'

Exhaustion was getting the better of me and I groaned, not seeing what Lincoln did. Everything seemed impossible right now and this, yet another test . . . It wasn't fair.

'Vi.'

Honey and cream.

Lincoln's voice was calm, soothing and powerful all at once. 'Concentrate.'

I shook my head and let out a frustrated sigh. 'Damn. I need coffee.' Merri's tea really hadn't hit the spot.

Lincoln chuckled, and the warm sound snuck its way into me.

Stupid, distracting laugh.

I didn't *want* to be eased. I wanted to be in panic mode. But I was defenceless against the way my heart beat for him, as my soul splintered with the physical pain of its unmet demands.

I took a deep breath. Lincoln waited calmly as I shook out my hands, regained my focus and directed it to the clearing by the water that he'd pointed out.

The glamour took longer to peel back than most and felt like pulling taffy away from a wall. But once I had a grasp on it, I kept going moving it away from the ground and up, eventually unveiling a white wooden cabin with heavy shutters over the windows and a verandah sweeping around all sides.

'Oh,' I said, mesmerised. I had never imagined Evelyn living somewhere like this. It was beautiful. Peaceful. Quiet.

'Looks like Lilith wasn't the only one who took a shine to this area,' said Lincoln, watching me rather than the cabin.

'Hmm,' I responded absently, already on the move, drawn towards the front door.

The verandah and the outside of the house were in remarkably good shape considering its abandonment. I looked around, trying to make sense of what I was seeing.

'How?' I asked.

Lincoln was equally spellbound, running a hand over the wooden railings and the paintwork, neither of which were nearly as chipped away as time usually demanded. He scuffed a foot along the decking, which was covered in a thick layer of dust but was otherwise untouched.

'Incredible,' he said. 'Jonathan must've found a way to manipulate his glamour to shield the place from the elements. It's as if . . . As if what is hidden under the glamour is protected indefinitely somehow.'

I pulled out the large iron key Merri had given us – like something from a fairy tale with its filigree design – and slid it into the lock. It all felt so surreal.

We opened the door and Lincoln entered, defensively. I followed, knowing we couldn't take our safety for granted. Evelyn hadn't mentioned any booby traps, but that didn't mean we shouldn't be prepared. Dust covered the floors and furniture, which had been draped in old sheets. I guessed she'd known she wouldn't be back for a long time.

Once we had passed through the main room – clearing it and the kitchen – we moved upstairs to the two bedrooms and bathroom. They were clear, too, and there were no obvious hiding places to check for nasty surprises.

We headed back downstairs and towards the basement next. It was locked tight, its door looking like the sturdiest feature in the cabin. We both put our ears against it to hear for any signs of activity but, like the rest of the house, the dust here was undisturbed and looked as though it had not been touched for many years.

Lincoln let out a breath. 'It's clear. We'll probably find a key around here somewhere.'

I'd already turned my attention back to the main room, wasting no time in starting to carefully pull back the sheets that covered the furniture, taking them out to the verandah with all their dust. Lincoln followed and in a few minutes we had unveiled the simple decor. The cabin smelled woodsy, like we were inside a huge walnut tree, but also, it smelled of time gone by, of history.

My eyes fixed on the wide stone fireplace, burnt black around the edges – it had been used often. I ran my fingers along the worn brown leather sofa and wondered how often Evelyn had stayed there.

Lincoln looked around in awe. 'If I had a cabin like this, I'd never leave,' he said.

I gave him a doubtful look. 'Don't you, like, I don't know, have a gazillion dollars or something? If you wanted a place like this, you could just buy one, couldn't you?'

He rolled his shoulders back, uncomfortably. 'I don't have a gazillion dollars. But . . . Yeah, I guess I have enough money to make some choices.'

'Well, then, what's stopping you?'

He looked at his feet. 'Maybe one day. If I had someone to share it with.' My heart ached. He stood by the window looking out. 'Do you think they ever got lonely here?' he asked.

I didn't need to think for long.

'Yes,' I said, sure it was the truth and, with that realisation, understanding my mother that much more.

CHAPTER TWENTY-FIVE

'Who rises up for me against the wicked? ... against evildoers?'

Psalm 94 : 16

While Lincoln set about calling Griffin – for a strictly timed conversation – and hiding the car within the glamour, I swept the dust out of the living area.

Returning the broom to the kitchen cupboard, I spied a flat-bottomed ceramic ball resting on a shelf. It was about the size of a tennis ball and seemingly served no purpose. I picked it up and looked at the base, where a letter 'E' had been etched into it – the same mark Evelyn left on all of her pieces. I shook it. Nothing.

Why would she make a ceramic ball and close it away like this?

I took it over to the counter, found an old towel and wrapped it up tightly, before bringing the base of my palm down hard and fast, shattering it.

I felt a wave of triumph when I found a key, wedged into the base.

Lincoln whistled. 'I see you found the key,' he said, but his attention was on the same thing as mine. The now-open basement revealed a surprisingly modern vault-style space containing pretty much every weapon imaginable. If I'd thought Father Peters was well stocked – his collection looked like the local convenience store in comparison to Evelyn's supercentre.

Circling the large stainless steel table in the centre of the room, I marvelled. I didn't even think flamethrowers actually existed outside of the movies. And not just that, boxes of grenades, plastic explosives, swords, knives, daggers – hell, there were even two machine guns on the wall. I gasped when I opened the first of many drawers that were filled with different currencies and what looked like stock sheets.

'Impressive.'

'I never want to get on your mum's bad side,' Lincoln countered.

My senses were drawn to a more discreet row of daggers. Discreet but powerful. 'Grigori blades,' I said.

Lincoln came up behind me, his body so close I could feel his warmth and a faint smell of car grease.

'Evelyn and Jonathan were around a long time. I imagine they made some of these blades using shavings from their own daggers like Samuel does.'

I nodded. Samuel was a weapons expert. He used small metal shavings from his own dagger to mix into silver for new weapons. It took only the smallest amount of Grigori metal to enhance ordinary weapons to entirely new levels. It didn't make them as powerful as a pure Grigori blade, but good nonetheless for back-up.

'But some of these are the real deal,' Lincoln went on, fascinated. 'Possibly blades of fallen Grigori or maybe those who retired.'

'But I thought they were supposed to disappear once a Grigori dies?'

I felt him shrug behind me and found it increasingly difficult to concentrate.

'Some people say that if another Grigori is there at the time one of us falls it can be claimed by the other. The reason they usually disappear is more to prevent them getting into the wrong hands.'

My mouth was dry. 'So, I guess she was around a lot of Grigori who died, then.'

'Not hard to believe, since she was chasing Lilith for so long.'

I felt a pang of sadness for my mother. It couldn't have been much of a life for her, following in the wake of Lilith's destruction for so many years.

And then she tied herself to Lilith indefinitely . . . for me.

Lincoln reached around me, his arm pressing my side as he touched one of the blades. 'Hmm . . .' he said, low, throaty.

Oh, good God. Was that for the blade or for me?

A silence filled the room, both of us now acutely aware of our close proximity. We always worked hard to keep a certain distance, but sometimes it felt like we'd been tricked. Like some cosmic set-up had toyed with us and then, there we were.

Same upending feelings.

Same uncontrollable desire.

Same heart-wrenching longing.

Same ruinous consequences.

I waited for Lincoln to step away.

My eyes rolled back as I breathed him in again. I could feel his power swirling, and vaguely wondered why it wasn't pummelling into me yet.

His arm slipped away from the dagger and I braced for the inevitable separation.

But instead, his arm grazed my side slowly and his hand came to rest on my hip. I froze.

He'll move away any moment.

When I heard him take a deep breath, the sound vibrated through my body and my head swayed back. His other hand braced my shoulder and a thrill ran down my spine, my body warming as his fingers moved into my hair, pushing it aside so that I could feel his warm breath on my exposed neck.

Heaven.

Hell.

My heart raced. He was warmth and sun and everything that felt right in my world. I wanted it so much, like I'd never wanted anything in my life before. Everything. His touch, his lips, his heart, his . . . soul. God help me, I wanted it all.

Mine.

I let my shoulders roll back, tilting my head, inviting him.

His lips grazed my shoulders, travelling towards the curve of my neck, his other hand moving up my arm slowly, thoughtfully.

I locked my knees tight and closed my eyes, feeling the thrill of his lips on my skin and the heat from every deep breath.

He kissed me just below my ear and I thought I might faint from the feeling that the world was suddenly igniting around me.

He stepped in, pressing closer to me. I wanted so desperately to fall into him, or better, to turn to face him and give him my lips in return.

But he'd saved me so many times. He'd always been the one to keep us in check.

His lips grazed my ear and I knew whatever small, miraculous hold I had over rational thought would soon fade completely.

I hated myself as I did it, but I drew down into my power and brought it out, gaining strength and distance and bathing Lincoln in its effects – what he'd told me was like vanilla cream.

My soul protested as if trying to get free of its unworthy host, but I pushed on, building the walls, wanting to scream as I rebuilt the barrier between Lincoln and me, locking out the sun.

I felt his lips – still on my neck – tremble. His hand, on my arm, gripped tight. I wasn't sure if it was because he was trying to gain strength or just hold on. I gave him his time, as he had for me – staying where I was, trying not to make things worse.

When both hands had dropped from me and he had taken a step back, I wanted to tell him it was okay, that – of all people – I understood. But before I could get the first word out he was gone.

When I came upstairs from the basement Lincoln was stuffing things into a backpack. He didn't even look at me.

'We need to keep up regular patrols. I'm going to walk the perimeter and then I'll keep watch for a couple of hours while you sleep. You can take over when you wake up.'

'Linc, please. Are you mad at me?'

He closed his pack and looked up at me briefly as he shook his head, a sour expression on his face. 'I'm not mad at you. I'm furious with me. I just . . . I don't know what we're doing sometimes.' He ran a hand through his hair. 'It was selfish.' He shook his head again. 'Get some rest.' With that, he stalked out of the room and I let him, even though I wanted to wring his neck.

Does he think I'm the only one who is allowed to have trouble dealing with this stuff?

It was times like this that I really missed having Steph around. I grabbed the phone Griffin had given us and ignored the warning that we should only use it in emergencies. This *was* an emergency: I needed my best friend. I dialled Steph's number and sighed.

Message bank.

I eyed off the leather couch and considered sinking into it but grabbed my pack instead and went upstairs. I ferreted out a stash of musty-smelling towels that were going to have to make do and chose the room I thought was Evelyn's. It would have been nice to see more evidence of her around the place, knick-knacks or photos, or journals even – but the cabin, while charming, was personality sparse.

The biggest shock was when I turned on the shower and actually felt hot water. I didn't deliberate too long, jumping in to wash before it ran out.

Lincoln still hadn't come back and I didn't think he would for a while. I got it. Sometimes space was the only answer. So I settled for finding some well-packed linen that wasn't nearly as old-smelling as I would've expected, and made the bed. Unsurprisingly, I fell asleep as soon as my head hit the pillow.

I was in a long dark corridor. The walls, floor and ceiling all consisting of dark-tinted mirrors, reflecting things that weren't there and not the things that were.

I stared into the glass, focusing on the substance that lurked somewhere within the space that my reflection should have been. I looked behind me. Nothing. What was it? And why was it familiar?

My gaze travelled down the narrow corridor. I was not alone. Sitting in a simple chair at the end was Uri. Dishevelled as always, unshaven, shoeless. When I had seen him in the desert, the sands had seemed to roll over his feet as if they were a part of him. Disturbingly, the mirrored floor now did the same, like a liquid ocean beneath his feet. He nodded to me, expressionless.

I turned. Nox was perched on a high stool at the opposite end of the corridor. He was predictably pristine, today sporting a full tuxedo with tails. I wouldn't have been surprised if he produced a top hat. Unlike Uri, the metallic ocean seemed to move in currents away from him.

I nodded to them both, the awkward arrangement making it impossible for me to keep both of them in my sight simultaneously.

'Am I dreaming?' I asked, just to be sure. They'd never come to me in a dream before.

Uri nodded. 'We thought it might be easier if we visited you together. Dreams have their purposes as much as a crossover.'

'Have you seen everything that has happened?' I asked.

'And more,' Nox replied, smug.

I looked into the dark mirrors again. Something was definitely moving within them.

'Still intrigued by the reflections?'

I realised then, these were the same things I'd seen hovering in the background when Uri and Nox had visited me in the past.

'What are they?' I asked, as my hand stretched out to skim the glass surface. It was ice cold, but it wasn't solid. When I took my hand away, my fingers were tipped in silver.

'Only when you must know, can you know,' Uri answered.

I rolled my eyes, but my attention quickly returned to my silvered fingers.

'What is this?'

'Beginnings. And endings,' Uri said.

Nox stood, gaining my attention. 'Do they still call to you?' he asked, gesturing to the reflections in the mirror.

'Why are there more of them here?' I asked.

Nox tilted his head, studying me. 'There are not. You simply see them better.' He glanced down the hall to Uri, a small smile playing on his lips. 'She grows.'

Uri remained seated. 'She must.'

I watched the reflections cruise along the mirrored surface. Something about them was so lonely, so lost. I took a step towards the mirrors, felt my arm extend as if of its own will. They were beautiful and they were terrible and I understood them somehow. I took another step.

Nox sighed. 'As interesting as this could be, now is not the time – child of Sole.'

I heard Nox, but I couldn't seem to stop. They were calling to me. My hand went again to the mirror and towards one of the reflections that was wavering in mid-air.

A firm hand with long fingers pressed into my upper arm and yanked me back. Nox's voice sounded uncomfortably close to my ear.

'If you go to them, you may never return.' With his words a coldness bled into me, leaving me just a taste of the terrible isolation this place offered. I stepped back with a start. He let me go.

'You are running out of time,' Uri said, sounding bored.

'Time?'

'The Hag grows stronger. You must open your eyes, see who your allies are.'

I knew Hag was another term for Lilith.

'I know who my allies are.'

'No. You know who you can trust, but there is one who would give his life, his very existence, for you. You must see him before it is too late,' Nox said, smiling. 'The dark beckons you.'

'Phoenix,' I whispered.

'We have been granted permission to aid you. If you can command Lilith in her physical form, fully subdued, we can take her from you. But . . .' Uri stood now and took a few steps towards me. 'We can't take her from your world. You must bring her over to us.'

'Me? How? I . . . I don't know how to cross the realms.'

Uri blinked at me and seemed to go somewhere else in his mind. I turned to Nox.

He shrugged. 'You have already proven you can carry things between the realms.'

'Yeah – grains of sand and a button!'

'We will open the connection, like we have done before; you simply need to cross into our space. It will be like when you first learned to move, in Santorini. How do you think you did that?'

'Strength.'

Nox scoffed. 'Hardly.'

I took offence, which he enjoyed.

I looked at the mirrors again, wanting to see myself. I thought about it so hard that out of nowhere, my reflection suddenly appeared, repeated up and down the entire length of the hall as it bounced off the mirrors.

That was my answer.

'Willpower,' I said.

'Yes,' Uri said from my other side. 'Always.'

'Where do you go when you do that?' I asked.

'Where do you go?' Uri replied.

'I don't . . .' But I stopped. I did go places when I tapped into the ability we called Sight. I moved away from my body and went to the places I needed to.

'Oh,' I said.

'There is one more thing,' Nox said. 'When you cross the realms, you'll need an anchor.'

I thought about the times Uri and Nox had crossed the realms. They had only ever come one at a time, the other always having to stay behind to work as an anchor.

'How does it work?'

'It must be someone more than human and near to your body, and one with whom you share significance. Their very existence in your world allows you to be drawn back there when you are ready, though it isn't pleasant for your chosen anchor,' Uri said, giving a rare twitch of his nose.

'Significance?'

Nox turned his back to me and began to walk away down the long corridor. 'Love, blood,' he glanced over his shoulder at Uri. 'Insufferable hate.'

I caught an uptilt at the corners of Uri's mouth. 'One that invokes the passions.'

'Soul?' I asked.

They didn't answer.

'Lincoln?'

Was what we had strong enough?

Still no answer.

'Would our souls have to be bonded?' I called out.

To this Nox chuckled and threw a hand over his shoulder as if to say goodbye. 'Excuses, excuses.'

They were gone.

I bolted upright in the bed.

My wide eyes fell on Lincoln's. He was standing in the doorway, his expression guarded and intense.

I pushed the hair back from my face. 'How long have I been asleep?'

And how long have you been standing there watching me?

He swallowed. 'A few hours. Not long.'

I nodded, still getting my bearings. Lincoln shifted as if he was going to leave.

'Linc, do you hate me? Do you think I'm weak and cruel to you?'

'No. Why would you . . .' But then his eyes dropped.

'Did you think I was the only one allowed to struggle with this? Come on.' I gave him a quirky smile. 'To be honest, I'm kind of relieved.'

He looked up, caught my expression and raised an eyebrow. 'Oh, yeah?'

'Totally. It's been kind of crushing my self-confidence. You know, me falling all over you all the time, and you seeming to have it all together.' I was teasing now, kind of.

Lincoln grinned. 'Well, I guess we've solved that problem then.'

'I believe so.'

He just shook his head as I laughed, but his green eyes said only, Thank you, and hazel ones replied only, Of course.

CHAPTER TWENTY-SIX

*'I hope you have not been leading a double life,
pretending to be wicked and being good all the time.'*

Oscar Wilde

after ordering Lincoln to sleep, I headed out to walk the
perimeter just as he had. Everything was silent. When I
returned to the cabin I subconsciously reached out to him with
my powers and felt his heart beating rhythmically.

Home.

When I found the sandwiches he'd left in the fridge – which
he'd obviously turned on – I snorted a laugh but fell on them
gratefully then gulped down a glass of milk before heading
out to do another patrol, just to be sure. I wasn't about to let
anything slip by on my watch.

While moving through the woods, pushing out my senses
to scan the area, I thought more about what Nox and Uri had
said. They'd brought Phoenix into this. They did that all the
time. And yet I was sure, despite their unhelpful crypticness,
that they actually did want Lilith defeated.

*So why are they trying to turn me back in Phoenix's direction?
After all he has done. Knowing he can so easily end me?*

Maybe because he hasn't.

When Phoenix had broken into the Academy and we found him, he'd seemed almost relieved. Like he had been waiting for us. And down in the tunnel – he definitely sensed me and still, he'd fed us the information that helped us save that other child. Not to mention my dreams. Was there another reason, apart from taunting me, that he'd entered my dreamscape?

Yes, he did take the other child away that night in the tunnel, but did he have a choice? With Olivier watching over him, could he have really done anything else at that time that wouldn't result in the boy being harmed?

The thoughts swirled in my mind but I kept coming back to the same thing – the look in his eyes. He'd looked right at me as he let go of a burst of his own emotion. It had felt so real, so haunting.

He couldn't have faked that.

He'd come looking for me tomorrow night. He had my mother. He knew I'd do whatever I was asked. Lilith would know that, too. They must be laughing.

If you leave as much as a window open I'll find you before then.

I stopped dead.

Even the animals rustling in the nearby bushes stilled, the birds' chirps faded away. I had thought he was winding me up.

I'd been keeping my barriers up so high since arriving in New York, both because of my efforts to grow stronger and also to keep my defences at the ready. Plus, I'd been within Academy walls and their shields almost the entire time. Had Phoenix been trying then, but unable to get to me?

'Oh, my God,' I said to myself, remembering my dreams . . .
We need to talk.

He had been trying to reach out this whole time and I had
only shut him out.

Stupid!

Right there and then – refusing to let another moment go
by with all those children locked up and at Lilith's mercy – I
decided to do something I was sure I'd live to regret.

A few hours later, I was running through my workout
movements on the patch of grass between the house and the
river, when Lincoln emerged and slumped into one of the large
rocking chairs, still half-asleep. He was wearing grey cotton
sweat pants and a white T-shirt, his hair was all messy and I
could tell just by looking he was still bed-warm.

Breathe.

I almost fell over when he leaned back to stretch his arms
over the back of the chair, exposing more than a touch of bare
skin at his waistband. There was no denying all of our recent
time together was affecting me.

Breathe!

I turned my back on him. 'There's coffee on the table
inside,' I said, oh-so-casual.

I heard the rocking chair creak, the door swing open and
then again when he returned. 'Thanks,' he said.

I shrugged, still moving through some strength exercises.

'Want some company?' he asked, coming down the stairs.

Well, there's a loaded question.

I looked at him quickly, so as not to stare. He looked gorgeous and mostly because he was relaxed instead of tense with overthinking everything. Just him.

We ran through a few drills, mostly just for something to do. Neither one of us suggested we spar. We both knew that wasn't a great idea right now. Playing with fire and all.

Finally, we settled down on the verandah. As each of us claimed a rocking chair I thought to myself, *This will always be my rocking chair and that one will always be his.* As if we might spend a version of forever here, together.

'We need to talk about Phoenix,' I said, killing any kind of peace that had settled. Because despite my earlier thoughts – it didn't mean we shouldn't be prepared.

Lincoln's expression shut down and he took a sip of his freshly made coffee.

Okay, I'll start.

'There are kids involved, Linc, and we can't keep ignoring that the only reason you haven't returned him is because of me. I saw you fighting him at the Academy. You were merely fending him off.'

Lincoln raised an eyebrow at me.

'It's true,' I said.

He stared into his mug.

'Look, we don't even know if returning Phoenix would mean killing me. I could survive . . .' I said, even though we both knew that was unlikely. I had no control over my powers when Phoenix chose to reinstate the wounds that Onyx had given me that night at Hades and Lincoln's healing powers were simply not strong enough on their own.

Lincoln was silent and I thought he wasn't going to answer

so I opened my mouth to start argument number two, but he beat me to it.

'I can't do it,' he said. 'I know that you want me to step up to this, but I can't. I won't.'

My heart tightened at his words. They were enticingly dangerous. But we were Grigori and that meant other things came before us.

'Okay,' I said, the word sticking in my throat. 'Under one condition.'

'Which is?'

'You'll never put me before an innocent life. If it comes down to a choice, and Phoenix is a danger to others, you need to promise me you won't hesitate.' I looked at him, forcing his gaze up until it met mine. 'Promise.'

His shoulders dropped, deflated as he said, 'Jesus, Vi. Jesus.' He sighed. 'Okay.'

After arguing for over an hour, I managed to talk Lincoln into letting me call Steph on the disposable phone. I didn't mention I'd already given it a go earlier.

'One minute and I'll be timing you,' he said.

The argument and his bossiness on the subject had put me into a stubborn mood, so I turned my back to him as I dialled. Steph, Salvatore, Dapper and Onyx were still on their crusade and time between talks for Steph and me had been the longest we'd ever gone since first becoming friends. I waited nervously and almost jumped for joy when I heard her answer the phone with a cautious, 'Hello?'

'Steph!' I yelled in my excitement. 'It's me!'

'Vi!' she squealed back. 'Oh my God, we've been so worried. Griffin filled us in. Where are you?'

'I can't . . . I have to be really careful what I say in case your phones are being tapped. And I only have a minute to talk before Lincoln hangs up,' I said.

'Sounds like trouble in paradise.'

'How are you guys?' I asked, quickly, wanting to know as much as possible.

Steph didn't delay. 'Okay. Salvatore has been amazing. He barely sleeps, patrolling all the time. But he saved us big-time in Cairo when a couple of exiles spotted Onyx and recognised him. Apparently he's pissed off people and exiles all around the world.'

'No big surprise,' I said. 'Is he behaving otherwise?'

'Amazingly, yes. He's even used a few old connections to get us around and it looks like he found a source for the twelfth earthly ingredient for the Qeres. We go looking for it tomorrow and if we find it, we'll be heading in your direction by tomorrow night.'

'That's great!'

'I heard about your testing and for the record, Josephine is an evil bitch. When I get there I plan on having ugly words with her and her damn Assembly!'

I swallowed hard at the memory. 'It's okay. I don't care,' I said, then added quickly, 'How's Dapper?'

'Same as always. He's led us to all of the other ingredients. He is seriously connected and most people are scared shitless of him as well. They drop to their knees and all but hand over their first-born to him. I'm not sure if they worship him or fear him.'

Hmm.

'Oh,' Steph continued, 'Griffin said if I spoke to you to tell you your dad's doing fine. He's up and talking and confirmed that Evelyn had been waiting for Lilith to make her move.'

Lincoln tapped my shoulder, pointing to his watch.

'Damn. Steph, I have to go. Did Dapper have any success figuring out what the thirteenth ingredient is?' I asked quickly, even as I felt a tug on my memory. I couldn't fight the feeling that I was missing something here.

'Yeah, but I don't know anything about it. He's being very secretive, says he needs to talk to some elder first, but that it's definitely from the angel realm. Something to do with life-force, I don't know.'

Lincoln tapped me again.

'I miss you,' I told her, glum.

'I miss you too, babe. I'll see you soon so please don't get dead before I get there. I bought you a T-shirt with a bling pyramid on it!'

Still feeling sad from my conversation with Steph, I moved back out to the rocking chair, selecting my one and leaving Lincoln's free.

Lincoln disappeared for a while and returned with two instant coffees.

Not perfect, but caffeine is caffeine.

We sipped in comfortable silence. If felt normal and I pretended for a while that we were just ordinary people, even boyfriend and girlfriend, away for the weekend, enjoying each other's company. Lincoln must have been thinking the same thing, or just sensed my feeling, because he jumped into small talk and we bantered back and forth while munching on a packet of Oreos.

Finally, our make-believe chat ended when Lincoln asked, 'Have you had any thoughts about next year? Do you think you'll try for university?'

I lifted a shoulder.

'I know you had to give up your place on the Fenton course. I'm sorry, Vi. I've been meaning to tell you that I know a few people who could probably help get you a place there next year if you'd like.'

There was a time when I definitely would *like*. But I shook my head. 'Thanks, but don't bother. Even if we make it through this, there'll always be something.'

'That's not true. You don't have to give up on your dreams just because you're Grigori.'

We were silent again for a while. Lincoln checked his watch and I could tell he was thinking he should patrol again soon. I knew I should tell him what I'd done, about my crazy, impulsive act out in the woods earlier, but when I opened my mouth, something completely different came out.

'I don't love him,' I blurted.

I heard Lincoln's breath catch. But then he relaxed back into his chair. 'Did you?'

I swallowed, nervous now. Why had I opened this floodgate? 'I . . . I cared about him. I think I saw a side to him that no one else got to see and I don't think it was all fake. There is good in him and even for all the bad I know he cared.'

'Not exactly an answer, Vi.'

'No. I know.' I sighed. 'I was so mad at you and I *wanted* to stop loving you, I *wanted* to love him. I was confused and angry and about to jump off a really big cliff. You had just told me that we could never be together and . . .'

'And?'

'And he made it better.' The confession stung. 'He made the pain go away, replaced it with other things. I think I became kind of addicted to him, to his abilities. But,' I looked at Lincoln now, letting out the vulnerability I always tried to keep hidden. He needed to see the truth. 'The answer is no. And I'm sorry for everything that happened. I'm sorry to you and . . . I'm sorry to him, too.'

Lincoln studied my eyes, gazing at me with nothing short of admiration – which I knew I didn't deserve – and possibly more.

'Violet Eden, you have nothing to apologise for,' he said.

I felt his presence only a split second before he spoke.

'Speak for yourself,' Phoenix said, stepping out from the nearby tree-line, hands in his pockets. 'I'd rather like to have that apology.'

chapter twenty-seven

'For the son of man has come to save that which was lost.'

Matthew 18:11

everything happened so fast.

Lincoln leaped up from his rocking chair and over the railing of the verandah, landing on the lawn in front of Phoenix, who moved into striking zone with the speed of wind.

Phoenix grinned wickedly at Lincoln, his hatred on show. 'No dagger.' He made a tsk'ing sound. 'Sloppy.'

I was on the lawn by then, too, and stepped up beside Lincoln. 'But I have mine,' I said.

Phoenix didn't take his attention off Lincoln, the two of them circling each other.

'I'd be lying if I said I haven't dreamed of this moment – taking you down once and for all,' Phoenix said, tauntingly, moving in short gusts of wind.

Lincoln tracked him, keeping up. 'Funny. You don't seem to make it into my dreams.'

'That's because you're busy dreaming of things I've already had,' Phoenix said, gesturing to me but not taking his eyes off Lincoln.

'Stop it,' I warned him.

Phoenix smiled at Lincoln. 'Just wake up, did we?'

'Violet, go inside,' Lincoln ordered.

He did not *just say that.*

'You heard him, lover. He obviously has a lot of pent-up frustration.' Phoenix's smile broadened. 'Understandably. Best to let him try. You should run along while he gets a beating for his efforts.'

My eyes narrowed in on the two of them but as I did, I pushed out my senses, scanning the area as far as I could. There were no other exiles nearby.

Phoenix darted me a look before returning to Lincoln. The hate fuming between the two of them was dense in the night air.

Shit.

'I invited him!' I blurted, regretting that I hadn't made it a priority to tell Lincoln what I'd done earlier. The truth was I'd expected Phoenix to show up either instantly or not at all. When he hadn't, I'd started to wonder if I'd been wrong about his intentions.

At this revelation, Lincoln looked at me with disbelief. 'You *brought* him here?'

I bit my lip.

Using Lincoln's distraction, Phoenix launched himself onto his nemesis, bringing him down to the ground, ramming a fist into his jaw. I was fairly certain I heard something crack. Lincoln responded in kind – the impact of his own closed fist across Phoenix's jaw stunning him enough for Lincoln to throw Phoenix off him and into the air.

Phoenix landed on his feet, feline-like.

But before Phoenix made it back into the striking zone and Lincoln was up and ready again, I leaped between them.

'Move,' Lincoln snapped at me.

I ignored him and faced Phoenix. I knew who the real threat was.

'Lover,' Phoenix said, dabbing a finger at the cut on his lip, showing how hard Lincoln's hit had been; drawing blood from an exile was never easy. 'Be patient. This will only take a moment and then you and I will have all the time in the world for . . .' he glanced at Lincoln, 'other things.'

'Shut up, Phoenix. God, I'm so sick of hearing you call me "lover". You asked me for help. I know you did. I let down my shields, I showed you the way to us because, as crazy as it is, I think you might actually want to stop Lilith from hurting those kids.'

Phoenix's face twisted and I couldn't help but feel a little satisfaction to see my scolding was having an effect.

'Now,' I continued, hands on hips, 'you can come inside and talk with us. You will tell us what we need to know and how we can stop her, or you can go. But you,' I glanced over my shoulder at Lincoln, fury still raging in his eyes, 'and your male egos will *not* be fighting tonight because, let me break it down.' I looked between them again. 'If either one of you lands another punch then this conversation is over and those kids are going to die.'

Silence.

'I'm going to put the kettle on,' I said, taking their silence for agreement. For now.

We sat around the kitchen table, coffees in hand, tensions running high. Suddenly the cabin seemed very small.

Lincoln and Phoenix sat opposite one another, their eyes burning with malice.

It was strange seeing them together. It caused an awkward sensation in my gut.

Phoenix looked incredible as per usual. He was dressed in black slim-line pants and a fitted black shirt. His opaline hair rippled with dazzling silver highlights.

He's just a creature of lust, I reminded myself.

I couldn't deny that being in close proximity to him affected me. It wasn't in the same way as with Lincoln; it was raw and laden with guilt. Because I knew it wasn't real. What Phoenix did to me was a controlled manipulation of my own emotions, but I longed for it anyway. I'd just explained to Lincoln earlier that I'd been addicted to Phoenix's abilities and now, looking at him, I realised it was more than that. I was drawn to him on a deeper level, because of our connection and what we'd once shared.

'You helped us in the subway. You led us to the other child,' I said. Statement not question. When Phoenix didn't respond, I went on. 'You've been trying to get to me in my dreams – not to hurt me, but to help us.'

Phoenix was statue-still.

Finally, he shifted. 'You kept pushing me out and once you were behind the Academy shields it was impossible.'

I remembered the force field that divided us last time.

'Have you always known I could sense your emotions more than others?' I asked, noting that Lincoln was stewing silently. But I needed to know. What I felt from Phoenix was more than just his emotional run-off and unlike anything I felt from anyone else.

Phoenix flinched. He knew what I was asking. 'Ever since I healed you the connection has been there.'

I explained to Lincoln, 'I think I can sense some of Phoenix's emotions even when he doesn't intend me to.'

'Sensational,' Lincoln said, flat.

'It's not like that,' I said, blushing. 'But I think that it helps me understand him at times.'

'And she does seem to know every single inch of me,' Phoenix taunted.

'What are you doing here, Phoenix?' Lincoln ground out each word.

Phoenix's facade broke, just for a few seconds, but I saw it. The darkness around his eyes, the desperation that I'd sensed in the tunnels. I felt his weariness.

He put his hands palm down on the table, considering his words carefully. 'I don't have a solution. I can only confirm that it is likely we will all die very soon. Nothing I can do will change that but unlike some . . .' His eyes bored into mine, 'I'm not ready to confess all my sins and be absolved.'

'As if absolution would ever be yours!' Lincoln snarled.

'True,' Phoenix agreed.

I gnawed on the inside of my cheek. This wasn't going well.

'Then what are you here for?' Lincoln pushed. I could see one of his hands fisted on his thigh. I could only imagine how angry he was going to be with me after we got Phoenix out of here.

Phoenix shrugged and leaned back in his seat. But his apparent openness wasn't fooling me. He was highly strung. 'I don't kill kids. I'm here to help you save them. And make the agreement that we either destroy the Scripture or return it to you afterwards, whichever opportunity presents itself first.'

'You mean the Scripture Lilith wouldn't even *have* if it wasn't for you!' Lincoln raged. 'This reeks of a set-up and you know it.'

Phoenix tilted his head. 'Think what you will but I never told her about the Scripture. Not my fault every damn exile out there knew about it. I gave you lot a chance to get it back and you forced me into a corner.' His voice had lifted in a rare display of anger. 'Lilith found out about the Scripture within hours of her arrival. I hid it for as long as I could, but I couldn't very well withhold it forever!'

Lincoln half laughed and not in a nice way. 'Of course not! That would've required you actually doing the right thing.'

'Why do you work with every "damn" exile, as you say, when you clearly hate them all so much?' I asked, trying to understand.

Phoenix's jaw locked. 'We are what we are,' was all he said.

At that, my heart broke a little.

He pointed a menacing finger. 'Oh, spare me.'

I tried to pull in my emotions. 'What are you suggesting?' I asked.

'Two things,' Phoenix said. 'One, Lilith wants you as her guests tomorrow night. That's when I'm supposed to find you and bring you to her. She has Evelyn . . .' His eyes softened on me for a moment and Lincoln stirred beside me.

'She's still alive.' Phoenix swallowed and took a deep breath. 'Lilith is offering you the chance to surrender. She has condemned you both to death but in return for your submission she has offered to reward you with the lives of as many of the children as you can manage to save.'

My mouth went dry. A million thoughts were running through my mind and yet, somehow, it was completely and utterly blank at the same time.

'And how is it decided how many children we can save?' I asked.

That's me, Miss Practicality.

Phoenix's mask fell away to reveal the true pale horror of what was to come. 'Like me, Lilith hates the Cherubim.' His smile was wry. 'It's the only hobby we ever shared. But whereas I just like to destroy them, she fancies herself as being more creative, using modern-day representations of their rank – of which the Cherubim despise – to disrespect and send her twisted messages to them.'

I had to know, once and for all, why he hated the Cherubim so much, so I asked.

'They kept her locked out of Eden after she fled. They drew their flaming swords and guarded the place so she could never return. Angels might be many things, but forgiving is not often one of them. I actually suspect Lilith loved Adam – as much as she was capable of loving anyone. I never understood how love and hate could be so strong all at once. Not until recently.'

His words stung.

He kept going. 'When the Seraphim decided I wasn't angel enough and branded me one of the abyss – to have no home, no purpose – they took everything I was and stepped on it like I was no more than a piece of dirt beneath their mighty feet. The Cherubim were there, both light and dark. They cast me from the realm and locked me out with the seal of their given power. They hated me out of instinct because of Lilith.'

I could feel the pain in his words. He'd told me other versions of the same casting out, how he'd been rejected over and over in his life. The first rejection coming from Lilith herself.

Had I really been so awful? Had I made him come full circle, back to the very thing that first broke a piece of him?

'I'm sorry, Phoenix,' I said, and I meant it. My apology was many-fold and I couldn't even begin to voice it, so I just let it flow from me to him.

He gripped the table, bracing as he experienced the influx of my remorse. He covered it quickly, straightening, and I turned off the emo-tap.

'Back to the part where we die,' Lincoln said, unimpressed by what had just passed. 'How is it decided?'

I thought about what he'd said. The modern-day image of a cherub was a creature of love, tiny fat, winged babies that flew around shooting their arrows of passion.

'Arrows,' I whispered.

Phoenix nodded, his eyes closing briefly. 'Violet will be strung up and shot with finger-length arrows. A child will be freed for each arrow she can survive, until she can take no more.'

'You mean until I'm dead?'

'Until you're dead.'

I ignored my subconscious, the ultimate realisation that death was now beating at my door. Relentless, unwavering, certain death. I looked at Phoenix, unable to face Lincoln beside me.

'And what about Lincoln?' I heard myself ask.

'He is required to accompany you. He'll be made to watch.'

'But he doesn't *have* to go?' I asked.

Phoenix shook his head. 'He has to go. She wants him to see. Without him, the deal is off.'

'Will he live?'

Phoenix looked down. I closed my eyes.

They'd execute Lincoln after he'd watched me die.

Lincoln's laugh was bitter. 'So Lilith expects me to stand by and watch while Violet is tortured?' He shook his head and leaned forward. 'That's never going to happen. Tell your psycho-bitch of a mother to sit on the pointy end of her deal and twist.'

Phoenix didn't say anything in Lilith's defence, he simply continued grimly, like a doctor delivering news no patient wants to hear, but must. 'I can help, but ... There's only so much I can do. There's no way to stop her, but I can give you my word that I'll get your mother out afterwards, Violet. She'll keep her alive after ...'

'I'm dead.'

'There's something else.' He glanced at Lincoln now, as if trying to tell him something. But Lincoln was seething so much I didn't think he could see anything but red. 'She knows we're connected, she sensed the bond on me and Olivier was only too happy to confirm it. She'll order me to reinstate your wounds if you are too strong. She'll stand by her word to release the children but she won't want to lose too many.'

He looked between Lincoln and me and sighed, coming to some sort of decision. 'You'd ...' He swallowed as if it was hard for him to say. 'You'd be best off if you considered every way to make yourself as powerful as possible before then.'

Lincoln threw his mug at the wall, the pieces shattering, coffee staining the white paint as it dribbled down.

'This is sick. Vi, you can't listen to this,' Lincoln said, but he knew as well as me, it might be sick but it was also the truth.

'And if you refuse to hurt me?' I asked Phoenix.

'I'm of her blood. She can force me.' He looked down. 'She knows that I . . . Lincoln isn't the only one who will be expected to watch.'

I remembered how Irin seemed to have so much control over his Nephlim children. I wondered if Lilith had a similar kind of control over him.

Lincoln stood, scraping his chair roughly as he did. 'This is priceless! So, you're telling us to surrender to Lilith based on *your* assurance that you will free her mother *after* we are both dead *and* trust that you will keep Violet alive for as long as possible so her death can be slower and more painful! You're insane. We may as well take our chances and kill you!'

I heard Lincoln's words, the desperate plea that this was not happening. But we both knew he'd left out the one thing that made the difference. That in return for all of that, we would have a chance at saving those innocent children.

Phoenix simply shrugged. 'We all know complications arise from that solution, too.'

I looked at Lincoln, pain rippling through his features. 'He's right,' I said, quietly. 'And you know it.'

Death is racing towards me.

Lincoln didn't respond. Instead he stared at Phoenix while Phoenix stared back. Their hate for one another seemed to morph into a mutual resentment, a shared desperation and even heartache. Finally, Lincoln dropped back into his seat.

'Is there any other way?' he asked.

'If there was, I would've found it,' Phoenix replied.

And I believed him.

Before the reality of what we were discussing could hit me, I powered on. 'Where do you stand in all this, Phoenix? What happens – Lincoln and I both die and you go on your merry way with Lilith, letting her kill anything and anyone that crosses her path?'

Lincoln ground his jaw together and slammed a fist on the table. 'Jesus Christ! We are *not* having this conversation. She is *not* going in there to be tortured!'

I flinched, but otherwise ignored the outburst. Phoenix shook his head when he saw I was still waiting for his answer.

'When Lilith finds out what I've done, she'll kill me. I'll do everything I can to take her with me. I swear it. I thought . . .' Remorse filled his eyes. 'I didn't expect this to happen . . . It's not what I wanted.' He ran a hand around his neck and dropped it back on the table. 'I expected collateral damage and told myself it wouldn't matter.' He huffed. 'I even let you believe I'd had your friend killed.'

He was talking about Rudyard and at the mention of him both Lincoln and I straightened.

'I didn't,' Phoenix added.

'But you brought Lilith back,' Lincoln pushed.

Phoenix nodded. 'Yes. But killing kids wasn't ever part of it. Not for me. I'm prepared to give my eternity to put her back in the ground.'

Lincoln glanced at his watch. It had been almost two hours since one of us had patrolled the perimeter.

'I'll do it,' I offered.

He shook his head. 'No.' His eyes shot to Phoenix. 'I can't

be alone with him. I'll go.' He stood up, strapped on his dagger and headed out. I followed him to the verandah.

'Linc?' I said from behind him. He stopped, reached out and pulled me to him, arms wrapping tightly around me.

'Don't ask me to deliver you to her. I can't,' he pleaded.

I didn't respond. And we both knew why. He moved back just as quickly as he'd pulled me to him.

'I'd better get this patrol done. Back soon.'

He took off into the trees.

I sat down on the steps leading to the lawn and stared out over the river. Phoenix approached from behind, sitting beside me.

'I heard what you said. About never loving me.'

'I'm sorry. I didn't know you were listening.'

He shrugged. 'It's not like it was news, anyway. I've felt enough from you to know you could've loved me, though, that you came close, even. Maybe, if I hadn't destroyed everything . . . Maybe, if you'd given me a chance to explain . . .'

'Did you know what would happen after we were together?' I asked, finally deciding I was ready to hear it, ready to know if he had planned it all – sleeping with me and forming the connection that led to Joel and Onyx first attacking me.

'No. And yes. I felt it happening while we were together. I could've stopped but . . . I couldn't at the same time. There's a part of me made by darkness that's inherent in me and fundamental to my existence – I can't deny that. With you, when we first met, I tried.' He shook his head, lost in memories. 'So. Damn. Hard. I wanted to be everything you deserved and I wanted it for me too, but, when we were together that night, I was so drunk on you . . . I knew the right thing to do but I let the darkness take over. It's not an excuse but you have to understand–'

I cut him off. 'It's your nature.'

He gave a sad nod of agreement. 'I tried to explain the next day, but I saw the adoration in your eyes when you healed Lincoln and the temptation to use the new power I had over you was too much to resist. I thought if I could just sway you a little, encourage animosity towards him and devotion to me . . . But by the time it all came out and I'd healed you . . . I'd already lost you.'

I shook my head, hearing it all like this, I believed him. 'You're right, you know. I think I could've loved you, but even with everything that happened, that wasn't the reason we didn't end up together.'

He looked towards the trees. 'Him,' he said.

'Him,' I agreed.

He smiled ruefully. 'There is always that. I should've known better, of course. About a lot of things. Now it's too late to make amends.'

'I thought you didn't apologise?'

His smile turned a little playful and I was reminded of the Phoenix I had first become friends with.

'I don't. But if I can make it right . . . I will. This whole thing, it's my fault. I did this, not you.'

I leaned forwards onto my elbows. 'Because of you I have my mother back. Because of you, that volcano might not have erupted, but without you, all those people on Santorini would have died. Because of you . . . I'm alive.' I gave a cynical laugh. 'Maybe not for long, but still, I'm alive.'

He looked away and I saw his hand go to his face. I wondered if he was wiping away a tear.

'It would be easier if I didn't love you. Saying things like that, after all I have done,' he half laughed. 'You ruin me. Absolutely and totally obliterate me.'

We were silent for a while, both lost in our own thoughts.

'Did you really not mean for Rudyard to die?' I asked after a time.

He held my gaze and opened the channels to his emotions, showing me his regret. He'd thought he had been so clever, controlling the exiles and getting what he wanted. Death was not what had motivated Phoenix, despite all his threats.

'It was still my choices that led to it. Still my fault,' he admitted.

I couldn't deny that.

Lincoln chose that moment to reappear. His face was expressionless, his shields up, blocking me from any insight. I understood.

'Perimeter is clear.' He looked at Phoenix – his green eyes like steel, his voice dripping with contempt. 'Violet and I need to talk. You can come back to collect us tomorrow night. If we're here, we're here. If not, you have your answer and good luck ever finding her again.'

Phoenix nodded and we both stood, brushing off the dust we'd attracted as we did.

'Fair enough,' Phoenix said. Then, after a pause, 'I don't suppose you could offer me a ride into the nearest town? I'd prefer not to use my powers more than necessary here – I tend to work as a homing beacon for Lilith.'

That was the first I'd heard of such an ability. By the dubious look on Lincoln's face and his crossed arms it was the first he'd heard of it too, but again, something seemed to pass between them and I saw Lincoln nodding, looking to me.

'Will you be all right?'

I raised my eyebrows. The two of *them*, enclosed in a vehicle for the next twenty minutes, and he was asking if *I* would be okay.

'Will *you*?' I asked.

He nodded solemnly, going inside to get the keys.

When I turned a sceptical gaze back to Phoenix, his hair sparkled in the late afternoon sunlight. With the backdrop of the river he looked striking and my breath caught. Phoenix didn't offer any further explanation and instead cast his eyes out over the water. Surprising us both, the moment overcame me and I closed the distance between us. He actually braced in readiness for a strike, but nothing could have hit him harder than when I put my arms around him.

Tentatively, his arms returned the gesture, exhaling as though the heaviest of weights had been slowly lifted from him and pulled me close.

For once, Phoenix didn't try to play with my emotions. Instead, he was eerily still, emotionally and physically.

'We've all made mistakes,' I said quietly. 'Terrible mistakes. We've all played a part in where we are now – you don't carry this alone. You won't finish it alone, either. I promise.' I didn't tell him about the potion Steph and Dapper were working on, but I would make sure he got it when I was gone. I just held him tight and he held me back, his cheek resting on the top of my head.

'I've never felt . . . The way you get to me.' He was breathing deeply. 'I know what I've done but, I swear to you . . . If there is a way to save you, I'll find it.'

'I know.' And I did.

He leaned back, his hand cupping my face tenderly. 'Next time I see you, you'll be lost to me forever.'

I stared back into his sad eyes, caught in his spell.

What does that mean?

Lincoln cleared his throat from the doorway. 'For Christ's sake, when you're done groping her, can we go?'

Phoenix's chest trembled as he snickered. I found myself mimicking the silent response. After all, a couple of hours ago such a comment from Lincoln would have ensured physical combat between the two of them.

When Phoenix pulled back from me, his eyes were different. Somehow they seemed renewed, reflecting something of the old him that made me smile. I wondered fleetingly, if in another time, another place, the three of us could have been friends.

Probably not.

chapter twenty-eight

'You will not fear the terror of night, nor the arrow
that flies by day.''

Psalm 91:5

the water pelted down, hot and fast and I relished the extreme
sensation.

My life was officially on the clock.

I would never see Dad again. I would never hang out with
Steph or joke around with Spence. I'd never paint another
canvas.

And yet, despite all of this, like Phoenix, a weight had been
lifted from my shoulders. Did that make me terrible?

Perhaps.

Nonetheless I was relieved to know I'd make a difference
– for the better. Tomorrow night I would save innocent lives,
children who would one day grow up to become warriors.
This would be my death. It had to count as one of the better
ways to die.

Scared?

I was petrified. But it wouldn't help to fall apart – there
simply was not enough time.

I thought back to when Uri had first spoken to me, when I

had embraced – he'd said 'Even the greatest bringers of justice will only find salvation in surrender.'

This must be what he'd meant.

A shame he hadn't seen fit to enlighten me with that one crucial detail: that surrender would lead to a gruesome death.

I felt the first prickle of a tear. I held it back. But the thoughts kept coming.

Everything we've done – all for nothing.

Lilith would survive us, and Phoenix would be left to destroy her, something that would not be done easily.

But what other option is there?

Not one of us could stand by and let so many children be slaughtered. Lilith had played a masterful hand.

I braced my hand against the shower wall. I half expected to break down, but I didn't. Instead, breathing deeply, I withdrew to that place I had learned to go a long time ago, the one that forced me to stand strong, that had helped me survive the attack when I was younger. I hadn't let that teacher break me, nor would I let Lilith.

I don't run. I don't quit. I don't believe in fairy-tale endings.

I will face Lilith.

The time for falling apart was over. The time for contemplating Heaven and Hell and which one favoured me was over, too. I wasn't going to be one of those people who dropped to their knees in the final stretch when it had never before seemed a logical idea.

Standing there under the shower, my thoughts travelled to Lincoln and I broke into a fit of bitter giggles. After all that we had done to stay away from each other. Fighting the very core of our souls that demanded closeness which we only denied, denied, denied. It seemed crazy now that we'd actually considered it a possibility to live our long lives side by side in such a ridiculous pattern of partnership but not as the soulmates we really were.

Who were we kidding?

Now, ironically – life's last bitch-slap – we were going to die anyway.

Sure, we could call in Griffin and the cavalry, but at what cost? Lilith would no doubt kill the children and our lives were not worth that risk. We were Grigori. We were warriors. It was our duty.

But then, something else clicked in my mind. The rambling thoughts and the tears stopped and I blinked. I'd missed something.

Phoenix's words – *You'd be best off if you considered every way to make yourself as powerful as possible before then* – and the difficulty with which he'd delivered them.

'Oh my God,' I whispered. 'We're *both* going to die.'

The air left my lungs and I grasped hold of the taps to stop myself from falling to my knees.

There is absolutely no reason for us not to be together.

In fact, for the first time, everything was in favour of Lincoln's soul being bonded to mine. The power it would give us, the ability to share our strengths and healing. It would give me more time, which equalled more children. And afterwards ... Lincoln wouldn't have to consciously endure the torment of his own execution.

All the risks of causing each other pain and hurt, all the dread of awful consequences vanished.

We were free.

Tomorrow, we will die.

But not tonight.

I smiled as bittersweet relief filled my soul.

Then I shaved my legs.

I'd been in the shower for so long that by the time I emerged, Lincoln was back from dropping off Phoenix and I could hear him moving around downstairs. I threw on a pair of jeans and a T-shirt, wishing I had something more . . . But I didn't.

I took my time, excited to find my hairdryer along with my toiletries bag. Zoe had obviously packed for me.

It was dark outside when I finally emerged from my bedroom. I headed down the hall and gasped when I reached the top of the stairs. The lights were off and dozens of tea-light candles lined the path down. Soft music that I didn't recognise drifted up from below. It was an old instrumental piece, something Lincoln must have found in the cabin. Known or not, it would remain my favourite song. For eternity.

I padded slowly down the stairs, my heart pounding, but in an all-good, exhilarating way. In the living room the fire crackled, giving off a warm glow.

My hand went to my mouth.

White lilies.

Everywhere.

Frozen in place, I looked towards the kitchen. Lincoln was facing the stove, stirring something. He must have had a shower while I was drying my hair, because his was still damp, and messed about. He was wearing jeans and a white T-shirt.

Barefoot. His arm flexed as he concentrated on whatever he was cooking, but he knew I was there.

'Dinner's almost ready,' he said, without turning around.

Whatever had happened to Lincoln between the last time I saw him and now, we'd clearly come to the same realisation.

I chewed on a smile.

'So,' I said, casually. 'We're really going to die, huh?'

At that, Lincoln put down a wooden spoon and turned. He paused, looking me up and down, his eyes travelling over me in a way he rarely allowed himself. My pulse raced.

His gaze settled on mine and I noticed the bruise on his cheek. He took a step towards me, and any coherent thoughts I had, scrambled.

'Either way,' he said, his voice thick as syrup, 'Don't you think we've waited long enough?'

I hitched a shoulder. 'The foreplay was dragging on,' I said, my smile now cheeky.

He watched, biting down on his lower lip.

'And if we only have tonight, I know exactly how I want to spend it,' he said. Simple. Sure.

Hyperventilate later!

I looked right back at him. 'Me too.'

He nodded once and spun back in the direction of the kitchen. 'Sit down,' he said. 'I'll finish making dinner.'

Even with his back to me I could see his body heaving with heavy breaths that mirrored mine.

'Linc?' I whispered.

'Hmm,' he said, one hand gripping the kitchen bench as if trying to fasten himself there.

My heart thumped. I felt every nerve in my body come to life as my soul awoke with the sense of possibility.

Breathe.

'I'm not hungry.'

I didn't even make my first step towards him before he was there, crushing me into his body, taking my face in his hands. He paused only to look at me, to make sure I knew he was seeing me.

'I love you,' he said, and then his lips were on mine.

My hands were in his hair, then down the strong lines of his back. His arms lifted me into the air as my legs wrapped around his waist. I cried out with the sheer relief of knowing I could finally let go, of knowing I could finally allow my soul its freedom.

He carried me upstairs, stopping along the way to back me into the wall, to press against me and kiss me in that way of his that ignited every kind of fire conceivable. Slowly, meaningfully, his lips moved with single-minded purpose, telling me with every deliberate touch that he loved me. It reminded me of the first kiss we'd shared and I knew now, that was the moment my soul discovered his and decided they belonged together.

The burden of our choice had finally been lifted. As a result, Lincoln showed me exactly what it was like to be loved by him without restraint. He was strong and unwavering, but he didn't rush, taking his time with my clothes and letting me linger as I removed his. I needed the staring time, damn it. He was utterly beautiful.

He laid me on the bed and held himself over me, his eyes burning into mine with love and want and need and I knew the same emotions were reflected in my own. It was dreamlike. The world had taken on a new perspective and I could feel and see everything with more intensity.

He pushed my arms up over my head and pressed his palms into mine, each finger connecting with one of my own. He took his time and somehow it was the most sensual experience of my life – feeling his fingers pushing down on mine until they curled around my hand and then, undoing me, he started all over again – his eyes on me the entire time.

My soul pushed forwards, hungry, willing and demanding what it had desired for so long. What it *needed*. For the first time I let go.

I'd imagined this moment over and over, in my dreams. I thought I knew how it would feel, but it wasn't what I had imagined. This moment transcended everything, because when we joined, my soul – so much more intense than my angelic power – surged up and found his, entwining with it, drowning me in his essence and everything that felt like the sun.

And then came the power.

Like a whirlwind, our abilities opened up to each other and I felt the final bond form, creating a gateway from one to another. I felt the rush of his immense strength, and was immediately in tune with his shadow-finding abilities. If I wanted to draw on his powers, I could. It was all there for the taking, just as mine were to him.

Lincoln cried out. Not with pain, but overload.

His hand grabbed the side of my face, pushing my hair back, his eyes blazing green.

'You're incredible. I can feel your power and it's more than anything I . . . Violet,' he swallowed, watching me in awe. 'It's like . . . It's like you're as powerful as an angel.'

The words were momentous. But even so, I was restless. His strength was coursing through me, daring to be tested. I smiled and with barely a thought, flipped him over so fast I surprised us both.

He approved.

Then he pulled me down to him, closer and closer until it was impossible to tell where one of us began and the other one ended. And I didn't want to. For once in my life I was exactly *where* I was supposed to be, *who* I was supposed to be and *with whom* I was supposed to be.

I nestled into the crook of his neck, breathing in everything that was him and found the ability to talk for the first time since he'd pressed his lips to mine.

'I love you, too.'

He planted kisses on the top of my head. I was in heaven.

Me. Violet Eden. Grigori. Child of man. Child of warrior. Child of angel. Above all else – I was his.

And he was mine.

chapter twenty-nine

'I love thee to the depth and breadth and height

My soul can reach . . .'

Elizabeth Barrett Browning

I lay on my side, a huge bowl of strawberries and a ripped-open packet of pancakes in front of me and a still-shirtless Lincoln wrapped around me. I wasn't sure if what I felt was his power, our souls, or just . . . the afterglow of everything we'd just done.

I popped a strawberry in my mouth then grabbed another, holding it up to Lincoln. His lips closed around my fingers and I felt heat rush through me again. We'd been doing this for a while. In fact, I was full. Not that I was about to stop.

'Is it clichéd to say we were crazy to have waited this long?' I asked.

'Yes,' he replied and I back-elbowed him, but he just used the movement to pull me closer. 'Though I'm starting to think you're right,' he added quietly.

I smiled. He kissed my shoulder.

'How's this for clichéd: I love you with everything I am,' he whispered.

I snuggled into his arms. 'I love you, too. So much that I'm not even going to ask how much practice it took you to get so very good at . . .'

He chuckled into my shoulder and I shivered, considering whether I had enough energy to suggest a rematch.

'No, we are not having that conversation. Nothing I have ever done with any other girl would ever compare to what we are to one another, Vi. And anyway, there's a big difference between sex and–'

I put my hands over my ears. 'La, la, la!'

His eyes lit up as he rolled me onto my back. 'What?'

I lowered one hand. 'Please don't say what you were about to, it sounds so . . .' I shivered. Daytime soapie, I finished in my head.

He chuckled again. 'Well, you know what I meant and anyway, there are other things I'd much rather be saying to you right now.'

I wiggled around in his arms to face him, my fingers grazing his cheek. 'Would it have anything to do with the bruise that was here earlier?' It must have healed at some point, probably when our powers joined. But I hadn't forgotten.

'I'd rather not talk about that either,' he said, sounding guarded for the first time that evening. I felt it too, through our bond, his contempt towards Phoenix but also something else, some kind of clarity I couldn't understand.

Is he blocking me?

'How bad was it?' I asked. It didn't take a genius to know he and Phoenix had fought.

He shrugged, refocusing his attention on his hand travelling up and down my arm. I shivered with goosebumps.

'It was better to get it over and done with. And on this one occasion, it was probably justified.'

Well, that can only mean one thing.

I bit my lip. Phoenix had known what he was leaving Lincoln and me to tonight.

'Was he okay?' I asked.

'Vi,' he sighed. 'Phoenix and I will never get along. And if I didn't have you in my arms right now, I wouldn't be able to say this but . . . his love for you is real. I think his desire to be the man he ought to be is what's driving him now. And I think you're the person that gave him that desire to begin with. It doesn't excuse what he's done. He should be held accountable, but, I do *get* some of the things.'

I did, too. 'But you guys still had to hit it out?'

'Just a little venting.'

'Feel better?'

His eyes travelled down my body and he grinned. 'Considerably.'

I rolled my eyes, even if my smile did betray me. 'So, if not that, what did you want to say then?' I asked, getting back to our previous conversation.

He took a moment, his fingers playing with loose strands of my hair. 'I want you to know: you're it, everything I want. I know you think I want to be this warrior, and yeah, it's important on one level, but what you and I have – what we are . . .' He shook his head slowly, holding my gaze. 'Nothing else comes close.' He kissed me, and the last part of me that hadn't *completely* liquefied, melted. When he pulled back, his fingers brushed over my lips. 'No matter what happens tomorrow – no matter *what* – tonight was exactly what I wanted and for all the right reasons. For you. Because I love you.' His gaze grew intense as he stared into my eyes. 'Promise me, Vi. Promise me you will always remember that.'

'I promise,' I vowed, my voice hitching on something – the way he was looking at me.

He smiled, and dropped back onto his pillow stretching out. 'It's amazing. Like my whole existence, my body, my soul, everything now finally *gets* it. We're together and I'm finally alive. I can feel you, reach you, know you in ways I never imagined possible.' He demonstrated this by opening our connection and as easily as spreading butter on toast moved his powers through me, drawing us together.

'Scary?' he asked, watching my reaction.

I moved even closer, hating that I was mere centimetres away. 'No way. It's perfect. Beautiful.'

I kissed a line along his jaw and his arms encircled me again.

'If I ask you to do something for me tomorrow, would you do it?'

'What?' I asked.

'Trust Phoenix. I can't tell you exactly how I know – I just do.'

'Did you two discuss anything else I should know about?' I asked, studying his eyes. He was holding something back.

He put a finger under my chin and gently tilted it up to him. 'Vi, promise me.'

He poured all of his heart into the request. Whatever this was, it was seriously important to him and I just couldn't bring myself to deny him anything.

'You do realise that's the second promise you've asked for in a very short space of time?'

He smiled. 'I do. But after this, I can *promise you* there will be no more talking.'

'I promise.'

When we finally dragged ourselves out of bed, it was mid-morning – even though we'd only had a few hours' sleep, it seemed pointless to waste any of our time together. I made coffees. Lincoln scrambled eggs and we moved around each other in our familiar pattern that was now so altogether different. And utterly delicious. We were adjusting to our soul bond – the feeling of complete and total connection with each other.

It felt as though we were in a constant dance.

Lincoln was fairly certain he would no longer need his silver wristbands, saying that his senses would now flow from me to him and be stronger than anything he'd experienced before. It was heartbreaking to know we'd never get to spend time testing the theories.

We ate our breakfast outside in our rocking chairs with blankets over our knees.

'We should probably call Griffin. Steph and the others should be in the country – or at least on their way by now,' I said, absent-mindedly running through my mental check-list, while my eyes roamed over Lincoln – a different check-list.

He smiled, and not because of what I'd said. I blushed and poked my tongue out at him, which only made him chuckle.

It's a weird thing – knowing the end is near. You think it will be all panic stations, but . . . There's relief. And a certain quiet. You can finally be yourself.

'Seriously,' I said.

He nodded. 'Okay. Yes, we should call Griffin. But there's no point doing that yet. We'll call an hour before we leave.'

At first I didn't understand, then it dawned on me. 'You think he'll try to stop us?'

Lincoln reached over and tucked a wayward strand of hair behind my ear, his hand lingering. 'Either way – it's too cruel to put him in the position to choose. If he lets us go, he'll feel like he's sending us to our deaths. If he forces us to stay, he'll blame himself for whatever happens to those kids.'

He was right. Griffin was the master of self-blame. I decided it was Lincoln's call to make – he knew Griffin the best.

'I can feel your heart beating,' he said, changing the subject. 'I was always aware of you but it was more like instinct, or when you were hurt, a kind of transference. But this . . . Have you always been able to feel my heart?' he asked, awe in his eyes.

I nodded. 'Since Onyx first hurt you. I felt it the morning I embraced. I was listening to your heart when I leaped from the cliff.'

He looked down. 'Do you regret it?'

'Not at all.' Despite what we knew was ahead, I had never been more sure of my answer.

I talked him through my abilities, pausing to take time on a few things – my angelic Sight, for one. I warned him against using it. He totally agreed and even doubted that he'd easily tap into that power anyway. He certainly couldn't feel it as easily as he could the senses. I told him more about the dreams I'd had with Uri and Nox, and with my angel maker. I fidgeted as I explained how they could come to me and cross the realms.

He saw that I was nervous, finally explaining everything.

He put a finger over my lips. 'Slow down. Most of this I already knew. Griffin and I suspected you'd been dream-walking from what you'd told us. We knew you just needed time to work it all out yourself. We think you inherited that particular skill from your mother.'

'Oh.' It made sense, Evelyn being a dream-walker herself.

Settling in to the tell-all, I filled him in on my most recent dream, too. 'Uri and Nox offered to accept Lilith back into the angel realm, where they can deal with her immortal spirit, but we'd still need to end her physical form beforehand . . . They said I could cross her over. Maybe someone else can after we're . . .' I couldn't quite finish the sentence. I was damned if I was going to burst my love bubble just yet.

Lincoln's brow furrowed. 'What do you mean, *cross* over?'

I polished off the last off my eggs and gave him my most adoring smile.

'More?' he asked, seeming to enjoy my response.

'Please,' I said. Eggs on toast had never tasted so good. I followed him into the kitchen as he dished out what was left and answered him. 'If we return her, she'll go to the pits of Hell and we risk her finding a way out again. The angels can't take her from the human world. But they said I could bring her over to them and then . . . I'd need an anchor to get back.'

'What kind of anchor?' he asked, and I could almost see the cogs in his mind ticking over.

'A powerful person. They said it needed to be someone who was near my body. Someone who shared a bond with me, either blood or through one of the passions.' Which really, left my options quite broad. The 'passions' pretty much covered any intense emotion – fear, hatred, sorrow and, of course, love. 'You, for example, would be perfect.'

Lincoln swallowed hard and turned away. Of everything I'd said, this seemed to worry him the most. 'What if I . . . I mean, could anyone else work?'

I pondered. 'Maybe Evelyn, or I suppose . . .' I hesitated.

'Phoenix?' Lincoln guessed.

'It's possible,' I admitted.

I ran my hand down his worried face. 'It's not as if we're actually going to be around to make it happen.'

He saw my concern and his expression eased but I could still feel his anxiety through our bond and I didn't know why. He swiped the last piece of toast from my plate. I withheld the growl – he had cooked everything, after all.

'We're not giving up, Vi. We might be going to her willingly, but that doesn't mean an opportunity won't present itself to us. If we see a chance to end her, we take it.'

I nodded. We needed to be smart and consider everything. But still, it was too much to imagine we might actually survive this.

Our food demolished, we gravitated back to the verandah and I found my way onto his lap, where we stayed, wrapped in a blanket, whispering to each other all the things we'd never said before, sharing all the dreams we'd had for the future. Our future. All the things we knew we'd never have.

Eventually, fantasy gave way to reality.

'Everything is about to end, isn't it?' I asked.

Lincoln stroked my hair and ran his hands down my arms before kissing me – just a light kiss on my lips, but one heavy with his love and I soaked it up.

'Not us, Vi. Everything else may end, but not us. What we have . . . We're endless.'

chapter thirty

'Let your plans be dark and as impenetrable as night, and
when you move, fall like a thunderbolt.'

Sun Tzu

By late afternoon, the honeymoon was over and we were
arming up. Phoenix was due soon and we wanted to be ready.
I'd found a pad and pen earlier and while Lincoln patrolled the
perimeter I'd taken the time to write some letters.

Goodbyes.

I stared at the folded pieces of paper, before packing them
away in my bag. One for Dad, one for Steph and one for Evelyn.

It was unfair, having lived my whole life without a mother,
to suddenly have her back, and now, before I'd even given her
a proper chance, to be losing her again. We still didn't know
what would happen to her once Lilith was ended, but I hoped
for both Evelyn and Dad's sake that she wouldn't be taken
from the world, too.

I wrote a group letter to Griffin, Spence, Zoe, Sal and
Dapper. I wasn't sure at first whether to include Onyx in the
gang – him having made no secret that his loyalties should
always be in question – but I quickly realised that whether
he admitted it or not, he belonged there. I told him as much

in the letter. I didn't write to each of them individually as many of the same thoughts applied to them all – thank you, and wishes for their long and happy lives. I wished Spence good luck with his partner. It was comforting to know that in a couple of months he'd finally have someone by his side. I told him I was sorry I wouldn't be there to have his back like he'd always had mine.

Lincoln finally made the call to Griffin, telling him we had a way to try and get at least some of the captured children to safety. Griffin saw through Lincoln's many omissions – even over the phone – and insisted we wait for the others to get there. Dapper, Steph, Salvatore and Onyx had apparently touched down in New York and were on their way to the cabin. Griffin had sent Spence on ahead, while he remained behind at the Academy to try to convince the Assembly to send more Grigori reinforcements when the time came.

It was strange to think they were so close – and with the almost completed Qeres, too. But Phoenix had been clear there would be no way to delay Lilith that wouldn't result in deadly consequences.

Lincoln told Griffin what he could, without alarming him with the entire truth, asking him to make sure Dapper knew to expect an important call.

I could hear Griffin arguing, but Lincoln just carried on calmly instructing him to start readying the troops and that we would get Lilith's location to him as soon as we could. He failed to mention it wouldn't be us who would be sending the message and when Griffin wasn't satisfied, Lincoln simply said, 'Everything will be as it must be. You'll understand in time. Bye, Griff.' And hung up.

We stood opposite one another in the basement. Both in dark jeans and T-shirts, Lincoln's short-sleeved, mine long. Dark colours had been a conscious decision. I was going to bleed tonight and I had no intention of making it any harder for those who would be forced to watch and saw no point in giving Lilith more of a show than necessary.

In the bedroom closet I found a black leather vest, which must have been Evelyn's. I put it on and zipped it up. It was snug but it was nice to have something of hers. I'd never had a hand-me-down before and besides . . . it was kick-ass. Lincoln also hoped the leather might offer some resistance to the arrows.

It struck me, watching him arrange things, that I never believed he would accept this. And yet he had. I thought he'd try and drag me into hiding, kicking and screaming. My brow furrowed.

Trying to pull my thoughts into line, I mumbled, 'There has to be a way . . .'

Lincoln was looking over the weapons, deciding what we should attempt to hide on ourselves. There was little point. We knew that any weapons we had would be taken but that didn't mean we wouldn't try.

'A way to what?'

'To get the Scripture. If we're going to do this, just . . . die like this, we need to at least get the Scripture back. If we don't, she'll just keep using it and take more children.'

Lincoln looked down. He'd thought of this too and its absence from our plan was another flaw. Problem was, it didn't change our predicament. The value of the young lives we had a chance of saving was real, despite what dangers lurked in the future. Logic couldn't mess with that.

Fear – like a slippery snake – wound its way up my legs and wrapped tightly around my chest. We could not win this game. Lilith had backed us into a corner and now we would pay the ultimate price. The most we could hope was that the Academy would come through with troops, overpower Lilith and get the Scripture back once we were gone.

Lincoln braced his hands on my shoulders. 'Vi, everything will be okay.'

My eyes narrowed. 'What aren't you telling me?'

His features strained. 'Nothing. I just want to protect you.'

I cupped his face in my hand. 'I'm strong, Linc. With your power connected to me, I'll last. We'll save those kids.'

He nodded, determined. 'And you *will* take everything you need from me to survive every single one of those arrows, you hear?'

There were at least sixty children that we knew of. It would be impossible to withstand that many arrows. But Lincoln was pleading with me and I knew what he was really asking – that I take more than *he* could survive.

Is it for the children? Or for me?

I didn't know the answer, but for him, I nodded. Not long ago, I'd made him promise that if it came down to a choice between an innocent life and mine that he choose the innocent. I would have to stand by the same promise, even if it carried a truth I didn't want to contemplate.

He grasped my hands. 'Once we get in there we might think of another plan. There's only one way to find out.' He seemed too confident and again it sparked nerves in me. In fact, since coming back from dropping Phoenix into town last night, Lincoln had not only developed an unnerving acceptance, but also a certain belief in the plan.

Sensing my concern, he pulled me to his chest. 'I'm not afraid to die. After having you in my arms, knowing that we are together . . .' He stepped back, his hands bracing my shoulders and his eyes locked on mine. 'I was a fool to think there was any other way for us. I have no regrets, not one.'

It was true for me, too. Right now I had everything and I wouldn't have traded that for an eternity of life denying myself Lincoln's love. We were soulmates in the truest sense, heart-mates to the greatest depths. That we must now die . . . That was irrelevant to our love. Lincoln was right – we were endless.

As he hid the last knife inside my boot, I felt Phoenix's nearing presence.

'He's almost here,' I said. 'And he has company.'

Lincoln smiled, shaking his head in awe. 'I can feel it through you, every sense like never before.' His nose crinkled. 'Never liked musk,' he added.

I rolled my eyes and his smile broadened.

'What is it?' I asked.

'I can feel your emotions for him. It's real and intense on so many levels, the way you care for him. I can even see how deeply he scarred you.'

My brow furrowed. This was not a normal conversation. 'So, why are you smiling?' I wasn't sure if I needed to start defending myself or not.

Lincoln knelt on one knee to strap his own knife under his jeans. He looked up at me with a knowing grin. 'Because what you feel for him doesn't even come close to what you feel for me.'

I snorted, though I was smiling back. 'Ha, ha. Can you please get out of my head now?'

'Not in your head.'

I knocked him on the shoulder and he lost his balance, falling back. 'Male egos,' I grumbled as I walked past where he was on the ground laughing.

I walked out to the front of the cabin. Phoenix was standing on the grass, looking resigned. A small troop of six exiles stood back at the tree-line beyond the glamour. Lincoln came out behind me and, despite our fast-approaching doom, he was still chuckling. Countless expressions passed over Phoenix's face and through his eyes in one moment.

He knows.

I held my breath.

But Phoenix's reaction quickly dropped to zero. His eyes narrowed and he growled, 'Let's go.'

I glanced at Lincoln nervously. He had also registered the waiting exiles, but nonetheless was smiling. I could actually sense his satisfaction in showing Phoenix that we'd bonded.

Men.

Lincoln's smile broadened.

Phoenix gave a huff that would've put Dapper's efforts to shame and stomped towards us. 'At least try to control your goddamn emotions!'

I was already nodding apologetically, embarrassed.

Lincoln, on the other hand, simply chuckled again as he replied, 'I am.'

Jesus. Phoenix will kill us before we even get to Lilith!

We opted to drive the truck, rather than let Phoenix use his powers to get us to Lilith's estate. Right now, we were all keen to conserve as much of our strength as possible. It also meant that Phoenix could arrange us some privacy, separating us from his exile enforcers. Heading in the opposite direction from the town, they drove in front and behind in their own vehicles.

It was a long twenty minutes and yet every one of those minutes had become precious.

'Will Lincoln and I be held together?' I asked Phoenix.

'No,' he replied. 'Lilith will lock up Lincoln on the far side of the estate, where Evelyn is imprisoned. She'll most likely put you down in the dungeons until the ceremony tonight.'

I nodded, trying to ignore the spark of fear.

'This is it,' Phoenix said, pointing towards a massive estate coming into view.

When we neared I realised why no one had been able to pinpoint Lilith's location. She and her cohorts held a glamour over the entire building, which made it look like an ancient castle, with crumbling walls and large sections of the roof missing. To passers-by it would be considered a ruin.

It was genius. Hidden in plain sight.

The reality was quite different. The building stood in perfect isolation, with massive stone walls and wrought-iron gates. It was indeed a castle-like estate, but unlike its glamoured appearance, it was pristine.

It wasn't difficult to spot, and sense, the numerous guards patrolling outside. I pushed my senses out a little further and gasped.

Lincoln glanced at me. He had felt it too.

There must have been at least sixty exiles in there, both light and dark, and almost all of them were powerful.

We pulled over behind the first car. Lincoln grabbed my hand before I could open the door. 'Remember, you'll need to open yourself up to me completely so I can send you all of my power.'

I opened my mouth to argue, but he cut me off.

'This isn't about you or me, Vi. If things get that far, it's about saving as many of those kids as possible.'

Resigned, my mouth closed.

'I'll take the fear from you where I can,' Phoenix offered quietly from the back.

I nodded.

'Both of you,' he added.

Lincoln pressed his lips together as he too gave a small nod.

He dug out the phone from his pocket and passed it over to Phoenix. 'Griffin's number is in there when you need it. Tell him we did everything we could and that I'm . . . sorry.'

Phoenix took the phone.

'Get Evelyn out, okay?' I added. 'She's your best hope at killing Lilith. Tell her I've left some letters in my bag at the cabin. And tell her to look after Dad.' Evelyn was the only one who had ever defeated Lilith. I knew she would do everything she could to bring her down again.

Phoenix swallowed, looking away. 'I swear it.'

We stepped out of the truck and Lincoln came to my side, pulling me into him. It was strange to think we had only had this closeness for the last twenty-four hours. It was so complete I couldn't imagine life any other way now.

Lincoln tilted my head up to his. Shining green eyes looked down on me with so much adoration and respect that I felt my own eyes begin to well.

'You have more power than any Grigori that has come before and perhaps, of any that will come again.' He leaned down as I pushed onto my tippy toes. Our lips met and we were in perfect harmony. When his kiss deepened I felt the stirrings of the magic that bound our souls and shivered.

'It's my privilege to love you,' he said, his lips grazing my ear with each word. 'Don't ever forget, no regrets.' He kissed the spot behind my ear and breathed in deeply. 'Not one.'

Something slipped in my stomach. I leaned back from him and searched his eyes.

But he simply stared back at me with nothing but the truth and love of his words. My hands moved up to cup his face. 'Me neither. I love you, too. With everything that I am.'

Phoenix, who had walked ahead a few paces to give us a moment, cleared his throat. 'It's time,' he said.

We followed him to the massive black gates, flanked by the exiles that had escorted us. It felt like we walked a mile just to reach them, climbing a sloping manicured lawn that declared money and power. Fleetingly, I wondered who had been living here or maintaining it during the years Lilith had been gone.

Once through the front doors the sheer volume of exiles inside struck us. They sneered, excited and dangerously stimulated to see us in their territory. Phoenix continued to shield us, not missing a beat when one of the exiles lost control. It was incredible that he commanded as much rule over them as he did, but even so, by the time we reached the end of the hallway, Phoenix had left four exiles writhing on the ground. As per an agreement, Lincoln and I had refrained from assisting.

Phoenix led us into what must have once been a grand ballroom. Now it was more of a shrine. Black carpet ran down the middle towards a hugely elaborate and ugly golden throne, on which sat Lilith.

My senses registered her power and I stumbled, Lincoln's hand was at my elbow to steady me. I had seen her at the Academy, but hadn't sensed her like I did now. She sat tall, flanked by two exiles. One was Olivier.

He stepped forward and motioned to two other exiles. 'Disarm them.'

The exiles were thorough and found all our hidden weapons quickly.

Power emanated from Lilith like a living breathing force that she fed to the world. Her hair was mesmerising, long to her waist and a vibrant orange-gold colour, each strand like precious spun toffee. Her eyes were a soft peach colour but lined in heavy black to look altogether striking. She watched us approach; her unflinching birdlike stare studying every movement. And not just ours. She examined everyone and everything around her with the same intense scrutiny.

She shifted on her throne. Crossing her legs and sitting a little taller. It was an understatement to describe her as beautiful. The fact that she took my breath away only gave me a small indication of what she – Lady Lust – did to the opposite sex. As if sensing this thought, the corner of her lip curled as she looked at me and then Lincoln. Dressed provocatively in a revealing blood-red dress there was no doubt she enjoyed the control she could wield over men.

I glanced at Lincoln, half expecting to see him salivating, but his eyes were not even looking in her direction. I followed his line of sight and had to hold back a gasp.

Human men lay on the floor around her, barely dressed, exhausted and nearing death. They were chained to her throne and looked as if they had been there for weeks with no food or drink and yet each of them watched Lilith with desire. They were smothered in a dense black coating, which I suddenly realised was actually shadow. I was tapping into Lincoln's shadow-finding abilities.

Lincoln took my hand in his. There was a time I would have shrugged free of such a display, would have thought it weak. But I no longer cared. I didn't want to stand alone any more, or prove I didn't need anyone. I did. And what Lincoln and I had went beyond that now.

I didn't miss Lilith's look of frustration when she noticed Lincoln's attention was not on her, but she covered it quickly with a killer smile.

I glanced around quickly. Evelyn was nowhere to be seen.

'Remarkable really,' Lilith said, her musical voice and rounded accent timeless. She looked at me. 'Such a plain girl – nothing striking about you, and yet I find I must compete with you. And most disturbingly,' she turned a less friendly look on Phoenix, 'you hold the heart of my offspring, even though you have clearly given yours to another. My, my . . . well, I suppose I should thank you.'

She turned her smile up another notch and I was almost surprised a choir didn't start to sing in the background.

'I must assume that without your actions my son may never have discovered his backbone and brought me back. Unfortunately for you, my gratitude has always been short-lived and your heritage inspires a specifically ... passionate response.' She stood up and I braced myself for her to approach me, but she just looked down on us.

'We're here for the children,' I said, seeing no point in encouraging chitchat.

'Of course you are. And I am sure that it has been explained to you that I am not without compassion.' She moved towards one of the men at her feet and patted him on the head. His cheeks were completely sunken in starvation yet he moaned in delight at her touch. 'I will grant you the chance to win the lives of the children in my captivity. For as many arrows as you endure a child will be released.'

I nodded. 'I've been told. But we will need someone to take the children to safety once they've been freed.'

Lilith waved a hand dismissively. 'You may not bring another of your kind within these walls.'

We were ready for this. 'What about another that was once one of yours?' I asked.

She raised her eyebrows.

'I know an exile who is now only human,' I explained.

She stepped back with shock and then responded, appalled. 'He chose this?'

Time to learn a little something about me.

I held her eyes. 'No. I took his powers from him.'

She tilted her head as if replaying my words, her attention flitting around the room considering them. Eventually, she turned a thoughtful look back to me. 'And then we will have an agreement?'

'We will,' I replied.

She looked at Lincoln and waited. He took a deep breath and hesitated. Lilith's smile simply broadened.

'We will,' Lincoln finally conceded.

Lilith's eyes shot to Phoenix and she resumed her position on her throne. 'Make the arrangements,' she said to him, before dismissing him with a harsh flick of her hand. 'Take him to the south cell and put the girl below with the children. Let her see the filth she is about to die for.'

Out of the shadows emerged dark exiles. Two dozen of them quickly surrounded us and my instincts screamed *Fight! Flight! Anything! Something!* But I forced myself to still as they approached, gritting my teeth as they pulled Lincoln and I apart and started to lead us away in different directions.

When one of them elbowed me in the side, Lilith spoke up. 'No one harms the girl. Let her be at her best for tonight's festivities. You may, however,' she paused as if deciding, 'play with her love, if you must. Just make sure he can still stand by the evening.'

I closed my eyes as the exiles hovering around Lincoln snarled.

chapter thirty-one

'There is no chance, no destiny, no fate that can circumvent or hinder or control the firm resolve of a determined soul.'

Ella Wheeler Wilcox

'Go with Lincoln,' I snapped under my breath at Phoenix, who had remained by my side. He ignored me.

'They won't hurt me. Go.'

His eyes flashed to mine briefly. 'I'm not leaving you. We agreed to this,' he whispered back.

We? Not he and I . . . Since when have Phoenix and Lincoln been making deals?

We made it back into the halls and the exiles led me to a set of stone stairs. The exile behind me pushed me down and I almost lost my footing. I righted myself in time to see Phoenix take a step towards him in anger. I sent Phoenix a sharp look. He was supposed to be on their side after all.

When we reached the bottom of the stairs I struggled to control my reaction to what faced me, but I couldn't stop my despair and had to close my eyes for a moment. The basement was a similar size to the ballroom we had just left, except this room was all concrete. The space had been divided into square cells by floor-to-ceiling metal bars.

There were dozens of children.

Between five and ten per cell. A quick scan told me we had underestimated the number captured. My stomach turned. They'd been herded and locked up like animals. All seemingly alive, though some, like the men upstairs, appeared to be just hanging on. The stench was overwhelming. They'd been left with nothing more than a small bucket in the corner of each cage. There was nothing else – no beds, no blankets – nothing but a cold concrete floor and metal bars for walls.

I felt another jab at my back as I was pushed into an empty cage, then the gate closed behind me with a click and I heard a key secure the lock.

Don't panic.

I was acutely aware of the numerous pairs of young eyes fixed on me. Some looked as young as four or five, the oldest maybe ten or eleven.

Phoenix stood by the gate, looking over the cells, surprise registering on his face. He covered it quickly and turned to one of the dark exiles.

'She's been busy,' he said, his tone approving.

The exile grinned. 'Big group came in from Canada and the Antanov flew in yesterday from Russia,' he reported.

Phoenix nodded. 'Leave us. Post a guard at the top of the stairs. No one in or out,' he ordered.

Once the exiles had disappeared up the stairs I felt the blood drain from my face and leaned against the bars for support.

'There are too many,' I whispered frantically. 'And what certainty do we have that she won't just recapture the ones she releases after we're dead?' I wanted to take a deep breath to try and clear my head but the smell was overpowering and I was already fighting the urge to gag.

Phoenix shook his head, leaning close to me so the children couldn't hear. 'She won't if you can make her pledge on it. Angels must adhere to a sworn oath. Exiles are hazy on the issue. Some are bound by oaths and others can break them. But Lilith was such a powerful angel, her oaths are still strong. If she makes one, she will not break it. You need to make her swear to the children's eternal freedom before the ceremony.'

'Will she?'

'She's so confident, she probably will.'

I felt a sharp stabbing pain in my lower back. I grabbed the collar of Phoenix's shirt and pulled him against the bars. 'Please, go to Lincoln. They are hurting him.'

Phoenix looked at me sorrowfully, but nodded.

It was a sorry thing, but right then I was comforted by the knowledge that after my death, Lincoln would not have to suffer the pain of seeing me and feeling it – his soul would shatter the moment I died and then even his own death wouldn't hurt him.

I moved to the back of my cage, the children surrounding it as if I were some kind of magnet. Their eyes were alight with a dangerous emotion. Hope.

My chest tightened and I suddenly felt the weight of so many lives hanging in the balance.

'Breathe,' a young voice said.

I spun to see one of the oldest children.

'Breathe,' he said again.

I realised I was panting, on the verge of hyperventilating. I tried to calm myself down. I thought it wasn't going to work, but then I felt him.

Lincoln.

Our bond, our souls. It wasn't like when Phoenix had infiltrated my emotions, this was more intimate and natural. He was just there, wrapping himself around me and comforting me like afternoon sun seeping into my skin. I crouched and closed my eyes, concentrating on the warmth that was spreading through my body and into my soul.

'Good,' said the young voice.

I opened my eyes and watched the boy, amazed. He was maybe eleven and from the way the younger kids watched him, he was a leader.

'What's your name?' I asked.

'Simon,' he said, standing tall.

I nodded to him. 'Thanks, Simon.'

'That's okay. Took us all a bit of time to adjust, down here. Cages and stink don't make happy thoughts.'

I sat down, still buzzing from feeling my connection to Lincoln, regaining strength by the second. I could feel that he had been beaten, but just as he was there for me, I knew he was feeling me too. Together, we had a safe place.

And we needed it.

'Are you here to save us?' came a small voice from behind.

I turned to face a tiny blonde girl, no more than six years old. She was stick thin, wearing what looked like a nightie, ripped and dirty, her face bruised and her exposed feet blackened. Her huge brown eyes blinked at me as she waited for my reply. *All* their eyes were wide and focused on me.

So many. An arrow for each of them. There's no way. . .

I swallowed and glanced at Simon, who was watching me carefully. So young, but he seemed to look at me with understanding.

He turned to the others and spoke confidently. 'Of course she is. Why else do you think God sent her to us?'

The other children began to nod slowly, still watching me. Some were whispering in other languages while others attempted to translate with charade-style sign language. I had to give them something but . . . I couldn't lie.

'I'm here to try.' My voice shook, because suddenly I was questioning our choice. We had looked at the situation from every possible perspective, but we hadn't been able to see a way of bringing in forces en masse without risking the lives of the children. Yet like *this*, with Lincoln and I locked up, separated, unarmed and at their mercy . . . What had we done?

Instinct still told me we could trust Phoenix. I prayed that I was right. If he turned on us now, it would all have been for nothing.

I moved to stand up, but my legs shook and my vision blurred. I fell back down to my knees before everything went black.

I breathed in deeply. The air was stifling, instantly cooking my throat from the inside. I gagged and sat up, my eyes blinking into the bright light and trying to focus.

I was in the desert.

Goddamn desert, again!

I coughed uncontrollably, squinting into the light. One of them was there, I just couldn't tell which one.

'Is this it?' I asked, still struggling with each breath as I tried to get to my knees. I didn't care who it was, I just couldn't let my guard down. 'Is this the freaking "bright light" everyone talks about? Because if it is, let me tell you, your customer service desk is going to be overflowing with unhappy clients.'

'We don't provide service beyond expiry.'

Nox.

My eyes began to adjust and confirm just that, then they widened. 'You look ridiculous!' I said. I couldn't stop staring. He was dressed in full leathers, very different from his usual suave and sophisticated wardrobe. I wasn't about to admit it to him, but he looked hot. Like some kind of fantastical creature painted in a shade of honey to match his shoulder-length hair – that was currently blowing freely despite the still air.

'You could make a fortune as a portable wind machine,' I quipped.

Nox smiled knowingly.

'I thought you might like this. I believe I spy a tinge of pink in those cheeks.'

'If you're going to ask me out on a date, the answer is no,' I snapped, getting to my feet.

He threw his head back and laughed. 'I'd sooner throw myself into the pits of Hell.'

I blinked. 'That was harsh.'

'That was honest. Though . . . I will admit that of all humans you do . . . intrigue me at times.' He looked me up and down as if he could see Lincoln's and my bond. 'I see you've made your choice then,' but his smile was secretive and unnerving.

I put my hands on my hips. 'What is this, anyway? Where are we?'

'A dream.'

'You put me under? You can do that?' I questioned, alarmed.

He shrugged, looking his outfit over. 'If necessary.'

'Why? Why didn't you just cross the realms?'

'The Hag might've sensed my presence. We thought that unwise.'

'Do you think the colour is right?'

'What?' I asked, increasingly confused with his left-field comments.

'The outfit. Do you think I should've gone with the more predictable black?'

I huffed. 'Nox, there are children here. At least a hundred of them. Lilith is going to sacrifice them and I can't save them all! And you're worried about the colour of your stupid outfit? What's wrong with you?'

His eyes narrowed, his usual off-hand attitude gone. 'I'm eternal. I have time to ponder when it suits me. Do not group us as like beings.' The desert fell into darkness. Shadows, impossibly thick and opaque closed in around me, rising from the ground and falling from the sky. My throat started to constrict with fear.

'You think you know me?' Nox bellowed. 'Can you feel me?'

The shadows increased, moving through me, tearing at the very fabric of my existence, and somehow I knew that if left to their own devices they would happily hold me for all eternity.

'I am everywhere. I am not one, not many! I am Malign!' He roared, his voice surrounding me, his menacing power reverberating through every particle of air.

Suddenly, he was in front of me. I gasped. It would take barely a thought for him to kill me.

But just as quickly as it had fallen, the darkness receded into daylight. The searing sun returned and he moved in closer than usual, his hair blowing once more in the non-existent breeze.

He regarded me patiently.

I swallowed, careful not to make a sudden movement. 'I like the colour,' I said.

He nodded and stepped back to his place. 'I think you're right. It stands out. Says I'm a leader, not a follower.'

Silence rang loud until Nox chose to speak again. A chair appeared from out of nowhere. He sat. 'You should sit, too.'

I looked around, not wanting to upset him again. 'There are no more chairs,' I said.

He looked at me like I was an idiot. 'This is a dream. Create one.'

I shook my head. 'I'll stand.'

He shrugged. 'Are you confident in your choice?'

'Well, I don't know how to make a chair,' I argued.

He snapped a wrist at me. 'Keep up! Not the chair. You are locked in a cage. You are at the Hag's mercy. Your mother captured. Your love imprisoned.'

'We're trying to save the children.'

'Where is your army?'

I shook my head. 'I don't have an army. I . . . We had to come alone.'

A slow smile spread across his face. 'Come now, young one, tell me what we both know.'

I didn't respond.

His smile broadened. 'You have not come alone at all. You came with the dark.'

I stood tall, despite the fear in the pit of my stomach. 'Yes. We came with Phoenix. He's helping us.'

'Indeed. Darkness can achieve much. But are you ready to travel the road that it must take you on?'

'What do you mean?'

He stood. 'The playing field is soon to be evened. I do hope you survive Lilith. Perhaps you can be the power that they believe you already are.'

'Who? What power? What are you talking about?'

He gave me a smug look and I knew he would say no more, so I pushed on.

'Can someone else bring Lilith across the realms? If I'm . . . If I don't make it?'

He sighed, bored now. 'They can return her to the pits. It may be enough. But no, only you can bring her across the realms.'

'Why?'

He raised one eyebrow high. 'Because you are the Keshet.'

Something hard pinged against my head. Then again. My eyes opened and I curled into a ball, just as another hit came to my arm. 'Ow!'

'Wake up!' a small voice said.

Something else hit my back. I looked down and saw small rocks – no, chunks of concrete.

'Okay, okay! I'm okay,' I said, before another one hit me.

'What happened to you?' Simon asked, panting.

I put a hand to my head. I could sense Lincoln. He was worried for me, as if he hadn't been able to sense me during my dream.

I'm okay.

I kept thinking it, over and over, until I felt him calm. Then I turned to Simon. 'I guess I fainted. I'm fine now.'

His concern remained but he nodded.

Seeing the nervous expressions on the faces of so many children left a lump in my throat. Then one little boy caught my eye. Still in his blue-and-white pyjamas and huddled next to an older girl, it was the little boy Olivier had taken. He was alive.

I smiled at him and dug my fingernails into my palms to stop from crying. I didn't know how much longer I would have until they came for me, but I decided to try and focus all my attention on the children.

For the next two hours I listened to them tell me, one by one, how they had been taken from their homes, how their families had been tortured, burned, murdered. Each of them, having already known the loss of one parent, understood all too well what losing the other would mean. They had nothing left and nowhere to go, even if they were to survive.

I wanted to scream for them. I wanted to rip Lilith apart for doing this. Phoenix too. Even myself. We had all played a part. But I held back the emotion and devoted my attention to the children.

'There is a place where you can all go,' I told them. 'There are people who will look after you and keep you safe. You will become a part of their family. It won't be the same as your real families, but it will be amazing. And when you grow up you will have choices. If you want to you can become very strong and very powerful.'

'Like you?' One of the smallest boys named Tom asked. His face was covered in freckles and he had pale blue eyes and fire-engine red hair. I'd never seen hair that colour before. He couldn't have been more than six.

I nodded. 'Like me.'

'Would we be a part of your family?' Another little girl named Katie asked. You could tell she'd had a tough life already. She held herself in a way that suggested she expected nothing more than suffering.

I smiled at her. 'You'll have family all over the world.'

She smiled back and my heart broke.

I have to save these kids.

'Have you seen the man with the purple hair. The one who brought me in?'

The children nodded.

'We call him Midnight Stars. He sneaks us in some food every now and then and tells us to hide it,' Simon explained.

I smiled. Midnight Stars was a perfect name for Phoenix.

'Well, if anything happens to me, or if I can't get back to you, do what he says, okay? You can trust him. He'll keep you safe.'

The children nodded.

Simon leaned into the bars and they gave a little under the pressure, making me wonder if I could pull them down with my strength. He reached his hand through, stretching it towards me.

'We pray every night for God to protect us. Will you pray with us?'

'Oh,' I said, taken aback. 'I . . . The truth is, I'm not sure I believe in God.'

Simon's reaction was shock at first, followed by confusion, and then . . . He smiled.

'You're testing us. I can see that.' He nodded, more to himself than me. 'Our faith will not waver. You will not see us lose our way.'

I wasn't sure why he was speaking to me like that, but he seemed to find some kind of strength from it and as a result the other children did too. I smiled as he watched me. I was glad he had faith. I didn't know how I felt about it, but then I knew a lot more things about the world of God and angels than these kids and I wasn't about to strip away their beliefs when they had so little else to comfort them.

I shuffled closer to Simon and took his hand. 'I can pray with you.'

All around me, children dropped to their knees and bowed their heads, a few turning away. I waited for Simon to start a prayer, to beg for their survival, for their families to be in Heaven. I braced myself. But nothing, *nothing*, could've prepared me for what happened next.

A lone voice – small, innocent, beautifully composed – rang out, bouncing off the concrete walls to haunting effect.

Tom sang.

The words sounded like Latin. Tears pricked my eyes instantly, his voice cutting right to my heart. I had never heard anything more heavenly.

I looked at Simon who seemed to watch me with awe.

'It's called "Pie Jesu",' he said as Tom sang. 'It's for our parents. It means: Merciful Jesus, who takes away the sins of the world, grant them everlasting peace.'

I nodded, tears slipping down my cheeks. 'It's beautiful.'

CHAPTER THIRTY-TWO

'Thou hast, with deadly magic,
Poured poison into me.'
Heinrich Heine

Pounding sounds filtered down from above. The children huddled together. The drums seemed to perfectly echo a heartbeat of encroaching evil.

Lilith was making quite the event of my torture.

Probably sold tickets.

I consoled the children as best as I could and explained that the guards would be coming for me and not to be frightened. I promised them someone would be back for them.

For some reason they trusted me, as if the kindling to all of their fears had been stamped out by my presence.

It made me feel sick. And guilt-ridden.

I knew there was no way I would be able to save them all, but I had to try. Beyond that, I had to believe that Phoenix, Griffin and Evelyn would find a way.

I heard footsteps and stood, refusing to look weak or afraid.

It was Olivier who came to collect me. Phoenix must have decided it was too risky. A current of fear ran through me that Lilith had already discovered his betrayal. My hand went to my stomach to reassure myself. If Lilith knew, she would have killed him instantly and my wounds would've reappeared the second he died. As long as I was okay, I knew he was alive.

Olivier looked delighted to be the one who got to deliver me to the festivities.

'No one told me it was fancy dress,' I said with a mocking grin. He looked like he had on some kind of Dracula outfit – long black cape and all. It was even more ridiculous than Nox's leathers. And Olivier on the whole frightened me a whole lot less than Nox.

Olivier unlocked my cage and dragged me out by the arm.

'That's okay,' he replied, his own cruel smile growing. 'We're about to paint you in red.'

The children cried out as he violently shoved me towards the stairs. The sight of their trembling made me so angry. I couldn't let the kids think we were helpless. Without thinking about what I was about to expose them to, I released my power over Olivier. It moved eagerly from me to him, my amethyst mist coating the immediate area. Most of the kids couldn't see the glittering purple but I noticed a few put their hands out with expressions of wonder.

Huh. Some can already see.

Olivier's body stilled and I held him prisoner.

He watched me as he struggled to try and regain control of his body. But I was stronger than him. I leaned close to his ear.

'I could end you right now, or worse, make you only human.'

His pupils dilated with fear. I looked at the children and began to walk slowly around Olivier.

'All is not lost.' I prodded my captive, making a show that I could. 'They're scary, yes.' I gave Katie a reassuring smile. 'But so am I.' I caught Simon's wide eyes just before I let my power drop and released my hold over Olivier. 'Be strong,' I urged him.

Olivier almost leaped into the air. His fist went back, his arm shaking with the desire to strike me. I clicked my tongue at him, almost daring him, but his hand dropped – too afraid of Lilith's wrath. He settled for pushing me once again towards the stairs.

I glanced back at Simon. He nodded bravely.

That boy will make a fine Grigori.

They all would. I'd ensure they had their chance with my last breath.

Olivier pushed me every few steps until we reached the top of the staircase, where four more exiles waited.

They had a prop.

'Original,' I muttered, looking at the crucifix.

Olivier took his time, tying me to the heavy wooden cross with thin ropes.

It felt wrong in so many ways that they were doing this, and even more disturbing was seeing the sheer satisfaction it brought them.

The ropes dug into my wrists and ankles as the exiles hoisted me onto their shoulders and paraded me into the main room. Facing the ceiling I couldn't see much, but I heard the roars and hissing. I felt like the hunt being delivered to the barbecue.

Finally, I was placed up against a stand so that I faced Lilith and Phoenix, who stood behind her throne. In front of her was a small golden table. My breath caught before I could stop myself when I saw the modern automatic bow and rows of small arrows, each knitting-needle-slim and no longer than four inches.

Lilith was adorned in a golden gown complete with plunging neckline and cut-outs down her sides that showcased her curvaceous body, leaving little to the imagination. On anyone else it would have looked crude – on her, it looked iconic. Her golden hair almost blended into the dress and her lips were highlighted by vibrant red lipstick. Her only other accessories were the chains that flowed from her throne down to the collars around her human slaves.

A whimper fell from my lips as Lincoln's power ran through me and I saw the shadows. Each human was shrouded by thick venomous shadows which had an almost oil-slick quality that confirmed their will had been tainted by an exile. A shiver ran through me.

To Lilith's left, I finally spotted Evelyn. She was bound in silver chains with exiles on either side of her, holding her up. She had been badly beaten, only her eyes left untouched. My anger boiled and was only contained when my gaze locked with hers. Evelyn's body may have been sagging under the strain but her eyes were as fierce as ever and focused on me. I didn't need a soul bond to feel the love she was sending me.

I looked away. I would have broken down otherwise.

Finally, I let my gaze travel to the place I'd been purposely avoiding since first entering the room. To the right of Lilith, Lincoln was chained up. He stood tall and fearless despite the fact that, like Evelyn, he too had been badly beaten. From the angle he held his arm, I suspected his shoulder had dislocated again. Nonetheless, his strength was so overpowering I found myself half smiling at him briefly. He nodded me on as if that was exactly the right thing to do.

The ballroom was lined with spectators. I pushed my senses out, registering that there was definitely a favouring of dark exiles. With Lilith now in charge and Phoenix viewed as her second-in-command, I wondered if exiles of light would be so happy to continue their truce with the dark. I imagined it would not be long before they went back to the old ways and began warring with one another.

The man standing on the opposite side of Lilith's throne caught my attention. He didn't seem to belong; small and unassuming, he was bald with wire-rimmed glasses. Dressed in a conservative grey business suit and cream tie, black briefcase in hand, shoes nicely polished – I couldn't get a clear signature from him. He was definitely an exile, which was strange in itself – I'd never seen one who looked so . . . average; on the whole, exile physiques fitted the *GQ* ideal.

He looked back at me, nothing more than a hint of curiosity showing in his expression. The hair on the back of my neck prickled.

Something about him is very, very wrong.

The drums continued their relentless pounding and exiles started to walk towards me in time to the beat. One by one they moved closer, pushing their power out towards me. They were combining their forces. I didn't know what they were planning but my heart began to race in anticipation.

They want me frightened.

Be strong. Stay strong.

One by one the exiles morphed into their creatures of choice. First something bat-like swooped in on me. Then something with great talons streaked by so close I felt it graze my arm. Another came, more like a gargoyle, then another; a dragon. They were relentless. A horned devil covered in orange fire, a creature illuminated in blinding white light with a gigantic and terrifying wingspan all ablaze, a vampire, a human snake, a fairy-vulture... All moving into my space from the side, behind and above!

I can't breathe!

They surrounded me, infiltrating my mind – whispering and taunting. They kept coming, creatures of treacherous darkness and creatures of the brightest light equally frightening. None of them meant for human eyes, none of them meant for this world.

My breathing was shallow and fast and the terror started to consume me as they took over my mind. They would not stop.

I forced my mind to work for me and called on my power. It flowed from me, out and over the room. Exiles hissed and moved closer, never ones to run in fright, even though they could sense my strength building.

Utilising my power, I set my will free and painted the room back to truth. The exiles returned to nothing more than human form and I concentrated on breathing. My view to Lilith cleared. She was watching me with fascination.

She clapped her hands. The drumming stopped and the exiles, following an unspoken command, reluctantly moved back to the shadows edging the room.

'You do not know who made you, do you?' Lilith asked.

I refused to answer. I didn't want her to know just how little I really understood about the Sole and my angel maker.

She laughed, the sound echoing around the room.

'Are you ready?' she went on.

This was it. 'Once I have your oath,' I said.

Lilith's eyes widened a fraction, but her smiled followed quickly. 'Clever girl. What would you have my oath on?'

'That the children saved tonight will never again be hunted or harmed at your hand or by your order.'

She tilted her head curiously. 'You're my prisoner. Why would I adhere to such a demand?'

I gave her a sharp smile. 'Because you want me to agree to your terms. You want to shove my free will down my throat.'

Her eyes narrowed.

'I warn you, I tire of restraints being put on my desires. For too long I've had to abide by the oaths I once gave to angels. Trinkets and necklaces have caused me many missed opportunities.' She lifted her chin. 'I'm not inclined to agree.'

A shiver ran down my spine, thinking about how many children's lives had been spared by such trinkets as the amulet my mother had left behind for me.

Now my eyes narrowed. 'You already swore it would be so through Phoenix. Are you willing to go back on your word in front of everyone here? Have you not promised rewards and spoils to many exiles here tonight? Do you expect them to follow you when your word holds no weight?' I looked around the room. 'It could be a costly mistake.'

The small man holding the briefcase cleared his throat. Lilith's birdlike glare snapped to him, but he seemed unaffected.

'I for one should like an assurance of your word,' he said. 'Since I've paid such a great deal for it.'

Fury hardened Lilith's features. Something about the briefcase man unsettled even her, which made him that much more unnerving.

'My oath is yours,' she spat out each word. 'No child released tonight will come to further harm by me or mine. Now, for Hell's wretched sake, someone shoot her!'

Olivier moved quickly towards the golden table, but Phoenix was already there, bow and arrow in hand.

Lilith smiled at the sight. 'My son?'

Phoenix nodded. 'I believe I've earned the right,' he said, casting a dark gaze in my direction. It was so real, for a moment, I almost doubted him.

'I must admit, I do like what you bring out in him,' Lilith said to me, reassuming her place on the throne.

I braced myself for what was to come.

'Lilith, this is between you and me!' Evelyn screamed. 'It always has been! Let me take her place!'

My heart squeezed for my mother. Even though her words were useless, it was her way of telling me she loved me.

Lilith swam gleefully in Evelyn's pleas, her smile indulgent. 'You're right, Evelyn. But you brought her into it and now you can live the rest of your days knowing that this was all your fault.'

Playing his part perfectly, Phoenix did not delay. He loaded the first arrow steadily and took position about five metres away from me. His expression was blank, but his chocolate eyes burned into mine as he raised the bow and took aim.

The first arrow pierced my thigh.

Exiles hissed.

The arrows were small but they were fierce. I felt the sharp tip embed itself in the muscle that contracted around it. I bit down on the scream.

Phoenix reloaded and aimed.

The automatic bow made a muffled thump-like sound before the arrow sped towards me. This one pierced my upper arm. A tear slipped down my cheek but I didn't cry.

Staunchly, Phoenix reloaded, just as we'd planned. The faster he could shoot, the more children we would save.

The third arrow punctured my shoulder and burned all the way down my back.

That's three. Three children free.

After the first five shots, the exiles began to cheer, encouraged by the sight of my blood dripping to the ground.

I kept my focus and opened the channel to my healing abilities. It was awkward, since the arrows were still lodged in me, but it was more about patching things up and slowing the bleeding than making good.

Beyond myself, I could feel Lincoln's power pushing at me, offering its help. I looked at him and shook my head.

Not yet.

As Phoenix reloaded, I saw a new person enter the room. I recognised the stale senses that came from him alone.

Onyx had arrived.

Which meant they had managed to contact him through Dapper and extend Lilith's invitation.

Onyx strode down the black carpet and did not look at me once, his eyes for Lilith only. When he reached the end of the runway, he gracefully dropped to one knee.

'Onyx,' Lilith sang, gesturing for him to stand. 'It has been a time since our paths last crossed. When the child told me she'd managed to pet one of us, I never considered it could be you. Is she truly so powerful, or were you never so great?'

Onyx didn't miss a beat. 'I was almost certainly greater than you ever realised.'

Lilith smiled. 'You must think highly of her then.'

'No.' He glanced at me briefly. 'She was obscenely lucky.' He feigned boredom. 'What service is required of me here? I care not for watching torture if I am not the one reaping the benefits.'

Lilith seemed to appreciate this. 'She has nominated you to lead her flock.' She laughed. 'For each arrow she endures a child I have imprisoned will be spared. She has elected you to deliver them to safety.'

Onyx nodded, still not looking in my direction. 'So be it.'

'But . . .' Lilith said, her voice shrill, 'I have an alternative proposal for you.'

Oh God, what is she going to do?

I felt Lincoln's tension rise and saw Phoenix's fist clench.

'And what would that be?' Onyx asked, showing the first sign of curiosity.

'I can give you back your power – in *all* its glory. I can make you a true exile again.'

I heard Onyx gasp. 'And what price would such a gift carry?'

Lilith took a few small steps towards Onyx and laid a hand on his shoulder. 'No order will be given, for *you* are not one of mine to command.' Lilith winked at me. 'However, if once the children are handed over to you, you should . . . make a choice as to where your loyalties lie, I may feel that you have adequately proven yourself worthy of power once more.'

'And how do you suddenly have the ability to restore my power?' Onyx asked.

'I am the first dark exile. Do you question my strength?' Lilith asked, smiling unkindly.

'No,' Onyx responded. He seemed to ponder his decision. 'You want me to destroy the children?'

Lilith clasped her hands together. 'If that should be *your* desire, Onyx. I understand it was you who first began the quest for the lost Scripture? Is this not what you have dreamed of?'

Oh, it was. When I'd first met him he was indescribably evil and had tried to kill me without a second thought. He craved power like no other. With this ultimate temptation laid at his feet, I dreaded what he would choose.

'And if I should not wish to fulfil my previous desire?' Onyx asked.

I held my breath, a small tendril of hope dangling.

Lilith's voice hardened. 'If you are tainted so badly that that is the case, then you have become one of the rodents you so despised. But I have made my oath and will make no move against it.'

Onyx gestured towards me. 'May I approach your sacrifice?'

'Why?'

He stood and took a step towards the golden table, picking up an arrow, palming it. He turned back to Lilith and shrugged. 'I wish to add one of these arrows to her myself.'

My stomach sank.

Lilith beamed. 'By all means.'

Onyx walked towards me. He didn't bother with the automatic bow. He was going to do this by hand.

When he got close, he spoke. 'Lucky number thirteen.'

I had no idea what he meant. He took the arrow in his hand and positioned it at my wrist, just above the rope and at the top of my silver markings. Then, with as much force as his human body could muster, he drove the arrow into my wrist.

I screamed.

But Onyx didn't stop there. He moved his hand down to the wound and collected my blood on the tip of his finger. He held it up briefly so only I could see the tiny specks of silver blended with the red.

'Heard an interesting story on my travels,' he whispered, leaning right into my ear. 'That potion of yours has another name: "the breath of the afterlife". They say when it took an earthly form it looked like mercury.' He glanced at my marbled blood on his finger, his brow furrowing and voice becoming urgent. 'Without you, she cannot be stopped. You *must* survive.'

The thirteenth ingredient.

The silver halls.

What I seek.

Beginnings and ends.

The angels have been trying to show me, but couldn't tell me.

It's in me. *All this time, we've had the final ingredient.*

The truth hit me hard, taking my breath away. I felt the link between Lincoln and I, and I knew he knew. The difference was – he wasn't surprised.

I looked at Onyx, wishing we'd known about this before.

My eyes flashed to my wrist. 'Take the arrow,' I whispered. 'Give it to Steph.' If nothing else its tip had some of the silver blood on it. Maybe it would work. 'You're a good man, Onyx,' I nodded at him. 'No matter what you say.'

His dark eyes connected with mine for a moment before he spun back to Lilith, gesturing to my wrist. 'Would you mind if I kept a souvenir?'

'Please do,' she said, unfazed by our interaction.

Onyx pulled the arrow out, causing another bout of agonising pain. I bit down hard but couldn't stop the cry that fell from my lips. Exiles all around laughed.

'As tempting as your offer is,' Onyx began, 'I find myself with a humanly debt to repay another. Until then, as your oaths bind you, so mine binds me.'

I was glad then that I was already crying. I didn't want them to see my tears were now for Onyx. He had become a better human than most.

Lilith's rage at Onyx showed, but she wasn't about to let his denial derail her. The show would go on. She ordered him out of her sight to wait outside.

'Phoenix!' she snapped.

He nodded once, turned back to the golden table and loaded the next arrow.

I screamed when it hit my stomach.

He reloaded.

I tried to breathe and prepare myself. The desire to shut my eyes tight and close myself off from the world – to take myself to that other place – was intense. But I didn't. I kept my eyes open. I wouldn't give any of them the satisfaction of seeing my fear.

The arrows continued to fly – my legs, my arms – Phoenix aiming as carefully as possible, trying to cause the least damage. They hurt more and less at the same time, as new arrows didn't increase the pain that was already so extreme. But they were starting to wear me down.

I focused all of my energy on healing, on regenerating and keeping as much blood as possible inside my body.

I kept count of the arrows, each one reminding me of another life – another child that would live to destroy these exiles one day. By the twentieth, I was starting to tremble. I was weakening way too soon. I needed to keep going.

I felt Lincoln's power pressing at me.

I closed my eyes briefly. I wanted to keep him strong but I was unable to resist his help any longer. I opened the channel and his power flooded into me, rejuvenating my own power like a breath of fresh air. My healing kicked up a notch, the wounds closing around the arrows. Some of the arrows were even pushed out altogether, clattering to the ground as my body repaired itself.

Phoenix ignored all of this. He simply reloaded. And fired.

By the thirty-fifth strike, the world was spinning. I'd developed a cold sweat that felt like my life pouring out from me. I could hear my heart beating, too slow.

Phoenix fired again.

I healed myself.

This time, I felt Phoenix sending me his emotion. Solid determination. I could feel his undiluted belief in me and in my power. So much so, I sensed his belief that I would survive. It made me sad that he could think that, when I knew otherwise.

He also *took* emotion from me, like lifting weights from my shoulders, one brick at a time. First, he relieved me of despair, then sorrow, then the well-buried fear. He found them and absorbed what he could.

By the fortieth arrow, Lilith was on her feet. The exile spectators had started hollering. Lilith came right up to me, yanking a few of the arrows from my body, twisting them as she pulled them away. I cried out. She smiled.

'You are just mortal. You think you have purpose? You do not. You think you are powerful? You are not. Are you watching, Evelyn? Are you *proud*?'

Evelyn struggled under the hold of the exiles restraining her. 'Look at her, Lilith. Take a long hard look at the mere mortal who is going to destroy you for good.' Evelyn spat out the words.

Lilith's composure slipped and she spun to Phoenix. 'Speed things up!'

He nodded and loaded another arrow.

'Not that way!' she snapped. 'Bring forward her wounds.'

I struggled feebly against the restraints.

Oh God. I can't. This is it.

Lincoln's strength flowed into me, holding me together. Blood now covered my body and poured from my mouth and nose.

Phoenix moved a step closer to me, his eyes closing briefly. I could feel his sadness and regret at what he must do.

I looked up at him and ground out, 'Do it!'

And he did.

Onyx's first shocking wound to me, after I'd embraced – the sword in my back that went right through me – returned. Phoenix did his best to minimise the pain, but he couldn't do much in the face of such a horrific wound. Blood poured from me as I watched him – my vision blurring again – reload the bow, and aim.

Fire.

Fire.

Fire.

Fire.

I choked on blood. I suffocated in Lincoln's power, pouring – no, hammering – into me. I couldn't imagine how he had anything left to send, but it kept coming. So I took it, and I used it. My body convulsed against conflicting urges; my human body wanting to give up, my soul demanding me to go on, and my angelic ability forcing my warrior to fight.

I thought of Tom, singing with his divine voice. I thought of Simon, the warrior he would become. If this was my purpose in life – if this was why I had been created, made Grigori, given this power . . . If this was why I was Lincoln's soulmate – to survive these arrows – I could live with that. Or die with it.

Arrow number fifty-six.

There was little space left on my body that was not marked and bleeding. I hiccupped through short trembling breaths.

At least one of the arrows had punctured a lung.

I tried to heal it.

Arrow fifty-eight.

I coughed. Blood splattered. I couldn't draw on any more power.

I refused to close my eyes. I looked at Lincoln, my love. He was crying, his face twisted in agony as four exiles held him back.

I let him see the truth. It was time. He screamed till there was no breath left in him.

Phoenix turned to Lincoln. Then back to me. Lincoln started shouting at him, 'No! No! No more! Phoenix, no more!'

Phoenix reloaded.

I held on. He fired.

One more child.

Each breath more shallow, more broken. I was afraid.

Still refusing to close my eyes, I began to mentally say my goodbyes, first to Dad, then Evelyn. I thought of Steph and Salvatore, of Dapper and Onyx, of Griffin, Zoe and Spence. My family.

I looked to Phoenix and sent him my apology, my forgiveness, too. He blocked me and reloaded. But it was okay. Every arrow equalled one more life.

Finally, I looked back to Lincoln and let my heart go to him. With the last of what I had, I whispered, 'I love you.'

Another arrow jolted my body.

Good. One more life.

Lincoln pushed against the exiles restraining him and screamed, 'I'm yours! Always. Always!'

Then he sent me everything he had. I saw him fall to the ground as the rest of his power fed into me, helping me to survive a few more arrows.

Arrow sixty-four hit.

Arrow sixty-five.

Arrow sixty-six.

Evelyn cried out.

Arrow sixty-seven.

I was sinking.

Finally, I let myself go to that place. I forced my eyes to stay open, but I let myself shut down and go to that place I'd taught myself to seek. The place that locks the rest of the world out, the place that created the rules.

I will not run from you. I will not hide from you. I will endure anything you give to me. I do not believe in fairy-tale endings. I will stand and I will fight. I will . . . I will . . . I will . . .

Arrow . . .

Arrow . . .

I didn't know if my eyes were open any more. It didn't matter. Eventually, there was only darkness.

No tunnel.

No light.

Only the promise of nothingness.

And yet, suddenly, in those final moments, a sharp wave of fear lurched up and penetrated every part of me. I was sure, more sure than I had been of anything in my entire life, that something truly terrifying awaited me. But there was nothing I could do.

chapter thirty-three

'What! Could you not then understand?
This is the hell with which you were threatened.'
The Holy Quran 36:62–63

Conflicting smells hit me first. Something damp, pungent – like disinfectant. Then, salty sweat and heat. But above all, the tangy smell of fresh blood mingled with the rotten odour of dried.

The pain came next. From my forehead to the back of my neck, my shoulders, arms and down from there. Everywhere. It felt like my body was on fire.

I laboured to breathe. My throat was raw, every inhalation felt like knives to an open wound. On some level it registered that it was because of all the screaming, but the thought was too difficult to hold on to.

'She's coming round,' a voice said.

Footsteps sounded, moving nearer. 'Hey, Dapper just called. They're almost back.' Different voice.

Who? Was that . . . Spence?

'Good. Go back outside and stand guard.'

A pause. Then footsteps fading away.

'Get her some water,' said the same voice.

'I'm not leaving her,' a female, replied.

'She can barely breathe, get her some water,' the first voice growled in response.

'I don't trust you with her.'

'I brought her here, didn't I?'

Another pause. Scuffled footsteps followed.

Someone yelled out from further away. More sounds then a loud bang followed by a click.

My mind wasn't working properly. I tried to open my eyes. Panic started to slowly rise as I questioned where I was and what had happened. Was I somewhere I'd been before? I started to see glimpses of light. Something flashing through the air towards me.

Arrow.

A hand smoothed my forehead with a damp cloth. It didn't help the pain. There was a loud banging nearby.

'Violet?' the voice said. 'You need to try and wake up.'

I couldn't understand why. Nothing made sense. I saw more flashes.

Memories started coming back to me. My body jolted. Strong hands held me down. I remembered Lilith. I remembered the children – Simon, Katie, Tom. I remembered the arrows.

So. Many. Arrows.

I tried to speak but no words came out.

'Don't try to talk,' said the voice. 'You need to concentrate on waking up. When you wake up properly you can heal yourself.'

But why?

I was supposed to be dead. I'd felt myself slip away.

A flicker of irony ran through me. I thought when I died all the pain would go away.

Just my freaking luck it hasn't worked that way.

But who would talk to me if I was dead? And why did he sound so familiar?

God?

If so, then surely I wouldn't get a house call; I'd never even believed in him.

'Violet, I don't want to have to slap you. Open your damn eyes!'

Definitely not God.

My eyes fluttered. The lighting was dim and my face felt badly swollen. Slowly, the person standing over me came into view.

There was more banging, louder this time. I couldn't work out if it was coming from my mind.

'Phoenix?' I croaked.

'Concentrate,' he said. 'This is very important. Can you understand me?'

I tried to nod. I was alive.

'Good. Good,' he soothed, as if encouraging us both. 'Violet, you need to heal yourself. Dapper's power isn't going to cut it and I can't help you until you're strong. Jesus,' he sighed. 'We have to do this now or I never will. Do you hear?'

'Chil-dren?' I whispered, concentrating on simply breathing through the extraordinary pain. Coming to terms with dying was one thing, coming to terms with surviving in the face of so much awfulness, knowing if I recovered I'd have to relive over and over all that had happened was ... earth-shattering.

Phoenix's expression softened.

'You saved seventy-one.' His voice held a strange kind of bewilderment. 'Dapper and Onyx are making sure they get back to the Academy safely. I . . . I don't know how you did it, but you stayed conscious through it all. I monitored your heartbeat the entire time, waiting for you to pass out, but you just kept going. When you finally closed your eyes, Lilith was sure you were dead, but I healed your wounds and Lincoln sent you the last of his strength. It was enough to keep you alive. She forced me to shoot you with another few arrows, but you didn't stop breathing and she refused to let you have an unconscious death. She saw it as a waste. So she sent you away until you could be returned to her so she could kill you herself. I got you out of there, but this is only temporary and we don't have much time. Violet, you need to help me.'

I was confused, trying to process all I had just heard. And the banging was getting more insistent. 'Banging?' I asked.

Phoenix shook his head urgently. 'Don't worry about that. We need to do this now!'

'Do . . . what?'

I still couldn't believe I was alive.

How did I survive seventy-one arrows?

Just the thought brought the pain back – pain I never believed I would have to remember.

'Concentrate,' Phoenix demanded. 'You need to heal your wounds. I need you as strong as possible otherwise I can't help.'

'I don't . . . understand,' I said, struggling to speak.

He put a hand on my shoulder. 'I'll explain everything later. You have to trust me.'

The banging persisted and I realised now that there were other sounds too. There were people shouting from far away – people who I knew.

I remembered Lincoln's request. I felt him through our bond despite my weakness, and his. He was still alive. I felt the small flare through our connection – he knew I was thinking of him. He was willing me on. I remembered the promise I'd made to him that I would trust Phoenix.

I nodded and closed my eyes, concentrating on my abilities, calling them up. They were sluggish and tired, but my power slowly built and started to work its way through my body, healing the worst of the injuries. I could feel Lincoln adding his own power and I tried to block him so that he kept what I knew he would need, but it took a while before I was strong enough to effectively push him away.

Finally, I opened my eyes again. 'It's okay,' I said. 'I'm starting to feel better.'

Phoenix nodded, his expression now closed off.

'What next?' I asked, looking around. We were back at Evelyn's cabin, in the basement. 'Where's Lincoln?'

'He's still there.'

'And Evelyn?'

Phoenix just nodded.

I sighed. 'What about the kids?'

'She let Onyx take the seventy-one, but she still has almost thirty locked up and she's already planning to go after more.'

'Who else is here?' I asked, things becoming clearer. The banging I'd heard was coming from the other side of the basement door.

He shrugged. 'The whole damn gang by now. We don't have long before they figure a way through.'

Why is he keeping them out?

'So we're going back, right? We have to get the rest of those kids out of there,' I said.

Phoenix shook his head slowly. 'There's something else we have to do first.'

'What?'

What could possibly be more important?

'It's better if you don't ask.'

On his last word, Phoenix was on top of me, straddling and holding me down. I was helpless to stop him, my strength no match for his. My eyes went wide when his hand closed over my mouth and nose.

I kicked out and bucked beneath him, but it was useless. He was too strong. Every movement of mine was easily counteracted and I couldn't breathe as Phoenix suffocated me.

The solid door blocked my way to help. They would not break through in time.

I felt Phoenix shaking on top of me and his haunting eyes penetrated mine, a million words within them, yet I couldn't pluck out one.

Was this the way I was always meant to go?

The way that had been intended for me?

I had thought for so long it would be Phoenix who would kill me. Had he only lured me back for this final, most awful, betrayal? He must have planned this. He'd wanted me dead for so long.

This is his revenge.

I stopped struggling.

This is my time. I've done what I could and now I will end.

I stared at him. He was crying. I didn't understand.

The colour in my vision and the life in me began to fade away. As the last pixel of light disappeared, I was suddenly standing before my angel maker.

This time, I knew beyond all doubt – I was dead.

There was no desert. No art studio.

I was in a field. Long, air-light grass, sun shining, its heat going all the way to my bones. The pain was gone. And this was not my world.

If felt strangely like a dream, though it was not. This was something else – for starters, it almost always rained in my dreams. But just as the thought crossed my mind, the sky crackled loudly and rain began to pour.

My angel maker stood before me. He was perfectly dry, not one drop of rain touching him. His face was clearer than ever before. More human and yet less.

'I'm dead,' I said, the words sounding all around me.

'Right now? Yes,' he replied.

I spotted the odd floating things I'd seen so many times before in my visits with Uri and Nox. They hovered in the background, shimmering and jutting in an unpredictable fashion. With so much water falling, they reminded me of large jellyfish. I took a step towards them, more drawn to them than ever.

'Child, no. Not yet,' my angel maker said gently. But it was a command. I froze.

'Is this heaven?'

'Is this what heaven would be for you? A field of rain?'

'No.'

'Then, that is your answer.'

'Is this the angel realm?'

'We have no need for land and physical substance. We are beyond that.'

'Then where?' Even in death, he was still annoyingly cryptic.

'Where you must be. You are within the link, the place where we can be close to you. It is neither ours, nor yours. It is a place we make together.'

Suddenly I knew. This is what it was all about. This place. This was somehow what I was.

'Others don't come here, do they?' I asked.

'No. When we must, we can simulate a place for them. A place for their trials – a dream, a vision – but no other has the ability to create space in the universe with us. You are the only one.'

I closed my eyes and intuitively knew what to do. I willed myself to see the truth – to see this place as it really was. I opened my eyes again.

The first thing I saw was the limits, as if we were on an island surrounded by . . . not nothingness and yet, not something either. Space unknown. Then I noticed the sun. It was much closer than it should be, and the rain I'd started stopped instantly, clearing my view to the sky.

I gasped, backing up a few steps.

The now-dusky sky was filled with rainbows. Dozens. Hundreds. Rainbows were encircling the universe, connecting everything.

'What . . . What does this mean?'

'New possibilities.'

'For what?'

'Many things.'

'But I . . . I'm dead.'

'For now.'

'But Nox and Uri said this was the angel realm when they visited me, that the two realms were touching.'

My angel maker shrugged. 'In a way, it is true. They told you what you were ready to hear. How is Evelyn?'

His change of subject surprised me. 'She's . . . Lilith has her.'

He nodded. 'It is the way it must be. Those of us who chose our paths earliest are the strongest and Lilith was the first to exile – her power grows. Evelyn is no longer a worthy opponent. She did what she could, remarkable it was, but now it is time for this battle to finish. It is time for you to take your place.'

'How?'

'You have all the tools you need.' He glanced at my wrists and my markings began to swirl. I held them up, remembering what Onyx had said.

'The thirteenth ingredient,' I murmured.

He actually laughed, surprising me again. 'The only ingredient.'

I blinked. 'But . . . Onyx said . . . Why . . . Why the other ingredients, then?'

'Humans like to complicate things. It is time to go.'

'Do you care?' I asked quickly, not knowing what was going to happen, where I was going to go.

'For many things,' he replied.

Desperate for something to make me whole again I pushed. 'For me? Do you care what happens to me?'

He considered me for a moment. 'Enough to allow what I know must now happen,' he said, fire erupting behind his eyes.

When I just stared at him, he looked beyond me. 'Go. Win the war and ask what you will afterwards.'

He pushed a finger over my heart and I felt something heavy thump into me, throwing me clear of the universal island and into the abyss.

I floated.

Another slam.

Air rushed into my lungs. So much, I thought they would explode.

They didn't.

I was forced to breathe.

chapter thirty-four

'Oh, leave me not in this eternal woe,
For if thou diest, my Love, I know not where to go.'

John Keats

my lungs sucked in air greedily. It hurt. Every breath harder and faster than the last, trying to sate my oxygen-starved body.

Someone was with me, coaxing me. A low voice, speaking constantly, calling me. A hand touched me.

So familiar.

It brushed the hair from my face, shaking. The voice continued to murmur in quivering broken gasps, like crying.

Phoenix.

My body was coming back to life. I started to open my eyes, but as I did, I felt a terrible – and vital – snap.

The scream that escaped my lips was shrill.

It felt like I would never stop – *could* never stop – screaming. The pain went beyond the physical, beyond anything I'd ever known. I would have rather suffered an eternity of flying arrows than another second of this agony.

I was lost. Taken.

'Breathe. You have to breathe, Violet. Please, God, just let her breathe!' Phoenix cried out. He was shaking me.

What's happening to me?

I managed to open my eyes. Phoenix's body sagged. 'Thank you, God,' he whispered. And then, before I could scream again, before I could cry, or make any sense of what was going on, his hands went to my chest. The impact was like lightning.

I sucked in a sharp breath, my mind and body in extreme overload.

No death should last so long. Surely the end was near.

But what I saw was not the end. It was something altogether new. Phoenix's power shimmered all around him. I'd always seen the moving shadows that followed him, often with swirls of gold running through them, like spun toffee. He had told me once that he inherited them from his mother – but this was different. The shadows were gone.

What came from him now looked like black crystal fire. Dark – but beautifully so, with sharp lines and a reflective quality, it was like the midnight you long to see. And from within the flames dazzling silver strands exploded like fireworks.

They encircled us, bound us. Left him slowly.

And came to me.

At the core of Phoenix's power tornado, something hovered, reminding me of the reflections I always saw in the angel realm – if that was the right thing to call it any more.

Phoenix was struggling above me, unusually weakened and looking like he had used everything he had to put on this extraordinary light show. He stumbled back.

As he did . . . I remembered.

'You killed me,' I whispered. The pain that I'd been feeling since I first woke was continuing to build. It was insufferable.

'I'm dying again,' I moaned. I wanted it to happen soon, wanted this pain to end.

'Relax,' he said.

Before I could explain that was impossible, I felt the reality of what he'd done to me. A new and strange presence moved through me. It was foreign and my body began to violently spasm, trying to reject it, but another part, my angelic part, made room and pulled it close.

I could feel the power it offered. And more.

It was unlike anything I'd ever experienced except for with one other. An angel. I could sense Phoenix in a way I'd never done before. My heart broke for him. So much time. So much pain. Too much rejection.

I knew what he had done.

I grabbed his arm.

'New death?' I gasped, finally understanding, the unbearable pain still growing.

Coldness spread through me like burning ice.

He smiled sadly. 'And new life,' he whispered.

Tears rolled down my face. 'You gave me your essence.'

'Shh,' he soothed. 'It was the only way to release you from our bond. We still have one, but it's different now. This one cannot kill you. You're free.'

I closed my eyes. My body bucked. Something was wrong. Very, very wrong. Phoenix's essence was changing me, but that wasn't what was causing the world-shattering pain that was consuming me.

I heard the banging again, but this time it was from above. They were breaking through the ceiling.

Phoenix looked up, frustrated. 'The room is a vault!' he yelled.

'Let us in there, you bastard!' Steph screamed.

'Eden, are you okay?' Spence's voice followed.

I started to shake all over. 'I'm cold,' I said.

Phoenix turned back to me and attempted to hold me down, but it only got worse. My body started convulsing as if it were rejecting my very existence.

My eyes shot open.

Oh. My. God.

I grabbed at my chest. At my heart. I clawed at it, feeling as if it had burned away to nothing.

'I died!' I gasped. I turned my wide eyes to Phoenix. 'I died!' I screamed, the pain and the truth tumbling down on me.

Phoenix was wordless.

'No! Tell me, no!' I begged.

No words. He just stared at me.

'No!' I screamed.

But Phoenix didn't need to say it.

I pushed my power out, searched everywhere for the link. I beckoned my soul and cried out for his. I pleaded, I begged, I cried.

Nothing.

Nothing but a billowing coldness that blasted me, freezing me to the core.

I rolled off the table I had been lying on and dropped to the ground, gagging, not wanting the air that continued to enter my lungs and torture me with life.

'No,' I gulped. 'No, no, no!' My head shook trying to make it so. 'No, no, no!' I gasped, again and again. 'No!'

But there would only be one answer for me.

Yes.

The connection was gone.

I had died . . .

Lincoln's soul had shattered.

He was gone.

chapter thirty-five

'What can be worse; Than to dwell here,
driven out from bliss, condemned.'
John Milton

Phoenix held me from behind, his arm around my waist, as I collapsed to the ground and screamed with everything I had.

Every second that passed was a long, unbearable eternity without him. I couldn't go on. I couldn't possibly be expected to breathe, to live, without him. What was left of my soul battered me violently, demanding to know where its counterpart was, blaming me for its loss.

But he was nowhere to be found.

I grabbed at my hair, ripping clumps of it out as I grappled desperately for sanity. And failed.

Phoenix held on as I struggled against him.

First absent-mindedly and uncontrolled, but then, along with a dawning realisation, my screams focused on him.

'You did this!' I accused. I didn't even sound like myself. 'You killed me!'

He continued to hold me up.

I flipped around and jumped on top of him using strength that was not there. I don't even remember the first punch, or how many times I hit him, all I know is that he just lay there and let me until he was bleeding badly and I finally fell on top of him, crying.

He pulled me close, held me tight.

I screamed and cried. I screamed and cried.

Hours passed.

I heard the intermittent banging on the door as Steph and Spence and whoever else was out there tried to get in. But it was all so distant now. I lost track of reality and writhed with the pain and loss. The misery of everything Lincoln and I were and would never be again overwhelmed me.

Phoenix held me silently, so tightly I was sure if he let go my body would fall apart.

Finally, thoughts started to connect to form broken questions.

'Why?' I spat out, the one word breaking me all over again.
Was it revenge?

Phoenix kept his arms around me as he spoke. 'It was the only way. We thought of every alternative but you needed the bond with him first to survive the arrows and this was the only way to release you from our physical connection.'

No.

'We? Lincoln . . . He knew?'

'I told him you were our only hope to destroy Lilith. He wasn't surprised. He said Dapper had told him something before you left the city, something else that made him believe you were the key to her destruction.'

Dapper had always had suspicions about the thirteenth ingredient. He must have told Lincoln he thought it could be me.

'My blood,' I lifted a wrist then slapped it back down. 'The markings are poison. I'm the goddamn apple, snake, whatever!' I cried.

Phoenix nodded sombrely. 'They told me when I brought you here. Your blood is lethal to exiles in human form. Angels in human form, too, I would guess. That's what Onyx told you, isn't it?'

I nodded.

He sighed. 'Lincoln and I knew that if I tried to help you, Lilith would turn on me. She has maternal power over me. If she chose, she could force me to inflict wounds on you or she could just kill me. I told Lincoln I knew how to break the connection so that no matter what happened to me, you would be safe. When I told him what it involved he said a source had hinted as much to him, but as far as he knew no exiles were capable of sharing their essence.' Phoenix half smiled, bitterly. 'But then, I've always been different.'

I remembered how relentless Lincoln had been in his quest to chase down sources and informants before leaving the city.

I'm such a fool.

'When Lincoln drove me out of here the other night, we talked, we fought ... we reached an agreement.' Phoenix's hand moved towards my face but did not touch. 'We knew no matter what we said to you, you would still go there to save those kids – you would've just insisted on doing it without the soul-bond and we couldn't risk that.'

I gasped for air. 'For me, or for the children?'

'Both.'

Everyone had been planning everything. My life, my death, my purpose, their ends.

'Why not do this first? Break our connection before I bonded with Lincoln's soul?' My anger was building again.

Phoenix shook his head. 'We couldn't be sure your death wouldn't alter the soulmate connection. The risk was too high.'

'I was never going to die,' I said, arriving at the painful truth.

'Not for any longer than necessary,' Phoenix confirmed.

Lincoln had known what would happen since he came back that night with the bruise on his face. He'd already made his choices before we slept together. He had known that Phoenix would kill and revive me, that he would give me his essence to release me, that his own soul would shatter, that ... That I would be left alive ... without him.

More tears – sorry, sorry tears – slipped down my face.

'There was no other way. Trust me, Violet, we looked at it from every angle. There was no way to stop Lilith killing all those kids.'

My voice trembled. 'You could've let me die like we planned!' My self-control broke and I struck out at him again, this time with swipes and desperate slapping. 'You should've let me die! I don't want to live without him! I can't! I can't ... I can't breathe, I can't ... I ... You should've let me die!'

'I know,' he winced. 'But I couldn't.'

'I was there! They forced me back. I was so close I could almost reach out and touch the reflections. They wanted me to go with them, but the angels stopped me. I should've gone!'

'What are you talking about?' Phoenix asked, suddenly grabbing my shoulders. 'What do you mean *reflections*?'

'The shimmerings. I see them when the angels come to me. They're always in the background calling to me.'

Phoenix slumped down, defeated. 'Oh, damn them all. They're pulling way too many strings.'

I didn't know what he meant. Didn't care.

'I'll never be able to tell you how sorry I am,' he said. 'I know I brought Lilith here. I know how awful it is to lose the very thing you have started to live for. I'll hate myself for eternity for doing this to you. But there *is* a way to stop Lilith. Together. We can still get the rest of those kids out. We can get the Scripture back, your mum. And . . . we can get Lincoln, too, get . . . his body out so we can . . .' He looked away.

I punched him, then gripped his shirt, shaking him. 'So we can kill him? That's what you want to say, isn't it? That's what the two of you agreed, didn't you? That you'd kill him!'

Phoenix took my hits, still doing nothing to stop me.

'Yes,' he confessed. 'He didn't want to be . . . He wanted you to be free.'

I slumped away from him, exhausted, moving into the corner of the armoury.

'I lost the only thing I would fight for.' I hauled myself to my feet, my knees knocking together, colt-like. My body had been mostly healed from the wounds but I was broken and weak in every way that mattered. Phoenix moved towards me, the injuries I'd inflicted on him already healed.

'No!' I put out a hand. 'Don't come near me.' I made it to the door and unlocked it before pulling it open. Steph, Spence, Salvatore, Dapper and Onyx all stood from where they'd been sitting on the stairs. Steph was crying.

They had heard.

Salvatore barrelled into the room and I heard him hit Phoenix. Steph made a move towards me but I put up my hand to stop her, grabbed onto the railing and took a step. Onyx cast his eyes down when I passed. Dapper watched me with undiluted pity.

'Let us help you,' Dapper said softly.

I shook my head, climbed the first flight of steps and moved through the kitchen to the next. With every step I took, I remembered being in Lincoln's arms the night before.

I dragged myself into the bedroom and stared at the bed; sheets still rumpled. I could smell him. I bit down on my fist as I screamed again and crumpled to the floor, wrapping my cold arms around my legs and tucking myself into a ball.

I knew beyond all doubt that nothing in my life would feel good, ever again. And all that I had left to hold onto – those few brief hours when we had been free to love one another – had been robbed from me and stripped back to nothing but lies and devilish scheming.

I rocked myself, feeling a chill settle into my bones. Loneliness was all that awaited me now.

There is a reason a soul is supposed to shatter when the connection is broken between soulmates. I knew that now. It was simply intolerable; a pain that outstripped words and surpassed beginning and end. There would be no relief.

Shouting downstairs ensued as Phoenix defended his actions to Steph and Dapper. In time quiet returned, as they no doubt reached the same hopeless conclusion that nothing could change what had been done.

More time elapsed. Eventually, I crawled into the bathroom. I turned on the hot water in the shower, not bothering with the cold, and sat beneath what should have been a scalding downpour.

But I was only cold. Empty.

Some time later, the door opened. The water stopped. Steph crouched beside me.

'Oh, Vi. Oh my God!' She ran to the door and yelled for help. I heard arguments erupt and then Steph reappeared with Phoenix beside her. She wrapped me in a towel, and Phoenix lifted me off the floor.

'You've burned yourself,' he said, carrying me to the bed.

I felt limp.

Steph was crying beside me, holding my hand. I couldn't look at her.

'I swear if you're lying, I'll kill you myself,' Steph hissed at Phoenix through her tears.

'I'm not lying. I'm the best person to heal her now and nothing I do can cause her any more harm.'

Phoenix lay me down gently and focused his power on me. I vaguely registered my burnt arms returning to their usual fair complexion.

'Vi, honey, can we get you anything?' Steph asked, her voice shaking.

I shook my head. 'Just leave.'

She paused. I thought she was going to argue but then I heard her stand up.

'We'll be downstairs so just yell out if you need us.'

Footsteps moved towards the door and Phoenix started to walk out with her.

'Phoenix?' I said.

He stopped and turned back to me.

'I need you to do something.'

He nodded. 'Anything.'

'Make it stop,' was all I said. But he knew exactly what I meant.

His eyes looked so sad, so sorry. For me. 'Violet, I don't know if that's . . .' He dropped his head. 'I'm already absorbing some.'

I couldn't fathom that there could possibly be more that I wasn't already experiencing.

'Make it stop, Phoenix. You two decided to do this to me, but from now on, *I'm* in charge of what happens to me. If you want my help, turn it off, all of it. I need to think.'

Slowly, he stepped back towards me and, resigned, nodded. I felt my emotions slowly start to lift. Phoenix was working his power like a sponge, gradually soaking up all the pain, the loss, the anger, the grief until there was only a dribble left. For the first time since I had woken, I could think. I sat up.

Phoenix stumbled and fell to the edge of the bed.

'Are you going to be okay?' I asked, my tone bland.

He nodded, swallowing back the tears from experiencing my pain. I ignored him and, still wrapped in the towel, walked to the cupboard to take what I needed before returning to the bathroom. When I reappeared, I was dressed in a pair of black leggings and a leather jacket. I tied my hair back in a high ponytail and pulled on my black boots, ignoring my shaking hands.

Functioning on nothing more than some kind of disconnected robotic mode, I made my way downstairs, everyone watching me nervously. I paused when I passed Onyx.

'Did you get the children to safety?'

He nodded. 'We put them on a bus to the Academy.'

With that, I continued on down to the basement. Phoenix followed. I entered the weapons room and started making my selections. I strapped on weapons belts, securing grenades around my waist, knives at my thigh belts, and two katanas onto my back. I spun round, looking for more, and found Phoenix standing there, my dagger in his hand.

He held it out to me. 'Thought you would want this.'

I took it from him. 'I do.'

He leaned against the side bench. 'Lilith can shield the area around her using wind as a force field. You'll never get close enough to her to hurt her.'

I stared at him and waited.

'I can,' he finished.

I simply nodded. 'Okay. Tell me what the plan is and *don't* leave anything out,' I warned.

Thirty minutes later, I sat outside the front of the cabin, backpack at my feet. Phoenix stood by the doorway, giving me my space. Everyone else was less considerate, pacing around me like wild animals.

'This is ridiculous!' Steph said. 'You are not going back in there! We haven't even had a chance to test out your silver blood – how can you be so sure that's all you need?'

'Steph is right, Violet,' Salvatore said. His face was bruised from where he and Phoenix had fought.

'It's not open for discussion,' I replied.

'Especially if we hog-tie you until Griffin gets here,' Dapper tried to argue.

'I'm coming with you, Eden,' Spence threw in.

I appreciated that he didn't try to talk me out of it, but even so, I shook my head. 'Not part of the plan.'

He folded his arms. 'Don't care. I'm coming. I'll go invisible until the time is right.'

I shook my head stubbornly. No one else would be sacrificed. 'No. Your glamour won't hold around so many of them.'

He scoffed. 'I'm strong enough and you know it. You're not my keeper, Eden. I'm coming whether you like it or not. Same terms as always – I get dead, it's on me.'

'We could use him,' Phoenix said quietly from his place by the door.

I wanted to argue and yet I found myself shrugging.

'Promise you won't make a move until I say,' I demanded, glaring at Spence.

'I can't believe you guys are even discussing this! You can't go after her alone, Vi!' Steph shrieked.

We ignored her.

'My word is gold. You know that, Eden,' Spence said, not looking away from me.

That much was true. I sighed. 'I need a phone.'

Phoenix passed me the same phone Lincoln had given him before we'd entered Lilith's estate. I called Griffin.

'Violet?' he answered on the first ring.

'It's me.'

'Oh, thank God. Dapper called when they arrived at the cabin last night but he wasn't making much sense. He said Lilith called Dapper's phone, demanding to speak to Onyx. She told Onyx she had you prisoner. That's why he agreed to go with the exiles she sent.'

None of it was a major surprise to me.

'Violet, what the hell's happening out there? I sent Spence, is he there?'

'Yes,' I said.

'The way Onyx was talking last night . . . He said they were torturing you . . . That . . . We thought you were . . .'

'I was,' I confirmed, my tone flat. I guessed no one had spoken to Griffin since Phoenix had turned up with me.

'You sound . . . What's going on? Where are the others?' Griffin was frantic.

So many questions. No good answers.

When I didn't respond he said, 'Onyx gave us Lilith's location and Josephine's been readying the forces. We're on our way to you. I'll be at the safe-house within the hour.'

'Don't bother. I'm leaving now. Tell them to go straight to the estate and . . . Bring everything you have, Griffin. Bring everyone who can fight.'

'Violet, you're scaring me. Put Lincoln on.'

I swallowed. I stared at a tall tree with branches that swept down over the cabin. 'Can't.' The word caught in my throat.

There was a pause. 'Where is he?'

'Lilith still has him.' I closed my eyes. 'His soul has shattered.'

'God have mercy,' Griffin breathed.

'Apparently not. I'll put Phoenix on the phone.'

'Wait. What? Phoenix?'

'Yes. He'll tell you how to get past the outer guards in case any are still alive.' I very much doubted there would be.

'Wait, Violet! Wait until we get there, you can't go in alone!' He sounded frantic. I could hear his fast footsteps and people calling out to him. He'd be too late.

'It's the way it has to be, Griffin. I have to get them out.'

'Violet, you *will* wait till we get there – that's an order!'

Every word felt meaningless, nothing penetrating the numbness that now engulfed me. 'I'm not taking orders any more, Griff.'

I passed the phone to Phoenix and turned my attention back to the river. I could feel everyone's eyes on me but I ignored them. Instead I waited for Phoenix to give Griffin approach instructions for the estate, describing its weakest points and suggesting entry tactics.

It didn't matter to me of course. I would be going in through the front door.

Before he finished the call I heard Phoenix struggle to answer a question that was obviously about me.

'I don't know . . . She's . . . I've never seen anything like it . . . I don't know . . . Maybe never.'

He told Griffin to hurry before hanging up.

'Let's go,' I said, extending my hand. I wasn't waiting any longer.

'Violet, please don't do this,' Steph tried one last time.

'I'm sorry, Steph. I have to,' I answered.

Phoenix pocketed the phone and nodded as he took my hand and then Spence's. The three of us moved like the wind. But it felt different this time. I now had Phoenix's essence in me and I could *see* the wind-travel like I had never been able to before. I understood how he became it, moved as a part of it and not just within it. I wondered if I could now do it, too.

I started to pull my hand from Phoenix's to see if I could keep moving like he did. My feet caught in the momentum and I stumbled. Phoenix stopped, Spence rolling onto the ground as Phoenix tried to steady me. I looked around. We were in the middle of a forest. I started to run, faster and faster, so much faster than ever before.

But I was not the wind.

I'd picked up some of whatever it was Phoenix had. It would come in handy, but I couldn't harness the power of the wind in the same way. I stopped running. Phoenix was beside me, Spence holding his hand again. Wordlessly, I put out my hand. The three of us moved like wind once more.

Moments later we were on the outskirts of Lilith's estate. It was nightfall again and had just begun to rain heavily. Everything had changed in such a short time.

Dark clouds rolled in and thunder echoed around us, closely followed by lightning that struck so sharp it looked as if it had split the sky in two.

My heart turned inside out for the world to see.

Ignoring the heavy downpour, I pulled out two daggers and made my way towards the first line of guards. As I neared them, I started to run, using my newfound speed. I ran straight for them, not slowing even when my blade slid into the first, then the second, then the third. I took them all down, every one I passed. I didn't look back. Anything that came at me from the side or from behind, I knew Phoenix and Spence had covered.

We were fast. We were silent. We were deadly.

When we neared the front gates, I stopped and gave both of my daggers to Phoenix, then turned to face Spence, taking off the holster holding the katanas.

'Stay back and out of sight. When you spot the Scripture – that's on you.'

Spence nodded. 'I'll get it.' He took my blades and held them up. 'And I'll be ready.'

He started to move away from us until he had disappeared completely under an invisible glamour. I took my Grigori dagger out of its sheath and tucked it into the back of my pants, concealing it with my top.

I looked at Phoenix. 'Do it,' I said.

He didn't hesitate and I was glad. He struck me hard across the face. Once.

The pain was nothing.

He hit me again, opening up a gash on my forehead, and shook his head. 'Good enough.'

I turned, clasping my hands behind my back. Phoenix tied them together, carefully placing the pull tie in my palm so I could loosen them any time I wished.

As his captive, we walked out of the rain and right through the front doors to Lilith's lair.

Phoenix led me past groups of exiles, who started to follow us, and into the ballroom, where Lilith sat on her throne. When we reached the end of the black carpet, he kicked my feet out from under me and pushed me to my knees.

'I suggest someone kills the guards who were responsible for her,' Phoenix growled, throwing one of the daggers I'd given him onto the ground and out of my reach. 'I'm getting sick of being the only one who can capture her. It took me the whole goddamn day this time. If it weren't for my control over her, you would've lost her altogether. When I found her, she was dead. I had to revive her just to bring her back for you to kill yourself!'

He was convincing.

I noticed the small man in the business suit standing to the side of the room, watching with great interest. He adjusted his spectacles and his eyes flitted between the three of us as if he suspected shenanigans.

Lilith looked on suspiciously as well.

'Olivier was responsible for her,' Lilith said.

Olivier stepped forward. 'As I explained, we were attacked.' He eyed Phoenix suggestively.

Lilith stood and walked towards Olivier, her hips swaying and her hair flowing like liquid gold. I wanted to rip her heart out.

Patience.

I spotted a low black sofa beside Lilith's throne. Lincoln's soul-less body was lying on it, a collar around his neck from which a single golden chain led into Lilith's hand. He was breathing. I didn't look for long. Didn't react. Couldn't.

Evelyn was there as well. She was chained around her waist to a pole. I let my dead gaze connect with her fire-blue eyes. I could see she, too, was trying to work out what was happening. She raised her eyebrows, questioningly. I gave her the smallest nod, letting her know I had a plan. It was a good thing such a gesture couldn't also convey that she probably wouldn't *like* said plan.

Lilith took her time, sauntering up to Olivier and circling him, before her hand caressed his chest. Even now, she didn't consider me a threat, not bothering to have me searched or further restrained. Her ego would be her undoing.

'You told me you were strong,' she said to Olivier, tenderly.

'I am,' he hissed, failing to disguise his contempt for her. Despite what he may be willing to do to destroy the Grigori, he was still once an angel of light and Lilith would always have been an angel of dark. They were not friends.

'You told me you were the best of the light,' she said.

'I am.'

Lilith took a deep breath, closed her eyes briefly and began to walk away from him slowly. Without turning back, a breeze began to stir around her, lifting her long golden hair out into needlepoints. She paused and suddenly, as if working like an extra limb, her tresses flew backwards and whipped Olivier across the face. His body flinched at the contact, his face turning a ghostly shade and sinking in on itself, as if a hundred plagues had infiltrated him in a matter of seconds.

Lilith smiled at me, secretively. My stomach turned.

She spun round – arm out and fingers extended – and drove her bare hand straight into Olivier's chest and out again, just as fast, clasping his heart. Seeing Lilith, the bringer of death and disease, in action at any other time would've scared the crap out of me.

Now? Not so much.

'Phoenix, my son,' she said, once Olivier's body had disappeared and she had resumed her place on her throne. 'You surprise me, again.' She nodded in approval.

Phoenix moved away from me and bowed before Lilith. 'My place is to stand by you, always.'

Lilith seemed happy with his answer and motioned for her son to take his place behind her. He did.

'Violet, I confess you astonish me – for a mortal. Quite remarkable that you have found a way back to the living so quickly, but I am glad you have returned. I so wanted for you to see your love again.' She tugged on the chain she held like a leash, connecting her to Lincoln, yanking so hard that his head jerked up.

I didn't move.

Lilith sighed, looking over his body appreciatively.

I gritted my teeth.

'Alive. But not. The soul has more power than anything else. Wouldn't you agree?'

I focused my attention on her and not on the man I loved more than life itself. 'I would. Now I have a question for you.'

She laughed. 'Yes?'

'Did you really think you could beat me? Did you really think, even with all your power, that you could match the power of the Sole?'

'I'm yet to see anything that proves to the contrary,' she said, condescendingly.

I smiled, the action showed only the emptiness that filled me. Lilith flinched. Closing my eyes, I delved deeper into my well of power than I had ever done before. I called it forth. Then I used my Sight, knowing now that it was so much more than its name implied. I lifted my consciousness from my body and, for the first time, took my power with me.

Then I released it onto the room.

CHAPTER THIRTY-SIX

*'Adam's wife, his first. Beware of her. Her beauty's
one boast is her dangerous hair. When Lilith winds
it tight around young men she doesn't soon let go of
them again.'*

Johann Wolfgang von Goethe

Dozens of exiles were instantly trapped by my power. I felt a surge of energy; it was intoxicating to know that each one was rendered motionless under my command. Every exile was now at my mercy. All but two.

I deliberately left Phoenix untouched by my power, though he remained stock-still like the rest of them. Even if I hadn't, I suspected he would be immune to it now, due to our new . . . relationship.

Lilith, on the other hand, revelled in proving I could not disable her with my abilities. She walked through my amethyst mist, chuckling. But despite her boldness, her steps were slower; she was not as invulnerable as her angelic ego would have me think.

'Impressive,' she said, looking at my physical form and then to the ceiling, tracking my incorporeal movement easily. 'You are indeed of the Sole. But you and I both know you cannot hold the room like this for long. You certainly cannot strip every unwilling exile of their powers.'

It was true. It took all of my concentration to hold so many at once. But just to make a point, I honed in on one exile – one of the ones who had been so keen to beat Lincoln earlier – and stripped him of his angelic power, reducing him to only-human status, against his will. He dropped to the floor, screaming hysterically. With a look of disgust, Lilith flicked her wrist and sent out a gust of wind so powerful he was thrown into a nearby wall. He stopped making any noise.

Reluctantly, I pulled away from my Sight and returned to my body, tugging at the tie around my wrists to release my hands. Keeping my hold on the surrounding exiles, I yelled, 'Now!'

At the same time as my arm went up, the holder carrying my two katanas flew into my hand and I pulled them both free.

Thank you, Spence.

Lilith threw her head back and laughed as I began to move towards her. She took a step to the edge of her stage, completely unthreatened.

'You cannot break my shields, little girl. Air protects me. It loves me and I wield and replenish it faster than you could ever comprehend.'

I took another step closer, feeling the crushing pressure of her force field. My grip tightened on the hilts of my swords.

Lilith was so wrong.

Thanks to Phoenix's essence, I understood exactly how her shield worked – I could see the way the air solidified around her, becoming something entirely impenetrable.

I stepped into the zone of her power and felt my body tremble under its oppressive weight.

Lilith continued to give me her amused attention. 'You are powerful to stay on your feet. But *so* human. *So* stupid. Is *this* all you have to offer? Is *this* your big moment?'

I stared right into her eyes. I didn't look beyond her. I didn't give anything away.

'No.'

She shook her head. 'You'll *never* break my shields.'

He struck.

She gasped.

Her chin jutted out, her mouth wide open as a blade sliced through her chest, from behind.

'She knows,' Phoenix said, at Lilith's ear.

Only now did I look to where Phoenix had moved and thrust the hidden blade into his mother. At her back and within her field, he had been in a prime position. And Lilith hadn't even considered that he could be a threat. Pride had seen to that.

Stunned, she stumbled forwards, turning shocked eyes on her son.

Phoenix returned her look, his sadness evident. 'I was wrong to bring you back. I'm sorry for my mistake,' he said.

Lilith reached behind herself and pulled out the blade, snarling at the pain. 'You were *wrong* to try and betray me.'

I moved slowly. Silently. Pushing through what remained of her shields. Just as Phoenix had planned, the injury had caused enough damage to weaken her defences.

'You of all people should know that blade is not enough to kill me!' She lunged, Phoenix's dagger now in her hand.

Frighteningly fast, she was in front of Phoenix, her fingernails digging into his neck, the dagger now in his stomach. She hissed and twisted the blade before ripping it out of him again.

Phoenix fell to his knees, looking up at her with heart-wrenching understanding. And maybe it was true. Maybe there was a part in all of us that could not be denied. But Phoenix had already proved his nature was not set in stone and frankly, right then, I didn't give a damn.

He shook his head. 'I didn't need to kill you, Mother, just weaken you.' He sank to the floor.

Realising her error, Lilith spun, blade in hand. She lashed out towards my side.

But I was already through her shields, and I was fast, too.

I forced both katanas, imbued with shavings from Grigori weapons, through her chest and released my power, pushing it *all* into her, letting go of my hold over the other exiles as I did. Something burned above my hip but I ignored it.

She stumbled, grabbing at the blades, but the sheer force of my power weakened her so she could barely move. She finally managed to wrench the swords free, a clanking sound echoing through the hall as they fell. Even so, the arrogance in her eyes remained. She still believed she would kill me.

'For my mother,' I said.

I pulled my Grigori dagger from behind my back. The blade was fast across my wrist, the cut deep. I didn't care.

'For your son,' I said.

Lilith watched as I let my angelic blood, marbled with silver, cover the blade.

Her eyes widened. I half smiled.

'Impossible,' she whispered, managing to move a couple of steps back.

I simply moved with her. 'For those children and the parents you stole them from.'

I took the final step and didn't hesitate, thrusting the dagger, covered in my blood, straight into her heart.

'For Lincoln.'

Lilith fell.

In that instant, before she could disappear, I felt the shift in reality. The air became thick and gravity's hold seemed to falter. I closed my eyes and rode it out.

When I opened them again, Uri and Nox stood before me – the rest of the room still. Operating on autopilot I bent, lifted Lilith into my arms and walked towards them, willing us into this in-between place I still did not fully understand.

Uri nodded to me as I crossed the threshold and passed him Lilith, glancing at my bleeding wrist in the transfer. Even in this otherworldly place, the coldness came with me, eating away at me like defenceless prey.

Nox took in the scene curiously and turned to me. 'Surprises to be had all round, it seems.' He nodded with satisfaction. 'All is as it should be. The tilt has now been corrected.'

'What *tilt*?' I asked.

Nox looked to Phoenix, who was barely breathing, then back to me. 'It was never right that one as powerful as you should carry only the light. Now, you carry both light and dark. It is just.'

It took a moment for me to process his words in my sluggish mind. But eventually . . . Oh.

'My angel maker is of the light,' I said softly.

Nox snorted. 'Did you think any self-respecting Angel Malign would embrace the image of the lion?'

More pieces of the puzzle fell into place and fury raged within me. I spat blood at Nox's feet, looking down and only now registering the wound in my side. Lilith must have done it. I vaguely remembered feeling something when I stabbed her.

'This was your plan all along, wasn't it? All of it! You wanted this to happen so Phoenix would give me his essence, because *what*? The Angels Malign were *jealous*?' I was screaming. It wasn't like anyone else could hear; we had stalled time around us.

'It is as it must be. I neither wanted nor denied it.'

'Nox,' Uri interrupted, 'we must go.'

'And why is that?' Nox sneered, challenging Uri. He wanted to stay and gloat.

'Because we have shown her the tool to destroy any of us in physical form whenever she should so choose and right now she is not herself. It would not be wise to remain.'

Nox looked at me properly for the first time. 'True.' He tilted his head. 'Though I do like this look. Feral works for you.'

Uri cast his emotionless eyes over me. For once, I felt I matched his gaze with my own blankness.

'Extraordinariness will always carry great sacrifice. It must. But you must surrender, still.'

I ignored him, issuing a threat. 'Make sure she doesn't find a way back this time.'

He gave a small nod, looking beyond me to the dozens of exiles that would soon attack. 'I'll leave you to finish things here.'

'Of course you will,' I spat.

Uri glanced over his shoulder to where Lincoln lay. As he and Nox began to fade he looked back to me, his eyes fiercer than ever. 'Nothing is a certainty.'

And they were gone.

But I was still there in this twisted reality. I wondered if I could just stay there, ignore the rest of the world and simply fade away. But as soon as I formed the thought I felt the tug.

A whimper fell from my lips and I turned to see Phoenix lying on the ground, barely alive, arm outstretched.

'Come back, Violet. Come back!'

He was calling me back to the world. He was my anchor.

Lincoln must've told him.

I closed my eyes briefly.

There is still more to do.

I stepped towards Phoenix and the world around me came back into focus. Phoenix shook with pain as I crossed the border between reality and other. Around us, exiles began to scramble.

The combination of chaos combined with their vindictive natures made the exiles as furious with one another as they were with me. And now that Lilith was gone and Phoenix down it appeared the timeless rivalry between light and dark had been reinstated.

Helicopter blades sounded overhead, along with an explosion nearby. I heard voices yelling out commands from outside the ballroom. The exiles started to turn towards the new threat.

The cavalry had arrived.

My eyes sought out Evelyn, bracing for the worst. But there she was, alive, struggling against her restraints, while Spence helped her.

I fell to the ground beside Phoenix.

He was barely breathing. The sword he had used on Lilith had not been a full Grigori blade, so when she'd turned it back on him it hadn't killed him instantly. Still, I was amazed he was managing to hang on.

I grabbed his hand. It was cold, like mine.

'Ironic, isn't it?' I said, coughing up some blood, registering the pain in my side and wrist. 'After all of this, we're just going to die.'

He squeezed my hand.

'You won't die,' he said, each word an effort.

I didn't bother arguing. 'Just one more thing to do first.'

With the last of whatever strength Phoenix had, he pulled me roughly towards him. 'I need to tell you something,' he pleaded, pulling me close.

He whispered.

I listened.

And trembled with his words.

'It's too late!' I cried.

'I thought that once, too. But it's never too late. You taught me that. Love can make us eternal.' Phoenix's eyes closed, haunted to the end. 'I'm sorry,' were his last words.

'I forgive you,' I sobbed, gripping onto him desperately. 'I forgive you.'

It was too late.

All. Too. Late.

chapter thirty-seven

*'Angel, my little angel . . . I am small, you make me big, I am
weak, you make me strong . . .'*
Orthodox children's prayer

The double doors to the ballroom exploded in a mass of
flying debris and smoke, black-clad troops armed with
Grigori blades storming the hall to be met by a throng of
waiting exiles.

I kept staring at Phoenix's inert body.

Why hasn't he disappeared?

It took me a while to realise it was because he was part-
human, too. Unlike other exiles, this was his true body. Perhaps
that was why it had taken longer for him to die.

Within seconds of his last breath, all of the emotions from
which he'd spared me rushed back into me. It took everything I
had to endure the onslaught, but I couldn't let myself succumb
to them yet.

I cried as I crawled over and retrieved my katanas, still
lying where Lilith had dropped them. I struggled to my feet
just as I saw a pair of exiles coming towards me.

Spence appeared from nowhere, leaping in front of me
and taking the exiles' attention. While he took care of them, I

— 400 —

pushed my power out one more time as more Grigori entered the fray, to hold back as many exiles as I could.

Digging deep, I found something new tucked well within my power. It was part of Phoenix that had come to me in his essence. While the rest of me was dominated by my soul's pain, burning with an icy coldness, in this new part of me, there was . . . nothing.

I travelled down a long dark corridor in my mind, searching for its meaning. When I reached the end, an understanding dawned on me. Phoenix had had the abilities of an empath and could both give and take emotions, but when he'd transferred his essence to me, it had mutated.

I could neither feel the emotions of others, nor give them away.

Instead, I could lock everything – every emotion – down. All of them. It was as simple as flicking a switch.

And so I did.

Everything melted away.

Numbness spread through me quickly. I could think more clearly, move more easily. The pain in my soul was still there, lurking, but it was no longer attacking me. I was . . . nothing.

I started to move again, controlling as many exiles as I could, even as I headed away from them towards the basement.

This will not all have been in vain.

I was weak. I staggered and lost my hold on the exiles.

The Grigori will have to deal with them now.

I looked back at Spence. He was in the middle of the battlefield.

'Spence!' I screamed.

He turned. I must have looked a sight – covered in blood and no emotion to show for it.

Spence screamed back at me even as he fought off oncoming exiles. He pushed one down and when another Grigori jumped in to take the next off his hands he started to run towards me, pulling out something from his waist.

He'd done it.

He had the Grigori Scripture.

I put up a hand. 'No! Get Lincoln!'

Spence skidded to a halt. He was close to Phoenix and I caught him register his lifeless body. Spence's eyes quickly moved to Lincoln, still chained and lying motionless on the sofa.

He shook his head. 'I'm coming to help you!'

'No, Spence! Swear to me you'll get him out. Swear it!' I yelled.

Spence's eyes darted between Lincoln and me. 'I'll get him!' he yelled back. 'I promise, Vi. I'll get him out.'

He held my eyes. Spence would do as he promised.

I turned back to the basement as total war broke out around me. I gripped my katanas and slashed at exiles that got in my way. I didn't stop.

I fell into the doorframe, using it to hold myself up. Before I'd righted myself completely, a hand grabbed my bleeding wrist from behind, squeezed tight and spun me around.

He pushed me against the wall. The back of my head hit the sandstone hard and I felt fresh blood run towards my neck. His strength was surprising, but I wasn't at my best. The small man, whose presence had troubled me earlier, restrained me as he placed his briefcase beside him and pulled an open vial from his inside jacket pocket.

He smiled soothingly, pinning me to the wall. 'It's a problematic world we find ourselves in,' he said with a heavy sigh. He looked forlorn and yet his eyes were alight when he looked back at me. 'I'm simply *fascinated* by you.'

'Who are you?' I ground out.

'That's a complicated question. But on this occasion, a mere financier. And I must say, though not living up to my original expectations, it seems it may still be money well spent.' He looked over his shoulder at the battle still raging. 'I would've loved to spend some more time together.' He placed the vial under my wrist and watched carefully as my blood flowed into it.

He was patient as I struggled, but there was little I could do – my power was almost entirely spent, my strength gone.

'What are you doing?' I demanded as I squirmed.

'Unfortunately, this is not the best time for a chat, but let's call it research.' He glanced behind himself again. He was going to run. It was a most un-exile-like trait, and yet, it wasn't due to fear. It was worse . . . He was smart.

I pulled on the dregs of my power, sending the very last from me, just enough to try and hold him for a few seconds. My mist floated right past him as if he were immune to it.

His smile widened and he pulled back the large vial, now filled with my blood. I realised I had never had him under my hold at all. Like Phoenix, briefcase man had been pretending.

He released me and I slid down the wall.

He bowed in a gentlemanly fashion. 'I do hope you survive.'

I blinked and he was gone. He could've run, dawdled or disappeared into thin air. In my state, it was impossible to know.

I picked up my sword and used the doorframe to force myself back onto my uncooperative legs. Another explosion rocked the room, the large chandelier falling with a crash, taking out whoever was beneath it. The far side of the room began to fill with smoke.

Half walking, half falling down the basement stairs I moved on until the sound of fighting grew faint. Finally, I reached the bottom. I looked myself over, the bleeding at my side and my wrist beginning to slow, eventually you just run out of the stuff.

It took everything I had just to breathe and stay upright.

Phoenix was dead. Lincoln was lost. Everything was gone.

The screams were repressed but they were there nonetheless, clawing at my throat, waiting to pull me down with them.

I turned to the cages just as another massive explosion erupted. Concrete chunks started to fall from the ceiling. The thirty children who had not been spared by my arrows huddled in groups. When they saw me, they started to scream.

Simon was standing up against the bars. Of course he was still there. I'd be willing to bet he'd insisted on staying with the others, even if he had been one of the children offered freedom.

'Violet!' he yelled, but it sounded more like a question.

I tried to smile. It was unlikely it looked convincing.

I scouted around for keys and finally found a set in a wall box. Staggering over to Simon's cage, I opened his first. He reached me just as I started to fall to my knees. He stumbled under my weight but managed to sit me against the bars.

I took his hand and pressed the keys into it. 'Get them out.'

His eyes connected with mine.

Such a small boy. So brave.

He nodded and started to unlock the other cages. A few minutes later all of the remaining children were huddled around me. They were free, but they still had to get out of the building.

Another explosion shook the basement and more concrete fell.

I gripped onto the cage and pulled myself to my feet, praying it would be the last time. I needed to be strong for them. I looked at the children.

My vision was starting to blur but I could see the smoke that had started streaming down the stairwell.

'Listen to me, this place is going to go,' I gulped. The whole building was on fire. 'Simon, take everyone upstairs. Stay low. Try not to breathe in the smoke. Everyone hold hands and stay in a line.'

The children began to join hands. 'Stay together,' I ordered. 'When you get up there, follow the hall. The front doors are at the end. Find a man called Griffin. Tell him . . . Tell him I sent you to him.'

The children nodded.

Good kids.

'Go!' I said. They started to move up the stairs in a line.

'What about you?' Simon asked, unsure.

I forced a smile. 'I'm right behind you.' Then I nodded him on and he left. Finally, *finally*, I dropped to the ground, face down.

When I could no longer hear their footsteps, I knew they had reached the top of the stairs. Tears welled with the relief of knowing that they would make it to safety. Griffin would look after them.

Smoke filled the basement. I didn't care. Time slowed down. I could see myself dying. I doubted I would come back this time.

Only now, did I let myself think of him.

I thought of our love, how much Lincoln meant to me. But even as my life drifted away, Phoenix's last words – the ones he'd whispered into my ear – played back. Over and over.

Is it even possible?

I forced another fraught breath. All I wanted was for it to be over. I wanted to go away, to never have to fight again.

But Phoenix's damn voice kept whispering to me.

What if? What if? What if?

I growled, angry at him for doing this to me. It would be just like him to lie to me, to make me fight and live only to discover it was just another trick to force my hand.

But still . . .

What if there's a chance it could be the truth?

I'd once promised Steph I would fight with every last breath to survive, but how could I when every breath felt like a thousand deaths?

The floor vibrated with another explosion. A large piece of ceiling crashed to the ground nearby. I could hear the crackling of the fire above. The building's structure was starting to give. It could cave in at any moment.

Oh, God. What if he was right?

I cried out. Rolling onto my back, clawing at the ground, trying to grab hold of something, anything. Suddenly I was fighting to get to my knees and trying to pull myself up.

But I was too weak. I fell back and closed my eyes.

It was over.

I had failed.

I felt hands on my legs, on my arms. My eyes opened. Looking down on me from above was Simon and three of the other kids.

No.

'Get . . . o-o-out,' I stammered.

But they just crouched beside me and Simon shook his head. 'And what would we say to God when he asks us why we left one of his angels behind to die?'

'I'm not . . . angel,' I tried to explain, because no matter what I wanted, I knew they would not be strong enough to carry me all the way out in the smoke and if they didn't leave now, they would never make it.

'Yes, you are,' said the girl at my arm. It was Katie. 'I dreamed an angel would save us. It was you in my dream,' she said, her eyes perfectly innocent.

'So did I,' said another girl at my leg.

'So did I,' said the boy at my other arm.

'And I,' said Simon.

Everything started to go black. I tried to tell them to go again. I tried and tried.

The next time I opened my eyes, I was being carried up the stairs by the children. Their strength alone was inexplicable, but even more so given the oxygen-starved air and unimaginable heat. Hell had found us and they faced it head on, fearless. I blinked.

We moved through the burning hallway, the fire raging around us and yet, the children marched straight towards the belly of the flames as if they knew they would part.

And they did.

I realised then, it was my angel maker doing this.

I closed my eyes again. It didn't stop the flood of tears.

I was carried out the front doors and down the steps. I could hear voices, orders being shouted, people running everywhere.

Everything suddenly stopped. All the sound, all the movement. Still.

Then a woman's voice bellowed. 'Clear their path!'

The children began to walk again and I felt strong hands move under me.

I could hear Griffin. 'Hold on, Violet. Hold on!' he said, over and over.

I was put down on the grass and a figure crouched beside me. It was Josephine. It had been her voice I had heard. Our eyes met. Blood and soot covered her face. Oh, she'd been in the thick of it tonight.

I wondered briefly if Josephine might end me there and then. But she just turned away and started calling out orders to someone behind her.

'Get Evelyn! Tell her . . . Tell her her daughter is alive. And fetch the medics, now!' She paused, then opened her mouth again. 'You, you and you: she's one of ours. Protect her!'

She looked down at me. 'You foolish girl. I don't know how

you killed her or how you're still alive, but you're damn well
going to stay that way so you can explain it to me later.'

How ironic, I thought, that just as Josephine had decided
I'd proved myself to be one of them, I had realised that I wasn't.

She stood, issuing more orders as she moved away.

Griffin stayed beside me as the medics started to wrap
bandages around my wounds. I faded in and out of awareness.
I could hear him talking to me, telling me to fight.

Another body slid to the ground beside me. Hands grabbed
at mine.

'Violet,' Evelyn cried, 'I'm here, baby.'

But I couldn't speak.

Breathe in.

Breathe out.

It was the most I could do.

Evelyn seemed to understand, but she pulled me into her
lap nonetheless and began to rock me back and forth. And then
she told me the only thing that would make me want to keep
breathing.

'We got him out. I don't know if it helps, but we got Lincoln
out.'

I didn't know if it helped either. I didn't know if it meant
anything. The pain was crippling, almost breaking through my
tenuous hold on life. I closed my eyes as my mother rocked
me. I went within myself, down to the darkest corridor in my
power, and found the switch at the very end. I glided towards
it, something singing out, warning me to beware.

I flicked the switch.

'Thank you, Phoenix,' I whispered.

Everything went black.

chapter thirty-eight

'The sadness will last forever.'
Vincent van Gogh

It was quiet. Early mornings were always the quietest time.

I barely slept any more. Dreams brought little rest. I sat on my bed, looking out the window of my twelfth-floor apartment. The world moved on below, safe, for now.

It had been three weeks since that night at the estate. We had been the victors. Funny that the pedestal came with no joy.

I looked around my room. It used to mean home to me. Now it just reminded me of everything that I wasn't. I stood up. I was strong again. It had taken over a week for them to release me from hospital. I had healed in days, of course – a fact Grigori doctors had kept hidden – but they'd insisted on keeping me in, sedated. They didn't tell me why, but I knew they were all scared I would do something to myself.

Dad or Evelyn had sat with me every day. Eventually, other visitors were allowed in, too. Steph had been the first. She cried and told me all the things that had been happening. She told me how sorry she was. I tried to listen, but stopped her when she started to talk about Lincoln.

After that, others came, but I never spoke, even when Josephine turned up and stated that she still had questions. Part of me suspected she was tempted to imprison me and Evelyn again, but after everything that had gone down, there was no way she could do so and save face. On another, more generous level, I understood that Josephine was a true fighter. And when she looked at me now, it was different. She knew I could destroy exiles and to her, that made me worthy.

She informed me the Grigori Scripture was in her possession and assured me it would never again fall into enemy hands. Frankly, it seemed dangerous enough that it was in hers.

Her parting words were: 'Your Grigori testing has been re-evaluated, to a unanimous pass.'

I didn't respond.

Now, two weeks after Griffin had arranged my release from hospital and departure from New York, I was back home and stronger than ever, with both my angel maker's power and Phoenix's essence running through me.

I hadn't seen Lincoln. I hadn't spoken about him, except to instruct Griffin that he would be coming home with us. Every now and then someone would mention him. I didn't listen, just flicked the switch and tuned it out.

Even when my angel maker came to me in my dreams, I'd discovered I could hit my new switch, blocking him out when he told me we needed to talk. Night after night, I sent him away. Wisely, he chose not to override my will. Yet.

The coldness had remained. It seeped into my bones so I was frozen all the time. The only other thing I couldn't stop as hard as I tried was my mind, despite the numbness. Over and over I relived the events of those final days and nights – all the choices made by so many different people and how those decisions landed me where I now was.

Broken.

I pulled on my hiking boots. The time had come. Dad was waiting for me and I couldn't delay any longer. I walked out to the kitchen. Evelyn was there, cooking breakfast. Dad was lounging on the sofa, reading the paper. They were happy, in their way, but there was a sadness about them, too.

Almost eighteen years had been stolen from their time together. Dad was only getting older while Evelyn looked young enough to be my sister. And it would only get worse.

Evelyn came up to me with a plate of food. She was wearing cream pants and a navy silk shirt, her hair recently restyled to help her look older. She held out some scrambled eggs. I shook my head and looked away.

Our relationship had changed. For some reason, right now, my parents 'got' me better than anyone else. Maybe it was the understanding of loss, the pain you can't imagine unless you have felt it rip through your body and soul. But even as Evelyn put down the plate that only reminded me of Lincoln and wrapped her arms around me, I couldn't return her embrace. Empathising, she backed away and I was grateful.

Dad pulled up outside Lincoln's warehouse.

'I can come in with you,' he said, again.

I shook my head.

He sighed. 'Okay. Call me if you need me.'

'Thanks,' I said.

Walking up the front steps, it was so familiar. For a couple of beats I let myself pretend it was normal. That I would knock on the door. That he would answer.

I shut it down.

It was a warm day, but I wore layers, wrapping them tightly around me, trying to keep the cold away. It was useless. The cold came from within.

I stood on the threshold. I could sense people inside. It took me a long time to knock.

Griffin opened the door. He hadn't known I was coming and his surprise showed. He held the door open and I walked in slowly, trying to keep my legs from buckling under me. Steph and Salvatore were in the kitchen. They stopped talking when they saw me.

Steph automatically started towards me, but paused when she saw my closed expression. I hadn't been able to talk to her at all. Nor to anyone, really, but especially her. Of all people, I knew she was the one I had to keep at arm's length. I could tell it hurt her, but I think she understood.

Spence walked out of his room, in old faded jeans and an equally faded red T-shirt, and stopped in the hallway.

'Eden,' he said as I passed.

I didn't reply. Couldn't.

I heard someone talking inside Lincoln's bedroom. I stood at the open door. I didn't look at the bed. Instead I focused on Dapper, who sat beside it. He was reading a book aloud.

When he saw me, he stopped reading. I said nothing, so he simply closed the book, placed it on the bedside table, stood and left the room. His hand brushed my shoulder as he did.

I stepped inside and closed the door behind me.

Every step towards the bed was shakier than the last. I looked down at him, my eyes finally seeing him. The air left my lungs and every muscle in my face ached.

A feeding drip was connected to his hand. He was silent, like he was sleeping, but . . . he was not peaceful. He was not really there at all.

I didn't cry.

I crawled onto the bed and curled up beside him, resting my head on his shoulder. I stayed like that, silently, for the rest of the day.

Eventually, when the sun started to go down and the room became dark, I got back up and stood at the end of the bed.

'I know you asked Phoenix to kill you,' I said, my voice breaking on every word. 'I know you two made your deals, but Phoenix isn't here any more.' I shook my head and made my way to the door, looking back at him once before I opened it. 'Did you really think it would be that easy?'

I left.

Everyone was still there and watched as I walked back into the living room and picked up Lincoln's car keys. I could feel all of them holding their breath, waiting for me to tell them. I knew they all thought I had come to kill him. As his partner, the decision had been left in my hands.

I looked at Griffin. 'No one touches him until I get back.'

Griffin stood. 'Where are you going?' he asked.

'To give an angel a choice.'

Spence was at the driver's door the moment I unlocked it.

I looked at him with empty eyes.

He held out his hand, staring back at me. 'Screw it. You can beat the crap out of me if you want, but you're not going on your own.' He pushed his open hand closer to me. 'Keys.'

'You can't come where I'm going,' I replied rigidly.

'I'll come as far as I can, then. You and I both know it's the smart thing to do. I'm good back-up. Plus . . .' He looked at the car. 'You drive like shit.'

I swallowed. He *was* good back-up. And I did drive like shit.

'I can't . . . talk.'

He half smiled. 'Never much liked your conversation anyway.'

I rolled my eyes and slapped the keys into his hand.

'See, Eden. You can't resist me. No woman can,' he said, smiling as he got into the car.

I ignored him and pulled out the directions I had prepared.

'Where are we headed?' he asked, starting up the four-wheel drive that smelled of Lincoln.

I rolled down the window. 'To a cliff.'

chapter thirty-nine

*'There is no refuge from memory and remorse in this
world. The spirits of our foolish deeds haunt us, with or
without repentance.'*

Gilbert Parker

Spence was the only one who could have talked his way into
coming with me. And he stayed true to his word, not saying
anything except when essential, which was basically, 'Time to
get petrol,' and 'Left here?'

It was strange being back in the wilderness. Back to where
it had all begun. Now, I'd come full circle.

We set up camp, finding supplies in the back of Lincoln's
car and building a campfire. The place was as forbidding as
it had been the first time I was there. As Spence and I sat in
silence and, later, pretended to sleep, I couldn't help but think
of my last time in this forest . . . pretending to sleep.

I had dreamed of Phoenix every now and then – he'd
materialise in a flash and disappear just as quickly. I hated the
thought of where he was, but he had told me himself that there
is no other place for exiles than the pits of Hell.

On the night of the fire at the estate, Spence had tried to go
back into the building for Phoenix's body. He didn't care much

for Phoenix himself, but Spence knew he mattered to me and guessed I'd like to be able to bury him. He was right. But other Grigori had held him back at the last second, stopping him from returning into the inferno. That place was now Phoenix's coffin.

While Spence rested I got up and wandered through the dark woods. My Grigori enhanced vision made it much easier than the last time I was here. I soon found the spot where Phoenix and I had camped and sat down on the large rock where he had sat beside me.

'Sometimes, I still want to blame you,' I whispered into the darkness. 'Sometimes, I want it all to have been your fault. But I don't and . . . it wasn't.' I looked up at the sky. Stars shone brightly, shimmering attentively as if listening to my every word. 'You saved those kids. They have a chance now, a future. You did good.' I sniffed, trying to hold myself together. 'But I still hate you.' A tear slipped down my cheek. 'I hate what the two of you did. You both just . . .' I blew out a breath shakily. 'You left me and now I can't go, but I can't stay either.'

I stood and wiped away the tears with the back of my hand. Phoenix had been wrong about a lot of things. But he'd been right about one thing: 'Love *has* killed us all.'

In the pre-dawn hours, Spence climbed the mountain with me, insisting on escorting me to the top. His exact words were, 'In case you decide to jump at the wrong moment.' He was only half joking.

We hiked the steep rock face in silence.

When sunrise teased the horizon, I made my way to the edge of the cliff.

So many what ifs.

I toed the edge and waited for the first rays of sunlight to pierce the dark sky. The timing had to be right.

'You think this is gonna work?' Spence asked finally, unable to help himself.

It was a good question. Grigori aren't supposed to jump off cliffs whenever they like and expect an angelic audience in return. That one move is reserved for when we embrace. But I needed to do this my way, on my terms.

'I'll tell you at the bottom,' I said, as the sun's first pale pink rays speared the sky, illuminating a thick band of cloud.

Arms wide, I leaped.

I landed on my back with a thump in the desert. I jumped to my feet and gritted my teeth.

'No desert,' I commanded.

The desert disappeared and I was left in darkness, surrounded by nothing other than glittering stars, which cast little light.

Uri stood before me, somehow perfectly lit. 'Why do you call us, Keshet?'

'I'm not calling you. I want to see my maker.'

Uri's chin lifted. Pride. 'You think you are entitled to such an audience at your request?'

'Yes.'

He stared at me. I put my hands on my hips and stared back. For the first time, he gave me a small smile.

'I believe he may agree with you.'

I tried to hide my surprise. 'You know who he is?' As far as I was aware, neither Uri nor Nox knew his full identity.

'It has become paramount to our duties,' Uri nodded and, if I wasn't mistaken, there was something of a bow in there, too. 'Do you remember my words, Keshet?'

'I'm not surrendering any more, Uri.'

His look saddened. 'I'm afraid that will not serve you well. Surrender brings both despair and joy – but if you choose not to give in to it, you cannot expect either.'

I was so sick of this. 'Fine by me,' I responded.

His gaze dropped. 'As you wish.'

He disappeared and I was left with the hollow feeling that I had just disappointed him. But before I had a chance to ponder any further, the one I'd come to see was beside me.

'Would you feel more comfortable with a different surrounding?' my angel maker asked.

I ignored the question. The truth was, the nothingness surrounding me felt right. 'You told me I could ask for something when I won the war.'

'I did.'

'Have I won the war?'

'This one, yes, I believe so. Lilith will not return.' The corners of his mouth curled, reminding me he was a fierce warrior.

'Then I want three things,' I blurted out.

His eyes narrowed. 'I cannot offer so many. You must choose.'

'No, I must not. I will be your warrior. I will become a Grigori like no other. I will take down every exile that threatens humanity. I give you my word. But it will be my way, by my rules. If you want that, I have terms. So, you see, it's not me that has to choose anything, it's you.'

He shook his head. 'Just like your mother. Tell me.'

I stared out into the darkness. Some of the stars seemed to be moving, now floating around me. There were so many of them.

How can there be so many?

'I want them to have a chance. Mum and Dad. You can give Dad back the years that were stolen from him, give them a future together.'

'And are you a part of their future?' he asked.

'I . . . I don't know.'

'I can't give them what you ask but I can provide a choice that would give them something close. But they must choose this of their own free will, and desire it greatly, for it to be so.'

I knew he wasn't telling me everything but at least they would have a choice. I nodded and continued. 'I want Phoenix to have a chance at peace. I know where he is and he doesn't belong there. He deserves more.'

My angel maker's eyes lit up mischievously. 'Done.'

My mouth fell open with shock. 'Really?'

He nodded. 'Phoenix made his choices, too. Wrong though many of them were, in the end he chose to overcome his true nature. Very few – angel, exile or human – ever achieve this. Redemption was his.'

My legs buckled, my angel maker catching me by the elbow as I struggled for breath.

'He's in Heaven or something?'

He waited until I steadied myself. 'Something.' His smile faded as he studied me, awaiting my final request. 'I am quite certain I know what number three is, but that is not a gift for me to give.'

'I haven't even asked yet.'

His eyes were all too knowing. 'You want me to return your love.'

My heart skipped a beat. 'Yes,' I breathed.

'I cannot.' He sighed – such a human reaction that it affected me. 'It is not in my power to do such things.'

I felt hope slipping away from me. 'But Phoenix said . . . He said that if I came here I could find him. That there was a way.'

My angel maker considered this. 'You see them. We know that much, but we cannot risk losing you.'

'Wait, "see them"? What?' But then I realised what he was talking about. 'The shimmery things? Yes.'

'Do you know what they are?'

'No,' I said looking out into the dark night seeing now that the many moving stars were in fact reflections, moving closer towards us, hovering. 'Can they help me?'

'Perhaps. They are the imprints of lost souls. There is a chance your love lies within them.'

My heart started to race with possibility. 'So I can find him?'

My angel maker didn't share my excitement. In fact, he became forlorn. 'There are billions of them out there, child. An impossible and dangerous feat. And you are needed for other things.'

'Phoenix didn't think so. I've earned my right to try!'

He considered me for another long moment. 'Then this one will not be for me to decide.'

'Then who? Who the hell do I have to convince?' I yelled, desperate.

He held his arm out beyond me. 'The other one who is now entitled a role in your guidance.'

I spun around and gasped.

He looked so strong, so healthy. His hair was sparkling in the night-light. He was in black pants and a white shirt, rolled up at the sleeves. He looked the same but different . . . Something fundamental about him had changed. His eyes. Still chocolate brown and beautiful but no longer so deeply haunted.

Phoenix was an angel.

chapter forty

'The windows of my soul I throw
Wide open to the sun.'
John Greenleaf Whittier

my legs wouldn't stop shaking. I tried to take a step towards him but fell to my knees.

I looked to the ground, waiting for the tears. But I couldn't cry. Even in this most tremendous moment I was still numb. Still cold.

'We were wrong. I see that now,' Phoenix said, his voice heavy with regret.

I knew what he meant, but I just couldn't go there. I looked up at him, my eyes begging him to stop.

'You're . . .'

'Angel once more,' he said. He didn't sound ecstatic about it.

I half smiled. Still Phoenix. 'Is this what you want?'

'Better than eternity in the pits of Hell,' he answered.

'But?'

He was silent. He glanced around as if only now noticing the darkness that surrounded us. When he looked back at me tenderly, so much more emotion showed on his face than ever before and . . . I understood.

Hell is in the eye of the beholder.

'I have no reason to be anywhere else, I suppose,' but his words were edged with a longing that I could not ignore.

His eyebrows furrowed and he took a tentative step towards me. 'I'm so . . .' He swallowed the words. 'I know you were attacked when you were younger.'

I froze. 'How?' I'd never willingly told anyone other than Lincoln.

'I'm an angel. Knowing just comes with the territory.' When I didn't respond, he added quietly, 'Why didn't you ever tell me?'

The memories washed through me – a wave that was now part of a much greater ocean of agony. 'I didn't see any point. It doesn't define me.'

'No, but I wish I'd known. I'd never have pushed the way I . . . It explains a lot.'

I bit my lip, fighting to control my emotions. 'I'm sorry, Phoenix, I . . .'

'Don't apologise. It's me who loved you beyond reason,' he said, shaking his head and I was sure his eyes were glistening in the starlight.

I looked to the sky, noticing there was no moon, and that my angel maker had disappeared.

'So you want to be here?' I asked, still unsure.

'I want to be where I am needed. For now, it is here but . . .'

The strength of his gaze – full of promise – drew mine back to him.

'If the day should come, for any reason, that you would prefer me . . . elsewhere, it will be so.'

I shook my head. 'I shouldn't have that kind of power, Phoenix. Those aren't my choices. I don't want them to be.'

He nodded sadly. 'Until I decide otherwise, then, I will be here. For you.'

We were silent. Phoenix standing, me still kneeling.

'I'm faster,' I said.

'Yes.'

'I can't feel things the way you can. At least, I don't think I can, but . . .'

'You can shut down your emotions.'

I swallowed. 'Yes.'

He took a tentative step towards me. 'Power takes many forms and mutates as it is passed on. It is the way of evolution. This is no different, but treat this power carefully. Emotion is raw. Meddling with it rarely works as we intend. Often by the time we see our error, it's too late to turn back,' his voice caught at the end.

There was another stretch of silence.

'It hurts too much,' I finally confessed.

'I know,' he said. And he did.

'You'll need to empty yourself of everything. It's not easy and the way you are at the moment – I don't know this is the best time.'

I took a few deep breaths and absorbed this information along with all that Phoenix had been explaining to me for the past . . . I wasn't sure how long. Time moved differently here.

'It's now or never,' I said, determinedly.

He sighed, resigned. 'Okay. When you go to them, they will all want you. You represent life and everything they long for. Whatever it was that led them to this place, to this in-between, they crave what you have. They will suffocate you with their desires. You won't have long to find him.'

I nodded, looking out into the infinity of the universe and the countless reflections, floating and diving through the air.

'What do I do once I find him?'

'Can you feel your power inside you?' he asked.

I pressed a hand over my abdomen. 'Yes, it's like a deep well.'

'Exactly. If you want to bring him back, you'll have to find a way to bring him into you. He must be absorbed *into* your power, otherwise when you leave this place he won't be able to hold onto you.'

'How will I do that?'

'His soul will be confused. You'll have to show him what he wants most.'

I knew what Lincoln wanted most. 'My soul,' I said, nodding.

Phoenix reached forwards, surprising me by placing a warm, soft hand against the side of my face. His gentle eyes bored into mine. 'Oh, Violet.' His lips pressed together and I could see his utter sadness for me. 'It's much harder than that. It's your heart.'

I cast my eyes to the side. I couldn't think about what he had just said, couldn't think about what that would do to me.

I gulped. 'Okay. I'm ready.'

Phoenix stood from where he'd been crouched beside me and nodded. 'I can't go with you. When you have him, I'll know and I'll send you back.'

There was a part of me that didn't want to have to walk away from him. 'Will I see you again?'

'That'll be up to you. When you're ready, call for me in your dreams. I'll be there.'

I walked into the unknown and the reflections that glowed ahead. They seemed to respond to my presence and started moving towards me, slowly at first and then faster and faster. I could sense their eagerness.

I kept moving, knowing that I needed to go as far as possible. They swirled around me, vibrating with anticipation. I was what they craved, what they remembered in some far recesses of their minds. It was both haunting and distressing and I wanted to stop, to fall back into the nothingness and weep for them, but I did not.

Instead, I ran into their midst.

They whipped around me, becoming frenzied as more of them became aware of my presence. I felt them fighting and pushing to get closer to me until eventually I could no longer move, their combined pressure creating a prison that trapped me.

I threw my head back, stared at the stars above and started the process of emptying myself. Just as Phoenix had told me, I pushed away my family, my friends. I cleared my mind of my joys, my passions, my sorrows, my hopes and my many regrets. I pushed away the exiles, the scars I carried from the wars I'd fought and those that were yet to come. I pushed away the angel guides, my maker. And finally I pushed away Phoenix so that all that was left was Lincoln.

I felt my body start to shudder under the sheer pressure of the lost souls as they tried to break me or, more accurately, to *take* my life force, as if they could somehow absorb it and claim back some of their own. I wanted to panic, but I pushed that away too.

Then I saw it.

It didn't come from the sides, or push through the masses. It came hesitantly from above, almost as if it had been hiding up there, behind a star. A small cry fell from my lips.

I knew it was Lincoln's reflection – his soul. My body ached to reach out to him.

It shone brightly as it floated down to me from above. I waited patiently, concentrating on keeping my focus on him and nothing else, making sure I continued to act as a homing beacon for him. And he came for me, sure and straight.

My falling star.

Eventually, he hovered right above me. My face tilted up towards his reflection – a mere disturbance in the air – and I closed my eyes briefly to draw in his presence. I felt it . . . the sun. Even in the darkness, the nothingness, he was still the sun.

He waited, moving around the edges of my face as if trying to caress me, as if worried for me.

I could barely take it. I had to bring him into me. I let go of everything that held me together. I cut the last thin ties that guarded what was left of my heart and I gave it to him.

As I screamed in agony, Lincoln's soul poured into me.

The moment I had him, I was falling again.

The next thing I knew, I was in Spence's arms. He was carrying me through the woods.

'You okay?' he asked as I blinked.

No. I wasn't.

'Vi?'

He shifted me in his hold and I heard a beep. We were at the car.

I swallowed through a dry throat. 'How long?'

'You've been out of it for about twenty minutes. I made it down the mountain and you were already there, where you told me to go. Fell with a thump, too.'

He opened the passenger door and sat me in the car, then grabbed a bottle of water from the back seat and twisted the top, passing it to me.

I took a sip. 'We need to go,' I said.

'Where?' Spence was looking around, no idea what to expect.

'Back to Lincoln's.' I turned to the front and dropped my face in my hands. Gradually, all the things I'd pushed aside were coming back and it hurt. Overwhelmed, I let out a moan.

'Jesus, Vi, what the hell happened to you out there?'

I shook my head, bracing a hand on the dashboard. 'We have to go,' I gritted out.

But Spence wasn't having it. 'Come on, Vi, you gotta give me more than that. Griff's gonna have my ass on a platter for this. What happened?'

I shook my head again. 'Please, *Spence*,' I begged, because every word – *every* second – hurt, and would for the rest of my life, but I had to put this one thing right. And having Lincoln's soul so close to me – *in me* – where it had once belonged . . . I could barely hold myself together.

Spence shifted from one foot to the other. 'Okay, Eden, we're going, we're going.' He jumped into the driver's seat and we took off while he mumbled something very imaginative about exactly what he suspected Griffin was going to do to his ass.

chapter forty-one

'What shall a man give in exchange for his soul?'

Mark 8:37

When Spence and I walked back into Lincoln's apartment, everyone was there. Even Onyx.

They watched me, barely breathing as I made my way to Lincoln's room. When I didn't close the door behind me they seemed to take it as an invitation and followed. I didn't mind. I had no idea what was about to happen and I might need them.

Griffin pulled Spence into the corner of the room and started demanding answers. Spence stuttered a series of defences that began with, 'Don't blame me,' and finished with 'I don't know.'

Onyx and Dapper stayed at the back of the room with Zoe and Salvatore. Steph came up behind me. 'We're here for you, Vi. Whatever you need. We're here,' she said.

They thought I had come back to finish things. They were wrong, but I suppose in other ways . . . they were right.

I turned to face Steph and she gasped.

'What?' I asked.

'Your eyes; they're green!'

I just stared at her, unwilling to fully contemplate what she was saying.

'They're not mine,' I said, eventually, turning back to the bed where Lincoln lay.

'Well, whose the hell *are* they?' Steph shouted, her voice high-pitched.

I didn't reply. Instead, I leaned down, knowing what I had to do. 'It's always a kiss,' I mumbled. And then I pressed my lips to his and let him go.

As I kissed him, his soul broke free. It was so painful, as though my very insides were torn away as it leaped from my body and back into its rightful owner. I screamed into his mouth, but I stayed there, forcing myself to keep going, to keep pushing his soul from me until it was all gone.

The moment I knew it was done, I sank to the ground, gasping for air.

Steph dropped beside me. Her hands were shaking as they clung to me. 'Vi, what was that?'

'Eyes are the window to the soul,' Dapper said from the doorway. 'The girl went and found his soul. Insane as those damn exiles. She should be dead.'

'What do you mean?' Griffin pushed. 'Lincoln?'

Dapper grunted, as Steph held me tight, trying to calm my shakes.

'Ask her yourself, but I'm betting she just pulled off something only the likes of her could do.'

Griffin crouched in front of me. 'Violet, is Dapper right? Did you . . .' But he couldn't finish the sentence. Lincoln was his best friend and I knew he blamed himself on some level for telling us to run that day, felt responsible that he hadn't been there in the end.

I looked up at Steph and saw her sharp intake of breath; my eyes were back to normal. Not that I needed her reaction to tell me that, I could already feel the change. The emptiness in me had returned and I could feel a presence I hadn't felt in weeks.

Griffin watched me anxiously.

'He's back,' I said.

We could have heard a pin drop. No one knew what to say. Perhaps they thought I'd finally lost it completely and was having delusions. Maybe they thought it was too good to be true.

But not Griffin. He stared right at me. He was a truth seeker; he knew what I said was right. I suspected he simply couldn't talk. Instead he pulled me from Steph's arms and into his.

'You're a miracle.'

I was stiff in his arms. Just like with everyone else . . . I couldn't. Gradually, I wriggled away from him.

'Phoenix said it will take a few days for him to recover.' I stood up, still shaky on my feet, though I tried not to show it. I looked at the floor, avoiding the bewildered gazes.

'Phoenix?' Griffin repeated, shock rippling through the group again.

I nodded. 'Phoenix is an angel.'

'Well, that figures,' Onyx snorted. 'Redemption, that sly bitch.'

Everyone ignored him.

'I'll be staying here until he wakes up. Phoenix said it would be safest that way since I was the one who brought him back.' I pressed my lips together.

Griffin nodded. 'We'll bring in a mattress and get you settled.'

I shook my head. 'A pillow and the chair will be fine.'

Griffin nodded, running his hands through his hair. 'Everything is going to be okay,' he said, relief flooding his face.

I gave a sorry attempt at a smile.

Gradually, when they realised I wasn't going to be telling any more of my story everyone filtered out. Steph and Spence were the last ones to leave. Spence didn't bother trying to hug me – he knew I wasn't capable. Instead, he got right to the point.

'Eden, you reckon since you could bring Lincoln's soul back that you might . . . Do you think you could find Nyla?'

I had known this question would come up from the moment I considered that this might work. I just didn't know who would be the one to ask. I was sorry it had to be Spence.

'If I thought there was any chance, I would. But it was only because of our . . .' Love. 'Connection, that I was able to find him. There were thousands, millions, out there. They go on forever.' I looked down and shook my head. 'I'm sorry, Spence.'

He put his hands in his pockets, shrugging to try and hide his disappointment. 'Yeah. Figured that might be the case, just thought I'd ask.'

I nodded. 'You're off to find your partner soon, aren't you?' I asked, keen to change the subject.

He smiled. 'Yep. Can you believe it – I'll finally be able to stop relying on you to fix me every time I'm hurt. Griff says we'll start tracking her down in a couple of weeks. You never know, maybe things are starting to look up.'

I wished it were true. 'You never know.'

After Spence left, Steph stayed with me for a while. I appreciated the distraction. Even though I knew I would be in this room for the next few days, I wasn't ready to be alone with Lincoln yet.

'You're strong, you know that?' Steph said.

'I know,' I replied.

'You can get through this. What happened, it was . . . And you had to survive when everyone around you . . .'

Died. Left.

I nodded. 'It's okay, Steph.'

'Are you ever going to let me back in?'

I looked at her properly; her lower lip was trembling, her eyes had dark rings around them. She had been keeping vigil over Lincoln since I had not been able to. She'd been there for me and she was exhausted.

'You're my best friend, Steph. You'll always be my best friend, but . . .'

'You're doing what you have to do to survive?' she finished.

'Yeah.'

She grabbed my hand and squeezed. 'Just know that I'm here. I'll always be here.'

I swallowed and tried to think of something else to say. 'So you and Salvatore are going well? Does he know what he's going to do next?'

She shrugged. 'Not really. But for now, he and Zoe are going to stay in the city and help Griffin out.'

I nodded. 'Have Dapper and Onyx been here a lot?'

'Yeah, they're in and out. Dapper brings food and Onyx brings . . . Well, nothing, but he comes. I think that's the most he can manage.'

I sat in my chair and cuddled the pillow. 'You know he could've become an exile again. Lilith offered him everything and he turned her down.'

She wasn't surprised. 'What can I say? He's one of those moves-in-mysterious-ways types.'

I actually felt the corner of my mouth twitch. 'He is.'

Steph raised an eyebrow. 'Hey, do you think . . . I mean, have you noticed how Dapper and Onyx are always together and how they fight but don't at the same time?'

I nodded, remembering having the same conversation with Lincoln. 'Yep. Totally together.'

'They're a good match,' Steph said, approvingly. She looked at Lincoln and back to me. 'He'll be okay. I can feel it.'

'I know he will,' I replied. 'I can feel it, too.'

After Steph left, I settled into the chair and tried to sleep. I failed and eventually had to look at him. I leaned forward, putting my face close to his, and reached forwards, my hand shaking as my fingers skimmed his hair. His chest moved up and down and when my hand touched him, his breathing became faster, just like mine.

'I can feel you,' I whispered. 'I know you're back.'

I inhaled his scent, letting everything about him surround me, his warmth building. Sun and honey. I breathed out, resting my head beside him. I slept a blissful, dreamless sleep.

The next morning Evelyn was in the room, too, clearly waiting for me to wake up.

I sat up and rubbed my eyes, moving away from Lincoln, who seemed to have moved closer during the night.

'We heard what you did,' she said.

'Is Dad pissed?' I asked.

'Yep. But he's also doing that thing he does when you do something he's proud of.'

I nodded, understanding. Dad had a signature proud-to-be-Dad smile that went with a particularly cocky walk.

'It seems collecting Lincoln's soul isn't the only thing you've been up to,' she added raising an eyebrow. 'I had a visit last night. I'd almost forgotten how intimidating your angel maker is.'

I shrugged. 'He grows on you.'

'Hmm,' she said, moving to the edge of the bed and sitting opposite me. 'He's offered me a choice and since I'm fairly certain you opened up the opportunity for me, I wanted to ask you what you thought before I make a decision.'

I leaned towards her, taking her hands in mine. 'Mum, do you know what you want to do?'

She froze. Her eyes welled.

'What?' I asked, worried.

She shook her head. 'It's just . . . That's the first time you've called me Mum.'

I sighed. 'It shouldn't have taken me so long.'

She pulled me into a hug. I tried to hug her back, I really did, but I just couldn't.

She eased back, studying me carefully. 'If I do this, I won't be Grigori any more. And we might have to move away.'

I nodded. There were no surprises there. 'If you know what you want, and if Dad wants it too, just do it. You don't need my permission.'

She smiled and nodded. 'Okay.' She glanced at Lincoln. 'And what about you? What are we going to do with you, my girl?'

I bit down on my lip. 'Actually, I wanted to talk to you and Dad about that.'

'Oh?'

'Yeah. I've made a decision.'

chapter forty-two

'I'm not upset that you lied to me, I'm upset that from now
on I can't believe you.'
Friedrich Nietzsche

for the next two days I sat in the chair, leaving Lincoln only to shower and make the occasional phone call. On the third day, Dapper came to see me, after I had asked him to drop by.

I could feel that Lincoln was getting stronger. I knew he would wake up soon.

I knew something else, too. Our souls were no longer joined. We were still soulmates – the familiar tug had returned instantly, combining with the coldness I imagined would now be with me forever – but the connection we'd made in the cabin . . . Gone.

'Why do I suspect this is a business call?' Dapper asked as he entered the room.

I stood up and closed the door behind him. 'Because it is.'

He grunted. 'And why do I have a feeling I know where this is leading?'

'Because you probably do,' I admitted.

He sighed and leaned on the windowsill.

'You said once that you owed me a favour.'

'I remember.'

'And you said not to talk to you about it again until I was ready to collect.'

'Mighta said something like that.'

I nodded. 'I'm ready to collect.'

After Dapper left – unhappy but with our debt settled – I sat back down in my chair and waited. Sure enough, that afternoon, Lincoln started to become restless and at 4 p.m. I could tell he was ready to wake up.

I stood over him, ran my fingers through his hair and leaned down.

'I love you,' I whispered.

He made a sound that ran through my body and reminded me of all the things we had shared.

I turned and left the room, going out to the living area, where everyone was waiting. They all looked up like expectant meerkats when they saw me. I half smiled.

'He's waking up.'

Griffin jumped to his feet, the rest of the squad behind him. They smiled and laughed and ran into Lincoln's room, leaving me alone.

I loved Lincoln's warehouse. In many ways it had become my home, too. I looked up to the enormous arched windows that were at either end. Afternoon sun flooded through them, drenching the space. It was beautiful.

Walking over to the kitchen, I ran my hand along the breakfast bar, remembering all the times I'd sat there eating food Lincoln had prepared for me, while listening to his advice and hanging off every word. I closed my eyes and imagined the smell of basil – how much he loved to cook with it.

I stopped by my wall, still covered by the drop-sheet. I left it where it was. The image beneath now seemed so naive.

I found a notepad and pen and wrote a few words, leaving the folded piece of paper on the dining table.

I could hear everyone moving about, the occasional cheer. He was awake and I could sense that he was looking for me.

Before I could stop myself I made my way to the front door. I had it halfway open when Steph ran down the hall.

'Hey, Vi. Lincoln's asking for–' She broke off when she saw me. 'You're . . . leaving?'

I couldn't talk. I just looked at her, trying to explain somehow without words that I couldn't possibly stay knowing everything I now did, having gone through everything I had gone through.

People had made sacrifices and died. For me. *Because* of me. I couldn't stay and watch those I cared about most continue to make choices that put me first. I had made promises to my angel maker and I knew he'd hold me to them. But the only way I could do that would be alone, where the danger and consequences of my choices would be my own.

And the simple truth was, I couldn't face him. Lincoln was back and now he had a chance to live. I wanted that for him – I certainly didn't bring him back just so he could die defending me. The only chance for his survival would be to be apart from me, and the only chance for mine would be to finally – completely – embrace the Grigori I am.

Steph stood frozen, staring back at me until her shoulders dropped and the tears started to fall down her cheeks. 'But you can't,' she whispered.

I cleared my throat. 'I left a note. Will you give it to him?'

She nodded as she cried and sniffed. 'Will you call me? Please, Vi, promise me you will call me.'

'He can never know where I am.' Because despite what I had decided, Lincoln would come for me if he knew where I was. He wouldn't accept this. We were partners. As far as he was concerned, like it or not, that meant we were together.

Steph shook her head. 'I wouldn't tell if that's what you wanted. Just promise you will stay in touch. Please, Vi. You're my best friend.'

I looked down. I should have said no to her. But I found myself nodding. 'When I get settled, I'll call you with my new number.' I gripped the door. 'I have to go.'

Before I could get away, Steph was hugging me tight. For just a moment, I let myself hug her back.

'Love you, Vi.'

'Love you, Steph.'

And then I left.

Dad and Evelyn had arranged everything while I had been watching over Lincoln. They had made their decision, too – whatever that meant – and were happy to leave the city, something I had resolved to do a while back. I was relieved now to be going with them.

They had packed everything up and put it into storage for now, until we made our final decision about where to settle. It turned out Evelyn had more than one safe-house and we were going to start by visiting them. I used my key for the last time and walked into the apartment.

Dad came out of his room, smiling. I was a little surprised to see him looking just the same.

'I thought you guys decided to . . .' I started, but then Evelyn walked out of the bedroom behind him and I realised . . . they had.

'Wow,' I said, transfixed by my mother, who, for the first time, actually looked like my mother and mature enough to be Dad's wife. 'You're beautiful,' I said, and truly meant it. She was even more stunning than she had been, just older.

She beamed. 'I know it isn't what you expected, but I've wanted to grow up for a long time and although your dad and I won't get back the years we lost, this way . . . The years ahead will be all ours,' she said, cosying up to Dad. I'd never seen Dad look so content.

I smiled. 'It's perfect.'

'Are you sure you want to do this, sweetheart?' Dad asked.

'I'm sure,' I said, heading to my room to find it stripped bare, a lone suitcase sitting in the middle of the floor. I grabbed it and headed back out. I knew that Lincoln wouldn't be up and about for another couple of days, but I didn't want to wait around to find out. Dad and Evelyn were by the door when I re-emerged, waiting for me.

'Ready,' I said.

We rode the lift down and headed straight for the taxi Dad had waiting, but as soon as we cleared the doors I saw that Spence was standing by the car. I headed to the boot and threw in my bag. The taxi driver gave me an odd look and I realised I should've made it look as though it was heavy.

Whatever.

After gawking at my mother's changed appearance, Spence stalked around the car, nodding to my parents as they got in the back.

'You weren't even going to say goodbye?'

'Don't sulk,' I said, trying to concentrate on organising my travel wallet.

'This is bullshit and you know it, Eden! You're not even giving him a chance to talk to you.'

'There's no point. Look, I've spoken to Dapper. He's promised to look out for you until you have your partner. If you're injured, he'll heal you. Griffin and . . . Lincoln, too. For as long as you all need it.'

Spence's fist went down on the car. 'That's not what this is about and you know it!'

I tried to press on. 'Tell Griffin that . . . That technically I died so maybe Lincoln is within his rights to request a new partner. Even if he isn't, I won't protest if he lodges an application.'

Spence shook his head. 'You're running away!'

My throat ached as the permanent lump grew larger.

'I know.'

Spence's eyes squinted and his mouth twisted as he tried to hold himself together. 'You're the only damn family I have!'

I placed a hand on his shoulder. 'I'm not. Your family is all back at that warehouse. I . . . I don't know what's going to happen to me, but I have to go.'

He looked down at his feet. 'I could come with you,' he said quietly.

'Not this time, Spence. You need to find your partner. I need to find myself. We'll both be better for it in the end.'

He stepped back and opened the taxi door for me. Dad and Evelyn were waiting patiently.

'I've always got your back, Eden.'

'And I've got yours. Anytime, anywhere.' It wasn't the first time I'd made Spence that promise and I meant it just as much now.

We waited in the airport lounge for our flight to board. Only then, once I was safely checked in and ready to leave, did I allow myself to exhale.

He was alive.

Part of me wished that meant happily ever after, that I had been able to write something in that note that meant that there was hope. But there was none. Any resolution that ended with us near each other as partners or together and in love didn't end well. He would always be the one trying to die for me.

And that wasn't enough.

I closed my eyes. I don't know if I actually slipped out of myself and into my angelic Sight, or simply dreamed, but one moment my eyes were closed to blackness, the next they were above Lincoln. He was on his sofa, propped up against pillows. He was panting heavily and sweating.

'I told you; you can't move yet, Linc. It's going to take a few days for everything to come back online,' Griffin said, sounding out of breath himself. Something had happened – they were surrounded by broken furniture and both looked worse for wear. Lincoln was staring straight ahead, the drop-sheet now gone, exposing the mural on my wall. I looked at the painting that had started as a solitary white lily, and now depicted a whole field of them beneath a violet sky and a golden sun. It was us . . . a lifetime ago.

'I have to get to her,' he said, his voice barely there, every word hitting me like a freight train.

'She's gone, Linc. She's gone.'

A cry fell from Lincoln's lips that speared my heart. His hand dropped down to his lap and my note fell from his fingertips.

> *Nothing is endless.*
> *I know that now.*
> *Let me go.*
> *V*

'Sweetheart,' Dad said, shaking my shoulder gently. 'They just called our flight. You ready?'

I looked up at him, still feeling Lincoln's nearness, feeling the fading rays of sunlight. I picked up my backpack and let Dad pull me to my feet. I hated that I was hurting Lincoln, hated that I was hurting myself.

But there was no other way.

He'd move on, find another partner – a better one – and until he did, Dapper would be there to heal him. He'd be stronger without me, and alive.

Dad was still looking at me with raised eyebrows and worry in his eyes. He was so happy right now that I knew the concern was solely for me. I smiled and hitched my bag onto my shoulder.

'Let's go.'

ANGEL HIERARCHY

THE SOLE

Violet Eden (G)
Violet's Angel Maker

SERAPHIM

Uri (AL)
Nox (AD)
Lilith (ED)
Griffin (G)
Josephine (G)
Drenson (G)

CHERUBIM

Nahilius (EL)
Rudyard (G)
Beth (G)
Adele (G)
Hakon (G)

1ST CHOIR

THRONES

Phoenix (ED)
Jude (EL)
Becca (G)
Evelyn (G)
Wilhem (G)

Grigori (G) Angel Light (AL) Angel Dark (AD) Exile once light (EL) Exile once dark (ED)

POWERS

Lincoln (G)
Nyla (G)
Gressil (ED)
Nathan (G)
Decima (G)

DOMINATIONS

Onyx (once ED)
Spence (G)
Gray (G)
Archer (G)
Rainer (G)

VIRTUES

Salvatore (G)
Morgan (G)
Valerie (G)

2ND CHOIR

PRINCIPALITIES

Irin – The Keeper (EL)
Kaitlin (G)
Max (G)
Seth (G)

ARCHANGELS

Zoe (G)
Olivier (EL)
Mia (G)
Father Peters (G)

ANGELS

Magda (G)
Samuel (G)
Hiro (G)

3RD CHOIR

ackNowLeDgements

there have been so many people who have played a part in bringing this series together. Sincere thanks to my agent, Selwa Anthony, whose friendship, guidance and support is invaluable.

Thank you to my publishers, Hachette. To Fiona Hazard and Chris Raine, who have supported the series from the outset. Special thanks to Vanessa Radnidge: I simply do not know a better person, let alone absolute industry pro and all-round support system. And thank you to Kate Ballard, editor extraordinaire, who knows these characters inside out and makes every scene simply better. I am incredibly grateful to you both; these books would not be what they are without your expertise and incredible attention to detail. Thank you to Airlie Lawson, who I am so lucky to have working on the series rights, and to Christine Fairbrother in marketing and Theresa Bray in publicity for everything you do (the list is long!) to bring these books to the readers.

Many thanks to my family and friends, whose support is truly endless. (See what I did there!)

To my husband, Matt: I will never have the words to express how much your encouragement to follow my dreams has meant to me. You believe in me so much, I think it's actually you who makes them come true! And to our girls, Sienna and Winter, who are so young and gorgeous but never afraid to barge in and drag me away from the computer. Never change, girls. My time with you is diamonds (precious and perfect).

Finally, to my readers – you are who books are made for. Thank you for giving up your own precious time to read my stories. I hope they make for a good escape!

Look out for

EMPOWER

the final book in
Jessica Shirvington's
stunning series.

COMING 2014

IF YOU LIKED ENDLESS, YOU'LL LOVE

Pbk 978 1 40833 075 3 £6.99   eBook 978 1 40833 076 0 £6.98

Stunning romance and relentless suspense – discover the first incredible book in **THE GODDESS WAR** trilogy.

From the bestselling author of **ANNA DRESSED IN BLOOD**.

From the bestselling author of KNIFE comes
an extraordinary story for older readers

ONCE UPON A TIME THERE WAS A GIRL
WHO WAS SPECIAL.

THIS IS NOT HER STORY.

UNLESS YOU COUNT THE PART WHERE
I KILLED HER.

WWW.ORCHARDBOOKS.CO.UK

Discover a thrilling world
of angels and romance

OUT NOW